# Always Us

## The Jade Series #8

# Always Us

## The Jade Series #8

By

## Allie Everhart

Always Us
By Allie Everhart

Cover Design by Sarah Hansen of Okay Creations
Photograph by Toski Covey Photography

ISBN: 1942781016
ISBN-13: 9781942781011

# Chapter 1

**JADE**

*Y*esterday when I got home from class, Garret was acting really strange. Actually, he's been acting strange for a couple days now. It's like he's trying to act normal but something's off. He seems on edge but not outwardly. It's one of those things that, when you know someone really well, you notice tiny details that tell you something's not right.

I asked Garret about it last night and he said everything's fine. But he's not fine and I think I know why. Ten years ago last Monday his mom was killed in a plane crash. He says that day doesn't bother him anymore but I know it does and I think that's why he's not himself right now.

I thought he'd feel better after seeing his dad, but it didn't seem to help. Yesterday Pearce came by the house while I was at class. He was in California for a meeting and wanted to stop and see Garret and me. But he only stayed for an hour so I never got to see him. When I got home, Garret seemed even more out of it than before I left. It was like his mind was elsewhere. I asked him about his dad's visit and he just said they talked, but he didn't say what they talked about.

This morning, as we were getting ready to leave for the airport, he still seemed off, but he keeps telling me nothing's wrong. I think he's just saying that because tomorrow is Thanksgiving and he wants me to enjoy the holiday. If something's wrong, I know he wouldn't tell me until we get home next Monday.

"Jade, we're almost there." Garret kisses the top of my head. I'm leaning against his shoulder, which is where I've slept for the past few hours. We're on the plane to Des Moines and the pilot just announced that we'll be landing in a few minutes.

I sit up and rub my neck. "I must've slept funny. I can barely move my neck."

"Here." He reaches behind me and starts massaging it for me.

"Mmm. That feels sooo good." I close my eyes, tilting my head side to side. He hits a pressure point that releases the knot in my neck. "Oh, yeah. Right there."

"You like that?" He puts a little more pressure on it.

"Yes. Don't stop." He puts his thumb at the base of my neck and runs it up to my hairline but I need more pressure. "That's good. But go deeper." I lean forward a little.

I hear him laugh, then clear his throat. "Jade." He takes his hand off my neck.

"What?" I sit up and see the old lady across the aisle staring at us with a disapproving look on her face. I peer back at the crack between our seats and see two businessmen working on their laptops. They smile when they see me looking at them. I replay the words I just said and realize how it sounded. Shit!

I whip back around, my cheeks on fire. "Garret!" I whisper. "Why didn't you say something?"

"About what?" He's trying not to laugh.

"Why didn't you tell me people were listening?"

"We're crammed in here, Jade. Everyone can hear. They don't even have to try to listen."

"I was talking about my neck!" I'm still whispering. "That's it! They saw you rubbing my neck. So why are they looking at me that way?"

He leans in, lowering his voice. "Because you just recited the dialogue from a porn film. Doesn't matter which one.

2

They're all the same." He laughs. "It sounded like you were auditioning for one of them."

"This is not funny." I bury my face in his chest as he hugs me.

"Actually, it's freaking hilarious," he says by my ear.

"I've never seen porn. How would I know what they say?"

"You've never seen porn?" He keeps his voice low.

"No! When would I have seen porn?" I whisper. "I don't have those kind of movies."

"You can see it on the Internet."

"I don't go to those sites!"

He looks at me. "Seriously? You've never seen it?"

"No." I cross my arms over my chest. Now I feel like an idiot. He's right. How could I be 20 years old and have not seen porn? Not that I'm interested in that stuff, but still.

He pulls me back into a hug. "I had no idea you were so innocent." He kisses my head. "I might have to dirty you up a little. But not too much. I like you sweet and innocent."

I peek over his shoulder and see that the old lady has gone back to reading her book. She's obviously seen porn or she wouldn't have given me those looks. So she's seen it and I haven't? I need to go online and check this out.

The flight attendant walks by. "Tray tables up. Seatbelts fastened. We'll be landing in a couple minutes." Her head moves left and right as she checks that we're all following orders, then she takes a seat up front behind the cockpit.

Cockpit. It sounds like a dirty word now that I've got porn on the brain. *Cockpit. Cockpit. Cockpit. Cockpit.* The word keeps repeating in my head, sounding dirtier each time. I start laughing and can't stop.

"What's so funny?" Garret's smiling at me. "Thinking about the neck rub?"

"No. Yes. Kind of." I'm still laughing. "I think I just need to get off this plane."

"We're landing right now." Our hands are joined and Garret squeezes mine a little. "You good?"

"Yes." I close my eyes and feel the wheels touch down. I get nervous on planes, especially the takeoffs and landings, but Garret always calms me down.

The plane comes to a stop and Garret reaches overhead to get our stuff. We're in first class, so as soon as they open the plane door we get right off.

"Well, that was embarrassing," I say, as we walk through the airport.

"And informative." Garret puts his arm around me. "Learn something new about you every day, Jade."

We go down the escalator and I see Frank and Ryan standing there.

"Welcome home." Frank gives me a hug while Ryan says hi to Garret.

"It feels like I haven't been here forever."

"We ordered up some snow for you," Frank says as I give Ryan a hug.

"It snowed already?"

"No, but it's supposed to on Saturday night," Ryan says. He looks at Garret. "You up for shoveling? You're part of the family now, which means we put you to work."

"Sure, I don't mind." Garret takes my hand as we walk to baggage.

"You guys need to get a snowblower," I say to Frank.

"We already have one. Ryan's just testing your husband."

Ryan laughs. "I wanted to see if pretty boy would agree to shovel."

"Hey." I punch Ryan. "Be nice."

"And enough with the pretty boy shit." Garret smiles as he says it. "I don't get why you call me that, but keep it up and I might have to come up with a nickname for *you*."

4

"We should totally give him a nickname," I say to Garret. "What should it be?"

"Okay, kids," Frank says, all Dad-like. "Everyone be nice. This is Thanksgiving."

"Ryan started it," I say like a kid would.

Frank shakes his head, smiling. "This is going to be a long weekend."

We all laugh.

Garret takes our suitcase off the conveyor belt and walks with Ryan toward the parking garage. "You gonna let me drive the new car?"

"It's not really new anymore, but yeah. We can go when we get home."

Frank and I are behind them. I look at Frank. "What is with those two and cars? It's a BMW. Aren't they all the same?"

"It's their thing," Frank says quietly. "They both like cars. It's something they can bond over. And going for a drive gives them an excuse to spend time together."

We stop at the white Honda CR-V Frank bought last summer after I gave him some of the money from my trust fund. Ryan puts our suitcase in the back, then comes around and gets in the driver's seat.

"Why aren't you driving, Frank?" I slide in the back seat, next to Garret. Frank's in front of me on the passenger side.

"I didn't sleep well last night. I don't like to drive when I'm tired."

His comment worries me. Frank looks healthy on the outside but I wonder if he's not feeling well. If he was, I know he wouldn't tell me. He doesn't want me to worry, but of course I still do.

"You guys haven't even complained about the cold." Ryan turns the heat up. "It's only 30 degrees. I thought you California people would be freaking out by now."

"We've only lived there a few months." I look at Garret. "I don't feel that cold. Do you?"

"Didn't even notice it." He aims his cocky grin at Ryan. "I'm not some pretty boy who can't handle the cold."

Ryan glances at him in the rear view mirror. "Then maybe we'll go throw the football around in the back yard. Get some of that cold Midwest air in your lungs. Unless swimmers don't play football. Might be too rough of a sport."

Garret knees the back of Ryan's seat. "I was quarterback in high school."

"Pretty boys are always quarterback," Ryan mumbles, loud enough for us to hear.

Garret laughs and shakes his head.

Guys. This is obviously how they bond, insulting each other, challenging each other. I don't get it, but if that's their way of becoming friends, it's fine with me.

We get to the house a half hour later. When Frank said his new house is on the west side of the Des Moines metro, he meant it. It's really far west. The house is off by itself on a couple acres of land, surrounded by woods. It's a one-level house with dark tan siding, multicolored stone, black shutters, and a black front door. The house blends in nicely with the wooded setting.

"You did a good job with the colors, Frank." We're standing in the driveway, admiring the house.

"I drove around and looked at other houses and copied one that I liked. The property goes way back into the woods. We've already seen a lot of wildlife, even out here in the driveway."

I latch onto Garret. "What kind of wildlife? Like snakes?"

"Snakes, raccoons, fox, deer, coyote."

Garret laughs as I grip him even tighter. "You shouldn't have told her that. Now she'll lock herself in the house the rest of the weekend."

"You're afraid of wildlife?" Frank asks me.

"Yes! You know how scared I am of snakes. At least at the old house we didn't have any, or any other wildlife."

"What are you talking about?" Ryan takes the suitcase out of the car. "We had snakes at the other house. And raccoons were always getting in the garbage. We even had a bat in the house."

"A bat?" I shudder. "You never told me that."

"You were at school when it happened. We got it out before you got home."

"Where was it? In the living room?"

Ryan looks at Frank, who shrugs and says, "We don't live there anymore so you might as well tell her."

"It was in your bedroom." Ryan starts laughing.

"And you didn't tell me?" I huff. "It touched all my stuff! It was probably in my clothes. I could've got rabies."

"You can't get rabies from a bat touching your clothes," Ryan says. "Besides, we washed everything before you got home. We figured it was better if you didn't know."

"I have to go inside." I check the area by my feet, making sure there aren't any snakes around. I'm still clinging to Garret. "I can't be out here."

"You need to get out in nature more, Jade," Garret says as we walk to the door. "I grew up playing in the woods. Snakes won't bother you if you leave them alone."

Ryan walks past us with the suitcase. "Huh. So pretty boy's not afraid of snakes. Interesting."

"Last time, Ryan." Garret jabs his shoulder. "Last time."

He laughs. "Check out the house, then let's go for a drive."

When you walk in the house, there's a small entryway that leads to a big, open space with the living room on the left and the kitchen on the right. Dividing the two rooms is a narrow stone-covered wall that has a see-through fireplace in it. The floors are a reddish-brown cherry wood and the walls are a dark beige color. The back of the house is mostly windows with a view of the woods.

This is exactly where I pictured Frank living. He loves the outdoors so this is perfect for him. He can sit and look out at the trees and the birds and the changing seasons. At the old house, the views were ugly power lines and other houses.

"This is a great house, Frank," Garret says as he walks into the living room. There's a flat-screen TV mounted on the wall with built-in bookcases on each side. "I see you upgraded the TV."

"I talked him into the 60-inch screen," Ryan says. "He wanted a 36-inch, which is way too small for this big of a room.

"Did you break down and get a satellite dish?" Garret asks Frank.

"Yes. I didn't want it, but Ryan insisted we have it."

Ryan hangs his arm off Frank's shoulder. "We need it for sports, Dad. You can't get all the games on regular TV."

"Yeah, you gotta have the sports channels," Garret says.

"Let me show you the kitchen." Frank leads us to the other side of the room, past the fireplace.

"I love this wall divider," I tell him. "We should do that with our house, Garret."

"Are you guys building a house?" Ryan asks.

"Not yet, but eventually. We have the land." As soon as I say it, I want to take it back but it's too late.

"You bought some land?" Frank asks.

"Um, yeah." I haven't told Frank or Ryan about the land we got from Grace. And I can't tell Ryan that Grace gave it to us since he doesn't know she's my grandmother.

"Grace sold it to us," Garret says casually. Sometimes it concerns me how good he is at lying. "She had it up for sale and Jade and I decided to buy it. Since she's a close friend of the family, she gave us a deal."

Frank's eyes are on me. I'm sure he assumes Grace gave us the land for free, but he's probably wondering why I didn't tell him. The reason I didn't is because I try to avoid talking about the Sinclair side of the family with Frank. He still gets angry whenever he thinks about what Royce did to my mom.

"Where's the land?" Ryan asks me.

"It's about an north of Santa Barbara, right along the coast."

"So you're staying in California after college?" Ryan seems disappointed, but he knew I didn't want to move back to Iowa.

"Yeah, we really like it out there. And I love living on the ocean."

Frank smiles. "Well, it sounds like a beautiful location. We'll have to come out and visit when you get the house built. You think it'll be after you graduate?"

I look at Garret. "We don't know yet. It's only an hour from where we live now so we might build it sooner than that so we can live there in the summers. And you're definitely coming to visit."

Garret pulls me into his side. "You guys are welcome any time. We'll make sure it has plenty of guest rooms."

"That's going to be a big house," Ryan says to me.

"What do you mean?"

"You want guest rooms, but you also need rooms for all your kids." He snickers as he reaches in the cupboard for some glasses. "You'll need at least eight bedrooms to accommodate the guests, along with you and Garret and your four kids." He snickers again.

Garret rubs my arm. He thinks I'm upset because of the kid comment, but Ryan teases me about this all the time because I tell him I don't want kids. And for whatever reason, his kid comments never bother me.

"Ryan, don't—"

I interrupt Garret. "Four? We were planning on having five or six. Right, Garret?" I smile at him.

He looks totally confused. "Um, sure. As many as you want."

"Six grandkids?" Frank smiles. "It's a good thing I bought a big dining room table." Frank motions to a room off the kitchen. "That's where we'll be having dinner tomorrow."

I go and peek around the corner at the dining room. There's a long table that seats 10. The table has an orange runner down the center topped with small white pumpkins and greenery.

"Did you decorate the table?" I almost laugh imagining Frank doing that.

"No, Chloe did it," Ryan says. "You guys want something to drink?"

"Just water." Garret and I both say it, then I say, "We're both thirsty from the plane."

We take a seat at the kitchen island as Ryan hands us our glasses of water. The kitchen is big and open. It has stainless steel appliances, dark cabinets, and the counters are covered in granite that has a brown, black, and beige swirl pattern.

We talk some more and then Frank shows us the bedrooms, which are on the other side of the house. The room Garret and I are staying in has its own bathroom and a walk-in closet.

I'm impressed with how well Frank did picking stuff out. The wall colors, the lighting fixtures, the flooring. It all looks good together and it fits his style, not too contemporary but more of a traditional look. Frank told me his girlfriend, Karen, helped him pick stuff out.

Ryan's phone rings. "It's Chloe. I'll be right back." He goes in his bedroom to talk to her while the rest of us go back to the kitchen.

"So Karen's coming over tonight." Frank says it casually, but his lips are creeping up just mentioning her.

"Good. I'll finally get to meet her." I gulp my glass of water down.

"She wanted to meet you before the race tomorrow. She'll be here at seven for dinner. Ryan's going to throw some steaks on the grill and Karen's bringing over a salad."

"Are you going to the race?" I ask him.

"Yes. Karen will meet us there. Ryan is staying here with Chloe. She's coming over early in the morning to start the turkey. Are you going to the race with us, Garret?"

"Yeah, I'm going." He gets up and refills my water glass from the fridge dispenser. "I've never seen Jade race before."

"I'm not going to race. I'll just keep pace with Karen."

Garret gives me my water. "I'm gonna go unpack."

"Right now? Why don't you do that later?"

"I want to clean up a little. Change my shirt."

"Okay." I watch him walk away. He's still acting strange. It's subtle and Frank doesn't notice, but I do.

Frank starts telling me more about Karen. His face lights up as he talks about her.

I can't wait to meet this woman. I still can't believe Frank has a girlfriend.

# Chapter 2

**GARRET**

*I* go in the bedroom and shut the door. I need just a few minutes to myself. I need to get my mind focused on tomorrow and this weekend. I want this Thanksgiving to be a good one for Jade, so I need to put on a smile, act happy, and pretend nothing's wrong. I did that for most of my teen years so this should be easy. Of course, back then I had alcohol to help me out. And I didn't have this huge secret to hide.

But so far, I'm doing pretty well. I've managed to act halfway normal since my grandfather's visit a few days ago. I've shoved that whole conversation in the back of my mind and when it makes its way to the front again, I tell myself it never happened, then shove any memory of it back in its place. If I don't, Jade will know something's wrong. She picks up on stuff, even the tiniest things, so I need to be aware of my tone, my expressions—anything that might give me away.

I hate hiding this from Jade but my dad practically ordered me not to tell her, and he's probably right. She doesn't need to know, at least not yet, and maybe not ever. How exactly would I tell her something like that anyway? *My grandfather plans to kill you, Jade.* Yeah, I can't even *think* those words, let alone say them.

My dad said he'd deal with my grandfather and I believe him. I just need to give him time to do that. I'm worried he'll sacrifice himself somehow to get my grandfather to back down. Like agree to do whatever his father tells him to do in exchange for him leaving Jade and me alone. My grandfather could make my dad run for public office, something he would hate doing. He has no interest in being a politician and never has. But my grandfather always wanted his son to be in politics because of the power and prestige that comes with those positions. So when my dad didn't go down that route, my grandfather wanted *me* to, which is why he was thrilled when I was chosen to be president, then furious when I destroyed my image, thus ending my future political career. So maybe my grandfather will force my dad to run for office, like maybe run for governor, or for Congress. The organization would make sure he'd win.

I don't want to see my dad's life ruined like that, but my grandfather has us backed into a corner. He's made this ultimatum. Divorce Jade or he'll kill her.

I haven't slept much since he gave me that ultimatum. A couple hours a night, max. The rest of the time I'm wide awake, watching Jade sleep, worrying about her safety, and trying to come up with ways to get out of this. Trying to figure out how to make my grandfather accept Jade, even though I know he never will. I even considered working for the company. Maybe if I agreed to take over Kensington Chemical someday, my grandfather would leave Jade alone. If he did, I would do it. I would dread going to work every day, but I'd do it if it meant he'd leave her alone.

Problem is, he won't agree it. He hates Jade and he hates that I'm with her, and he's determined to break us apart. Which means I have to rely on my dad. He's the only one who can fix this. I just hope that he can.

"Hey." Jade comes into the bedroom. I'm unpacking the suitcase and hanging clothes in the closet. She comes over and gives me a hug. "You want to take a nap? You look tired."

"I'm okay. We should go hang out with Frank and Ryan."

"Ryan went to pick up Chloe. They're getting stuff for tomorrow. And Frank is resting in his room. Do you think Frank's okay? It worries me that he's so tired."

"I'm sure he's fine. He said he didn't sleep well last night."

"But why isn't he sleeping well? That could mean something, Garret."

"Don't read so much into it." I kiss her forehead. "He just didn't sleep well. That's all."

I don't know what Jade will do if Frank ever gets really sick. Last year when he was in intensive care, Jade was a mess. She couldn't handle seeing him like that. I tried to be there for her, supporting her, helping her get through it, and I think she was glad I was there. It was hard to tell back then. She hid so much of herself that I was always left guessing what she needed from me. She's better now, but I still have to guess sometimes.

"Come on." She leads me to the bed. "Just take a short nap. I know you haven't been sleeping much the past few nights."

Shit. How did she know that?

"I'll take a nap, but only if you sleep next to me."

She smiles. "I will."

We lie on our sides, her back against my chest, and I hold her there, not wanting to ever let go. As hard as I try to shove that conversation with my grandfather out of my head, I keep hearing his words and rage erupts inside me, making my muscles tense up, my jaw clench.

"That's a little too tight, Garret," Jade says. "What is with you and these super tight hugs? You keep doing it. You've been doing it since Monday."

I relax my arms. "I don't know. I guess I don't know my own strength." I use my cocky tone to steer her off course from any suspicions she has that something's wrong.

14

"You *are* really strong." She turns her head back and kisses me, then rubs her neck. "My neck still hurts."

"You want me to massage it again?" I laugh as I say it. "If I do, you better keep quiet this time or Frank will think we're doing something in here."

She laughs. "I promise I'll be quiet this time."

"Don't do it on my account. Feel free to practice your porn lines again. I don't mind. You're the one who gets all embarrassed."

She reaches back and swats at my leg. "Which is why I'll be quiet."

She leans forward a little and I massage her neck.

"Garret?"

"Yes, Jade."

"I'm so happy being here. Having a real Thanksgiving with you and Frank and Ryan. And it's so great seeing them living in a house that's new and doesn't have a leaky roof and peeling paint. All of it just makes me happy."

I lean over her shoulder and kiss her cheek. "Good. I love seeing you happy."

And that's why I can't tell her what's going on. All her happiness would disappear if she knew the truth. Jade hasn't had much happiness in her life and now that she finally does, I'm not going to take it away from her.

"Did you mean it when you said we would have lots of guest rooms in our house?" she asks.

"Of course I did. We'll need lots of rooms for when people come visit us."

She flips to face me, her face beaming. "That's what I want. I want both our families to come to our house for the holidays and summer barbecues and birthdays."

It's sweet how Jade gets so excited about family. This family thing is all new to her and she loves having them around.

I kiss her. "We'll make sure there's plenty of room for everyone. Maybe we'll build a guest house. We have all that land. Might as well use it."

"That's a great idea! Let's do that. Then people can have more privacy if they want it. They can stay with us or in the guest house."

"And that'll keep the main house from getting too big. If we get too many rooms we'll end up with a house the size of my dad's and we don't want that."

"We won't have *that* many rooms. Your dad's house is huge."

"I don't know, Jade. Like Ryan said, with the guest rooms and the rooms for our six kids, it's gonna add up to a lot of rooms."

She rolls her eyes. "I was joking about the six kids. I had to get Ryan to shut up."

"That's a relief. I mean, if you want six, that's fine, but it seems like kind of a lot. And you'd have to be pregnant for almost six years of your life."

"Not if I had two sets of triplets." She laughs. "Can you imagine us trying to take care of triplets?"

Jade has been bringing up the kid topic a lot more now. She doesn't say she wants kids, but she'll at least talk about it or joke about it like she did just now. I think she's been talking about it with Jennifer, her counselor. Jade usually doesn't tell me what she talks about at her counseling sessions, but I can guess by the topics she brings up at dinner or when we're just sitting and talking. And this kid topic has come up several times the past few weeks.

"Garret? Are you awake?"

I realize I haven't responded to the triplets comment. "Yes. The triplet thing threw me. I was trying to figure out how that might work. I think we could handle it, but I don't think it's something we should try for. One at a time seems like a better option."

Now that she's more comfortable with the kid topic, I sometimes just pretend we're planning to have kids and see how she reacts.

"I don't think we have any control over it, Garret. We may try for one but end up with three."

"Well, we'll just have to wait and see what we get."

"Yeah." She looks directly at me and smiles. Like *really* smiles.

Wait. Did she just agree to have kids? What was the 'yeah' referring to? That we'll wait and see if we have kids? Or that we'll wait and see if we have one or triplets? And what's with the huge smile?

"Jade, did you just—"

She interrupts my words with a kiss. "Just give me a little more time, okay? And then we'll talk." She smiles again. "But yeah, I want that."

Holy shit, is she serious? I think she just told me she wants to have kids. But she said she needs more time. More time for what? To be 100% sure? From the look on her face, I think she's already there. Damn. I did not expect that. At all. It's not like she's telling me she wants them right away. Neither one of us wants that. But to have her admit to wanting them at all is a huge deal.

Ever since we got married, I've been telling myself I might just have to accept the fact that kids aren't in our future. Before today, Jade didn't really act like she wanted them. She'd joke about having them, but she was never serious. But just now, she was serious. She even seemed a little excited about the possibility. Maybe it's because she's around family and it makes her think of us having our own family someday. Who knows? But whatever the reason, it made my heart jump a little. Who knew a simple 'yeah' could have so much meaning?

"I love you." They're the only words I can come up with after hearing her say that. I'm too shocked to come up with anything else. I hope this isn't just temporary and that this really is what she wants. Because it's definitely what *I* want. I love Jade so damn much and I want to have kids with her. One. Two. Six. Triplets. Doesn't fucking matter to me. I'll take whatever she'll give me.

"I love you, too." She flips around and pulls my arm down around her middle. "You need to sleep. Let's just take a short nap."

A few minutes later, she's asleep. But am I? Hell, no. My body is freaking exhausted but my mind is wide awake, even more so now that Jade's agreed to have kids. Well, almost agreed. We've got this whole future ahead of us. We're making plans. A new house. Kids. Holidays with the family. And instead of being happy about it, like I should be, I'm scared shitless that it's nothing more than a dream. A dream that will never come true because of my psychotic, controlling grandfather. I don't know why he won't just leave me alone. I don't know why he's doing this. What the fuck happened in his life to make him this way?

A half hour later Jade's still asleep and I'm still lying here, wide awake. My phone vibrates on the nightstand. I carefully take my arm off Jade and reach over to get it. There's a text from my dad asking if we made it to Iowa. I text him back that we did. Then I slowly move off the bed.

"Garret?" Jade turns over and notices I'm gone.

I lean down and kiss her. "I'm just using the bathroom. I'll be right back."

"Okay." Her eyes are closed and she curls herself into a ball and goes back to sleep. I stand there a moment and look at her. She's smiling as she sleeps. She's so freaking happy right now that she's smiling in her goddamn sleep. All I ever wanted was to make Jade happy, and now she is, but it's all going to come crashing down if I don't fix this shit with my grandfather. Or if my dad doesn't fix it.

That's why I got up. I need to call my dad. I need to know if he has a plan. I go in the bathroom, shut the door, and call him.

"Dad, what's going on?" I ask when he picks up. "Did you decide what to do?"

"Garret, I told you I'd take care of it. I don't want you involved in this."

"I already *am* involved. So just tell me."

"This is between my father and me. I told you that yesterday. I also told you to stay out it. And I mean it. Do you understand?" He's got that threatening tone he always used when I disobeyed him in high school. I can't stand that tone. I always feel like a kid when he uses it.

"No. I don't understand. This isn't just about you. This has to do with—"

"I am NOT going to say it again!" His threatening tone is replaced by something darker, more ominous. It doesn't even sound like him. "Stay the fuck out of it." He pauses, but I hear him breathing. "Now I'm asking you again. Do you understand?"

My heart's pounding in my chest. I notice my hand's shaking a little. What the hell? My hand never shakes.

"Garret. Answer me." He lowers his voice, but it's still fucking scary. "Do you understand?"

"Yes. I understand."

"When this is over, we'll talk. Until then, don't call me."

"When is it going to be over?"

"I will see him tomorrow. We'll be having a conversation."

"You think this is going to be settled in one day?"

"It will be the start of what could be a very long battle if he doesn't cooperate."

19

"Why can't we talk?"

"Rule number one, Garret. You've already broken it several times during this conversation, which is the reason we can't talk. I can't answer your questions, and all you have are questions. You haven't said one thing to me on this phone call that doesn't relate to your grandfather."

"Because this is all I can fucking think about!" I said it too loud. Shit. I hope Jade didn't wake up.

"Have a nice Thanksgiving, Garret. Tell Jade to as well."

And then he hangs up. Just ends the call. No goodbye. Nothing. I call him right back. I know he said not to, but he pissed me off by hanging up like that. His phone goes straight to voicemail. Great. Now my own father won't talk to me. I slip my phone in my pocket and go back to the bedroom and lie next to Jade.

"Who were you talking to?" she whispers. Her eyes are closed so I thought she was asleep.

"My dad. I just wanted to wish him a happy Thanksgiving."

"Why? Aren't you calling him tomorrow?"

"No. We'll be busy with everyone here, and my dad's having my grandparents over for dinner so it was just better if we talked today."

"Don't you want to talk to Lilly tomorrow?"

"No. Katherine will just be a bitch about it, so I'd rather avoid all that and call Lilly some other time. I didn't talk to her last Thanksgiving and she was fine. It's not a big holiday for her. She doesn't like turkey."

"Really?" Jade leans back into my chest. "Who doesn't like turkey?"

"She's never liked it. But she eats the other stuff. Mashed potatoes. Sweet potatoes. All that stuff."

Jade turns to face me. The smile she fell asleep with is still there. She gives me a kiss. "Did you get some sleep?"

"Yeah," I lie.

"You still look tired." She puts her hand on my forehead, then down the side of my face. "You're not getting sick, are you?"

I take her hand off my face and kiss her palm. "I'm not sick. I feel fine."

"Good." She hugs me. "I love you."

"I love you, too." I hug her back, probably too tight again but I can't help it. I know my grandfather said she was safe until the end of the year, but I still feel like I can't let her out of my sight. I just want to keep her in my arms like this until I know she's safe.

"I think I heard Ryan come home," Jade says. "We should go help with dinner."

We both get up and Jade goes in the bathroom. While she's in there, I check my phone to see if my dad called back. He didn't. But I notice a call coming in. It's Sean.

"Hey, Sean. Are you at your parents' house?"

"Yeah. Got here this morning. My sisters are here, too. They're in the kitchen with my mom, making pies."

"You still going tomorrow?"

"Yeah. I'll be there Friday morning."

Sean's going to LA for Harper's shoulder surgery. Even though she broke up with him, he still loves her and wants to be there for her. The surgery is on Friday and he's taking the red eye tomorrow night to get there. The guy has no money since his job is shit and he maxed out his credit card buying Harper's engagement ring, so I don't know how he's paying for a hotel. I tried to give him money but he wouldn't take it.

"Where you are staying?" I ask him.

"Don't worry about it."

"Sean, you better not be planning on sleeping on some fucking park bench or in your rental car."

21

"Rental car? I can't afford that. I'm taking the bus."

I sigh. "Did you get a hotel or not?"

"I'll figure it out when I get there."

"Dammit, Sean. I'm giving you my credit card number and you're going to stay at a hotel." I get my wallet out and take out my card and start reading off the numbers.

"Garret, stop. I don't want it. I know some people out there. I'll see if I can stay with them."

"I swear, you're as annoying as Jade was last year."

"Did you just call me annoying?" Jade's laughing behind me.

I turn around. "I was telling Sean how annoying you were when you wouldn't let me give you money. Now he's acting the same way. What's the deal with you people not taking money?"

Jade takes the phone from me. "Sean, are you okay?" She puts the phone on speaker so I can hear.

"Yeah, I'm fine."

"Sean. How are you *really*?"

"Yeah, it sucks, but there's nothing I can do. She won't even talk to me. She won't take my calls."

I give Jade a look, reminding her not to interfere. She can't fix this thing with Sean and Harper. Kiefer will soon officially join the organization, and when he does, Harper and her sisters will only be allowed to date men who are members. Jade is desperate to do something, but I made her promise me she wouldn't. We are not getting involved in anything even remotely related to the organization.

"I'm sorry, Sean." Jade nods at me, telling me she'll stay out it. "But you're still going to the surgery?"

"Yeah, I'll be there."

"Okay, well, have a nice Thanksgiving."

"You, too. Garret, I'll talk to you later, okay?"

"Yeah. Bye."

"I didn't mean to race you off the phone," Jade says.

"It's fine. He's at his parents' house. He couldn't talk long."

"He shouldn't be going to Harper's surgery on Friday. It's just going to cause problems."

"I know, but he really wants to be there."

There's a knock on the door and I hear Frank's voice. "Jade? Garret? We're having dinner in a few minutes."

Jade opens the door. "We're coming. We fell asleep and didn't realize it was so late. Garret, are you ready?"

"Yeah." I follow her out to the hallway, taking a deep breath to get control of myself again. That call with my dad put me on edge and I need to relax.

It's time to put on a show. Smile and act happy. Pretend everything's good.

# Chapter 3

**JADE**

*G*arret and I walk into the living room. Frank is standing there, next to a tall, thin woman with blond hair, who I'm guessing is Karen. She has on dark jeans and a light blue, v-neck sweater. Her hair is chin-length and straight, but cut in layers so it has some fullness to it. It's a cute haircut. Very modern. I pictured her looking older, with an old-lady haircut. I don't know why. She's 50, but could easily pass for mid-forties.

Frank has this big grin on his face. "Karen, this is Jade and her husband, Garret." He looks at us. "Jade. Garret. This is Karen."

"It's nice to finally meet you both." She shakes our hands. "It sounds like you live in a beautiful area. I've always wanted to visit California."

"You'll have to come out there sometime," I tell her.

"Yes, we should do that," Frank says.

*We?* I didn't think Frank and Karen's relationship was at the point where they'd take a trip together. But I guess it is. I guess their relationship is more serious than I thought. They've only dated a few months, but maybe when you're old, things move faster.

Ryan comes up behind Frank, tongs in his hand. "The steaks are almost ready."

"I can help with dinner," I tell him. "What do you need?"

"Karen took care of the rest, so we're all set. We'll eat in a few minutes." Ryan goes back outside.

"Let's head to the dining room." Frank puts his hand on Karen's lower back and keeps it there as they walk in front of Garret and me on their way past the kitchen.

Garret nudges me and raises his eyebrows, like he thinks Frank's getting lucky later. I nudge him back and mouth 'stop it' which makes him quietly laugh.

"Frank said you're a nurse," I say to Karen as we sit down.

"Yes, I work in obstetrics. Delivered two babies today." She smiles. "Well, the doctor did, but I assisted her."

"Do you like being a nurse?"

"I love it. And I love working with new moms, especially first time moms. Some of them are convinced they'll never make it through labor, but they always do. And once they see their babies, they forget all about the labor."

That's another reason I'm scared to have kids. Being pregnant and going through labor. It sounds horrible. And I'm sure these moms Karen's referring to don't forget about the labor part. How could they? You're in excruciating pain for hours. That's not something you'd forget.

"Do they scream a lot?" I ask her.

"Newborns sleep for most of the day, so no, not really."

"Not the babies. The moms."

Garret starts laughing. I don't know why that's funny. I really want to know the answer. On TV, women are always screaming during labor.

Karen smiles. "They don't usually scream. We have ways to deal with the pain."

"I would scream. I can't handle that kind of pain."

Garret puts his arm around me. "You'd be fine. You're tough."

"Are you two planning on having children soon?" Karen asks.

I feel like there's a giant spotlight on me as Karen, Garret, and Frank all await my answer. I decide to keep it vague. "No, not anytime soon."

25

"The steaks have arrived." Ryan walks in with the platter and sets it on the table next to the side dishes.

Frank starts passing the food around while Ryan sits down and says something about the weather. I'm not really listening. I'm just glad he showed up when he did. We needed to get off that childbirth and kid topic. One, because thinking about labor and delivery while people are trying to eat is gross. And two, I didn't want Karen asking more questions about Garret and me having kids.

When Garret and I were in the bedroom earlier, I hinted that I want kids. And although I usually joke about it, this time I was serious. A few weeks ago, I started talking to Jennifer about my mom and my childhood and my fear of having kids. And we've continued to talk about those things at every session.

What I've realized is that I *do* want kids someday. I proved that to myself when I thought I was pregnant. I was scared and I wasn't prepared for it, but part of me was happy about it. And ever since that happened, I've felt this strong desire to have kids someday. I love being around Sara's baby and being around Lilly, and even that little girl I helped at the swim lesson.

I've thought about this a lot, and I know it's what I want. But I don't want to tell Garret until I'm absolutely, 100% sure, and I'm not quite there yet.

Dinner continues and Garret and I tell everyone about our classes and the town we live in. Karen keeps asking us questions, which makes Frank smile. He really wants me to like her. And I do. I think she's really nice. She seems smart, too. And she's pretty. Most of all, she seems to really like Frank. She keeps smiling at him and touching his hand—in a loving way, not an I-want-to-have-sex-with-you way. Although if she *was* touching him that way I wouldn't notice because I'm blocking those thoughts from my head.

Karen brought over a pie for dessert. We all have a slice, except for Garret. He rarely eats dessert so that's not unusual, but what *is* unusual is that he didn't eat much of his dinner. He hasn't eaten much at all the past few days. Maybe he's coming down with something. There was some kind of respiratory virus spreading around campus before we left. Maybe Garret caught it. He never gets sick, but his lack of sleep the past week could've lowered his immune system.

"Well, I should be going," Karen says when we're done with dessert. "I need to get some sleep. I have to be up early for the race and I have to work tomorrow night."

"You have to work on Thanksgiving?" I ask her.

She nods, smiling. "Babies arrive every day of the year. But I don't mind working the holiday shift. I always volunteer to work Thanksgiving so the other nurses can be with their families."

Karen seems like someone who doesn't complain much. She's very positive. Frank needs someone like that because sometimes he can be kind of negative. She's good for him.

We say goodbye to Karen, then watch TV. Everyone goes to bed at ten because we have to get up early. The race starts at eight but we're getting there at seven-thirty to check in.

When Garret and I are in bed, I put my hand on his face to see if he's warm. He's not.

"What are you doing?" he asks.

"Checking to see if you're sick. I know you wouldn't tell me if you were."

"I'm not sick, Jade. Why do you keep saying that?"

"Because you didn't eat much at dinner and you haven't eaten much for days. And you're not sleeping and you look really tired."

He kisses me and pulls me against his chest. "Stop worrying about me. I'm fine."

He's not. Something's bothering him. He just won't tell me. I'll have to figure it out myself.

"So what did you think of Karen?" I ask him.

"I liked her." He laughs a little. "And Frank *really* likes her."

I jab him with my elbow. "Don't start talking about them that way."

"I'm just saying. He couldn't take his eyes off her all through dinner. And she couldn't take her hands off him."

"She was just holding his hand. That's it."

"I'm pretty sure they do more than that when there isn't a roomful of people around."

"What are you saying? You think they've had sex?"

"Just forget it. Let's go to sleep."

I flip back around to face him. "They haven't even dated that long! They can't be doing that yet. You're wrong. They're definitely not doing that."

He's smiling. "Yeah. I'm sure they're not. Now would you go to sleep?"

I lie against his chest again. "I'm starting to freak out about Saturday."

This Saturday I have to talk about myself in front of a group of women. I'm supposed to inspire them with my story. My high school algebra teacher asked me to do it. He and his wife volunteer for an organization that helps young women who are struggling. Most of them grew up in bad homes, like mine, and some have been in abusive relationships or are trying to get over addiction. My teacher thinks I could be a role model for them. I'm scared to death of public speaking so I didn't want to do it, but then Garret talked me into it.

"Jade, you practiced your speech a million times. There's nothing to freak out about."

"I don't want you to go to the speech."

"Why not?"

"Because I don't want you to see me screw up."

"You're not going to screw up. You're going to do a great job."

"See? You're putting all this pressure on me and now I'm afraid I'll screw up."

"Stop worrying about screwing up. This isn't a performance. Nobody's going to be grading you. This is about you helping other people. Think about the women in the audience. Think about what they're going through. Think about how you felt when you were just a kid, living with your mom. How did you feel back then?"

"Hopeless. Like nobody cared. Like I'd never survive. Like I had no future."

"So pretend you're talking to your old self. What would you say to that Jade to give her hope? To make her believe things would get better? That's what you need to be thinking about when you're up there giving your speech."

He's right. I need to focus on the audience and not myself. I keep making this about me, thinking I need to give a perfect speech as if I'm back in high school and need to impress my teacher. But this isn't about that. This is my chance to maybe help someone see just a hint of light in the never-ending darkness that they think is their future. I lived in that darkness for years, but I made it out and these other women can, too.

"You think you can sleep now?" Garret asks.

"Yeah. Goodnight. I love you." I don't go to sleep right away. Instead, I lie there awake, replaying the words of my speech in my head. I have it memorized, but now I might change it a little. It sounds too formal and too much like the speech I gave when I was valedictorian, which was supposed to inspire my classmates, but really just bored them. It bored *me* and I wrote it. I start reworking my speech in my head and eventually fall asleep.

The next morning we arrive at the race at seven twenty-five. Luckily, it's not too cold. It's about 45 degrees, which is warm for November in Iowa.

Karen sees us and comes over. She's wearing tight black running pants and a bright green workout jacket. I see Frank checking her out. She *does* have a good body. He gives her a hug and a kiss on the cheek.

Garret gives me a sideways glance and smiles. He needs to stop this. I cannot think of Frank and Karen together that way.

"Should we get our registration packets?" Karen points to the long line of people at the registration table. I've never done one of these races, so I'm not sure how they work. I follow her to the line while Frank and Garret wait by the race course.

It's kind of awkward being alone with Karen. I'm not sure what to talk about.

"Thanks for doing the race with me," she says. "It's hard to find people who like to run."

"Yeah, I don't run as much as I used to because I don't have anyone to run with me. Garret doesn't want me running alone."

"Do you two ever go running together?"

"We do, but he doesn't like running. He only does it for me."

"I just recently convinced Frank to start going on walks with me." She glances back at him and waves. "I don't think he likes it, but he'll do it if I ask."

"Yeah, he doesn't like to exercise." We inch forward in the line.

"He needs to, though." Her tone turns serious. "It's good for his health. I'm trying to get him to be more active at home, as well, and not sit so much."

"How's he doing? Does he tell you? Because he never tells me anything and I've noticed he seems more tired than normal."

"People with MS have good and bad days, and the past few months he's had some bad days, but he's doing better now."

The past few months? Why didn't he tell me this? Why didn't Ryan say anything?

"What was causing the bad days?" I ask her.

"His doctor thinks it was stress. Selling the house and moving to the new one was good, but stressful. And he worries about you and Ryan."

"He does? Why?"

She smiles. "Because that's what fathers do. They worry about their children."

"He doesn't need to worry about me."

"He doesn't as much anymore. He knows Garret takes good care of you. He really likes your husband."

I look over and see Frank and Garret talking. Garret keeps glancing over at me, like he's checking on me. He did this at the airport, too. He wouldn't let me out of his sight, except when I went to the bathroom. And even then, he waited outside the door. I like that he watches over me, but sometimes I think he's a little too overprotective.

I turn back to Karen. "So why is Frank worried about Ryan?"

"Because Ryan won't move forward with his life. He thinks he needs to live with Frank so he can take care of him, but Frank doesn't want that."

"I kind of thought that was going on. The two of them were fighting about it last July when they came out for my wedding."

"They were fighting up until just last month, but it's better now. They came to some type of agreement. I don't know what. I didn't ask." We step forward in the line and her hand brushes

31

my arm. "Jade, I'm sorry. I shouldn't have said all of that to you. It's really not my place."

"Frank would never tell me this stuff, so I'm glad you did. And it's good to know Frank's feeling better. I wish he'd tell me when he's not feeling well."

She puts her hand on my shoulder. "I'm doing whatever I can to make sure he stays healthy. Even though I'm a nurse, I didn't know that much about MS until I met Frank. But since then, I've done a lot of research and I'm trying to help him have more good days and fewer bad."

I watch her face as she says it. She seems determined, like she really wants to help Frank get better.

"You care about Frank, don't you?" It's a stupid question. She obviously does and yet my mouth just spit out the words before I could think.

"Yes, very much so. I love spending time with him. He's very smart. And funny." She looks back at him. "And handsome."

The way she's talking about him, it's almost like she's in love with him. Holy crap! What if she is? And what if he's in love with her? Would they get married? How did this happen so fast? I'm overreacting. They may be in love, but they're not getting married. Frank moves at a snail's pace when making decisions. Then again, he didn't take long to decide to buy that house, so who knows?

"Name, please." I wake from my thoughts and realize we're at the front of the line. Two high school girls are handing out packets.

"Kensington, Jade," I say to one of the girls as the other girl helps Karen.

"Kensington." The girl flips through a stack of papers, finds my name, and checks it off. "Did you watch that show?"

"What show?"

"That reality show. Prep School Girls." She hands me my registration packet. "Every time I hear the name Kensington, I think of that guy who was on the show. Garret Kensington. Do you know who I'm talking about?"

"Yeah, what about him?"

"I'm totally in love with him. I stalk him online, trying to find out where he is so I can go find him and ask him to marry me."

The girl next to her at the table overhears and says, "She's not kidding. She's totally stalking that guy. She has a boyfriend and yet she's still stalking some guy from TV."

The girl shrugs. "It's not like I'll ever meet him. My boyfriend has nothing to worry about. Anyway, what size t-shirt do you want?"

"Small." I check to see where Garret is so I can warn him about this girl.

She hands me the t-shirt, then Karen and I bring our stuff back to Frank and Garret.

"Hey." I pull Garret down to talk in his ear. "That girl checking people in told me she's stalking you online and wants to marry you, so you might want to move so she can't see you."

"What girl?" He looks back at the table.

"Don't look! She'll see you."

"Why didn't you tell her I was married?" He smiles and gives me a kiss.

"She probably wouldn't believe me."

He nods toward the table. "Let's go tell her. You can show her your ring. That way she'll stop stalking me."

"No. Just forget it."

"Is there a map of the race course in there?" He points to the plastic bag the girl gave me.

"I don't know. I didn't look. Here." I hand him the bag.

He opens it and sifts through the sheets of paper.

"Why do you want the map?"

"I just want to see where you'll be." He checks the map.

"I'll be with all the other runners. Just look for the crowd."

He's acting weird again. Why does he care about the route? It's a 5K. It's a short loop, down and back.

He puts the map away and sets his hands on my shoulders. "When you're out there, stay with the other runners, okay? Don't go off the race route."

I give him a funny look. "Why would I go off the route?"

"Just be careful. And don't get hurt."

I reach up and kiss him. "I love you, but you worry way too much about me. If anything, I should be worried leaving *you* here with Stalker Girl."

"Jade, we should head over to the starting area," Karen says as she stretches her arms behind her back.

"Okay." I give Garret another kiss. "See you later."

"Good luck." He hugs me and says quietly to me, "You look really hot, by the way. Love you. Have fun."

I'm wearing tight black running pants and a hot pink running jacket with black gloves. The jacket is tight like the pants because when it's cold out, I like having the fabric close to my skin. I used the gift card Garret's dad gave me to buy a whole new running wardrobe. I love buying running stuff. Sports bras, tank tops, running shorts, headbands. I love all that stuff.

The race starts and I keep pace with Karen, who runs what I'm guessing is a nine-minute mile. It's slow for me but I don't mind. This is for fun, not competition. We finish it in a half hour, then meet up with the guys who are waiting with bottles of water. Then Karen goes home to change, and Garret, Frank, and I head back to the house.

When we get there, Chloe is in the kitchen with an apron on, mixing something in a bowl. She comes over and gives me a hug. "Jade! Welcome home."

"Thanks. And thanks for making dinner for everyone. It smells great in here."

The whole house smells like turkey, but also like a bakery. She must be baking rolls.

"I was happy to do it. I love to cook." She goes up to Garret and gives him a quick hug. Chloe's a hugger, just like Harper. She hugs everyone.

I offer to help her cook but she won't let me. She said Ryan's her helper today. She has him wearing an apron and making some kind of casserole. It makes me laugh how she gets him to do this stuff. It's only because he's totally in love with her.

Chloe looks cute today. She's about my height and has shoulder-length, straight brown hair with blond highlights. She's wearing a dark orange, short-sleeve knit dress that hugs her curves. I notice Ryan eyeing her as she moves about the kitchen. She's not fat, but she's a lot curvier than I am, and Ryan likes a curvy girl.

As Chloe and Ryan make dinner, the rest of us watch the parade. Karen arrives at eleven, wearing a dark green dress with a patterned scarf. Frank has on a shirt and tie. He almost never wears a tie, but he wanted to look good for his girlfriend. Garret's also wearing a shirt and tie, and I have on a dark purple dress, which is one of Garret's favorites because he loves seeing me in purple.

We have Thanksgiving dinner at two, stuffing ourselves to the point we can barely move. The rest of the day we play games, watch TV, and talk. Frank has the fireplace going, which makes the house feel warm and cozy. Speaking of cozy, Frank and Karen were getting awfully cozy on the couch when we were watching TV. There was hand-holding and some kissing going on. Just on the cheek, but still. They thought nobody was looking, but I caught them several times. And when Karen was leaving to go to work, they were kissing good-bye at the door.

That night, the guys watch football while I look over my speech again. Then I call Harper. I was hoping to talk to her before the surgery but her phone goes straight to voicemail.

On Friday we hang out at the house, just being lazy. We watch movies and stuff ourselves with leftovers. It's my kind of day. Karen and Chloe come over for dinner, then we all play cards. I keep my eye on Karen and Frank, watching them interact. I've decided they're definitely in love. Garret thinks so, too.

Before going to bed, I call Harper again but she doesn't answer. She's probably still too out of it from the surgery. But I did get a text from her mom saying that everything went well.

Garret called Sean but he didn't pick up. That's probably not a good sign.

We haven't heard from Pearce either. He didn't call us yesterday because he had his parents over for most of the day. But I thought he'd at least call us today and ask about our Thanksgiving and tell us about his, but he didn't. We haven't heard a word from him, and Garret hasn't tried calling him. I was going to call Pearce myself just to say hi but Garret told me not to. He said his dad's busy and not to bother him. It seems weird, but whatever. I can't worry about it. I need to focus on my speech, which is tomorrow. I don't know if I can do it. I'm so nervous.

# Chapter 4

**GARRET**

*I*t's been two days and I haven't heard a word from my dad. He said he was going to talk to my grandfather on Thanksgiving, but it must not have gone well because my dad said he'd call when this is over and he hasn't. It's not like I thought this would end after just one conversation, but I thought my dad would at least give me an update.

I still haven't slept more than a few hours a night. I have no appetite but I've been forcing myself to eat so Jade doesn't think something's wrong. Well, she knows I'm not myself, but she's convinced I'm coming down with a cold or the flu. Maybe I should just pretend I'm sick to throw her off track. I hate lying to her like this. I told myself I'd stop hiding shit from her and here I am doing it again. My dad needs to hurry up and end this because I can't keep this up for much longer.

Now it's Saturday and time for us to leave for Jade's speech. She's so nervous I thought she might throw up. She hasn't yet, but she looks like she could. The speech is at her old high school in the auditorium. There's supposed to be about 50 people there. Jade gave her valedictorian speech to 350 of her classmates and their parents so this should be easy, but I think she's nervous because for today's speech she has to talk about herself and she's not comfortable doing that.

We arrive at Jade's high school at noon. Her algebra teacher, the guy who helped plan the event, greets us in the hallway. The guy is old and bald with thick glasses, wearing a plaid shirt and khaki pants. He gives Jade a hug and thanks her for doing this, says hi to Frank and me, then takes off to get the auditorium ready.

"How's it feel to be back?" Frank asks Jade.

"Not much has changed. It still smells like sweaty gym socks and notebook paper."

Jade's holding my hand. Her hand is all clammy because of her nerves. I need to get her mind off the speech so I say, "Why don't you show me around?"

"There's nothing to see. It looks like any other high school."

Actually, mine looked nothing like this. My prep school looked like a castle, all stone on the outside with ivy growing up the sides. And the inside was kept immaculate with shiny hardwood floors, walls that were kept freshly painted, and a hand-carved wooden banister on the staircase.

Jade's school has cracks in the walls and floor, banged up lockers, and it smells like sweaty socks, just like she said.

I pull on her hand. "Come on. Give me a tour. We have some time to kill."

Frank takes a seat on the bench outside the auditorium. "You two go ahead. I'm going to wait here."

Jade shows me her old classrooms, her locker, and the gym. Her hand isn't as clammy anymore so I think my distraction technique is working.

We walk outside and check out the track. Jade was on the track team sophomore year and the cross-country team junior and senior years. The football field is next to the track and some guys are out there playing football.

"I told you there's nothing to see." Jade starts moving side to side and shivers a little and I know it's from her nerves and not the cold.

"Hey." I put my hands on her shoulders. "Relax. You're going to do great. Just remember you're doing this for them. Not you."

38

She takes a deep breath. "Keep telling me that because it helps. It really does. Otherwise I feel like I'm in speech class being graded."

"I'll tell you again before you go on stage." I hug her. "But you need to relax, Jade. Seriously. You're shaking. Let's go back inside."

As I go to open the door, it swings open and a guy walks out. He does a double-take of Jade and says, "Jade?"

Jade looks up and sees the guy. She seems surprised. "Um, hi."

"Didn't expect to see *you* here. How have you been?"

"Fine." She must've gone to school with this guy, but she must not have liked him because she's not acting happy to see him. "What are you doing here?"

"My parents moved, so now we're in this district. My little brother goes here." He nods toward the football field. "He's over there playing football."

"What grade is he in?" Jade hides her hands in her coat pockets and glares at the guy. She definitely doesn't like him, which means *I* don't like him.

"He's a sophomore." The guy's eyes haven't left Jade for a second, and I don't mean just her face. He was checking her out. All of her. She has her coat unzipped and I just saw him trying to look down her shirt. I don't know who the fuck this guy is, but he's not going to look at my wife that way.

"Hi, I'm Garret." I shove my hand in front of him. "Jade's husband."

The guy ignored me until I said 'husband.' Then his eyes shot up and met mine, but he's too shocked to say anything.

"Don't know how to shake hands?" I'm still holding my hand out. "It's pretty simple."

I hear Jade snicker as the guy shakes my hand. He has a weak handshake. I hate weak handshakes.

"Might want to work on your grip, there," I say, just to be an ass. "And *you* are?"

"Josh." He stands up straighter, shoulders back. I'm still taller than him. He's about 6'1. I'm just under 6'4. He looks at Jade. "Was he joking? You're not really married, are you?"

Jade holds up her hand and shows him the ring. "Actually, I am. Garret and I got married last summer. I met him in college."

"The college you got the scholarship to?" He flips his hair back. He has one of those haircuts where it's too long in front, which he probably thinks is what girls like, but it just looks stupid because it's always hanging in his eyes.

"How'd you know about my scholarship?" Jade asks him.

"I dated some girls here who knew you."

"Why were they talking about me?"

He shrugs. "I don't know. That's what girls do. They talk about each other. So you're really married?"

"How many times does she need to say it?" I raised my voice, which I didn't mean to do, but this guy's really getting on my nerves.

He ignores me and keeps talking to Jade. "You live out east somewhere?"

"I used to, but now we live in California." Jade pulls her coat closed because the guy keeps glancing down at her chest.

I've had enough of this asshole. I put my arm around Jade. "Come on, we need to go."

I lead her past the guy, opening the door for her.

"Jade, wait. Why are you here?"

She pretends she didn't hear him as we both go inside.

"Who was that guy?" I ask as we walk down the hall.

"Just some asshole I used to date."

Jade didn't date much before we met. She told me she only dated like five guys in high school.

"How long did you date him?" I don't know why I care. I can't stand thinking of her with another guy so I shouldn't even be asking.

"About a month. We went to homecoming together."

Jade only went to homecoming one time. Senior year. And the guy she went with is the guy she lost her virginity to. She told me the story. She said he went to another school, they dated for a few weeks, he invited her to his homecoming, had sex with her that night, and never called again.

"That asshole was the guy?" I spit out the words as I think about the idiot with the weak handshake and floppy hair sleeping with Jade. That guy took her virginity. Never called her again. And now he tries to act like they're friends? Like he did nothing wrong? That fucking pisses me off. And this is not the time to mess with me. I'm already fired up with rage over my grandfather and this guy's adding gas to the flame.

Jade sees my anger and doesn't answer my question.

I stop walking. "Jade. Was that the guy?"

"Garret, it doesn't matter now. It was a long time ago. He's an ass. Big deal. A lot of guys are."

"Not with you they're not." I storm back toward the door.

"Garret, stop!" Jade grabs my arm and yanks on it. "I'm giving a speech in 20 minutes. You can't go beat up Josh." She puts herself in front of me.

"I can take him down in 30 seconds. Plenty of time to make it to your speech."

"Yeah, and you'll go to jail. You already got in trouble last year for beating up Blake. You can't beat someone up again."

"After what he did to you he deserves to have his face bashed in."

"And you could end up in serious trouble."

"I'll take the risk." I can't get past the door because she's blocking it. "Jade. You need to get out of the way."

41

"No. Stop it. I mean it. He's not worth it." She looks into my eyes and I can see that she's scared. Scared I'll do something that'll take me away from her.

Fuck. She's right. What am I doing? I'm a grown man. I'm married. I can't do this shit anymore. Two years ago, I would've beat the guy unconscious. But now? As much as I want to do that, I can't. I have responsibilities. I have Jade.

I relax my shoulders and take a breath. "Fine. But I still want to kill him."

"I know you do." She smiles a little. "But I'm already stressed enough about the speech. I need you to calm me down, because right now you're stressing me out. Let's just go." She gets a firm grip on my arm and leads me away from the door.

"Can I kill him *after* the speech?" I'm kidding but she thinks I'm serious.

"Garret, no. Please don't do anything."

I kiss her. "I was joking. I'll leave him alone. Unless he talks to you again. Then I'll have to hurt him. And if he looks at your breasts again? I'll definitely kill him."

She sighs. "You're stressing me out."

I hug her into my side. "Sorry. We're done talking about him."

We walk back toward the auditorium and find Frank still sitting on the bench in the hallway. "How was the tour?"

"Boring," Jade answers.

"They want you to go wait behind the curtain on stage," Frank says to her.

"Right now? I still have 15 minutes."

"They want you back there while they do the introductions."

"Crap. I'm not ready."

I face her toward me, my hands on her upper arms. "You're ready, Jade. You've practiced this a million times. Just relax. And remember, it's about the audience. Think of the audience."

42

She nods.

I hug her. "I love you."

I let her go, then Frank wishes her luck and she goes through the side door that leads to the stage.

Frank smiles. "She'll do fine."

I sit next to him on the bench. "So how have you been, Frank? We haven't talked much."

"I'm doing well. It's good to finally be settled in the house. The move was more work than I thought it would be. But Karen helped a lot." He pauses, then says, "Has Jade said anything about Karen?"

"She said she likes her. Other than that, she hasn't said much." I smile at him. "Why do you ask? Are you thinking of marrying this woman, Frank?"

"Not anytime soon, but it could happen." He glances at his watch, then back at me. "But don't tell Jade that. I want her to get to know Karen first. If things get more serious between Karen and me, I'll tell Jade myself."

"Fair enough." Another secret I have to keep from Jade. Although I think she already knows Frank and Karen are serious enough that they might get married someday.

"How's Jade's therapy going?" Frank asks.

"She doesn't talk about it much. But she likes her counselor."

"I'm glad. If Jade can deal with all the issues from her past, it'll really make a difference in her life."

"It's already making a difference. Jade's starting to open up to me more and talk about stuff she wouldn't talk to me about before."

"That's good to hear." Frank stands up. "We should go inside. They'll be starting soon."

The auditorium is huge, so with the 50 or so people in here, it almost looks empty. Everyone's sitting up front but Frank

43

and I sit in the back. We don't want to make Jade even more nervous.

The program starts and some lady talks about the purpose of this event. I'm so tired I'm not really listening, but then I hear her introduce Jade and I pay attention again.

Jade comes out on the stage and goes up to the podium. She looks beautiful up there, in her navy skirt and white button-up shirt with the sleeves rolled up a little. Her hair is down, hanging in soft waves, and she has just a touch of makeup on. She looks much more sophisticated than when I first met her. Back then, she looked more like a high school kid. Now she looks like a young woman. She's grown up a lot this past year.

She begins speaking. Her voice is shaky and she stumbles on a few of her words. She stops mid-sentence and takes a breath.

*You can do this, Jade. Just relax.* I try to mentally send her the message.

She starts over from the beginning. "I'm here today to talk about—" She stops again.

Damn. This is bad. She was already nervous and now that she messed up, she'll be even more nervous. *I'm* nervous just watching her there, standing at the podium, unable to speak.

The people in the front row start checking their phones, coughing, messing with their hair. A few of them start whispering to each other.

"You know what?" Jade says. "I had this formal speech planned with inspirational words like hopes and dreams and all that stuff, but I don't think that's what you want to hear."

What is she doing? This is not what she practiced. But her words have everyone intrigued enough that their focus is back on the stage.

Jade continues. "I think what you want to hear is the truth. Because that's what I would've wanted to hear back when I was struggling to figure out how to escape the hell that used to be my life. Hopes and dreams mean nothing when your life is hell. When you're so far down that deep, dark hole that you no longer believe light even exists. When I was in that place, you know what I would've wanted someone to tell me?"

She pauses. The room is completely silent. All attention is on Jade.

"I would've wanted them to tell me that sometimes life sucks. Sometimes it's lonely. Sometimes it hurts so bad you feel like you can't go on. And it's not fair. It's not fair that some people have perfect lives and other people have to suffer. It's not fair that some people are born to drug-addicted, abusive, alcoholic parents while other people are born into loving homes. I was one of those unlucky people born into a home with a drug-addicted, abusive, alcoholic parent. It sucked. And it was lonely. And I felt like I was trapped in a deep, dark hole with no light. I thought there was no way out." She stops to breathe. "But there *is* a way out. You know what gets you out of the darkness?" She pauses again. "Choices. You may not think you have any. You may only see one road ahead of you, a road that leads nowhere. But the truth is, there are many roads and they all start with choices."

She takes a sip of the water that was left for her on the podium, then continues. "When I was 12, I decided to try my mom's vodka. It was out on the kitchen counter and my mom didn't care if I drank it. She was too drunk to care. But as I held the bottle up to my mouth, I realized I had a choice. If I took a drink, it would lead to another, and another after that, and soon I'd be her. I'd be my mom. And it wouldn't be her fault. It would be mine. I made a choice that day. Not just with the vodka, but with my life. I decided I didn't want to be my mom and I didn't want to use her as an excuse for having a crappy life. Although that would've been a lot easier. It would've been easy to drop out of school, become an alcoholic, do drugs, be homeless, and blame it all on my mom. But why would I do that? Why would I give her all that power? This is *my* life. Not hers. And I wanted something better. I wanted to have a real life. A real job. I didn't want to struggle. I wanted a different road than she took. And the only way I could get there was by making choices. Alcohol? Drugs? I had opportunities for all that. But I chose not to go down that road, because although that might've made my teen years more fun or more exciting or would've made me more popular, that road would've led me to a dead end. And it literally could've been a dead end, because sometimes that road leads to death. Like it did for my mom. She died. She overdosed on drugs and alcohol. And I found her. Dead. On the bathroom floor. Two days before my 16th birthday."

Jade's voice is shaky, but not from nerves this time. Now it's from emotion. Pure, raw emotion. She's putting it all out there. All of it. And I'm so damn proud of her. And fucking amazed she's able to do this. I actually have chills just listening to her speak. She's braver and stronger than anyone I know or will ever meet. I could never do what she's doing right now. I don't know anyone who could.

I glance over at Frank. He's got tears streaming down his face. Big, messy tears, but he's smiling.

Jade continues to tell her story. She owns the room. Nobody can take their eyes off her. Nobody's checking their phone. I don't even notice anyone moving. Not even a leg cross. They just listen, taking in each word.

After 30 minutes, I see Jade glance at her watch. Her time is up. She looks back at the young women in the audience and says, "I have an amazing life now. I'm in college. I have a great family and great friends. And I have a husband who I love more than anything in this world." She looks back at me and smiles, then directs her focus back to the women. "And it all started with one good choice that led to another. The choices weren't always easy. Sometimes I wanted to say screw it and give up. But I didn't, because after that first good choice, I saw a flicker of light from that dark hole I was in. And the more good choices I made, the more light I saw. And now all I see is light." She smiles. "Thank you for your time."

She walks off the stage, and as she does, everyone stands up and starts clapping so loud it fills the entire room. I'm clapping so hard my hands hurt.

That was incredible. *Jade* was incredible.

I go out of the auditorium to the hallway and see her there.

"Did I do okay?" she asks.

I hug her. "You did more than okay. You were freaking amazing. Words can't describe it. I had chills."

She pulls away. "You did? Really?"

"Yes, Jade. Really." I kiss her. "I think everyone did."

Jade notices Frank behind me. "Frank, what's wrong? Why are you crying?"

"I'm just so proud of you, Jade." He hugs her really tight, then lets her go and dries his face with his hand.

I put my arm around her. "When did you decide to change your speech?"

"When you told me to think about my audience and not myself. You were right. I needed to think about them, not me."

"When did you write all that stuff?"

"I didn't. I just jotted down some ideas for what I wanted to say and that was it."

"You didn't practice that?"

"No. I just talked."

"Jade, it sounded like you spent weeks practicing that. You didn't even stumble on your words."

"I know. It was weird. I just pretended I was talking to my old self. And as soon as I did that, the words just came out."

Jade's teacher comes out the stage door and goes up to Jade. "The women have asked if you'd be willing to go back in there and answer some of their questions."

"Isn't there another speaker now?"

"Yes, but she said she doesn't mind if we delay her speech. In fact she was so impressed with you, she'd like you to speak at a youth conference next March in San Francisco."

"She does?"

He motions to the auditorium. "Would you be willing to go back in there? Everyone is asking for you."

"Um, sure." She turns to Frank and me. "Do you guys mind waiting?"

I steer her to the door. "Just get in there, Jade. Take all the time you need."

She spends the next half hour answering questions. And she could've stayed even longer but they needed to move the schedule along. Before we left, the woman who wanted Jade to speak at that youth conference gave Jade her business card and asked her to call her. She told Jade she'd get a speaker's fee of $2000. Jade just about passed out when she heard that. She didn't know people got paid for this stuff. I didn't tell her, but my dad gets paid $50,000 for giving a speech at a business conference, sometimes more. Speakers can make a lot of money.

We leave the school and go back to the house. Ryan and Chloe are there, then Karen arrives and we all go out for an early dinner. During dinner, Frank and I tell everyone about Jade's speech and what a great job she did. Jade's embarrassed, of course, but I don't care. I'm so damn proud of her I want to tell the whole freaking world.

I was amazed by my wife before, but now I'm even more amazed. I knew she would do great things in her life and today just proved it. This is her calling. To share her story with people who need to hear it. People who are struggling like she was not that long ago. Jade doesn't think her story is anything special, but it is. She made a success of herself despite her childhood and she worked her ass off to do it. And she can inspire others to do the same. That speech she made was amazing. I bet she changed lives today. All with her words and her story.

Ever since Jade decided not to go to med school, she's felt lost and unsure of herself. But today, her path was made clear. This is what she needs to do. And if she doesn't realize that herself, I'm going to help her see it.

# Chapter 5

**JADE**

We just got back from dinner and said goodbye to Karen because she has to work tomorrow. Then Chloe left because she's behind on studying after spending so much time here the past couple days.

Frank and Ryan are lucky to have those two in their lives. I feel like I don't have to worry about Frank as much with Karen around. She really does take good care of him. And I've always liked Chloe. Last year, she used to make Frank go on dates with her and Ryan just to get Frank out of the house. She didn't want him to be lonely. She treats Frank like a dad, which he would be if Ryan would just marry her.

Now the four of us are watching a movie on TV. The fire's going and I'm lounging on Frank's new couch. It's so comfy I could fall asleep on it. I wish Garret and I could stay longer. The time went so fast. I can't believe we're leaving tomorrow.

"Jade, get over here." Ryan's standing by the back window.

I go over to see what he's looking at. "It's snowing! Let's go out there."

"No way I'm going out there," Ryan says. "It's too cold."

"I'll go with her." Garret grabs our coats from the closet. "Who's the pretty boy now? Can't take the cold, Ryan?" He smirks at him as he gives me my coat.

"Just wait," Ryan says. "Once you feel that wind, you'll be back here in a few minutes."

"Boys," Frank calls out from his chair. "Be nice."

50

He's just kidding. Frank loves his dad role. Now with Garret, he's got three kids to scold.

Garret and I go out to the back yard. The ground is already covered with a couple inches of snow and giant flakes are dropping from the sky. I tilt my face up and watch them fall.

"Hey." Garret circles his arms around my waist.

I take my eyes off the snow and look at him. "Yeah?"

"You were amazing today."

"Thanks, but you don't have to keep saying that."

"I need to, because you need to hear it. What you did up there was amazing. I can't stop thinking about it."

"It *felt* amazing."

He smiles. "Tell me why."

"It just felt good to be up there and look out at the faces of people just like me and have them understand me and what I've been through. I've never had that. I used to think I was the only one stuck in the darkness, unable to get out. I mean, when I got older I knew there must be other people who felt that way but I'd never met them. And today I did. I didn't know those women in the audience, but when I looked at them, I could tell they felt just like I used to feel. So maybe something I said today will help them stop feeling that way. Maybe it will help them get to the light."

"It will, Jade. You had that whole room focused on your every word."

"How do you know?"

"Because I sat in the back and watched it. And then they asked you to go back in there. That shows how much of an effect you had on them." Garret wipes the wet snowflakes off my cheeks. "Jade, I think you should give more speeches like you did today."

"I told that lady I'd do that conference in March."

51

"I mean more than just that conference. I think you should consider making this your career."

"That's not a career. It's just a thing I might do on the side."

"It *is* a career. You can get paid for giving speeches. A lot of people do. And if you don't want to get paid, you can donate your speaking fee to charity."

"But it's not really work. I actually *liked* doing it."

Garret laughs. "Jade, do you hear yourself?"

"Yeah. Why?"

"This whole semester you've been trying to figure out what to do for a career. And I told you to find something you like doing. Something you had a passion for. This is it, Jade. What you did today is what you should do for a career."

I take a moment to think about that. Could I really be a speaker? Could I go around telling my story to other people? If I did, I'd be helping people, which is what I want to do. And once I got past the nerves, I *did* like what I was doing today. It gave me energy. I could feel the energy from the audience. They actually listened to me. They wanted to hear what I had to say. And when that lady asked me to speak in March, I was excited about it.

"I think that might be a good idea." I peer up at the snow again. "But I still don't know what to do for a major."

"What about psychology?" Garret says it like he's already thought about this. "You like your psych class. You tell me about it all the time. And you liked the psych class you took at Moorhurst."

"Yeah, but what does that have to do with giving speeches?"

"You'll be speaking to people who are struggling with a lot of different issues. Ones that aren't the same as you had growing up. If you major in psych, you'll learn about all those different issues. You'll understand people better. And maybe you won't just give speeches. Maybe you'll work with smaller groups. Do workshops. Group counseling. I don't know. I'm just throwing out ideas here."

I'm getting even more excited because I like everything he just said. I would love to take more psych classes. I never even considered majoring in it, but what he said makes sense. A psychology degree might be the perfect fit for me and would be a good degree to have if I decide to help people like those women I met today.

"I need to think about this some more, but you might be on to something here."

"Don't overthink it, Jade. Just go with what feels right. And if what you did today feels right, then don't question it. Same with your major. Go with your gut, not your head. Always works for me."

I close my eyes and listen to the snow. People think it doesn't make a sound, but if you listen, you can hear it crackling as it hits the trees.

"When did you get out of the darkness, Jade?"

My eyes flip open and I see Garret looking at me.

"Like when did you get completely out so that it was all light?"

I smile at him. "When I met you. When I got to know you and you made me feel like I mattered. Like I was worth fighting for even when I pushed you away. When you agreed to be my friend and didn't force me to be more than that. Like I said today, I always had choices and those choices helped me get into the light so I could have a future and be able to support myself. But I was still lonely and afraid to get close to people. I still had darkness until I met you."

He hugs me into his chest. "See? Another good speech. You just keep getting better and better with these."

"And I didn't plan that one either. I guess I should just wing it from here on out."

A strong gust of wind blows, swirling the snow around our heads.

"Guess that's the wind Ryan was talking about. You want to go inside?"

I lift my head up. "Can I have a kiss first? I love kissing you in the snow."

"You can have as many as you'd like." He cups his hands around my face and presses his warm lips to mine. It reminds me of when we kissed in the snow on our first date. I still get that same fluttery feeling I felt when he kissed me that night just over a year ago.

The wind blows again and I shiver. Garret breaks from the kiss. "You want to go inside now?"

"Yeah, the wind's too cold." I huddle next to him as we walk toward the house.

Ryan opens the door. "Jade, you might want to call Harper. She's called twice since you came out here. I didn't answer it but I saw her name on the screen."

"Really? I hope she's okay." I race inside to the table to get my phone. "I'll call her from the bedroom."

Garret follows me in there. "I'm guessing it's about Sean. You want me to listen in?"

"Yeah, because you'll probably have to call Sean when I'm done with Harper."

I call her and she answers right away. "Jade, I'm sorry to bother you when you're with your family. Can you talk?"

"Yeah, of course. How are you feeling? Did the surgery go okay?"

"Yeah, it was fine. That's not why I'm calling." Her voice is shaky and it sounds like she's crying.

I look at Garret. "Harper, is this about Sean?"

"He came to the hospital. I told him not to. I knew he didn't have the money for a plane ticket, but he came anyway."

She sniffles. "But my parents wouldn't let him see me. They told the hospital staff to keep him away. Now I don't know where he is. I've called him a million times. Texted him. I'm worried about him, Jade. He always answers his phone. What if something happened to him?" She sniffles again. "I talked to one of the nurses and asked her if Sean told her where he was staying. She said he didn't tell her, but that she thinks she saw him sleeping in the park last night." Harper's crying even more now.

Garret's shaking his head, annoyed with Sean for not taking the money we offered him for a hotel room.

"Harper, don't worry. Garret will call Sean and we'll figure out what's going on."

"Can Garret call him right now? I have to know if Sean's okay."

"Yes, he'll call him right now."

"Thanks, Jade. And you'll call me back, right?"

"Yes. Bye, Harper."

We hang up and Garret's already got his phone out. He calls Sean, putting the phone on speaker. It rings and rings but Sean finally answers.

"Hey, Garret."

"Sean, where the hell are you?"

"I'm at my apartment."

"I thought you weren't flying back until Sunday."

"Plans changed. I came back early."

Sean sounds strange. He's talking slow and his words are kind of drawn out.

"Jade just talked to Harper."

"So you know what happened."

"Yeah, but you need to call her back. She's freaking out because you're not answering her calls or her texts."

"Why would I answer her? We're not dating anymore."

55

"What the hell's going on with you? Why are you acting like this?"

"Because it's over." He slurs the last word. Garret noticed it, too. "And I need to accept that and move on."

"Have you been drinking, Sean?"

"It's Saturday night. That's what people do."

"You sound drunk."

"Whatever. Maybe I am."

"Just call Harper and tell her you're okay."

"Have Jade call her. I'm done talking to Harper."

"Jade shouldn't have to get in the middle of this and neither should I. You need to call Harper yourself."

"Can't do it. Sorry."

Garret sighs. "Fine. Jade will call her, but we're not doing this again."

"You won't have to. I told you, Harper and I are done. It's over." He slurs his words even more.

"Sean, put the damn bottle down. It's not going to help. And hey, what the fuck were you doing sleeping on a park bench in LA? You could've been killed."

"Who told you?"

"Harper said a nurse saw you sleeping there."

"Must've been Deloris. She's a nice lady. She was the only one at the hospital who didn't treat me like shit."

"Sean, we've gotta go. Stop drinking and get some sleep. I'll call you later." Garret hangs up. "He's too out of it to talk. I'll call him tomorrow when we get back."

I call Harper again. She answers on the first ring. "Did you talk to him?"

"Yes, and he's fine. He's back in Connecticut."

"Why didn't he answer my calls?"

I don't mean to be harsh, but there's really no nice way to say it. "You broke up with him, Harper. He's not going to answer your calls."

"I just thought maybe we could—"

"You can't be friends with him. It won't work."

"Did he say that?"

"No, but you know you can't."

"I miss him, Jade. I miss him so much." She's crying again. "I just want to talk to him. I just—" She doesn't finish.

"I'm sorry, Harper."

"I have to go." She's sobbing now.

"Harper, wait." I check the phone. "She hung up," I say to Garret.

He's in a daze, staring at the wall behind me.

"Garret, what's wrong?"

"They got to him."

"Who? What are you talking about?"

"They got to Sean. That's why he's acting like he doesn't give a shit. That's why he came home early."

"Who got to him? Harper's parents?"

"No. The organization."

"What do you mean they got to him?"

"They threatened him, or they threatened to hurt his family if he doesn't stay away from Harper."

"Are you sure?"

"I'm sure. There's no other reason he'd suddenly act that way. He wouldn't even call Harper back after she left him all those messages. You know that's not Sean. The Sean we know would've called her back right away. He wouldn't let her worry like that. He cares about her way too much. That's why he's drinking. He can't handle hurting her like this, but he had no choice. They threatened him." Garret holds my arms and looks me in the eye. "This is serious, Jade. I mean it when I say to stay out of this. If Harper wants to talk about Sean, just change the subject. Don't even mention his name."

"Doing that will just cause her to ask more questions."

"I don't care. She'll have to get answers from someone else. She's not getting them from us."

Once again, the organization is interfering with our lives. But this time, they're going after our two closest friends.

# Chapter 6

**GARRET**

Jade and I are flying back to California in a few hours and I'm not sure how I feel about that. I like our beach house and I like where we live, but I don't feel safe there. What if my grandfather is having us watched? What if he changed his mind and decides to do something to Jade *now* and not wait until later? If he wants me to transfer to Yale, he can't wait years to hurt her. He'd have to do it soon.

I feel like I can't let Jade out of my sight, so how is this going to work? I can't be with her every second of the day. But when I'm not with her, all I can think about is if she's okay.

My dad still hasn't called me. I've been sending him texts just to see if he'd respond, but he hasn't. And now I really need to talk to him. If he won't talk to me about my grandfather, I at least need to ask him about Sean. I need to know what's going on with Kiefer.

The organization sent their people to threaten Sean, which means they want to hurry this along. They want to make Kiefer a member, but they can't until he's met all the requirements, and breaking up Sean and Harper was one of those requirements. I'm guessing the organization found out Sean wasn't giving up on Harper so they took matters into their own hands.

What I can't figure out is why Kiefer took so long to force Harper to break up with Sean. I'm sure Kiefer's membership offer came with a deadline. Just like my grandfather, the organization likes deadlines. They probably gave Kiefer several months to do whatever they asked him to do in order to become a member. And yet he waited until last week to give Harper that ultimatum. So was Kiefer purposely stalling because he's not sure he wants to be a member?

I need to know the answer to that. If he's wavering, maybe my dad could talk to him and convince him not to do this. It would be risky for my dad to do that, but someone needs to talk Kiefer out of this and it can't be me.

If Kiefer joins the organization, his life, and the lives of his wife and daughters, will be destroyed. And if he joins, Jade can no longer be friends with Harper. I haven't told Jade this because I thought she'd figure it out herself, but she hasn't so I'll have to tell her soon. It's going to be a huge loss for her to lose Harper, but we can't be friends with someone who has ties to the organization. Obviously, Jade and I are already tied to the organization by way of William and my dad, but they're family so we can trust them. But I don't trust the other members, and Harper will eventually be married to one of them, which will make being around her too much of a risk.

"Garret, are you done in there?" I hear Jade in the bedroom. I'm in the bathroom, shaving.

I open the door, wiping the towel over my face. "Yeah, I'm done."

She comes up to me like she's going to kiss me but instead starts sniffing my face. "I love the smell of shaving cream. I have to sniff you before the smell is gone."

"You're funny." I kiss her, mid-sniff, then walk past her into the bedroom. "Did you pack everything?"

"Almost. I just need to grab my makeup bag." She comes out of the bathroom with it and tucks it in the suitcase. "Ryan has breakfast ready so we should get out there."

As I walk to the door, she stops me, her arms around my waist. "It's Sunday and I can't go to Garret's Pancake House."

I brush the wispy strands of hair off her face and kiss her. "You can go next Sunday."

"Can I pay for them ahead of time? Like when we get back?"

"There's no pre-payments allowed but we can still do stuff, Jade. You don't have to wait until next Sunday."

"Good, because it's been almost a week and that's just way too long." She leans in and whispers. "And we never got to celebrate our sexiversary."

"We'll celebrate it." I kiss her, then open the door. "Let's go eat."

Jade wouldn't have sex in Frank's house so we haven't done it since before we left. Truthfully, I haven't been in the mood because of everything that's been going on. I'm distracted and stressed and exhausted from my lack of sleep, so right now, sex isn't even on my mind. That's totally messed up and I don't like feeling this way and I'm pissed that I do. I have a beautiful wife who wants to be with me and we're newlyweds so I should be as eager as Jade is to get back home so we can do it. But I'm not.

I don't know how long I can go on like this. Hiding this from her is nearly impossible. She knows I'm not sleeping, she notices when I don't eat, and if I give her any indication I'm not in the mood for sex, she'll definitely know something's wrong.

"It's all ready," Ryan says as Jade and I walk in the kitchen. "Help yourself. We're just eating at the counter today."

"Works for me." Jade hands me a plate and takes one for herself.

Ryan has platters of scrambled eggs, hash browns, and bacon set out on the kitchen island.

"I went out this morning and got you these." Ryan holds a tray of donuts in front of Jade.

"Donuts! Thanks, Ryan." She takes two. "Frank, are you eating?"

"Yes." He's sitting in the living room, watching one of those Sunday morning political shows. "I was just listening to our new president to see what promises we can look forward to him breaking when he takes office in a few months."

Frank walks to the kitchen and I hand him a plate. "Not a fan of Kent Gleason, huh?"

"It's not just him. They're all liars. Doesn't matter what party." Frank scoops some eggs on his plate. "And Gleason never should've been elected. Part of me thinks they rigged the voting machines to make him win."

Jade looks at me, her hand frozen in place over the piece of bacon she was about to pick up. Luckily, I'm the only one who notices. She needs to get better at hiding what we know. She can't react every time someone says something like that. People will get suspicious.

"Look, Jade. Name brand." Ryan's holding up a carton of orange juice. "Remember when we used to have to buy the generic brand and water it down?"

Jade relaxes and picks up her bacon. "Yeah, it was gross. That's why I drank soda for breakfast."

"Real orange juice." He takes a sip of it and smiles. "Having money is awesome."

Just like Jade, it doesn't take much to make Ryan happy. He's used to having nothing, so undiluted, brand name orange juice is a big deal to him. Even though he has money now, he's still careful with it. He doesn't spend much. But at least he got some new clothes. He used to have on the same clothes every time I saw him. It's like he only had one pair of jeans and a few t-shirts and they all looked really old. Other than clothes, Jade said he's only used his money to pay for school and to buy his car.

"We never took the car out," I say to Ryan.

"Yeah, I was just thinking that. Let's go after breakfast."

Jade reaches across me for the salt. "Garret and I need to be at the airport at ten, Ryan."

"We won't go very far. And your flight leaves at noon. You don't need to be at the airport at ten."

"He's right, Jade." I grab a piece of bacon. "That's way too early."

"Okay, but if we miss our plane, I'm blaming both of you."

We finish breakfast, then Jade offers to clean up the dishes so Ryan and I can go for a drive. It's only nine-thirty, but Jade's already getting anxious, convinced we'll miss our plane if we don't leave for the airport soon.

"We'll be back around eleven," I say as I follow Ryan to the garage.

"You better not be gone that long!" Jade yells from the kitchen. "Garret, did you hear me? Turn your phone on."

I just laugh. "We should probably get back by ten or she'll have a panic attack."

Ryan hits the garage door opener. "Jade's always been one of those people who likes to be early. Like way too early." He gets in the car and waits until I'm in the passenger's side, then says, "In high school, Jade went to a party at seven forty-five because her friend said it started at eight."

"Which means it really starts around nine or nine-thirty."

"Yeah, exactly. So she got there and nobody was there. Nobody showed up at eight either so she just left. I had explain to her that you always add at least an hour to whatever time they tell you."

He backs the car out, then stops. "Did you want to drive? Sorry, I didn't even think to ask. Here, let's switch places." He undoes his seat belt.

"No, that's okay. You can drive."

Ryan nods. "I guess you've already driven one of these before. You have a six series so this is a step down. Or several steps." He fakes a smile. "We can just skip the drive. We don't have to do this."

"What are you talking about? I want to take it out." I motion him to go. "Hurry up. Show me what it can do."

"Okay." He smiles for real this time as he backs out onto the street.

This is one of the downsides of being rich. You can't share stuff with people. I don't mean material stuff, but experiences. Like the orange juice thing. I grew up drinking fresh squeezed orange juice, so I can't really share in Ryan's excitement over a carton of brand name orange juice. And even if you do show excitement, the person doesn't believe you. I'm sure Ryan thinks I'm just playing along, pretending to be excited about his car. The truth is, I *am* excited. The car is brand new and I haven't been in this year's model and I love cars, especially BMWs. So I *want* to take it for a drive. But even if I tell Ryan that, he won't believe me. He'll think I'm just being nice.

"I'll take it on the interstate," he says, "but I can't speed because there's always cops sitting there."

I glance around the inside of the car. "I like the interior. Newly designed this year, right?"

"Yeah, and part of the outside, too. They narrowed the front and changed the hubcaps."

He turns onto the on-ramp and hits the gas. We take off, merging onto the interstate.

"Nice acceleration, huh?" Ryan's beaming. He loves this car. I love mine, too. So that's an experience we can share. Doesn't matter what car you have. If you love it, you get that same feeling. That same excitement from driving it.

"You better slow down," I tell him. "I see a cop up ahead."

"Shit." He taps the brakes. "Thanks."

"How's school going?" I figure I should talk about more than just the car since Ryan and I don't get to talk much.

"It sucks. I've got really hard classes this year. Seems like I never stop studying. But at least the semester's almost over."

"So what do you think of Karen?"

"She's great. She takes really good care of my dad. I can't remember anything about my mom, but my dad said Karen's like her in a lot of ways." He merges into the left lane. "So how's Jade doing?"

"She's fine. Why? What do you mean?"

"I mean, does she ever like, hear stuff anymore?"

He means the voices. Ryan and I are the only ones who know about Jade hearing her mom's voice in her head.

"No. She doesn't."

"Do you think she'd tell you if she did?" He turns the vent so the heat isn't blowing on him.

"Yeah, she'd tell me. She's going to counseling now. You knew that, right?"

"Dad told me she was. But she's been to counseling before and it didn't help."

"It's different now. She wants to go. Nobody is forcing her."

"Good. She needs to deal with that stuff." He pauses. "When I first met Jade, she was so skinny I thought she was anorexic. Her face was all sunk in, her bones were sticking out everywhere. Then I found out she was skinny because she didn't have any food at her house. She was 12 when I met her. She saw me moving into the house with my dad and came over and said hi, a big smile on her face. She was desperate to make a friend. I invited her for dinner that night, and before she came over, my dad told me about her and her mom."

Part of me wants to hear more about Jade's past, but the other part of me doesn't. I don't want to think about her not having food or friends or anyone to take care of her. It's the past, but it still breaks my heart.

"Anyway," Ryan says. "I love her and I just want her to get past all that."

"We both do, Ryan. It's just going to take some time, but I'm doing everything I can to help her."

He shrugs. "I've decided you're not so bad. Jade could've done worse."

I laugh. "Thanks. That means a lot."

"Speaking of Jade, I better turn around or she'll yell at us for being gone too long." He gets off at the next exit. There's nothing out here but farm fields and an old gas station. "You want to drive back?"

"Sure."

"I'll pull over at the gas station." Ryan turns right, heading toward it just as my phone rings. It's Jade.

"Garret. You need to get home."

"Yeah, I know. We're turning around."

"Did your dad call you?"

"No. Why would my dad call?"

"You need to hurry." Jade's voice is rushed, urgent.

"Why? What's wrong?"

Ryan turns into the gas station. I nudge his arm. "Don't pull over, just go."

"You don't want to drive?"

"No. Just get back on the interstate and head home." I speak into the phone again. "Jade? Are you still there?"

"Yes, but—" Her voice gets cut off. I check my phone and only see one bar lit up.

"You don't have cell reception out here?" I ask Ryan.

"It gets spotty when you're out in these rural areas."

I hear Jade again. "Garret?"

"Yeah, we got cut off. What's going on there?"

"You need to get home. Your grandfather—" The phone cuts out again.

"My grandfather what? Jade? Are you there?"

I check my phone. It's dead. Shit! I forgot to plug it in last night. "Ryan, can I borrow your phone?"

"I left it on the kitchen counter." Ryan's on the interstate now, going the speed limit.

"You need to drive faster," I tell him.

"I can't. I'll get a ticket. That cop we passed earlier might still be there."

"I don't give a shit. I'll pay the ticket."

He mumbles something about his insurance rates going up. I'm not really listening as I try to figure out why Jade sounded so frantic. Did someone show up at the house? Is my grandfather there? Or did he send someone there? Shit, what if he did? Is that why Jade asked if my dad called? Does she know what's going on? Does she think my dad's involved?

In my mind I see images of Jade and Frank being held hostage in the house, guns pointed at their heads.

"Ryan, drive faster. I'm serious."

"What's wrong? What's going on?"

I keep my eyes on the road. "Do you have a gun?"

"A gun? Why would I have a gun?"

"So you don't have one? Frank doesn't have one?"

"No. Why?"

"Something's wrong and Jade wouldn't tell me anything. But she sounded really upset so we need to hurry up and get home."

"Why did you ask about a gun? You think someone's at the house? Like trying to rob us?"

I squeeze my hand into a fist, clutching my phone with the other. "I don't know. We just need to get home."

He steps on the gas and five minutes later we're back at the house. Nothing looks out of place, at least not on the outside. I jump out of the car while it's still running and we're still in the driveway. The front door is locked so I bang on it and ring the bell a few times.

Jade opens the door and pulls me into the living room and points to the TV. "It's your grandfather."

An image of my grandfather is at the top right corner of the screen.

I walk closer to the TV and hear the newswoman talking, "...suffered a severe stroke that has left him in a coma. Kensington was found earlier this morning in his Manhattan apartment and immediately rushed to the emergency room. He's currently in critical condition. In a statement just released, Holton's son, Pearce Kensington, said his father appeared to be in good health just last night when the two of them met for dinner. Pearce has asked the press to give his family privacy during this difficult time. In other news..."

My gaze remains on the TV as Jade hugs me. "I didn't want to tell you over the phone. But I thought for sure your dad would've called and told you." I feel her pull away. "Garret?"

I glance down at her. "No, he didn't call."

"You should call your father," Frank says.

I look over and see Ryan standing next to Frank. Everyone's staring at me, waiting for me to say something.

"Could you change the channel?" I ask Frank. "Find another news channel."

He comes over and hands me the remote. "It's all yours."

I flip through the channels until I see my grandfather's photo again. I turn up the volume. It's a financial news show with two older men talking to each other at a round table.

One of the men says, "If Holton doesn't recover, how will that impact the future of Kensington Chemical?"

The other man answers, "I doubt that it will. Holton is chairman of the board but his son, Pearce, is the one driving the success of the company. Kensington Chemical has seen tremendous growth since Pearce took over as CEO. With him at the helm, I foresee many profitable years ahead." He smiles. "Now if the company is ever turned over to Pearce's son, Garret, I would predict it would go out of business."

Both men laugh. Then one of them says, "Yes, he certainly made a spectacle of himself last year, didn't he? He's not the type of person you'd want running a company."

I change the channel again and see my dad walking fast toward the entrance of Kensington Chemical.

"I'm not answering any questions," he says to the reporters gathered around him. "I ask that you give my family privacy during this difficult time." He goes inside the building and security guards block the door so the reporters can't get in.

I hand Frank the remote. "I need to call my dad." I walk down the hall with Jade following behind me.

"Garret, wait. What should I do? Should I get the next flight to Connecticut?"

"We're not going to Connecticut. We're going home."

"Oh. Okay. So when are we leaving for Connecticut?"

"We're not." I walk into the bedroom and over to my phone charger on the dresser. I plug in my phone and turn it on.

"Don't you want to see your grandfather?"

"He's in a coma. He wouldn't even know I'm there."

I'm really pissed right now. Why didn't my dad call me? Or my grandmother? Or Katherine? My grandfather's in a coma and nobody tells me?

"You're not going to see him?"

"No." I stand there, my mind racing, my muscles tight. I'm still on edge from thinking Jade was here with a gun to her head.

69

"But he's your grandfather. You need to go."

"The news said he's in critical condition. He's probably not going to make it. He'll probably be gone before I even got there."

"Then we should be there for your dad." She says it softly. "And the funeral."

"I'm not going to the funeral."

"You're not?"

Jade's staring at me like she can't figure this out. Like she thinks I should be crying or something. But right now, I'm not able to put on a show and pretend that I'm sad. Because I'm not sad. Not even a little.

"Garret, if he doesn't make it, you have to go to the funeral."

"Why? You didn't go to *your* grandfather's funeral."

Shit. I didn't mean to say that. My mind's all over the place right now and I'm not thinking straight.

Jade looks down at the floor.

I pull her into a hug. "I'm sorry, Jade. I never should've said that. I know you wanted to be at Arlin's funeral. Dammit. I'm really sorry."

"It's okay." She wipes her eyes and looks up at me. "I know you're upset. What can I do?"

"Just give me a minute to talk to my dad."

She nods. "Okay."

She leaves, closing the door behind her. I call my dad. After the third ring, he picks up.

"Garret, I have some news," he says.

"Yeah, I heard. When did you find out?"

"Earlier this morning."

"And you couldn't fucking call me?"

He's quiet, and I realize I need to calm down. I don't know how my dad's feeling about this and I need to at least consider he might be sad.

"I'm sorry, Dad. I didn't mean to yell at you. I just didn't like hearing about this on the news."

"I know. And I should've called earlier. I was at the hospital and then things got out of control with the media and—well, I should've called. I'm sorry about that."

"So someone found him?"

"Yes. The housekeeper went in to clean and she found him on the floor in the living room."

"Where was Grandmother?"

"At home, in Connecticut. But now she's here in New York, staying with me at the apartment."

"How is she doing?"

"She's dealing with it. My mother isn't one to show emotion. You know that."

"How about *you*? Are you okay?"

"Yes." There's this odd moment of silence and then, "He's not expected to recover, Garret."

More silence. Dead silence.

My family uses silence like other people use words. Silence is a form of communication to us. And I think my dad is telling me something with his silence.

A cold chill runs through me as I consider what the silence means.

"Dad, you didn't—" I can't say it. I shouldn't even be thinking it. He would never do that. Not to his own father. But he answered my phone call. And he said he wouldn't talk to me until this was over. Until he took care of it. He promised he'd take care of it.

And now it's taken care of. Or it will be if my grandfather dies, and it sounds like that'll be happening very soon.

"Garret, I need to go."

"Wait. So you were with him last night for dinner?"

"Yes, I was here for a meeting so we met for dinner. He was tired so we didn't stay out late."

"What caused the stroke? Do they know?"

"They're not sure. It could've been caused by a number of things."

I've heard that story before. Someone has a sudden heart attack or stroke that can't be explained. I don't know much about strokes other than stuff I've heard on TV. I know they can kill you and I know there aren't always warning signs, so maybe it just happened.

But I also know there are certain drugs that can induce a stroke or a heart attack or a brain aneurysm. That's one way the organization takes out their enemies, especially people who are important. People whose deaths would be investigated. If they wanted to kill someone like Sean, a nobody, they'd just shoot him and then pay some cop to make a fake police report saying it was just a random crime. But if they need to kill a senator or a governor or some other well-known person, they plan a car accident or a plane crash. Or they make it look like the person died of a stroke or a sudden heart attack.

That's what I think happened to Arlin. I think one of the members slipped Arlin a drug that caused his heart attack. I didn't come to this conclusion until just last week, when my grandfather made that comment about Arlin. My grandfather acted like he knew Arlin was involved in the plan to destroy my image. And if *he* knew, then others might've as well. If so, Arlin would've been killed, maybe by my grandfather himself. Arlin and my grandfather were good friends for many years. And yet I know for a fact that my grandfather would have no problem killing his friend. Just like he had no problem killing his daughter-in-law. And no problem plotting to kill Jade.

I want him gone. I want that bastard dead and I don't feel bad about it.

"How long?" I ask, without an ounce of emotion.

My dad knows what I'm asking. "The doctor said he won't make it through the night. He'll be gone by morning."

There's more silence. This time it's conveying relief. Overwhelming relief. By tomorrow, this will all be over.

"We'll talk soon. Goodbye, Garret."

He hangs up and I sit on the bed, the relief I felt just seconds ago replaced by a heaviness in my chest as I think about how this happened. Was it really just a stroke? Or did my dad do this?

I never asked him the question. I couldn't, because I didn't want the answer. He said he didn't know what caused the stroke. But he's an expert at lying. All my life, I've never been able to read him to know if he's telling the truth.

As much as I wanted my grandfather gone, I didn't want it to be at the hands of my dad. Killing his own father? It seems too evil. Like something my grandfather would do, but not my dad. He's different.

My dad didn't do this. He couldn't. I know he's had people killed before, and even done it himself, but he couldn't kill his own father. Could he?

I think back to last week, when I told my dad what happened to my mom. How his father had planned my mom's death. Planned the timing of it. Made my dad think she was safe when she really wasn't. Is knowing that enough to drive my dad to kill his own father?

# Chapter 7

**JADE**

*I* knock on the bedroom door, then open it slightly and see Garret sitting on the bed, his forearms resting on his knees as he stares at the floor.

I walk over and stand in front of him. "Did you talk to your dad?"

He sits up. "Yeah. He agreed I shouldn't go out there. He said my grandfather won't make it through the night."

I hug him. "Garret, I'm sorry."

He hugs me back but doesn't say anything. I'm not sure what to do for him. I don't know how he's feeling. I know his grandfather wasn't speaking to him, but I thought Garret would be more upset by this. Maybe he's still in shock. He needs time to let this sink in. Right now, I just need to be here for him.

I pull away. "I don't mean to rush you, but we really need to head to the airport. Or we could take a later flight if you want."

He stands up. "No. Let's go. We need to get home." He points to the suitcase. "Is everything packed?"

"Yeah." I kneel down and zip it up, then turn it upright.

Garret takes it and we go to the living room. As Garret brings the suitcase out to the garage, I go over to Frank and Ryan. "Pearce said Holton won't make it through the night. I think Garret's kind of in shock right now so don't ask him about it, okay? Just act normal."

Garret comes back in from the garage. "I wasn't sure which car we're taking to the airport but I put the suitcase in the Honda."

We all stare at him. He's almost acting like nothing happened.

"Yes, that's perfect." Frank grabs his keys from the counter. "Everyone ready?"

It's weird to act like this, but how else are we supposed to act? We have to follow Garret's lead, and right now, he wants to ignore the fact that his grandfather is dying.

Frank makes small talk on the way to the airport. Ryan and I add to the conversation but Garret says nothing. At the airport, Frank parks at the drop-off area and we do the usual hugs and goodbyes.

"Call us when you get there," Frank says to me.

"I always do."

"I know. I'm just reminding you to."

I hug him. "Love you, Dad."

"Love you, too, honey."

I hug Ryan. "You need to give Chloe that ring for Christmas."

"You need to stop pushing me to get married. It's really getting annoying."

I laugh. "Get used to it. I'm not going to stop until you propose."

Garret's standing there, waiting. He already said his goodbyes.

"See you guys later." I wave as they get in the car.

Garret and I check in, then go to the gate and find that they're already boarding. We get our seats and Garret takes my hand, like he always does before we take off.

I lean over, keeping my voice down. "Are you okay? I'm worried about you."

"I'm good. Everything's good." He squeezes my hand a little, his eyes straight ahead. "We're gonna be okay."

Be okay? What is he talking about? Why *wouldn't* we be okay?

He leans his head back and closes his eyes and takes a deep breath. "It's almost over."

He said it so softly I think he was talking to himself, not me. But what does he mean? What's over?

The plane engines roar and I feel us taking off. I rest against Garret's shoulder and fall asleep.

When we get home, Garret brings the suitcase to the bedroom, then comes back out to the living room and turns the TV on. He's standing behind the couch as he flips through the channels. He stops on a news channel.

"...is still in critical condition," the newswoman says. "Holton Kensington is well known by those in the financial world, but other people know him because of his grandson, Garret Kensington, who appeared on Prep School Girls, a reality TV show. Garret dated one of the stars of the show, Ava Hamilton. We spoke to Ava briefly and asked her about the news."

They cut to video of Ava coming out of a coffee shop. She looks different. Her hair is longer and she has on less makeup than normal. She's wearing skinny jeans and a short black coat and sunglasses, a giant gold purse hung over her shoulder.

"I was so sorry to hear about Holton," she says. "I'm hoping he'll make a full recovery." She walks up to her silver Mercedes.

"Do you ever talk to Garret?" the reporter asks.

"Of course I do. Garret and I are close friends." She gets in the car.

"Have you spoken with him since this happened?"

Ava doesn't answer as she shuts the door and starts her car. The video ends and they cut back to the newswoman at the desk. "People close to the family say that Garret has been estranged from his grandfather since last spring. It's not known if the two of them have reconciled, although our sources tell us Garret has not yet been to the hospital to see his grandfather. We'll take a short break and when we get back we'll be…"

Garret clicks the TV off. "Where do they get this shit?"

I take the remote from him and lead him to the couch to sit down.

"I don't know." I really don't, and it kind of scares me that they know all that. It's like someone's watching us or something.

"And they ask *Ava* about me? Seriously? Why are they even talking about me? They should be talking about my grandfather, not me."

I give him a hug because I don't know what else to do. I can't tell what he's thinking or how he's feeling, and he's not ready to tell me.

I sit back and look at him. His eyes are heavy and his face looks tired. "Garret, maybe you should try to sleep a little."

He doesn't answer. He's gazing behind me at the TV that's no longer on. I get off the couch and take his hand and pull on him to stand up. "Come on. Let's just lie down for a few minutes."

He gets up, not saying anything, and we go in the bedroom and take off our shoes. We lie down on the bed and he pulls me against his chest. He's holding me a little too tightly, which he's been doing all week and I've been kidding him about it. But today, I don't say anything. After a few minutes, he loosens his hold on me and his breathing changes as he falls asleep. I try not to move because I want him to sleep. He needs to. He hasn't slept much all week and I don't know why. Whenever I ask him about it, he denies it and says he's been sleeping.

His breathing becomes slower and heavier as he falls into a deeper sleep, his arm now relaxed around me. I'm not tired since I slept on the plane, but I remain there next to him so he doesn't wake up.

An hour later, I'm still wide awake, thinking about Garret's family. I wonder how Pearce is doing. He didn't get along with Holton, but Holton is still his father so I'm sure this is hard on him. I think about Lilly, too, and how she'll feel when Holton's gone. I hope someone's there for her, comforting her. I know Katherine won't do it. She'll tell Lilly not to cry or act sad. And Pearce will be too busy planning the funeral to deal with Lilly.

My phone rings from the living room. Shit. It's going to wake Garret up. It rings again and keeps ringing, then finally stops. It's probably Frank. I forgot to call him to tell him we made it home. I lift Garret's arm off me and slide to the edge of the bed and get up. He's still sound asleep.

I sneak out of the bedroom and gently shut the door. I check the phone and see that it was Sean who called, not Frank. I text Frank and let him know I'm home, then call Sean back.

"Sean, it's Jade."

"Hey. I saw the news and I wanted to check on Garret. How is he?"

"He's okay. He's sleeping right now."

"When he wakes up, tell him I'm really sorry about last night. I drank too much and was being an ass."

"Don't worry about it. We know you're going through a rough time right now."

"Did you talk to Harper?"

"Yeah. I told her you're okay. She was really worried about you, Sean."

"I know. I just—" He stops and I know he wants to tell me what's really going on and how he was threatened, but he can't. "I just couldn't call her back. She made it clear that we're over, so I can't keep talking to her. It only makes this harder."

It's true, but I know Sean would still be calling her if he hadn't been threatened like that. He wouldn't care how much it hurts to hear her voice. He loves her too much to never talk to her again. So I know this is killing him, being forced to stay away from her.

"Has she called you again since last night?" I ask.

"Yeah. She left me a goodbye message on my phone. She cried through most of it so I couldn't hear her that well. But she said she wouldn't call again." Sean's voice cracks and he clears his throat. "Anyway, I should let you go. Tell Garret to call me when he's ready to."

"Sean, you don't have to hang up. We can talk if you want." I feel like he needs to talk to someone. Garret is his best friend, and although Sean has other friends, I don't think he talks to them about this kind of stuff.

"I'm moving," he blurts out.

"To a new apartment?"

"I'm moving to LA."

"What? When did you decide this?"

"Last Friday. After I went to the hospital and they kicked me out, I knew Harper and I were done. I knew there was no chance of us ever getting back together."

It's a lie. Sean would never give up that easily. He was definitely threatened.

He continues. "So I called up my old boss from that place I worked at last summer."

"The one who offered you a job last September?"

"Yeah. I wanted to see if he had any openings. I met with him at his restaurant in LA on Friday. He gave me a tour of the kitchen, introduced me to the staff, and offered me a job on the spot. So I took it. I told him I'd need an advance on my pay in order to get an apartment. He agreed to it, so I'm moving there next week. I leave Thursday morning."

"Is this really what you want?"

"This job could actually turn into something, so yeah, it's good. And I'll get paid a lot more."

"But you don't know anyone in LA."

"Doesn't matter. I'll meet people. And you and Garret will come and see me, right?"

"Yes. Absolutely. And you can come up here. We don't have a guest room but we'll get you a place to stay."

"Jade, I hope we can still be friends even though I'm not with Harper anymore."

"Of course we will."

"You say that now, but things change when people break up. People pick sides."

"Sean, I'm not going to do that. And neither is Garret."

"I need to start packing. I still have some of Harper's stuff here. What do you think I should do with it?"

"Put it in a box and take it to Moorhurst. Just leave it with Jasmine. She's the RA on Harper's floor. Tell her to give it to Harper when she gets back later this week."

"Okay, thanks. I'll talk to you soon."

I hang up and check on Garret. He's still asleep. I hope he sleeps the rest of the day. He really needs the rest.

I go back in the living room and call Harper. She left me several messages while I was on the plane.

"Jade, how's Garret?" she asks as soon as she picks up.

"He's okay. We're back home now and he's sleeping." I almost start to tell her I talked to Sean, but then remember I can't talk about him anymore.

"Tell him I'm sorry. I know his grandfather was mean to you guys, but still, it's hard when something like this happens to your family."

"The doctor said Holton probably won't make it through the night."

"Really? I thought maybe he'd get better."

"It doesn't sound like it."

"Well, tell Garret I'm really sorry and I'm thinking about him."

"I will. So when are you flying back to Connecticut?"

"On Wednesday, as long as I get the okay from the doctor."

"Sean is leav—" Shit. I wasn't supposed to say that. This is really hard. I'm so used to talking about Sean with her.

"Sean is what?"

"Nothing. So how are your parents?"

"What were you saying about Sean?"

"I'm not going to do this, Harper."

"Do what?"

"I'm not going to tell you stuff about Sean now that you two are broken up. It will just make you sad, and you both need to move on."

"Please just tell me if he's okay." She sniffles. I think she's cried almost nonstop since they broke up.

"He's okay."

"Is he really, or are you just saying that?"

"He just needs some time."

She sniffles again. "I can't do this, Jade."

"Can't do what?"

"I can't be without him. I feel like I've lost a part of myself. I didn't realize how much I loved him until I didn't have him anymore. I kept telling myself that something was missing. That he wasn't the one. I guess because my parents didn't approve of him. But now that he's gone, I realize I made the biggest mistake of my life by letting him go. I know that he's the one, Jade. I know it now. I know it with all my heart."

Now she figures this out? Now? When she can't have him?

"You'll find someone else. Maybe not for a while but—"

"Jade, didn't you hear me? I don't want anyone else. I want Sean."

"What are you saying?"

"I'm saying I want him back."

"What about your parents?"

"I'm not speaking to them. Let them disown me. I don't care. I don't need their money. I'll get a job to pay for college. After everything they've put me through, I'm not even sure I want them in my life anymore."

"Harper, I know you don't mean that. You're really close to your parents."

"Not anymore. They lied to me, Jade. They said they'd support me in whatever I wanted to do. They always told my sisters and me that all they wanted was for us to be happy. And they know that being with Sean is what makes me happy. Happier than I've ever been. And yet they're still trying to take him away from me. They know how much I love Sean and they don't care. I had a huge fight with them last night."

"You did? With both of them?"

"Yes, and it was really bad. There was screaming and yelling and then my dad stormed out of the room and my mom followed him. I'm done, Jade. I love my parents, but I can't let them do this to me. They have no reason to. I've asked them a million times why they don't like Sean and the only thing they can come up with is that he's not right for me. And they can't explain why. So I'm done trying to please them. I'm getting Sean back."

"But you just left Sean a goodbye message." Damn! I did it again. Why can't I keep my mouth shut?

"How do you know about that? Did you talk to Sean today?"

I sigh. "Yes, but we didn't talk long."

"I'm calling him as soon as we hang up. I'm going to apologize to him a million times or however many times it takes for him to forgive me."

"He won't take your calls, Harper."

"Then I'll go to his apartment as soon as I get back in town. I'll surprise him." Her voice sounds happy just saying it.

"You can't. He won't—" I seriously need to stop talking.

"He won't what? Won't be there? Why? Does he have to work? Then I'll go there the next day."

Maybe I should tell her he's moving. She'll find out in a few days, anyway. And then she'll know I was keeping this from her, which will make her mad at me. What do I do? Garret told me not to talk about Sean, but he also told me to encourage Harper to stay away from him, so I guess this is my chance.

"Just let him go, Harper."

"Jade, why would you say that after what I just told you?"

"Because Sean's moving. He'll be gone when you get there."

"Moving where?"

"To California. He got a job at a restaurant in LA. It's a really good opportunity for him, so you need to let him go."

She's quiet.

"Harper, are you still there?"

"Yes." She sniffles. "I don't want him to leave. What should I do, Jade?"

This is so hard. I know what they both want, but I also know they can't have it.

"Let him go. He's already given up a lot for you. And what if you change your mind? You can't do that to him."

"What do you mean? What has he given up for me?"

What is wrong with me today? I keep telling her things I shouldn't. I must be tired or too distracted thinking about Garret.

Now that I've hinted at it, I might as well tell her the truth.

"Sean was offered a job last fall. Back in September. The guy he worked for last summer told Sean he was so impressed with him that he wanted him to work at one of his restaurants. He told Sean he could see him being head chef someday."

"And he turned it down? To be with me?"

"I shouldn't have told you this. Sean didn't want you to know. But Harper, I only said it because I don't want him missing out on another opportunity. He was lucky this guy gave him another chance and still wanted to hire him. Sean needs this job, Harper. He needs to go."

"You're right." She says it quietly, almost whispering it. "I'll talk to you later."

"Wait. You don't want to talk anymore?"

"I can't right now."

"Are you mad at me?"

"No. Not at all. I just need to go."

"Okay, but call me if you want to talk."

"I will. Bye, Jade."

This day just keeps getting worse. It's six now, so at least it's almost over. I turn my phone to vibrate and go back in the bedroom and lie next to Garret.

He stirs a little, then notices me there. "Where did you go?"

"I was just getting a drink of water." I don't want to tell him I talked to Sean and Harper. If I do, he'll ask me about it and then he won't go back to sleep.

"I missed you." He whispers it by my ear and kisses my neck as his hand moves under my shirt. Does he want to have sex? Now? I hope he's not thinking he *has* to because of what I said last night, telling him how it'd been too long since we did it.

"Garret, we don't have to. I know you're probably not in the mood with everything that's going on."

"I want to." He sits up, his face hovering over mine. "I need to be with you."

He looks into my eyes, his hand on the side of my face, his thumb brushing my cheek. He's thinking something but

I'm not sure what. The way he's looking at me reminds me of how he looked at me last March, when I was at his house after I learned about the plans for his future. Garret thought he'd lost me, but then he had hope again after we made that plan to destroy his image.

Why would he look at me like that again? Maybe he's not. Maybe he's just sad. I can't really tell.

He leans down and kisses me, softly, just once. He sits up and reaches behind his neck and yanks his t-shirt off, tossing it aside. Then he kisses me again, this time on my stomach as he undoes my jeans. He slowly undresses me, leaving kisses where my clothes used to be. Gentle, loving kisses like he's savoring every inch of me. The touch of his hands, the feel of his mouth, and the warmth of his breath cause tiny bumps to rise up on my skin and heat to well up in my core. I want to speed this along, my body aching to be with him. But he's not in a hurry so I let him continue, kissing and caressing me.

I don't know how he's holding out this long. Usually we'd be done by now, especially since we haven't done it for almost a week. But it's different this time. I'm not sure why.

Garret takes off his jeans and his boxers, then lies over me, his lips covering mine, his tongue teasing my mouth. He kisses me for several minutes, then finally puts himself inside me. Again, his movements are slow. Gentle. I love our usual fast, can't-get-enough-of-you type of sex, but I love this kind, too.

After a while, his thrusts get harder and faster until I finally get the release I've been waiting for. He stops for just a moment and kisses my forehead, then my cheek, then my lips. He starts up again, until he gets his own release. And then he lies on his back and holds me against him.

"I love you," I hear him say. I feel his lips kiss the top of my head as his arm tightens around me.

"I love you, too," I whisper back.

We fall asleep, and when I wake up, it's midnight. My stomach is growling because we missed dinner, but I don't feel like eating. We're both still naked on top of the bed. I feel cold, but if I get under the covers I'll wake up Garret. I quietly sneak to the closet and grab a blanket and take it back to the bed, laying it over us. Garret's sound asleep but he instinctively puts his arm up when I get next to him, letting me into my spot.

I'm relieved Garret's finally getting some rest, but I'm still worried about him. Something's not right. He's not himself. I snuggle closer to him and hug his chest and fall asleep again.

# Chapter 8

**GARRET**

*I* wake up and Jade's not in bed. The blinds are closed but I can see light peeking through the edges.

"Jade?"

There's no answer. I turn to check the time and see a note sitting on the nightstand. It's from Jade.

*Went to the library. Forgot I had to meet with my lab partner today. I'll be back after my meeting. Eat something. Then go back to sleep. Love you!*

It's ten. I'm supposed to be at class. Guess I'm not going. I get out of bed and stumble to the bathroom. I feel like I have a hangover, but it's just that groggy feeling you get after sleeping for 15 hours or however long it's been. It's strange how sleep can sometimes make you tired.

I see my reflection in the mirror and, shit, I'm a mess. My hair's sticking up everywhere and I almost have a full beard. For me it only takes one day without shaving to get a beard going. I take my razor from my travel bag, which Jade left on the counter. I didn't even unpack yesterday. Jade must've done it because the suitcase is put away. I didn't hear her unpacking. The only thing I remember from last night is having sex. And then I fell asleep again. I didn't even hear her leave this morning.

Jade left. And she's alone. Shit!

I drop my razor in the sink and race back to the bedroom to get dressed, then stop, realizing she's okay. He can't hurt her. This is over.

I relax and go back in the bathroom and turn on the shower. *It's over. This is over.* I keep repeating the words as I stand under the hot water.

I finish my shower, get dressed, and check my phone. I see a string of messages but I call Jade first to make sure she's okay.

"Hey, you're awake." She sounds happy, probably trying to cheer me up.

"Yeah. Where are you?"

"I'm still at the library. I'm done with my meeting but I had to look up some stuff. Do you want me to come home? I can do this later."

"Just stay there and finish. You want to meet for lunch?"

"Okay. Can we go to the coffee shop? Maybe meet at noon?"

"Sure. I'll see you then."

"Garret, how are you feeling?"

"I'm fine. I feel better now that I slept and took a shower."

"You grew a beard overnight." She laughs a little.

"Yeah. I'll shave. See you soon."

"Wait. Garret?"

"Yeah."

"You heard, right?"

"Heard what?"

"About your grandfather."

When she says it I realize I forgot to check the news this morning. I didn't even think to check. I just assumed he passed away overnight. But if he had, Jade wouldn't have left this morning. She'd want to be with me. And she'd sound sad. She doesn't sound sad.

"What happened?"

"Your grandfather made it through the night." She sounds happy, hopeful.

I'm neither of those. Truthfully, I'm disappointed. Fuck, that's messed up. He's my grandfather, but shit, he's pure evil and I wanted him gone.

"Garret, did you hear me?"

"Yeah. So they said he's getting better?"

"I'm not sure. He's still in a coma. You should call your dad."

"I will. I'll do it right now. I'll see you at lunch."

After we hang up, I turn the TV on and search for any updates. I find one on a financial channel.

"...condition remained the same overnight. His wife, Eleanor, has asked that her husband be transferred to a medical facility closer to their home in Connecticut." The camera pans to the other news anchor. "The stock market took a nosedive yesterday as reports of—"

I click the TV off and call my dad.

"Yes, Garret." He sounds like he's in a hurry.

"What's going on?"

"It's not a good time to talk. I'm in crisis mode here. One of our plants had a fire last night and this morning one of our distributors wants to—"

"Not about the company. What's going on with Grandfather?"

He sighs. "My mother is moving him to a different facility."

"Wait. Back up a minute. So he's better? He's recovering?"

"His condition hasn't changed. And it doesn't look like it will."

"By different facility, you mean the clinic?"

"Yes. Not the one you were at, but a different one. It's in the Hamptons. It has the latest equipment. A top notch staff."

"What does this mean? You think they can help him?"

"I don't think so. I'd be surprised if he made it through the week."

"You said he wouldn't make it through the *night*, but he did."

"Garret, I really can't talk right now. I have at least 10 people waiting outside my office. We'll talk later." He hangs up.

So it sounds like my grandfather's still going to die, but now it's happening later this week. Dammit. I just wanted this to be over. And it will be. In a few more days. Until then, I need to start acting normal so Jade will stop wondering what's wrong with me. I need to start eating and sleeping and going to class. And when my grandfather dies, I need to play along and act sad.

At noon I meet Jade at the coffee shop for lunch. She's sitting at one of the small round tables but she gets up when she sees me. She has on jeans and a light pink sweater that reminds me of the pink flowers we had at our wedding. Her hair is pulled up in a ponytail with a few loose strands falling down around her face. I see her every day, but sometimes I have these moments where I see her and realize how lucky I am that this beautiful woman is my wife. That she's all mine.

"Hi." She gives me a hug and I smell the fresh, flowery scent of her hair. I hold on to her for just a moment longer when she tries to pull away.

"You look beautiful." I kiss her head, then slowly let her go.

"Thanks." She gives me a funny look as she glances down at herself. She obviously disagrees, which I don't understand, but maybe if I keep telling her, she'll eventually realize that she really is beautiful.

"So did you call your dad?" she asks as we sit down at the table.

"Yeah. He said my grandfather's condition hasn't changed." I put my arm around her. "Let's not talk about this. I need a break from it. Talk about something else."

"Well, it's not a fun topic, but Sean called yesterday. And then I called Harper."

"I don't like the sound of this. Did something bad happen?"

"Kind of." She tells me about Sean moving to LA for that job he was offered back in September. Then she says Harper wants Sean back and doesn't care if her parents disown her.

"But you told her to leave him alone, right?"

"Yeah, but I don't know if she will. She really wants him back."

I'm not surprised she's trying to get Sean back. I kind of thought she would. She doesn't know the real story behind why her parents threatened to disown her if she didn't break up with Sean. And I knew if she thought about it, she'd realize that her parents' disapproval of him was not enough of a reason for her to lose the person she loves.

Sara comes up to the table. "Sorry I haven't been over here. It's been super busy." She turns to me. "Garret, I'm really sorry about your grandfather. Jade told me before you got here."

"I'm surprised you hadn't already heard about it. It's all over the news."

"I don't have time to watch the news. I barely have time to take a shower." She gets her order pad out. "Do you guys know what you want?"

We give her our order, then she leaves and I look back at Jade. "You have to tell Harper to let Sean go."

"I did. And I'll keep telling her that. It's just hard because she really misses him and doesn't want to accept that it's over. Maybe when she starts classes again she won't have time to think about him." Jade threads our hands together. "I tried that last spring. I tried to keep busy so I wouldn't think about you, but it didn't work. You were all I could think about."

"At least you had stuff to keep you busy. I was stuck in a house in the woods every weekend. I thought about you constantly."

She gazes down at our hands. "Someday I want you to tell me what you did all those weeks we weren't together. I don't want to know right now. It's still too fresh in my mind. But years from now, when I know for sure you'll never be taken from me, I want you to tell me."

"Jade, I'm not going anywhere. Nobody's going to take me."

She nods. "I'll believe that someday. I'm just not there yet."

If she only knew how close we were to being separated again. This time for good.

I can't tell her what almost happened. I don't want her ever knowing what my grandfather had planned. He'll be dead soon, and once he is, I don't want to think about this ever again.

Our food arrives and as we're eating, Grace calls to check on me. She worries about me as much as she worries about Jade. She's such a nice lady. She's more like a grandmother to me than my own grandmother.

I called my grandmother several times yesterday and again today and she hasn't returned my calls. I haven't talked to her since the Fourth of July. I know she's been avoiding me because my grandfather forbid her from talking to me. But now he can't control her so I don't know why she hasn't called me back.

Sometimes I get so freaking tired of my family and all their drama. I don't know why we can't just act normal and get along. Why does everything have to be so damn difficult? I just want to live my life and be happy, without them interfering. So today, that's what I'm going to do. I've been miserable ever since my grandfather showed up last week. But today, I'm going to be happy.

When we're finished eating lunch, I put my arm around Jade and say, "You know what we should do?"

"What?"

"We should get a Christmas tree." "But it's still November."

"Yeah? So? December's only three days away. And when my mom was alive we always put the tree up the day after Thanksgiving. Well, my mom did most of the work while my dad and I watched football, but I'd help her with the ornaments." I slide Jade's chair closer to mine and kiss her cheek. "Come on. I need this. It'll make me feel better."

She smiles. "Then let's get one. We'll go right after class. Do they sell them already?"

"They've had the fake ones out since before Halloween. I don't know about the real ones. You want a real one?"

"Maybe we should get a fake one. If we get a real one it might be all dried out by Christmas."

"We'll get a fake one now and when it's closer to Christmas we'll get a real one."

"Two trees? Really?" She gets that excited look I love so much. She's a millionaire and yet she still gets excited over the littlest things.

I kiss her. "Yes. Two trees. Or maybe three."

She laughs. "Two is good."

I grab my backpack and stand up. "I need to go. Come home right after class and we'll go shopping."

As I leave, I look back and see a huge smile on her face. I'm going to make this the best Christmas she's ever had. It'll be the best one for me, too, because I no longer have to worry. There's no deadline. Jade is safe.

# Chapter 9

**JADE**

*G*arret takes off out the door just as Sara comes over. "What are you smiling about?" She sits down across from me. "Why do I even ask? You're smiling because you have the hottest, sweetest husband in the world."

I laugh. "That's true, but that's not why I'm smiling. Garret wants to get a Christmas tree today and I'm smiling because I've never had one."

"I haven't either. My mom had this small green metal one she put on the kitchen table but it was more like a decoration. It wasn't an actual tree."

"Are you getting one this year?"

"I don't have the money for one, but Alex will have one up at his place."

"Hey, are you on break? I need to hear about your weekend."

"Yeah, I've got a few minutes. Tell me about yours first."

"We didn't really do much. We ate a ton of food and watched movies. Oh, and I gave that speech I told you about."

"How'd it go?"

"Really well. One of the other speakers asked me to talk at a youth conference in March, and now Garret thinks I should give speeches for a living, but I don't know. I need to think about it. So tell me about going to Alex's house for Thanksgiving."

"It was great. His parents' house isn't very big and there were 40 people there, so it was packed." Sara props her elbow on the table and rests her chin on her palm, a big grin spreading across her face. "But I loved being there. It was so much fun. His sisters are awesome. They both have young kids but not babies, so when they saw Caleb, they went all baby crazy. He got so much attention. I didn't talk to Alex's brothers much, but I talked to their wives. They went all crazy for Caleb, too. And Alex's parents are super nice. His mom even invited me there for Christmas. Oh, and the dinner was so good. Caleb kept trying to feed himself sweet potatoes with his hand and it got all over his face. It was really funny."

"See? I knew you'd have a good time. You worried for nothing. How was the hotel situation?"

"It was fine. I had my own bed and the hotel loaned us a crib for Caleb."

"So again, you didn't need to worry. Nothing happened."

"I know but," she lowers her voice, "I kind of wanted something to."

"You did? Like you wanted to—"

"Shh. Don't say it." She sits up, checking to make sure we're alone. "But yes, I wanted to do that. I wouldn't, with Caleb there, but I wanted to."

"Do you think Alex did?"

"He's a guy. Of course he did."

"So are you saying you're done being just friends?"

"Yes." She leans across the table, the grin appearing again. "Alex officially asked me to be his girlfriend. When he picked me up to go to his parents' house, he brought me flowers and asked me if I'd go steady with him. He actually said 'go steady' as a joke and then he got serious and told me all this stuff about why he likes me and asked if I'd be his girlfriend."

"That's really sweet."

"Yeah, it was. And then he asked Caleb for his permission. He gave him a mini football to sweeten the deal. His words, not mine." She laughs.

"And what did Caleb say?"

"He threw the football at Alex's face." We both laugh. "Alex took that as a sign Caleb was okay with it."

"So now what? I mean, you were kind of already dating him so does anything change?"

"Well, we can kiss without feeling like we shouldn't be. And maybe do more than that." She smiles again. "But other than that, not really. Friday, Alex is making dinner at his place so I'm bringing Caleb over there. He'll be asleep by eight and then Alex and I can watch a movie or something."

I raise my brows. "Or something?"

She swats my arm. "Not *that*. Not with Caleb there."

"You said he'll be sleeping."

She rolls her eyes, but she's still smiling. It's good to see Sara so happy. She was convinced Alex wouldn't stick around, but I think now she's realizing that he will. It sounds like he really cares about her and Caleb. I've only seen Alex a few times so I don't know that much about him. But maybe now that those two are dating, we can all go on a double date and I can get to know him better.

"Oh. I almost forgot to tell you." Sara sits back in the booth, checking her phone, then setting it on the table. "That guy was here again yesterday."

"What guy?"

"The one who was asking about you last week. Justin, or whatever his name was. I think it was Justin."

I get a sick feeling in my stomach. I'd forgotten about that guy. I told myself he was nobody and to forget about it.

I shiver and Sara notices. "What's wrong? Are you cold?"

"No, I'm just freaked out that that guy's still hanging around. You didn't tell him anything about me, did you?"

"I didn't talk to him. He just came in to get a coffee and left. Someone else waited on him at the counter."

"Was anyone with him?"

"No, it was just him."

"And what did he look like? What was he wearing?"

"Just dress pants and a shirt and tie. Like he was going to work or something."

He wasn't wearing a suit. So he's probably not from the organization. Then again, Walt didn't wear a suit and *he's* connected to the organization.

"Jade, I have to get back to work."

"Yeah, go ahead."

As she leaves, I get my phone out to call Garret and tell him Justin's back in town, or maybe never left. But Garret's in class now and there's nothing he can do, so I change my mind.

My phone alarm goes off, reminding me I have an appointment with Jennifer in a few minutes. When I get there, the first thing she asks about is my trip to Des Moines. I tell her about seeing Frank and Ryan, but I mostly talk about that speech I gave and how Garret thinks I should consider doing that as a career. When I tell her I'm not sure about it, she brings out those personality tests I took a few weeks ago that help you choose a career. Being a teacher was one of the careers that fit my personality, and speaking to people is kind of like being a teacher.

"Jade, what did you like the most about giving that speech?"

"I liked feeling like I was helping people. People who are just like I used to be. I don't know if what I said helped them or not, but maybe my story made them feel like there's hope."

"Are there any reasons why you wouldn't want to do this as a career?"

"I don't feel ready to. I feel like I need to try it some more and make sure I still like it. And I don't feel like I know enough to help these people. Garret thinks I should take some more psychology classes."

"I agree with him. I think it's a good idea. Maybe you'll decide to major in it."

"Actually, I *have* been thinking about doing that."

She smiles. "This trip was good for you, Jade. I'm glad you agreed to speak at that event."

"Garret forced me to. He said I had to face my fear of public speaking."

"And look where it got you. Because of that, you might have your major and your career figured out. You see how one person can influence you enough to change your life? *You* could be that person for someone else, Jade. Think about that as you consider your options for careers."

After our session, I leave thinking this might just be the right career choice for me. I have time to kill before my next class so I stop by my advisor's office to make an appointment. He's there, and has the next half hour free so he offers to meet with me now.

I tell him about my interest in psychology and he suggests I take a couple psych classes next semester to help me decide if I want to declare psych as my major. Then I mention the speech I gave and he suggests I take a speech class to see if I really like public speaking and to get better at it. Even though I gave that speech, I'm still scared to death of public speaking. I only did well last week because I ditched the speech I'd memorized and just talked. But if I really want to consider doing this for a living, I should learn how to give a proper speech, which means I need to take the class.

I leave his office with a marked-up course catalog and another appointment with him later this month to go over what I decide. But I think I've already decided. I like his recommendations. I'm even getting excited about next semester.

And it all started with Garret making me do that speech. Jennifer's right. One person can make a huge difference in your life. Garret is proof of that, and not just with his career suggestion. He's changed me completely since we met. He's made me a better person, and he just keeps continuing to do so.

# Chapter 10

**GARRET**

*D*uring my afternoon class, I didn't hear anything the professor said. Instead, I imagined my grandfather, comatose in a hospital bed. And it finally sunk in that this is almost over. My grandfather will soon be gone, and when he is, I'll be able to relax.

All the stuff I worried about the past few months all linked back to him. I kept worrying about that fake burglary and the fake cop, wondering who was behind it and what they wanted. But that was all my grandfather's doing. And maybe the incident with Roth last July was orchestrated by my grandfather, too. It wouldn't surprise me if he sent Roth out here to scare me into not marrying Jade. My dad said my grandfather recently went to Roth's house for dinner, which means they were becoming friends or already were friends. So maybe that's why Roth agreed to do that for my grandfather. Or maybe he owed my grandfather a favor.

I'm home now and waiting for Jade to get back from class. Then we're going to buy a Christmas tree. I don't want to wait to start celebrating the holidays. I want to start now. It's almost December and I'm going to make it a whole month of celebrating. And it won't just be about Christmas. It'll also be a celebration that my grandfather is gone. That he's out of my life. And my dad's life. For good.

I hear Jade's car in the driveway and I open the door as she approaches. I love that pink sweater on her. The color looks good against her skin and her dark hair. And the fabric clings to her breasts, causing my eyes to linger. We might have to have sex before we go shopping.

"Hi." She hugs me and I lift her up and into the house, kicking the door shut. "Were you waiting for me?"

"I was." I set her down and kiss her.

"You're really in a hurry to get that tree."

"Actually, I'm in a hurry to do something else." I slip my hand under the back of her sweater, feeling her soft skin. "You feel so damn good. You smell good, too." I inhale the scent of her hair. "You're beautiful, you know that?"

"What's with all the compliments today? I mean, I like it, but I'm not used to getting so many in one day."

"That's my fault." I look into her gorgeous green eyes. "I'm going to give you more, starting today."

"What's gotten into you? Why are you in such a good mood?"

"Because I love you. And I love being with you and I love our life together. It puts me in a good mood. That's all."

"I know, but your grandfather—"

"Jade, stop. I don't want to talk about it. And I'm not going to cry about it or be depressed about it."

"But he might not make it." She says it softly and her head drops down.

"Jade." I lift her chin up. "I know you expect me to be more upset about this, but honestly, I wasn't that close to my grandfather. He and I never got along. He treated my dad like shit and he treated me almost as bad, and he never accepted my mom." I wasn't going to tell her all that, but I feel like I need to explain this somehow or she'll keep expecting me to be sad.

She nods. "Okay. I understand."

"Good. Now can we go back to what we were doing?"

"Which was what?" She smiles and bites her bottom lip, which is sexy as hell.

"Getting you naked." I scoop her up and carry her to the bedroom. I set her down and pull her sweater over her head, then flick open the clasp of her bra. She tosses it on the floor and gets to work on my jeans. Our mouths crash together as we continue to undress our lower halves.

We're both hot for each other so it's not going to be the slow, gentle sex like we had yesterday. That was great and I loved it, but right now I'm too turned on to take this slow. And so is Jade.

As I lower her to the bed, she yells, "Chocolate chip pancakes!"

I stop for a moment. "What?"

"I want chocolate chip pancakes." She whispers it this time and I realize what she's asking for. She's just too embarrassed to say it. I love my sweet and innocent Jade, but I wouldn't mind if sometimes she just came out and told me what she wants me to do to her. I'd find it totally hot.

"Say it, Jade," I hover over her as she lies on the bed.

"I already did." She's blushing. She really needs to stop being embarrassed about this stuff. We're married. There's nothing to be embarrassed about.

"Tell me what you want." I smile, and as she opens her mouth to speak, I put my finger to her lips and say, "And don't mention pancakes."

She turns her head and nods toward the wall. "I want to do it over there."

I'm still smiling. "And what exactly do you want to do over there?"

"Have sex?"

"What's with the question? You're not sure?"

She rolls her eyes, smiling. "No. I'm sure." She pushes on my chest. "Come on. Hurry up."

I lift her up from the bed, her legs around me, her arms around my neck. I take her to the wall and push inside her. She arches back, putting her breasts on display as she takes a fist of my hair and holds on. I pump in and out, hard and fast, my hands gripping her tight round ass. It's freaking hot, and I have to work hard to hold myself back until I know she's satisfied. When she is, I get a firm grip on her and finish up myself.

As I lower her to the floor, I kiss her softly on the lips. "You ready to go buy a tree?"

She laughs. "Why do you always do that?"

"Do what?"

"We have this hot, wild, crazy sex and then you just go back to normal, like it never happened."

"What do you *want* me to do?"

"Nothing. It's just funny. It makes me laugh."

"So next time we do this, are you going to tell me what you want?"

She gives me her shy smile. "Maybe."

"I think you should." I run my hand down her arm. "I liked it. I'd like you to do it again."

She's still smiling. "I'll think about it."

I kiss her, then swat her ass as I walk past her. "I need a shower before we go."

"Is that an invitation?" She follows me into the bathroom.

"We just did it. You want it again?"

"No. I just like feeling your warm soapy hands on me."

I turn on the shower. "Which always leads to sex."

"Guess we'll just have to see."

Jade doesn't realize that guys can't always recover that fast. Either that, or she's testing me to see if I can do it. And so far, I've been able to, probably because I'm only 20 and she turns me on like no other girl can. But I hope she knows it's not going to work the same way when I'm 40.

As usual, our time in the shower leads to sex. And then we get dressed and go shop for our tree.

"What do you think of this one?" Jade points to a tiny five-foot Christmas tree.

We're in a strip mall at one of those pop-up stores that's only here for the holidays. In October it was a Halloween store where Jade got this smoking hot cheerleader costume. She needs to put that thing on again. Damn, that was sexy. I'm getting worked up just thinking about it.

I lean down and whisper in her ear. "You need to wear that costume for me."

She thinks a moment, then smiles. "The cheerleader costume?"

"Put it on tonight when we get home."

"We're decorating the tree tonight. But how about tomorrow?"

"I can't wait that long."

She laughs and pushes me away. "Back to the tree. You like this one or not?"

"It's not big enough. We need the biggest tree we can find that will still fit in the house." I walk over to a display of bigger trees and point to a seven-footer. "This one's better."

"You sure it'll fit?"

"We have eight-foot ceilings. There's plenty of room."

"Okay, let's get it!" She claps her hands. It's so damn cute. She's so excited about buying a tree. It's the first one she's ever had.

I take the sales slip for the tree, then walk over to the lights. "What kind of lights do you want? And please don't say white because I don't like white."

"No, definitely not white. Let's get the multicolored ones."

"Flashing or steady? Or they have ones that do both."

"Ooh, get the kind that do both!" Her face lights up and she looks like she wants to jump up and down like Lilly would. She doesn't, but I know she wants to.

Again, so cute. Cute enough that I have to pull her into my side and kiss her. "You're freaking adorable, you know that?"

She doesn't answer. She's too mesmerized by the lights display, twinkling all around us. I let her go and grab a shopping cart. I take 10 boxes of lights and load them into the cart.

Jade's watching me. "Why are you getting so many lights?"

"Because you like lights, and so do I."

"But 10 boxes?"

"We need some for the tree and some for the windows and wherever else you want them. You want me to switch out the blue lights in the bedroom for the multicolored lights?"

She looks like she wants to say yes, but instead she says, "That's too much work. The blue lights are fine."

I grab two more boxes of lights. "I'll switch them out. I'm tired of the blue ones."

She smiles really wide. I knew she wanted them changed out.

"Let's go look at ornaments." I take her hand and lead her to the next aisle. The shelves are full of boxes of shiny glass ornaments, the kind I hate because they remind me of Katherine. She'd only allow the decorators to use those fancy glass ornaments on our Christmas tree, along with white lights. That house is white enough. It doesn't need even more white, especially at the holidays when you want a warm, homey feel.

When I was a kid, my mom decorated our tree with colored lights and a mix of ornaments we collected over the years. Every Christmas, my dad would give her an ornament. And every year, she'd take me to the store and let me pick one out for myself. I always picked ones that were sports-themed or superheroes, which didn't match the nice ones my dad got her, but she didn't care. To her, the tree was about family memories, not looking like it came out of a magazine. She'd even include the ornaments I made in school that were ugly, but special to her.

"I don't really like any of these," Jade says, picking up a box of blue glass ornaments. "They look like they'd shatter if you touch them. And I hate to say this, but they kind of remind me of Katherine. All of these do." She motions to the rack.

I laugh. "I was thinking the same thing. So you want to look somewhere else? We don't have to get the ornaments here."

"Maybe we could just go with the lights."

"You don't want ornaments?"

"I do, but I don't want to get them all at once."

"Why not?"

"I was thinking that maybe we'd collect them over the years, like get a couple this year and a couple more next year and make them special for each year so they mean something. Like this year we could get some that would remind us of our first Christmas together as a married couple."

I never told Jade about the Christmas tree I had as a kid so it's odd that she'd suggest that. It's almost exactly how my mom's family did their tree and how she did ours.

Noticing my silence, she shrugs. "I guess it's a dumb idea. You don't want a tree with just two or three ornaments. We'll just go to another store."

"Jade, it's perfect." I lean down and kiss her. "I love that idea. Come on. Let's check out and go home so we can get to work. We'll stop for dinner so we don't have to make anything."

I take her to her favorite Mexican place for dinner, then we go home and start assembling the tree. Well, *I* do, while she watches.

"You sure you know how to do this?" She laughs as she watches me try to figure out which piece is the bottom.

I'm sitting at the kitchen table, looking at the diagram on the flimsy instruction sheet. "There are only four pieces, Jade. I think I can figure it out."

"But your dad said you weren't handy around the house."

I stand up, tossing the instructions aside. "No, he said *he* wasn't handy, not me. And this isn't the same as installing a light fixture."

"You think you could do that? Install a light fixture?"

"Yes. But I'd rather hire an electrician." I pick up the tree section that appears to be the largest of the four and set it in the metal base. The base wobbles a little and I see that I forgot to put in the stabilizing pins.

"It's not sitting straight," Jade says, laughing. "Do you want me to do it?"

"Okay, that's enough." I pick her up and throw her over my shoulder. "You're waiting here until I'm done." I drop her on the couch and toss the remote on her lap. "Watch TV so I can do my work."

"But I was helping." She sits up, hanging over the back of the couch, watching me.

"You weren't helping. You were disrupting my concentration. Now turn around."

"You're so bossy." She smiles, then flips around and turns on the TV.

I get the pins in the base and the wobbling is fixed. Then I find the second piece of the tree and slip it into place. This is way easier when Jade's not watching.

"Are you going to put together other stuff?" she asks.

"Like what?" I slip the third tree section in place.

"I don't know. Like tables and stuff." She lies down, her legs dangling off the arm of the couch, swinging back and forth.

"We're not buying furniture we have to assemble. We have plenty of money to buy furniture that's already put together." I slip the last piece of the tree in place.

"Well, other stuff has to be put together, like lawnmowers. Outdoor furniture. Cribs."

I freeze, my hand still on the tree. Cribs? Is she trying to tell me something?

"Jade, you're not—"

Her head pops up over the couch. "No. I was just using that as an example."

I breathe again. Neither one of us is ready for a baby. Jade still hasn't told me for sure if she even wants one.

"Maybe use a different example next time," I tell her as I push down on the tree, locking the pieces in place.

Jade does this all the time now. She brings up the baby topic out of the blue, like she did at Frank's house. And all it does is confuse me and get my hopes up. Then she says she needs more time to think about it, which is fine, but I kind of wish she'd stop bringing up the topic until she's made a decision.

"Okay, I got the tree together."

"Already?" She looks back at it. "How'd you do that so fast?"

"Because I didn't have someone watching me, criticizing everything I did."

"I wasn't criticizing. I was helping."

"You weren't helping." I go sit next to her on the couch and kiss her cheek. "But now you can. You get to fluff all the branches. They're all matted down from being in the box. Have fun." I put my feet up on the table and flip to a sports channel.

She stands up, her hands on her hips. "You're not going to help?"

"I did my part. Now it's your turn. Tell me when you're done and we'll do the lights together."

She goes over to the tree. I'm quietly laughing as I listen to her complain.

"This is going to take a really long time. There are a lot of branches here."

"You can do it," I yell back at her. I have to give her a hard time after she acted like I was too incompetent to put the tree together.

"I can't reach the top branches. I might need a ladder." She mumbles it to herself and I hear her straining to reach.

I flip around and check her progress. "What's taking so long?"

"I just started!" She's so annoyed with me I want to laugh but I try to be serious.

"I would've been done by now." I give her my cocky smile.

"There's no way you would've been done by now."

"That branch in the middle isn't fluffed enough." I point to it.

"How do you know if it's fluffed enough?" She actually takes me seriously, so I play along.

"There needs to be even distribution of the evergreen tips. Some up, some down, and a couple shooting out each side."

"Really?" She adjusts the branch, making it just like I instructed. She starts mumbling again. "I don't know why it matters as long as it fills in the space."

I laugh. "I'm kidding, Jade. I made that up."

"Garret! I thought you were serious."

"I know. It was hilarious. You want some help?'

"I thought you said you wouldn't."

I hop over the couch and meet her by the tree. "I was joking. Of course I'll help."

She fluffs another branch, shaking her head, smiling. "Why were you teasing me? You know I don't know anything about Christmas trees."

"Because you're fun to tease. You always believe me when I make shit up." I glance over and see that she's doing every branch the way I told her to. "Jade, you don't have to follow my instructions. I told you I was kidding."

She stands back to look at the branches. "I know, but your stupid technique actually works. They look better when I do it that way."

"Then you shouldn't say it's stupid." I kiss her. "We need music." I shut the TV off and put my phone in the speaker dock and turn on some holiday classics. The song about roasting chestnuts on an open fire starts playing. I grab her from behind, hugging her. "How's that? Feeling Christmasy yet?"

She flips around. "When did you load Christmas songs on your phone?"

"I always keep a few on there. I like Christmas music."

"I love this song." She closes her eyes, presses her cheek against my chest, and just listens, smiling contently.

It may still be November, but I can already tell this is going to be a great Christmas.

# Chapter 11

**JADE**

I could stay like this for a very long time. Hugging Garret while listening to Christmas music. Last year I was with him at Christmas but that was at his dad's house. This year we get to have our own Christmas with our very own tree. Well, actually, we'll be at his dad's house again on the actual day, but we'll spend most of December here at home, enjoying our tree and our lights and doing whatever holiday traditions we decide to start.

The song ends and I pull away. "Let's keep fluffing so we can do the lights."

He doesn't let me go. "You sure? This is kind of nice."

"It'll be even nicer when the lights are up and we can turn all the other lights off."

"True. Okay, you keep working on the branches and I'll get the lights."

Garret rummages through the closet and comes back with extension cords and power cords. He takes the lights out of the boxes and checks that they work, then helps me finish the tree.

I keep watching him to see if he's okay because I still find it odd that he's acting this way when his grandfather's dying. Is he trying to pretend it isn't happening? Hide his sadness with holiday fun? Or maybe, like he said, he really isn't that sad about it. I just find that hard to believe after seeing how upset he was last Fourth of July when his grandfather rejected him. Garret was really hurt by that and I know he

110

was hoping that someday he'd have a relationship with his grandfather again. So did something happen since then to make him not even care that his grandfather is in a coma and going to die soon?

"You want to put them on or do you want *me* to?" Garret has the lights stretched out and ready to go.

"You do it. I'll hold them for you."

He weaves the strands in and out of the branches and when he's halfway up the tree I say, "Is that a certain technique or are you just making it up as you go?"

"This is how my mom did it when I was a kid. She said the lights fill the tree better if you go from the inside of the tree to the outside, instead of only going around the outside. And it's true. You end up with a better looking tree."

"Did your dad help with the tree?"

"He'd take us to the tree farm and chop it down and get it set up in the stand. Then my mom would do the lights and I'd help her with the ornaments. My dad doesn't like doing that stuff."

"Did your grandfather? I mean, was he into Christmas?"

Garret stops stringing the lights.

"I'm sorry, Garret. I shouldn't have asked."

He starts weaving lights into another branch. "He's never been into Christmas. My grandmother isn't really either. She has her staff decorate the house for her and everything's very formal. The tree at their house looks just like the one at my dad's house. White lights and glass ornaments."

Garret's now at the very top of the tree. He tucks the end of the light strand behind a branch and stands back. "Done. Hit the lights and we'll see how it looks."

I turn off the overhead lights.

Garret puts his foot on the switch that turns on the power strip, but doesn't turn it on. "You want to do a drumroll like on Christmas Vacation?"

I laugh. "No, that's okay. Go ahead."

He turns the switch and the room fills with a warm glow. The tree is amazing. Garret's trick for stringing the lights worked great. Lights sparkle from both the inside and the outside of the tree.

"That's the blinking version," he says. "I could put it on steady if you want."

"Leave it on the blinking. I like how it looks all sparkly."

He comes over and hugs me, my back against his chest, and we gaze at the lights. The Christmas music is still playing, making the scene even more magical. This night is one of those memories I'll tuck away and take out again when I want to relive it. Because I'll definitely want to relive it. It's perfect.

"I love you, Garret." I lean my head back, checking out the top of the tree.

"I love you, too." He kisses my forehead.

And we remain there, listening to the music and watching the twinkling lights. Later, when we go to bed, we leave the tree on so we can see the warm glow of the lights from the bedroom. It's calming and I fall right to sleep.

The next day I get up early because I have chem class at eight. I only have two classes on Tuesdays, but they're spread out in the morning and afternoon, so I end up staying on campus all day, doing homework between classes, either at the library or at the coffee shop.

Garret usually sleeps in because he doesn't have class until ten, but today he got up with me. When I get out of the shower, I go in the bedroom and see him checking his phone.

"Any update?" I ask him. Every morning and all day long, he checks his messages to see if there are any updates about his grandfather.

"He's the same. No change."

Yesterday, Holton was moved to the clinic, the special medical facility that only rich, important people have access to. Garret said the clinic has several locations but he didn't tell me which one his grandfather is at, and I didn't ask.

Garret's acting strange about this whole thing and I've decided not to force him to talk about it. He's not ready to. He needs time to work this out in his head. He has a complicated relationship with his grandfather and I think he's struggling to figure out how he feels right now.

"Did you hear from your grandmother?" I ask him.

"No." He keeps his eyes on his phone. "She has too much going on. She doesn't have time to call me."

I'm dressed now and I go over to the bed and kiss his cheek. "I have to go."

He kisses me back. "Have a good day." He focuses back on his phone.

I rub my hand along his scruffy cheek. "Garret, I know I keep asking you this, but are you okay?"

"Yeah. I'm fine."

I wait for him to look up, and when he does, he says, "Jade, stop worrying about me. I'm fine. I really am. I know what's going to happen and I'm prepared for it. It's okay. He's old. It's not like I thought he'd live forever." He kisses me. "Go to class. I love you."

I hug him. "I love you, too."

On the drive to campus, my mind is still on Garret. I wish his grandmother would call him back. I don't know why she's ignoring him. I know she's busy with everything going on, but you'd think she could take a minute to call her grandson.

After class, I go to the library and study for a quiz I have later. During lunch I call Garret but he doesn't answer. I forgot he has physical therapy at noon. When my afternoon class lets out, I go outside and am surprised to find that it feels like a summer day. It's way hotter than normal. It's the perfect weather for laying out on the beach, which is exactly what I'm going to do.

I go home and change into my bikini and grab my beach towel and suntan lotion and find a spot on the sand. Since moving here, Garret and I haven't taken full advantage of living on the beach. I never run on it because Garret still thinks it's too dangerous for me to run alone. And he can't surf because of his shoulder.

As I lie on the beach, the warm sun and the sound of the waves make me sleepy and I feel myself drifting off. If I do, Garret will wake me up. He'll be home from class soon.

"I finally found you." I hear a man's voice and open my eyes to see someone standing above me. I'm looking right in the sun and it's so bright I can't see his face.

"Who are you?" I grab my beach towel and pull it around me, tossing sand everywhere.

"Don't you recognize me? We were friends all last semester." He takes his sunglasses off. "I even drove you home for spring break."

"Carson?" I look closer. Holy crap! It *is* him! What is he doing here?

"It's Justin."

"What are you talking about?" I stand up, wrapping the towel around me, keeping my eyes on him. "Your name is Carson. Unless Carson has a twin."

He smiles. "Carson was a fake name. My real name is Justin."

Justin. That's the name of the guy Sara said was trying to find me. But it wasn't Justin. It was Carson.

I stare at him. He looks different. Older. He's wearing dress pants and a shirt and tie, and his hair is shorter, cut close to his head.

Why is he here? Why was he trying to find me? And why the hell was he using a fake name?

"What are you doing here?" I back away from him toward the house.

"Jade, you don't have to be scared of me."

"I don't know why you're here but you need to leave."

"I just want to talk."

"We have nothing to talk about. Just go, Carson. I mean it."

"My name's Justin." He motions to the deck behind me. "Why don't we go sit down? I don't need to go inside."

"Tell me why you're here."

"I need your help."

"For what?"

"Let's go sit down and I'll explain."

"No. Explain right here. Right now. Why aren't you at Moorhurst anymore?"

"Because I'm done with college. I'm 24."

"What? So you were just pretending to be a student? Why?"

"So I could get to know you and some of the other students there."

Okay, that's really strange. Like psycho strange. I shiver as a chill runs down my spine.

"I can't help you, Carson. You need to leave."

"I heard you married Garret. A little young, aren't you? And weren't you two broken up last semester? Or was that all for show?"

"What are you talking about? You're not making any sense." I feel like it's last semester all over again. Listening to Carson's conspiracy theories and trying to steer him off track. And just like last semester, his theories aren't that far off.

"What's going on, Jade? You broke up with Garret in March and now you're married to him? After he slept with all those girls and did drugs and destroyed hotel rooms and cars? Doesn't seem to add up."

"Garret's changed. He doesn't do that stuff anymore. And I forgave him, so yeah, we got married."

"I'm not stupid. I know something's going on here."

"Garret will be home any second, and if he sees you here it's not going to be good. He has a gun, so you really should leave." Now I'm making up lies. That's just great.

"Is it the same gun he shot himself with last year? You said that was a shotgun. Are you saying he's going to show up here with a shotgun? Does he take it to class with him?" He laughs a little.

"It's not a shotgun. It's a handgun and he's not afraid to use it. So you need to get out of here."

His expression turns serious. "What happened to you, Jade? Why are you involved in this? I told you to get out while you still could and now you're married into his family. Why didn't you get away from him when I told you to?"

"Why would I listen to you? You really think I'd believe your crazy conspiracy theories? You're the only one who believes that stuff. Even your dad thought your theories were crazy."

"That wasn't my dad. And that woman wasn't my mom."

I stare at him, trying to see if maybe this is some kind of joke. But why would he joke about that? He doesn't look like he's joking. And this isn't funny. Just having him here is freaking me out and the things he's saying are just plain eerie. Why would he say those people weren't his parents? I met them. They told me stories about his childhood. Is he saying he was adopted? But they'd still be his parents.

He continues. "The people you met were actors. They're good at playing parents, don't you think? Very realistic."

More chills run down my spine and I shudder. "Why would you do that? Why would you hire actors to play your parents?"

"Because I had to get you to believe my story. I never thought you'd actually take me up on my offer to drive you across the country like that. So when you did, I had to come through on my story about living in small-town Illinois and my dad being a doctor and my mom being a nurse."

"What about that house? Who did it belong to?"

"Nobody. It was just a model home that real estate agents show people who are looking to build a house in that neighborhood. They let us rent it for the day. We hung some fake family photos on the wall to make it look like we really lived there."

"You're saying everything you told me was a lie? Even that stuff about your sister dying from cancer?" I'm getting really angry now. He lied to me for months. Made up those stories. Made me feel sorry for him.

"My sister *did* die. But not from cancer." His eyes fix on mine. "She was murdered. She was killed because she knew too much." He pauses, then says, "She was the reporter, Jade. The reporter who discovered the election fraud in Ohio and Florida. She was killed before she could tell people."

"You said the reporter was a guy."

"It wasn't a guy. It was my sister."

"You're lying. You admitted to lying about everything else, so why would I believe this story about your sister?"

"Because it's the truth. I wouldn't lie about that. My sister was everything to me. Our parents died years ago in a car crash. She's all I had left."

"What about your uncle in Chicago? The one you said got you into all this conspiracy stuff?"

"There was no uncle. I was talking about myself. I'm a reporter in Chicago. Well, I was until I started doing this."

"Doing what?"

"Can we just sit down and talk?"

I glance back at the deck. Maybe it would be better to be closer to the house. My phone is on the kitchen counter. I could run in and get it if I needed to. Or I could get a knife from the drawer.

"Fine. We'll sit on the deck. You first." I don't want to walk in front of him, so I let him lead the way. We go up the short set of stairs and sit at the table.

"I'm listening," I say. "Start talking."

"I know for a fact that election fraud is going on. My sister proved it happened during the presidential election four years ago. She told me all about it, but she didn't give me her evidence and they took it when they killed her. She said that a powerful secret society is behind the election fraud, along with some people planted inside the government. We just don't know who those people are. We haven't been able to identify the members of this secret society, other than Pearce Kensington and his father, Holton, who I know is now in a coma."

"Pearce is not a member of a secret society. I promise you, he's not."

Carson watches me as I say it. I swear he's one of those body language experts that can tell when you're lying by your eye movements or nose scratching or whatever the signs are that someone is lying.

"We've been watching Pearce and we're almost certain he's a member. Now we need to find the others."

"Who's 'we'?"

"I work for a very wealthy businessman who ran for president four years ago. Aston Hanniford."

"Yes, I know him. He almost won."

"He *should've* won. But he didn't because this secret group rigged the election to make sure their candidate won. Mr. Hanniford is determined to expose what they're doing and take these people down."

I roll my eyes. "Some rich guy is mad that he didn't win the election so now he's making up stories that people cheated?

Why? Does he think if he gets enough people to believe his made-up story he'll somehow end up being president someday?"

"It's not a made-up story. It's the truth. And he wants to expose the people who did this. Not only because rigging elections is illegal and wrong, but also because in their efforts to keep it hidden, they hurt innocent people. Like my sister."

I sit back in my chair, my arms crossed. I can't believe this is happening. That Carson is here. That he tracked me down and that he's not the person I thought he was. He's not a college student. He's a reporter. Someone who knows way more than he should and someone who could get Pearce in some serious trouble. Maybe even killed.

Garret needs to get home. Fast.

# Chapter 12

**GARRET**

*I*'ve been checking my phone all day to see if it's happened yet. I just checked again and it hasn't. He's still in a coma. It's Wednesday, so it's been four days now. I didn't think he'd make it this long. I talked to my dad earlier, and he, too, is surprised. Maybe this will go on longer than we thought. Some people are in comas for months, or years. But at least if he's in a coma, he can't hurt Jade.

As bad as it sounds, I'd rather have him dead than in a coma. I want this to be over so I can stop worrying about this and focus on my future. Today, during my afternoon class, I began thinking about my career, and by the time class was over I was all fired up, wanting to start my business.

It's an entrepreneurship class and today we had a speaker as part of the ongoing lecture series my dad started here at Camsburg. Today's speaker was Luke Canfield. He opened a sporting goods store about five years ago and the business has really taken off. He started with just one store in San Diego, a surf shop, and it did so well that he opened another store but added other sporting goods, not just stuff for surfing. Now he's got stores all over California and he's started to expand east into Nevada and Arizona.

The guy's only 29, which means he opened his first store when he was only 24. Hearing that made me feel like I need to get my ass in gear and get to work on creating my business. I'm just not sure what business I want to be in. I didn't think

I'd want to be in retail, but after hearing this guy's story I think I want to look into it.

After class, I talked to the guy and told him who I was. I don't usually use my last name to impress people, but this time I did because I wanted to get his attention. And it worked. He asked me if I wanted to visit the company headquarters in LA and spend a day shadowing him. Then he offered to be my mentor, answering any questions I had about starting a retail business. He gave me his email address and phone number.

He wouldn't be doing any of this if it weren't for my dad. I'm nobody, other than a former reality TV star, which is embarrassing. I'm sure he heard about the bad shit I—or the fake me—did last spring, but he didn't mention it. He seemed impressed that I was going to Camsburg, which is known for academics, not partying. And I told him I was married, which makes me seem even more responsible.

But despite all that, I know the only reason Luke offered to be my mentor is because of my dad. My dad is a rock star in the business world and this guy thinks if he spends time with me he'll eventually get to meet my dad. I know how it works. Luke's trying to grow his company and being connected to powerful people will help him do that. Or just getting advice from someone like my dad could be very valuable. I usually don't like it when people use me like that, but in this case, I'm using him, too, hoping to learn from him just like he wants to learn from my dad.

I should also be learning from my dad. I need to start asking him for business advice. I didn't before because he's my dad and I don't see him the same way everyone else does; as a great businessman with a ton of knowledge to share. But he *is* a great businessman and I need to start seeing him that way. He'd be happy to teach me whatever I want to know.

My dad is actually a really good teacher. When I asked him to teach me about the stock market, he did, and he didn't make it overly complicated. He taught me the basics, then gave me some companies to research and asked me which ones I'd invest in.

It was like a school assignment, but I didn't mind. It was way more useful than just reading a book about investing. My dad wanted me to apply what he'd taught me using real world examples, and by doing that, I learned much faster. Then he let me invest some of my money. He purposely let me pick some bad stocks so I would know what it feels like to lose money, because you have to be willing to accept losses when you're investing. After a few bad stock picks that cost me a lot of money, my dad went over my research and showed me why I shouldn't have chosen those stocks. That's when it hit me that he really knows what he's doing. And he's not just good with investing. He knows how to successfully run a company. I'm amazed at what he's done with Kensington Chemical, and so is everyone in the business world. That's why my dad's always being asked to speak at conferences and being interviewed for magazines.

So yeah, I piqued Luke's interest when I dropped the Kensington name. I told him I'd love to shadow him for a day and I accepted and thanked him for his mentorship offer. I like the guy and I could see us being friends. He likes a challenge and he goes after what he wants, just like me. He also loves surfing and football and basically all sports, which makes sense given that he owns a sporting goods store. But what I like is that he still does all that stuff even though he runs a business. He still makes time to surf. He's on a flag football team and a basketball league. Doing all that shows his passion for his business and makes him more like his customers. That's why he's so successful. He knows what his customers want because he's just like them.

I'm really excited to start working with him. I'm going to take full advantage of this opportunity and learn as much as I possibly can. I've learned a lot taking this class, but learning from real life examples is so much better than listening to a lecture or reading a textbook.

I can't wait to tell Jade about this. I'm driving home now and I just called her but she didn't pick up. She's probably outside. I think I'll take her somewhere nice for dinner tonight to celebrate. She loves that sporting goods store, so she'll be almost as excited as I am. Unlike most women, Jade doesn't like shopping for fancy shoes and clothes. She'd much rather shop for running shoes than high heels, and I love that about her. I like seeing her all dressed up in skirts and heels, but she's also damn sexy when she wears a sports bra and shorts.

As I drive up to our place, I see a silver car I don't recognize parked on the street. It's right next to our driveway and I immediately panic. It could just be parked there but why is it so close to our house?

I force myself to calm down. It's nothing. Nobody's after us. My grandfather's dying in a hospital bed thousands of miles from here.

I park in the driveway and go inside the house and look for Jade. She's not there. I check the garage and see her car, so she must be around somewhere. I walk over to the sliding glass door and see her sitting on the deck across from some guy, her beach towel wrapped tightly around her.

I shove the door open. "What's going on here?" I put myself in front of Jade and face the guy. "Who are you?"

As I get a better look at him, he almost looks like Carson, that asshole who bothered Jade last year. But it's hard to tell with his sunglasses on and the sun glaring off his face.

"Garret, good to see you again."

It *is* him. I recognize his voice. He stands up and extends his hand like we're good buddies. Instead of shaking his hand, I shove it away.

"What the fuck are you doing here, Carson?"

"Garret, don't." Jade's standing behind me, holding on to my shirt so I don't hit the guy. As if she could hold me back. If I wanted to hit him, there's nothing she could do to stop me. And right now, I want to hit him. But first, I wait for him to answer.

"I came here to talk to Jade. And you."

"I had enough of your shit last year, asshole. Jade and I are married now. She's not interested in you. She never was. So get the fuck out of here before I call the cops."

"I'm not interested in Jade that way. I only acted like I was in order to get close to her. To make her tell me stuff."

Jade sneaks around me. "You would've dated me just to get information?"

He shrugs. "I do what I have to do."

"I told you to leave," I say to him. "And if you show up here again, I won't be as nice as I'm being right now."

"I just need to talk to you."

"You did enough talking last semester. We're done listening to you, Carson."

"His name is Justin, not Carson," Jade says. She doesn't seem that freaked out by this. "He used a fake name last semester. And he's not a college student. He's a reporter."

I grab Carson's shirt and shove him against the deck railing. "Why the hell would you do that? What kind of fucked-up game are you playing here?"

"Let me go and I'll explain." Carson's a big guy and he could fight me but he's not. His arms are at his side.

"Why is he here, Jade?" I keep my eyes on him, my hand still clutching his shirt.

"He said he works for Aston Hanniford, the guy who ran for president four years ago. Hanniford thinks he didn't win because the election was rigged and now he's going after the people he thinks did it."

I let go of Carson and take a step back. "You're still obsessed with that conspiracy shit? You seriously need to get a life, Carson."

"It's not a conspiracy. And my name is Justin. Like Jade said, I used a fake name last semester. I was working undercover for Mr. Hanniford. I'm 24 and was just pretending to be in college, although I actually did have to take the classes in order to make it look real."

"Why would you work undercover at Moorhurst?"

"Because Hanniford is trying to identify the members of the secret society that was somehow able to rig the election. The same secret society your father belongs to. And your grandfather." He smirks, acting all proud of himself for knowing that.

"Nobody belongs to a secret society. You're delusional, Carson. Justin. Whatever the hell your name is."

"We can't prove it yet, but we know they're part of it. And since you're born into it, that means you're part of it, too."

"Yeah, right. And what do we do again? We rig elections? I don't even pay attention to politics. I didn't even vote in the last election."

"Because you didn't need to. You already knew the outcome."

I shake my head. "You are seriously messed up. I don't know who told you that shit, but you're wrong. And coming onto private property, uninvited, and accusing people of things, is going to get you arrested."

Jade was behind me but she sneaks around to my side. "So you went to Moorhurst to spy on Garret?"

"Mostly Garret, since Pearce and Holton are the only two members we've identified so far. We were hoping Garret would lead us to the other members, or the members' children who attend Moorhurst."

"If you were interested in Garret, why were you so obsessed with getting to know *me*?" Jade asks.

"I knew Garret wouldn't tell me anything so I tried to get close to you instead. I thought maybe you'd tell me things. Things about his family that you didn't understand. Things that might give me clues about what was going on with them. But you never did. You're good at keeping secrets, Jade."

"There aren't any secrets to keep. I told you that repeatedly, so I don't know why you stayed there all semester."

"We have reason to believe that Moorhurst isn't your average college. We believe it's where the members send their children. The children who aren't good enough to attend the Ivy League."

I laugh. "So now an entire college is a secret society? You're even more messed up than I thought. You should get on meds or something."

"I didn't say it was the whole college. But we think at least some of the students there are connected to this group. The same wealthy families send their kids there generation after generation."

"A lot of people end up going to the same college their parents went to," I say. "That's not unusual. And *I* have no family connections to Moorhurst, so there goes your theory. My dad went to Yale, not Moorhurst. I'm the first person in my family to go there."

Some of what Carson is saying is right. A lot of the members do send their kids to Moorhurst. Not everyone there is connected to the organization, but some of them are. When I went to the meeting last March, I saw Courtney's father, as well as the fathers of two guys who lived on my floor. Guys who would soon be initiated as members. All of us knew this secret but none of us spoke of it.

And now Kiefer is going to become a member. So maybe he encouraged Harper to go to Moorhurst in order to get her immersed in that world. Let her start getting to know the people she'd be forced to interact with in the future. Kiefer's the one who suggested she go there. He probably got her the tennis scholarship so she'd agree to go.

"I didn't say everyone who attends Moorhurst is part of this," Carson says. "I'm just saying we're looking into the families that have a history of sending their kids there and we're seeing if there's a connection. We're going to find out who these members are and we're taking them down. This is going to end. They got Kent Gleason elected, but the next president will be chosen by the people."

Jade tries to move, but I hold her against my side as I keep my eyes on Carson. "I've heard enough of your bullshit stories. Just get out of here. And if you show up here again, you *will* get hurt."

He crosses his arms over his chest. "I might be able to get him out. And you as well."

I sigh. "You never shut up, do you?"

"We might be able to get both you and your dad out of the secret society. You'd have your freedom back. You wouldn't have to do what they tell you anymore."

"Leave." I glare at him. "Last time I'm saying it."

He doesn't move. "If Pearce gave us some names, we could shut it down. We could bring down this group, or at least weaken it to the point where they couldn't control the system anymore."

Is he really that naive? That stupid? He really thinks he can take down the organization? He has no fucking clue how powerful they are. Carson, Hanniford, and whoever else they're working with, would be dead before they could even think of doing something to the organization.

I let go of Jade and step closer to Carson. "Are you gonna leave or do I have to throw you off my property?"

"I'm going." He reaches in his pocket and pulls out a business card and hands it to me. I glance at it and see that his name is listed as Justin. It's probably another fake name. "Just think about it. Talk to your dad."

"There's nothing to say to my dad because he's not part of some secret group. He'd laugh if I even mentioned your theory. And he'd make sure you never worked again if he knew you were spreading rumors about him. So if you care about your career, I'd strongly suggest you stop talking about him."

"Just present our offer." He walks down the steps.

"Did you hear me? He's not involved in anything so let it go. Trust me. You don't want my father as an enemy."

"Goodbye, Jade." Carson stands at the bottom of the stairs. Jade doesn't say anything so he says, "Goodbye, Garret. I'm sorry to hear about your grandfather. I hope he recovers. But if not, at least you were able to see him last week."

"What are you talking about?" Jade asks.

Shit! I fucking hate this guy. How the hell did he know my grandfather was here?

"Get out of here!" I yell at him. "Now!"

Carson sees Jade's response and can tell she doesn't know about my grandfather's visit. He probably thinks she doesn't believe him, which is why he explains. "Mr. Hanniford flew me out here on one of his private planes, and the Kensington jet was at the airport when I arrived. I saw Holton getting off the plane. I assumed he was here to see Garret. Why else would he be in this small town?" He smirks at me. "See you later. Stay in touch."

He walks off. He's such an ass. I already hated him for hitting on Jade last semester. Now he's after my dad. And he just spilled a huge secret I wanted to keep from Jade. I really fucking hate him.

# Chapter 13

**JADE**

"Your grandfather was here?" I ask Garret. "Last week?"

"Jade, we need to talk about Carson." He takes my hand and pulls me inside, locking the sliding door behind us. "Was he here when you got home?"

"No. I was lying on the beach and he just showed up. He knows too much, Garret. You have to tell your dad."

"I will, but I might have to fly out there to tell him. I don't think I should talk to him over the phone about this, just in case someone's listening in."

"You better tell him soon. Carson's got other people helping him. That Hanniford guy is wealthy and powerful. He could do real damage to your family."

"He won't. They don't have proof of anything. They just have theories." Garret goes in the hall closet and takes out a thing that looks like a silver wand. "Was Carson in the house?"

"No. Why?"

Garret runs the wand thing over the furniture, making his way around the room. "You sure he didn't break in before you got home?"

"I don't think so. Nothing looked out of place." I point to the wand. "What is that thing?"

"It checks for listening devices."

"Where did you get it?"

"I don't remember. I just had it."

It's a lie. I can tell because he's talking fast and won't look at me. I get in front of him as he wands the door to the deck.

"Garret, stop." I put my hand on his arm. "Tell me the truth."

"I told you, I can't remember where I got it. I probably bought it online."

"I'm not talking about the wand thing. I want to know about your grandfather. Was he here last week?"

I look directly at Garret, but he avoids my gaze, his eyes on the glass door just behind me.

"Garret. Was he here or not?"

He doesn't respond, which just tells me Carson was right. Holton *was* here and Garret didn't tell me. Why wouldn't he tell me? We agreed we were done keeping secrets from each other.

"Dammit, Garret!" I shove him back. "Why do you do this to me? Why do you keep hiding stuff from me?" Tears fall from my eyes before I can stop them. "I need to be able to trust you. You're my husband and I need to be able to trust you."

I'm so mad at him right now. I've worked so hard this past year to learn to trust people, and the person I trust the most keeps lying to me. I walk around him and stand by the couch. He turns to face me but remains by the sliding glass door with that stupid wand thing still in his hand.

"Jade, I'm sorry. But you don't understand."

"There's nothing to understand. Your grandfather was here and you hid it from me. Why would you keep that a secret, Garret?"

He sighs, heavily, and stares down at the floor. But he doesn't answer.

"Is that why you were acting so strange when we were at Frank's house? Because Holton came here and you didn't want to tell me?"

Silence.

"Garret. Answer me. Was Holton here?"

"Yes."

"When?"

"Monday. A week ago Monday."

"Why? What did he want?"

Garret finally looks at me. "I can't talk about this right now. I need to deal with this thing with Carson."

"There's nothing to deal with. You'll tell your dad and *he'll* deal with it. There's nothing else we can do. Now answer my question. Why was your grandfather here? He wouldn't show up here for no reason. So tell me what it is."

Garret stares at the floor again and shakes his head side to side.

"What does that mean? You're not going to tell me?"

Silence. Again.

I take a deep breath and wipe the tears from my face. "Fine. I'll see you later." I storm into the bedroom and slam the door.

Garret opens it and meets me at the dresser. "Jade, where are you going?"

"Where do you think?" I take out a sports bra and some shorts.

"You're not running, Jade. I promise you, we'll talk about this. Just not right now. I need some time."

"You *had* time! You had over a week to tell me and you didn't. And you *wouldn't* have told me if it weren't for Carson. I only found out because of him."

"Jade, just wait." He tries to take my running clothes but I yank them back.

"I'm running, Garret. I know you don't want me to, but I don't care. I'm running. I have to. Because I can't handle having you lie to me like this. Not answer my questions. Stand there in silence without even trying to explain. I can't handle how I'm feeling right now and I have to run. I admit it. I'm messed up and that's what I do. I run. Deal with it."

I go to the other side of the room into the walk-in closet and grab a t-shirt, then change clothes as fast as I can. When I turn around, Garret's blocking the door. I don't look at his face. I just push on his chest as hard as I can. "Get out of the way."

His hands are bracing the door frame and he doesn't move. I can't even squeeze around his sides.

"Garret, I mean it. Move. I need to run. I can't stay here and listen to your silence."

"Okay." He says it quietly. "I'll tell you."

I look up at his face. His eyes are wet and there's a tear running down his cheek.

I didn't expect this. I didn't expect to look up at him and see tears. The only time I've ever seen Garret shed a tear was last spring when he thought he'd never see me again.

I take a step back. "Garret, what's wrong?"

He reaches for me and pulls me into his arms. "I almost lost you."

I swallow hard, fighting back my own tears. "What do you mean?"

He doesn't answer, but just holds me close to him and breathes. Deep, heavy breaths. He slowly lets me go, then sits on the floor just outside the closet. He's backed against the wall, his knees bent and his arms resting on them, his eyes on the floor.

I sit next to him, rubbing his arm. "Garret, talk to me."

"My grandfather came here last week. He broke into the house. I didn't have class that afternoon so I went home. And he was here."

"Why? What did he want?"

"A couple weeks ago he called me and told me I had to work for the company."

"Yeah, I remember. And you told him you wouldn't do it, right?"

"Yes. But he didn't like my answer. That's why he showed up here."

"To tell you to work for the company?"

"Not tell, but force. He was going to force me to work there. And force me to transfer to Yale. He already got me accepted."

"Yale? But we have a life *here*, in California. And what was *I* supposed to do? I can't get into Yale."

"You weren't part of the plan, Jade." Garret won't look at me. He won't even look in my direction.

"He told you to divorce me?"

"Yes. And to never speak to you again."

"What did you say to him?"

"I told him he couldn't control me like that. I told him I'd never leave you and I'd never work for the company."

"And what did he say?"

Garret shuts his eyes, then opens them again, his gaze still on the floor. "He said—" He stops and takes a deep breath and lets it out. "He told me if I didn't do what he said, he would—" He stops again. "He would kill you."

I inhale sharply and the muscles in my chest immediately tighten, making it hard to breathe. I turn so that I'm facing Garret. "No. Your grandfather wouldn't do that. He was just trying to scare you into doing what he wanted."

"He was serious, Jade. He would've done it." Garret pauses. "He killed my mom."

"What? No. That's not possible." Now I really can't breathe. I'm shaking. "The organization killed her."

"Yes, but it was his idea. The organization wanted to do something to the company to punish my dad for marrying my mom. But my grandfather convinced them that getting rid of my mom was a better punishment. It was all his idea. He had her killed. And he determined when it would be done. They wanted to kill her right after my dad married her but my grandfather made them wait. He wanted my dad to suffer. He wanted my dad to have all those years with her, to love her, to have a child with her, and then take it all away."

"No." I shake my head, tears falling again. "A father wouldn't do that to his own son. And his daughter-in-law. Your mom." I cry even harder as the realization of what he's saying hits me. "Oh my God. Your mom. She'd be alive if he didn't—"

He nods. "Yeah."

I hug his chest. "Garret, I'm so sorry. I'm sorry she's gone. I'm sorry he did that." More tears fall, my heart aching for him. "I don't even know what to say. I don't know how anyone could be that evil."

"Evil is everywhere, Jade. Your own father tried to kill you."

I sit back and look at him. "Yes, but he didn't know me. He didn't raise me. This is different. Holton raised your father. Pearce is his only son. Why would he do that to his son? And his grandson? You were just a little boy. How could he take away your mom?" I'm still crying, but Garret's expression is blank, his gaze on the bed behind me.

"Because he wanted to punish my dad. My dad didn't listen to him. He didn't divorce my mom. And he didn't raise me the way my grandfather told him to. My grandfather hates not being the one in control, which is why he was trying to take over my life. He was determined to make sure I followed orders. To do exactly what he had planned for my life. He was even trying to get me accepted back into the organization. That's another reason why he had to get rid of you."

My whole body is shaking. I don't believe this. It's too evil, too vicious, too cruel to be real. I wipe my tears and take some deep breaths.

My focus shifts from what Holton did in the past to what he'd planned to do in the future. To me. "When was he going to do it? When was he going to kill me?"

"He gave me a deadline. He said you were safe until the end of the year. After that, I had to make a decision. If I divorced you, you'd be safe. Otherwise, he'd kill you, but I wouldn't know when. He said he'd pick the time, just like he did for my mom. When he told me this, I swear I almost killed him with my bare hands. But he had a gun."

I'm so shocked, I can't even come up with a response. Why would Holton bring a gun? Did he plan to hurt his own grandson?

Garret continues. "After he left, I called my dad and told him to come out here right away. He flew out that night and that's why he was here Tuesday morning. He said he'd take care of it. He was going to talk to my grandfather on Thanksgiving. I don't know if he ever did. He didn't tell me."

No wonder Garret was so out of it last week. No wonder he didn't sleep and could barely eat.

I lean my head on his shoulder and take his hand, threading it with mine. "I wish you would've told me this, Garret."

"I couldn't do it, Jade. How could I tell you something like that? All I ever wanted is for you to be happy. And you finally were, and then this happens. I just wanted you to be happy for a little longer. I thought maybe I could find a way to fix this. Then my dad said he would, and I believed him. I wanted to give him time to at least try before I told you."

I understand why Garret didn't tell me, and part of me is glad that he didn't. If I'd known about this, I would've been so scared and so angry that I wouldn't have gone home for Thanksgiving. I couldn't have been around Frank and Ryan. They would've known something was up. I couldn't hide something like this from them.

"Were you ever going to tell me?" I ask him.

He rubs my hand with his thumb. "I was hoping I'd never have to. I was hoping it would just be over and you'd never have to know." He pauses. "I never would've let him hurt you, Jade. I would've done everything possible to protect you. I spent all last week trying to figure out ways to keep you safe. I stayed up all night, every night, thinking about it."

"Is this ever going to end, Garret?"

He wraps his arms around me and kisses my head. "It's over. With my grandfather gone, this will end."

"But what about that burglary and the fake cop? What if the organization was behind that?"

His body stiffens and I sit back again.

"What is it, Garret? Do you know something about the burglary?"

He slowly nods. "That was his original plan. But it didn't work. The burglary was set up by my grandfather. He hired a guy to break in here and—"

"Kill me?" A chill runs through my entire body.

"I'm so sorry, Jade." He pulls me back into his chest. "I'm so sorry I got you involved in this. I'm sorry I put you in danger. I'm sorry for all of it."

"It's not your fault. You didn't do anything wrong. It was all your grandfather."

"Yes, but I should've been more aware. More cautious. My job is to protect you and I didn't. That guy would've killed you. He almost did. He didn't because he was scared off by the security cameras."

"Why did the fake cop show up here?"

"My grandfather knows how my dad checks into stuff like this. He knew my dad would try to find out more about that guy who was lurking around our house. So my grandfather hired that man to pretend he's a cop and tell us our neighbors were robbed. That way we wouldn't think the guy was targeting us specifically and my dad would just assume it was a random crime. Anyway, when the robbery didn't work as planned, my grandfather decided to take a different approach."

We sit there in silence, Garret hugging me too tightly again, but it's what I need right now. I need to feel safe, and the only place I feel safe is in Garret's arms.

Holton's going to die any day now, but I still feel scared. I was almost killed. Holton wanted me dead. I'd be dead right now if that burglar had done what he was hired to do.

Is this really over? How can Garret be sure? He didn't know about his grandfather's plan, which means he may not know about other threats against me, or against us. I shudder just thinking about that.

# *Chapter 14*

**GARRET**

*I*t's done. I told Jade everything. Every last detail. And she's scared, just like I knew she would be, which is why I didn't want her to know. Her whole body is shaking, and no matter how tightly I hold her, I can't get the shaking to stop.

"Jade, get up." I push on her a little until she backs away. "Let's go to the bed."

"I'm not tired." Her eyes are red and teary, and I can see from her face that she's more than just scared. She's terrified.

"Let's just go lie down. You don't have to sleep."

I stand up and help her off the floor. We go to the bed and I shove the covers back and we get in. Then I pull the covers back over us.

"Just breathe," I tell her as her shaking continues. I have her body pressed into mine, my arms completely around her.

"What if he sends someone after me? Like Roth? What if they're in on this together?"

I didn't tell Jade about my grandfather being friends with Roth and I'm not going to. She can't handle any more than what I've already told her. I'll talk to my dad about Roth and see if he thinks Roth poses any kind of threat. I don't know why he would. He doesn't care if I run the company or go to Yale. And I don't know why he'd want me back in the organization after the embarrassment I caused him. He was the one pushing for me to be president someday and then I acted out last spring and made him look like a fool for picking me in the first place. If anything, the guy should want to kill *me*, not Jade.

"Nobody will hurt you, Jade. I swear. They'll have to kill me first. And if I'm dead, my dad will protect you."

"Don't say stuff like that. You're not going to die. You're not going to leave me. Say it, Garret."

I kiss her head. "I'm not going to leave you. Not ever."

We lie there quietly and eventually her shaking stops and she falls asleep. I didn't think she'd be able to sleep, but there's something about being in my arms that makes her sleepy. I don't move, even though the arm that's under her keeps going numb. I flex it a little, trying to get the circulation going again, but by the fourth time of doing this, I have to move it or I may not have an arm left. I slide it out from under her and she wakes.

"Don't leave," she whispers.

"I'm not leaving. I just needed to move my arm."

She turns around and grabs hold of my shirt. "He's still alive. He might still come after me."

"He's in a coma, Jade. He's not going to recover."

"What about the other members? I don't believe you when you say this will end."

"It will, Jade. It already has."

"You don't know that. You don't know who else is out there."

"My grandfather was the one who was obsessed with trying to control me. Nobody else cares what I do with my life. Nobody at the organization cares. They have other things to worry about. They're not going to waste time trying to go after me."

"What about Lilly?"

"Lilly? What do you mean?"

"What will happen to her? Will they force her to go to whatever college they choose? Marry someone she doesn't want to be with? Will she always be controlled by them?"

"I don't know. I think my dad's trying to get her out of it. I don't ask because I know he won't tell me anything."

"I don't want Harper to be part of this."

"We can't interfere, Jade. You know that."

"Yes, but it makes me sad." She lays her head on my chest and I feel her tears soaking through my shirt.

I kiss the top of her head and rub her back.

Jade was so happy last night, putting up the tree and the lights. Then Carson had to show up and destroy everything.

I have to find a way to make Jade happy again. Even just a little.

"I'll be right back." I move over and off the bed.

"Where are you going?"

"Just wait here." I go in the living room and slide the tree into the bedroom, dragging all the cords with me. Then I plug it in and the twinkling lights fill the room. I put my phone in the speaker dock on the nightstand and play the Christmas music.

I get back into bed and Jade returns to her spot on my chest. I look down and see her gazing at the tree.

We stay there, watching the lights sparkle, not talking about Carson or my grandfather or any of that stuff. I'll deal with the Carson issue later. Right now, I need to make Jade feel safe again. Then later, I need to convince her this is over so we can go back to how things were before my grandfather's visit.

The next morning, I have class but Jade doesn't. I offer to stay home with her but she insists I go. She seems better today than last night. Maybe now that she's had time to think about it, she believes what I told her. That this is over. Probably not, but she does seem more relaxed.

I moved the tree back in the living room, and as I was leaving the house, I noticed Jade plugged the lights in even though bright sunshine is filtering through the blinds. She loves the tree and the lights. She doesn't care if it's daytime. She wants to see the sparkling lights.

On my way to campus, I check my messages. There's one from my dad saying that my grandfather is still hanging on. I call him, but he doesn't have time to talk, other than to say he hasn't yet made it to the clinic to see my grandfather. But my grandmother's there and apparently Katherine has stopped by a few times. I have no idea why, other than the fact that she's one of the few people my grandfather actually likes. But he doesn't even know she's there so I don't know why she'd bother going to see him, unless she's trying to suck up to my grandmother.

After my morning class I go home for lunch, then take Jade with me back to campus since she has an afternoon class. I told her if she sees Carson not to talk to him and to go find security if he won't leave her alone. But I don't think he'll show up again. He said what he needed to say. Now he'll wait for some kind of response, but I'm not going to give him one. I'm going to have my dad handle this. Except I totally forgot to mention it to him when I had him on the phone. It's probably good that I didn't. I don't trust that the phone line is secure. We need to discuss this in person.

It's only one-thirty and Jade's class is at two but mine's not until three, so before my class I drive to the Christmas store, buy another tree and more lights, then go back home. I want Jade to feel better, and although another tree won't change what I told her, it might put a smile on her face for just a little while.

The tree is for the bedroom so I bought a small one. It's just three pieces, so only takes a few minutes to assemble. I add the lights and then tack another string of lights along the bedroom window. I don't have time to change out the ceiling lights but this is good enough for now. I also bought an ornament. I stuff it in my drawer to give to her later.

I go to class, then meet Jade at the coffee shop a little after four. She's smiling as Sara talks and laughs about whatever she's saying.

I sit down and put my arm around Jade. "What's so funny?"

"Just something Caleb did," Sara says. "You want some coffee?"

I look at Jade. "You want to stay or go home?"

"Let's stay." She points to a Christmas tree in the middle of the room. "They put up a tree."

"I decorated it," Sara says. "That's why it doesn't look very good."

Sara and Jade both put themselves down like that. I don't understand it. Jade doesn't do it nearly as much as she used to, but Sara does it constantly.

"The tree looks great, Sara," I tell her. "And yes, I'll take a coffee."

"I'll be right back." She leaves.

Jade kisses me. "She said they'll start playing Christmas music next week."

"Then you'll never want to leave."

"I have my own tree at home and my own music. And I'd much rather look at the lights while snuggling in bed with you. Thank you for doing that last night. It made me feel better."

"Good." Just wait till she sees the tree I got for the bedroom. Hopefully, she'll feel even better.

"So how was class?"

I'm surprised Jade's not asking about my grandfather. I was prepared for her to bombard me with questions now that she's had almost a day to think about it.

"It was okay." Sara comes back with my coffee, then takes off again. I turn to Jade. "I didn't get a chance to tell you yesterday but I met this guy at my entrepreneur class and he offered to be my mentor. He was speaking to the class about how he started his business. He owns that sporting goods store you like. WaveField Sports."

"Yeah, I love that store."

"I talked to him after class and he invited me to the headquarters in LA to follow him around for the day."

"That's great. What's he like?"

"He's 29, loves sports, loves surfing. I liked him. I think we'll get along well."

"Maybe he'd give you an internship this summer."

"I don't know. I just met him. We'll see how it goes after I spend the day with him."

"When are you going down there?"

"Probably not until January. He's traveling a lot in December."

"You seem really excited about this."

"I am. I think it'll be good."

We stay there a little longer and Jade tells me about the courses she's decided to sign up for next semester. She avoids any mention of what we discussed last night. I guess we both need a break from it. I'd prefer to never talk about it again, but I'm sure at some point she'll ask me about it.

Since we're already out and it's dinner time, we stop and eat before heading home. I didn't feel like making dinner. I haven't for weeks. There's been too much going on.

When we get home, Jade plops down on the couch. "You want to watch a movie?"

I drop the mail on the kitchen table and join her on the couch. "Maybe later."

"Do you need to study?"

"No, I don't need to study. Let's go in the bedroom."

She smiles. "Right now? It's kind of early, but okay."

Her mind goes straight to sex, which makes sense given what I said, but I didn't think she'd want to do it. I thought after the stress of last night, she might not be in the mood. But sometimes after something stressful happens, she wants to do it. I think it's less about the actual sex and more about the need to be close and intimate like that, which makes her feel more relaxed.

I stand up and offer her my hand. "Let's go."

I'll just let her think we're having sex. Who knows? Maybe we will.

As she gets up, I say, "Close your eyes."

"Garret, I don't want to try some crazy new sex thing tonight."

I laugh as I walk her to the bedroom. "It's not a crazy new sex thing. It's a surprise."

"That has to do with sex?"

"No. It has nothing to do with sex. Get your mind out of the gutter."

"Then why are we going to the bedroom?"

"Just wait right there." I face her toward the tree, which is in the corner, a few feet from the bed. "Keep your eyes closed." I turn on the Christmas lights. The blinds are shut, but I close the bedroom door to keep out the light from the living room. "Okay, you can open your eyes."

"You got another tree!" She turns and hugs me. "And you put lights on the window? When did you do all this?"

"I did it before class. Do you like it?"

"I love it! Thank you."

"I know you like having a tree in the bedroom and I didn't have time to get a real one so I got this one. We can still get a real one later."

She goes and lies down on the bed, propping her head up on the pillow. "I think I'll just stay in here all night and look at it."

I go over to my drawer and pull out the ornament. It's wrapped in red tissue paper. I lie next to her and hand her the ornament. "Here. I got you something."

"Just because?" She holds it up, inspecting each side.

"Just because." I kiss her cheek. "Open it."

The ornament is a silver heart that says 'Our First Christmas' with the year engraved below it. It's nothing great but it's something to put on the tree.

"Garret, it's perfect. Thank you."

"You're welcome." I take it from her and go put it on the tree, then return to the bed. "What do you think? Our first ornament."

"I like how the lights shine off the silver. It's really pretty."

I watch her as she looks at the tree.

"Jade." I cup her cheek, directing her gaze back to me.

"Yeah?"

"I don't want to talk about what I told you yesterday, but I need to know if you're okay. So are you?"

"I'm hoping this is over now, so I'm trying to move past it. Like you said, your grandfather will be gone soon, so he can't hurt me. And if other people are after us, or after me, what are we supposed to do? Live in fear for the rest of our lives? I don't want to do that. I've been doing that for months now and I'm tired of it. And as for this thing with Carson, maybe your dad could handle it and leave us out of it. He has connections with people who can maybe get Carson off track. Send him off in a different direction."

"Yeah, we're not going to be involved with any of that. I'll talk to my dad and let him handle it. Carson won't be bothering us again."

Jade smiles. "His name is Justin. We keep calling him Carson."

"He's Carson to me. I don't know who the hell Justin is. The whole thing is stupid. Like he really thought he'd uncover all these secrets by pretending to be a student? All he did was annoy people. Most of all you and me."

"Let's not talk about him. He's ruining my Christmas spirit." She sits up and takes her sweater off and then her bra.

"What are you doing? Getting into your pajamas? It's only six-thirty."

"I'm not putting pajamas on." She takes her jeans off.

"You're just stripping?"

"You said we were coming in here to have sex."

"Um, no. I never said that."

"You didn't?" She takes her panties off and tosses them on the floor. "I thought you did."

"No. You just assumed that because I asked you to go in the bedroom."

"Okay. Well, I'll just sit here naked then and look at the lights."

"Yeah, I don't think so." I get naked with her. I don't want to rush this tonight. I'm going to take my time, kissing and touching every part of her like I did the other night.

"You want a massage?" I say it in her ear and kiss the area just below it.

I see her smiling. "Okay."

She flips onto her stomach and I run my hands in long strokes up and down her back. My eyes wander to her cute round ass, the one that caught my eye the first time I saw her back at Moorhurst. That cute little ass was sticking out the back of the car as she reached in to get her stuff. My mind couldn't stop imagining what was under those shorts. And now here it is. Hot. Sexy. And all mine.

My hands keep going lower with every stroke, eventually skimming over the curve of her ass. She moans a little, which only makes me want to do it again. I slide my hands up her back, then down again, cupping her ass and squeezing a little.

Damn, she has a great ass. I leave my hands there, deciding she needs her ass massaged as well. As I'm doing that, I kiss her back, starting at the top of her spine and working my way down, then up again to the nape of her neck. I see her lips turn up and part a little. She's breathing fast. I've been teasing her a long time now and I can tell she's getting impatient.

"Garret."

I put my lips over her mouth and kiss her. "Yes, Jade."

"Do it. Don't wait."

"I'm not done with the massage." I give her ass one more squeeze, then slip my hand between her legs. "This is the best part."

She grabs the sheet with her hand, balling it in her fist. "Garret."

"You're so beautiful." I kiss her shoulder. "So damn beautiful."

She smiles. "Please."

I love making her wait. Making her beg. I leave soft kisses down her back and keep touching her until she's at the edge. Then I flip her over and slide inside her. I've tortured her long enough, and touching her got me so turned on I can't hold out much longer. I move fast and deep, and moments later, she digs her fingers in my back and makes the noise she always makes. As her body relaxes, I finish up, then remain over her, propped up on my arms.

I look into her eyes. "I love you."

"I love you, too." She brings my head down over her shoulder, running her hand through my hair.

This is how it should be. Jade and I going to class, having dinner together, and spending our nights having sex or just lying in each other's arms, sleeping or watching TV.

Just a normal day. A normal life. That's all I want. And in a few days, when my grandfather's gone, we'll finally have it.

# Chapter 15

**JADE**

*M*y phone has been going off nonstop since class started. I set it to vibrate and put it in my bag on the floor but I feel it going off against my foot. I know it's Harper. I had three messages from her when I woke up this morning, but I couldn't call her back because I got up late and didn't have time to talk. I texted her and told her I'd call her after class but I guess that's not soon enough.

She's calling because she wants to talk about Sean. She got back to Connecticut last night, and knowing her, she went to his apartment as soon as she got off the plane. I told her not to, but I knew she wouldn't listen. I'm hoping Sean wasn't there, because if he was, it'll just make this harder for both of them.

Class ends and I go outside and find a bench to sit on. I call her and hear her voice before the phone even rings. How is that possible?

"Jade?" She's sniffling. I bet she hasn't stopped crying since I talked to her last. "He's gone."

"I'm sorry, Harper." It's all I can say. I've said it so many times now it sounds meaningless. "But he had to leave. He needs that job."

"I know he does. And I'm so proud of him." She sounds happy and sad at the same time. "That place he'll be working at is one of the nicest restaurants in LA. All the celebrities go there." She sniffles again. "He's going to be so great there. I bet he'll be head chef in a few months."

"Yeah, I bet he will." I try to steer her off the topic of Sean. "So what happened with your parents? Are you talking to them now?"

"No. I haven't spoken to them in days."

"Harper, this silent treatment can't go on forever. Maybe you should talk to them."

"I'm not ready to. I'm still too angry with them. They're not the people I thought they were. They used to be nice to everyone. It didn't matter if the person had money or not. They didn't care. And now suddenly they've turned into these parents who only want me to date rich guys they pick out for me." She pauses. "I don't want to talk about my parents. I called because I wanted to tell you I went to Sean's place last night."

"Wasn't he gone?"

"He had everything packed, but he didn't leave until this morning."

"Did you talk to him?"

She takes a moment to answer. "We did more than talk."

"What? Harper! You had—" A guy sits down next to me on the bench. Can't he see I'm trying to talk here? I take my backpack and walk over to a different bench. "You had sex with Sean?"

"I know. It's bad, isn't it? But it's what we both wanted and it just kind of happened."

"How did you—" I try to figure out how to phrase this. "You had surgery last week."

"Only on my shoulder. There are many ways to do it, Jade."

"Yeah. Got it. So you did it? And then what?"

"I talked to him and told him how I felt. I told him I made a huge mistake and I apologized over and over again. Then I told him I knew about his job and that I was happy for him. After we talked, I didn't want to go back to the dorm and I knew he didn't want me to, so I spent the night there." She sniffles. "This morning he told me he loves me but that it's over and not to call him again. He said he won't be able to move on if we stay in touch."

"I know this sucks, Harper. What can I do?"

"Nothing. There's nothing anyone can do. Last night was our goodbye. Now I just have to try to move on."

"You will. It just takes time. Maybe I could fly out there some weekend. We'll shop, go to the movies, whatever you want."

"Will you be out here for the funeral?"

Funeral? I haven't seen the news all day and Garret didn't send me any updates. Maybe it just happened.

"Did Holton die?" I ask her.

"No. I'm sorry. I shouldn't have said it like that. It's just that the news makes it sound like he could pass away any day now so I just assumed the funeral will be soon."

"Yeah. I guess it will be."

"Jade, I hate to race off the phone like this but I have class. I have to go."

"Okay. I'll talk to you later."

I reach down for my backpack just as another person sits beside me. There are tons of open benches. Why does everyone insist on sitting next to me?

"Hey, what's up?"

I recognize the voice and turn back and give the owner of that voice a kiss. "Don't you have class?"

"Not for a half hour." He puts his arm behind me on the bench. "I saw this hot girl sitting on the bench and I had to come check her out. What are you doing out here?"

"I called Harper. Get this. She went to Sean's place and they did it."

"They had sex?" He says it just as someone walks by.

"Don't say it so loud," I whisper.

He laughs. "It's a college campus, Jade. People talk about sex all the time."

"Whatever. So anyway, they did it and she spent the night over there. And now he's gone and she's even more depressed than before."

"Why did she even go over there?"

"She wanted to say goodbye."

"By having sex with him? And spending the night?" Garret shakes his head. "Sean should've never let that happen. Poor guy's so damn in love with her I'm sure he couldn't help himself, but if someone found out—"

"They'd hurt him?"

"Just forget it. He's on the road now. He'll be fine." Garret gives my shoulder a squeeze and I slide over until I'm right up against him.

My phone rings and I'm thinking it might be Sean, but it's William, my uncle.

"Hi, William." I look at Garret as I say it. He looks as surprised as I am. William never calls me. I haven't talked to him since that weekend we all met at Grace's house.

"Hello, Jade. How have you been?"

"Um, okay, I guess."

"I'm sorry to hear about Holton. How's Garret doing?"

I glance at him. "He's doing okay. I mean, given the circumstances. He's been checking in with his dad to see if he has any updates. But so far, it sounds like nothing's changed."

William's quiet, then says, "When did Garret last talk to his father?"

"I don't know. He's here with me now. I'll ask him." I turn to Garret. "When did you talk to your dad?"

"About an hour ago. He has meetings all day in New York so he couldn't talk long but he said my grandfather's condition was the same."

I direct my attention back to William. "Did you hear all that?"

"Yes. I'm just a little confused."

"What do you mean?"

"I talked to Eleanor this morning to see how she was holding up and she said Holton had improved overnight."

I keep my eyes on Garret. "Oh. We hadn't heard that."

Why is William calling Garret's grandmother? Are they friends? And why does Eleanor answer William's calls, but not Garret's?

"I didn't know you knew Eleanor that well," I say to William.

Garret's giving me a strange look, trying to figure out what's going on.

"The Sinclairs have been friends with the Kensingtons for many years," William says.

"I know. I just didn't know you still talked to her."

"I haven't for quite some time. But when something like this happens, it's customary to reach out and offer any assistance."

I try to gather my thoughts because this whole conversation is throwing me off. "So what did she say about Holton?"

"Just what I told you. As far as I know, he's still in a coma, but he's improving a little more each day."

"That's good." I hope I don't sound as nervous as I feel right now. "I should let you go. I know you're busy."

"Yes, well, I just wanted to check in on you and Garret. Call me if you need anything."

"I will. Bye, William." I end the call and set my phone down.

"What was that about?" Garret asks.

"William said your grandfather is getting better." I'm in a daze as I say it, my mind slowly realizing what this means.

"How does William know?"

"He talked to your grandmother this morning."

Garret grips my arm. "What exactly did he say? Is my grandfather out of the coma?"

"No, but his condition is improving. I don't know what that means." I rub my forehead. "I feel sick. What if he recovers?"

"He won't. He's in a coma. A lot of people die in comas." He whips his phone out and makes a call. "Voicemail," he says to me, then says in the phone, "Dad, call me when you get this."

I stand up, picking my backpack off the bench. "I have to go. I have class."

Garret stands in front of me, his hands on my arms. "You okay?"

"I would be if I hadn't heard that news."

He hugs me. "Just forget about that. He's not getting better, Jade. There was probably just a slight improvement in his blood work and the doctors are making a bigger deal out of it than it is to make my grandmother feel better."

"I don't think so."

"Jade, stop worrying about it. Go to class, and when you get home we'll turn on the Christmas lights and watch a movie. We'll get a pizza for dinner so we don't have to cook."

I know he's trying to make me feel better but it's not working. But I smile and pretend that it is. "Okay. That sounds fun. I'll see you at home."

I walk to class, my eyes darting around to see if anyone's following me. I know Holton's still in a coma, but I feel like he can still see me. Like he's watching me. Plotting to kill me.

# Chapter 16

**GARRET**

*A*fter Jade leaves for class, I check my phone for any updates about my grandfather. I don't have any messages from my dad or anyone else in my family. But what William said had to be true. He wouldn't lie about something like that, which means my grandfather must be getting better. What if he comes out of the coma? Shit. This is bad. But even if he wakes up, he still has to recover from the stroke. That could take months, or maybe even years.

I'm too on edge to go to class so I skip it and go home. As soon as I'm there, I turn on the TV. There isn't a single story about my grandfather. No updates. No news that he's getting better. Nothing.

I fire up my laptop to see if there's anything online. I go to click on the Internet icon but notice something strange on my screen. An icon I don't recognize. I wonder if I accidentally clicked on an ad and it downloaded something to my computer. The icon looks like a dial with numbers on it. I'm not sure if I should click on it because it could be a virus. But my curiosity wins out and I click on it.

A series of numbers pop up on my screen, each one in their own little box. The last one keeps changing, scrolling really fast. Then I notice the second to last number has now changed.

An icy chill courses through me as I realize what this is. It's a timer. A countdown to the end of the year.

"Fuck!" I drop my laptop on the couch and back away, like it's possessed. The numbers keep scrolling, the seconds rolling by, the minutes right next to it. And then the hours and the days. I quickly calculate it in my head to make sure this really is what I think it is. And it is. Based on today's date and the current time, the numbers on the timer are set to count down to the end of the year.

I pick up my laptop and click on the icon to shut the timer down. The numbers go away, but in their place are the words, *Time's running out.* And then the program closes and I'm left with the icon again.

How the hell did that timer get there? Did my grandfather do that? Is he awake now? I get my phone out and call my dad. His voicemail picks up and I leave another message. Why isn't he calling me back?

I need to know my grandfather's condition. I need to know if he's still in a coma. William said he was, but that's just what my grandmother told him. Maybe she lied. Maybe my grandfather's out of the coma but she doesn't want anyone knowing until she makes an announcement to the press. And maybe my dad knows, but has been lying to me so I don't worry. Maybe that's why he won't answer my calls.

I call my grandmother for the millionth time this week. And like all the other times I've called, she doesn't answer. What the hell? I need someone in my damn family to pick up the phone.

I try to think of who else to call. Who else would know the truth about my grandfather? Katherine. I hate her, and she's the last person I want to talk to, but she's my only option right now.

She picks up on the second ring. As usual, she skips any kind of greeting. "Your father isn't home. And Lilly is at school."

"I called to talk to you."

"Is that so?" I can almost see the smirk I know she's making. "And what would you like to talk about?"

"My grandfather. Do you know how he's doing?"

"Yes. In fact, I just got off the phone with Eleanor."

"And? What did she say?"

"She said Holton was up and reading the Financial Times. He still has no appetite but—"

"Wait. When did he get out of the coma?"

She sighs. "Why aren't you asking your father these questions? I don't have time for this."

"Dad's busy. I keep getting his voicemail. Just tell me when he got out of the coma."

"Yesterday. He gradually became more alert and by this morning, he'd improved even more."

"How is that possible? Everyone said he was dying."

"He's getting the best treatment in the world. And he's a very important man. They're not just going to let him die." I hear her heels clicking as she walks. "I have other commitments to attend to. I'll tell your father you called."

She hangs up.

I feel like I might throw up. My grandfather's out of the coma. So why wasn't it on the news? Why didn't my grandmother tell the press? Do the doctors think he'll have a relapse? Why hasn't anyone called me? I should've been told as soon as he woke up.

My phone rings. It's still in my hand and I answer without looking. "Hello."

"Hello, Garret."

When I hear his voice, my heart shuts down. I stop breathing. And wait to see if it's really him.

"It's your grandfather. I wanted to let you know I'm doing well and am expected to make a full recovery."

I force myself to breathe again. I don't want my voice to be shaky. I need to sound strong. Let him know I'm not afraid of him.

I clear my throat. "How are you feeling?"

"My appetite isn't quite back to normal and I'm still a little tired, but other than that, I feel fine."

As he's talking, I realize his speech isn't slurred or impaired in any way. That doesn't make sense. If he had a stroke, he wouldn't sound like this.

"You didn't have a stroke." I blurt it out.

"No. Apparently I was drugged. The toxins in my system caused the coma."

"But the news said…" My voice trails off.

He chuckles a little. "Garret, please don't tell me you're that naive. After everything you've seen and heard over the years, you can't possibly tell me you still believe the stories you hear on the news."

I ignore his insults. "Who drugged you?"

"I can't say for sure. It could've been any number of people. I have no shortage of enemies. But when I find out who did this, it will be the end for them. I might even take care of them myself."

He says it like it would be fun. Like he's looking forward to it.

"Garret, have you made a decision yet?"

"There IS no decision. You're not doing this. The plan is off."

Shit. I shouldn't have said that. He has to be in control and I just told him he's not. He'll take that as a challenge. Shit!

"You know, Garret, when you're faced with death, as I was earlier in the week, you realize that time is precious. Hours. Minutes. Seconds. They pass by so quickly and then they're gone. It's a shame to see them wasted. Wouldn't you agree?"

"What are you getting at?"

"Your life, Garret. Your future. It needs to begin now. Today. Giving you this month to decide just seems wasteful. Think of all you could accomplish in that time."

My heart's beating again, going so fast I'm having trouble breathing. "You gave me a month. You're not taking it back."

"Things have changed. And after further consideration, I—"

"No! This is YOUR game! And those were YOUR fucking rules! You're not changing them now."

The only sound I hear is my heart thumping in my eardrums.

He's silent. And then, "Fine. The rules remain. Goodbye, Garret."

He hangs up and I toss the phone aside. I remain on the couch, my hands over my face, rubbing my forehead. My head is pounding, probably because I wasn't breathing for most of that conversation.

I sit up and notice my laptop next to me. I wake it up and click on that icon again to make sure the timer is still running. It is. It's still counting down to the end of the year.

How the hell did that get on my computer? He must've hacked into it. But how? He's in a hospital bed. He just got out of a coma. How did he have time to get this done?

Someone's helping him. There's no other way he could do it. And if someone's working with him, they could be anywhere right now. They could be in this town. They could be on campus. Watching Jade. Following her. Fuck!

I grab my keys and sprint to the door. When I open it, I almost run the mailman down. He's standing at the door, the mail in his hand.

He holds it out to me. "I was just putting it in the box, but if you'd like to take it."

I grab the mail. "Yeah, thanks."

I toss it in the house and as I go to close the door, I spot a large white envelope with the Yale seal. I step inside and pick up the envelope and rip it open. It's an official acceptance letter along with registration instructions.

"Shit!" I toss it on the floor and race out to my car. When I get to campus, I go to Jade's classroom and peer through the glass panel in the door to make sure she's there. She doesn't see me but some other girl does and rolls her eyes. What the hell's *her* problem?

I wait outside the classroom on a bench in the hall. I call my dad again. This time, he actually answers.

"Hello, Garret. Katherine said you called."

"Yeah, and she told me the truth about Grandfather. Why the hell would you lie to me about that?" I hear how loud I am and lower my voice. "I needed to know! I need to protect her!"

"I wasn't lying to you. I just haven't had a chance to call and tell you."

"And you knew he didn't have a stroke?"

"Yes. But that can't be public knowledge. Very few people know what really happened."

"Do you know who did it?"

He clears his throat. "No. But your grandfather has numerous enemies who would be happy to see him gone."

"What am I going to do? He called me just now and—"

"My father called you?"

"Yes."

"I'm surprised he'd call you. He hasn't even called *me* yet."

"He called to tell me the plan is still on. He tried to move up the timeline but I wouldn't let him. Dad, there's a countdown timer on my laptop. Who would've done that? You think he's working with someone?"

"I don't know but I'll find out."

"Until you know, what should I do? I'm waiting outside Jade's classroom right now because I don't want to leave her alone. I don't trust that she's safe."

"If my father set the rules, he'll abide by them. She won't be harmed."

"Maybe not now, but she could be in a few weeks. The end of the year isn't that far away. I need to stop him."

"Just stay out of it. I told you I'd take care of it and I will."

"I'm not going to just sit here and do nothing!"

"You need to calm down or Jade's going to figure out what's going on."

"She already knows."

"I told you not to tell her."

"I didn't have a choice. Carson was—"

"Garret, I can't talk right now. I'm meeting with some people and they just walked in. We'll talk later."

He hangs up just as Jade's class dismisses.

She spots me as she walks out. "What are you doing here?"

"I'll tell you when we get to the car." I take her backpack and hold her hand and walk her out of the building.

"What's going on, Garret? Is this about your grandfather?"

"Yes."

She sees the serious look on my face and knows I'm not here to give her good news. We don't speak until we reach our cars. I parked right in front of her.

I unlock her car and open her door for her. "You go first and I'll follow you."

"Wait. You said you'd tell me what's going on when we got to the car."

"Let's just go home. I'll tell you there."

We drive home and go inside and the first thing she sees is the letter from Yale, which is still on the floor.

She picks it up. "Is this an acceptance letter?"

I take it from her, tossing it back on the floor as I lead her to the couch. We sit down and I tell her what happened while she was at class; my talk with Katherine, then my grandfather, then my dad.

Jade's trying to be strong, but she looks terrified, her arms crossed tightly over her middle, her foot nervously tapping the floor. "So what does this mean? We just wait for your dad to do something?"

I shake my head. "No. I'm going out there. I'm going to go see my grandfather."

"What good's that going to do?"

"I don't know, but I can't sit here and do nothing. Maybe we can work something out. Maybe I'll just agree to take over the company."

"Garret, no. You'd hate that. That's not what you want to do with your life."

"It doesn't matter. I have no life if you're not in it. So if taking over the company means he'll leave you alone, I'll do it. I'll even go to Yale. Maybe you could go back to Moorhurst. We could get an apartment in between. It wouldn't be that bad of a commute."

"Are you seriously considering this?"

"I don't have any other alternative."

"But he wants you back in the organization."

"Maybe if I do this other stuff, he won't push me to be a member."

"So am I going with you?"

"I don't want you that close to him. I like the idea of keeping you thousands of miles away. But I also don't feel good about leaving you here alone." I stop to think of how to keep her safe while I'm gone. "Maybe William could help. He has really good security. Maybe he could loan us one of his security guards to watch the house."

"Why wouldn't you just ask your dad?"

"Because I'm not going to tell my dad I'm going out there. I'm going to try to talk to my grandfather alone first. If I can't get him to change his mind, I'll get my dad involved. But I can't tell I'm going. He doesn't want me there. He told me to stay out of it. If he finds out what I'm doing, he'll try to stop me."

"I don't like this, Garret. I don't think you should go out there. You should just let your dad handle this."

"I tried that, and he didn't do anything. And I can't keep waiting for him. I need this to end."

"How do you know your dad didn't do anything?"

"What do you mean?"

"Your dad was the last person to see Holton before he went in the coma. Do you think he—"

"Jade, no. It wasn't him."

She nods. "Sorry. I shouldn't have said that. I know he wouldn't do that."

Actually, I think he would. But when he talked about what happened to my grandfather, he didn't sound guilty or nervous or anything. Then again, he's good at hiding that shit.

"So when are you leaving?" Jade asks.

"I'm going to try to get a flight out today." I take my laptop, facing it away from Jade. When the screen pops up, I pull the timer icon to the trash bin. "But first I need to see if William can get someone out here to watch the house."

"Why do I need that? Holton's at the clinic and he said he'd leave me alone until the end of the year."

I was hoping I wouldn't have to tell her about the timer and my theory about how it got there. But I have to tell her in order to explain why she needs protection and why she needs to be extra careful while I'm away and even when I get back.

No more secrets. She needs to know the truth. All of it.

"I need to show you something." I pull the icon out of the trash and turn so that she can see my laptop screen. "I found this when I turned the laptop on earlier." I point to the icon.

"What is it?"

"It's a timer." I click on it and the numbers appear. "It's counting down to the end of the year." I shut the timer down and the message appears, telling me time is running out.

Jade inhales sharply and covers her mouth with her hand.

I set my laptop aside and pull her into my arms. "I'm sorry, Jade. I didn't want to show you that, but I had to because I need you to know how serious this is. I need you to protect yourself and not take any risks."

"How did your grandfather do that? How did he get that timer on your laptop?"

"I don't think it was him. I think he might be working with someone."

Her shoulders fall and she lets out a heavy sigh. "You said the other members didn't care about you anymore. You said they weren't in on this."

"I don't know if it's another member. It could be someone else. A freelancer he hired."

"To do what? Scare me? Kill me?"

I hug her tighter. "No, Jade. That's not what I meant. He'll keep his word. He won't do anything before January. But he could have someone watching you. And who knows? Maybe that person *would* do something to scare you. I have no idea. Which is why I need you to be extra cautious. And why we need the security guys."

She pulls back and looks at me. "What are you going to tell William? You can't tell him what's really going on."

"I'll just tell him I'm going to visit my grandfather and don't want to leave you here alone. He'll understand. He knows the risks involved in families like ours. He travels a lot and I'm sure he has a security team to watch over his wife. You can never be too careful."

I pick up my phone and call William. His voicemail answers and I leave a message. Then I take my laptop and start searching for flights.

Moments later, my phone rings. It's William.

"Garret, I got your message. You said you needed something?"

"Yes, I need to get someone to watch the house for a few days. I have to go to Connecticut to see my grandfather and I don't want Jade here alone. I want to hire a security guard for while I'm away. I thought maybe you could give me a recommendation."

"I'll do better than that. I have several security personnel who travel with me. They're all excellent and I'd be happy to send a couple of them out there to watch the place while you're away. You'll need two so they can work in shifts."

"That'd be great. Would it be possible for them to be here by tonight?"

"Absolutely. I'll have them leave right away. But Garret, why are you calling *me* instead of your father? He, too, has an excellent security team."

"We're kind of having a fight," I lie. "We're not talking right now."

"Oh. I'm sorry to hear that. Do you need anything else from me?"

"No, I don't think so."

"Okay, well, once I have it arranged, I'll send you the details about the men I'm sending out there so you'll know who to look for and when to expect them."

"You're sure we can trust these guys? You've done background checks? You know them well?"

"Yes, the men I'm sending out there have been with me for years."

165

"And they're not part of—they're not…freelancers?"

"No. They've never worked for them. Garret, I'm glad you're doing this. It's smart. After we met at my mother's house in October, I worried about the two of you. I didn't think you were taking enough precautions, given that you're a Kensington and have connections to—well, you know what I mean. Anyway, it's good to know you're being more careful now. I'll get everything set up and be in touch later with the details."

"Sounds good. Thanks for your help."

"What did he say?" Jade asks as I set my phone down.

"He said he'd have two of his security guys out here by tonight. I want to meet them before I go so I'll plan to leave in the morning." I take my laptop and search for flights. "There's a 6 a.m. flight. I'll take that one."

"Why do I need two guys? Isn't one enough?"

I get my credit card out and buy the ticket. "We want someone watching the house 24 hours a day, so we need two so they can alternate shifts. And actually, one of them should go to class with you. Well, not go *in* the class, but wait outside."

"Garret, you're freaking me out. If Holton's not going to do anything to me, I shouldn't have to be escorted to class by a security guard."

"I'd just feel better if you weren't alone. It's just for a couple days. I'm flying back on Sunday."

"That's not enough time to do anything."

"I have tomorrow and Saturday. That's plenty of time. All I'm doing is talking to him, seeing if we can come to some kind of agreement."

She's quiet. I know she's scared, and although I don't like scaring her, I'm not going to pretend I don't have concerns. Because I do. And I need her to know that so she doesn't take risks. She needs to be aware of her surroundings and never go anywhere alone.

We have dinner later, then wait for William's security guys to show up. They arrive at eight. I invite them inside and question them for a good hour. They're older, probably late thirties, and huge. Both of them used to be in the military. They're very serious and call me 'sir' even though I'm almost 20 years younger than them. By the time we're done talking, I feel better about having them here, although I still wish I didn't have to do this.

I hate leaving Jade, but I feel like I don't have a choice. I need to deal with my grandfather. In person. By myself.

And when I get there, I'm prepared to do anything to make this end.

# Chapter 17

**GARRET**

*I* almost couldn't leave this morning. Even with the security guys and the alarm system and the cameras, I don't believe Jade's safe unless I'm there watching over her. I'm putting all my faith in William that those security guys will take care of her. I like William, and he treats Jade like family now, so I hope I can trust him. I tell myself I can because if I didn't, I wouldn't have been able to leave her.

But truthfully, I feel like I can't trust anyone right now, or anything they tell me. I can't trust the doctors, who lied and told reporters my grandfather had a stroke. I can't trust the news, which kept saying he was dying. I can't even trust my own family. Everyone's lying and covering up the truth. That's why I'm here in Connecticut. I need to know what's really going on with my grandfather. I need to see him myself and see if he looks healthy or sick. I need to know if his mind is still sharp or if the drugs affected him in any way. I need to talk to him. Alone. And then I need to take action.

I arrived in Connecticut a half hour ago and just checked into my hotel. Jade was in class when I got off the plane, but I texted her and she texted back so at least I know she's okay.

She should be out of class now so I call her. "Hey. How's it going?"

"I just got out of class." She's talking really quiet. "Mike's here." Mike's one of the security guys. He must be standing right next to her. "Could you give me a minute?" she says to him. I don't hear anything but I assume he gave her some space because she says, "Okay, I can talk. Are you at the hotel?"

"Yeah. Just checked in. Tell me what's going on there. If those two aren't working out, I'll—"

"No, they're fine. Although everyone's staring at me for walking around with this guy. He's so huge, he stands out."

"It's just one day. Tomorrow you'll be home and he'll stay outside all day."

"So have you decided what you're going to do? Are you just going to show up there?"

"I don't know yet. And I don't want to talk about it until I get back. I'll tell you everything when I get home."

"Okay. I guess I'll talk to you later then. Can you call me tonight?"

"I'll try to. If for some reason I can't, I'll send you a text."

"Be careful, Garret."

"You, too. I love you."

"I love you, too."

As I unpack my stuff I watch the news to see if they have any fake updates about my grandfather. They don't.

Now I need to figure out where he is. I've never been to the clinic he's at. My dad said it's in the Hamptons. What if he's not there anymore? They could've moved him to the clinic that's closer to his house. Shit. I have no one to call to find this out. I can't call my dad.

I'll call Katherine. Oddly enough, she's the only one who's told me the truth about my grandfather.

"What now, Garret?" she says when she answers.

"Hello to you, too, Katherine."

"Your father's not home. Call his cell."

"I already did. He didn't pick up. I wanted to get an update on my grandfather. Is he getting any better?"

"Why don't you call him yourself?" She laughs. "Oh, that's right. He's not speaking to you. You're too much of a disappointment to him. To all of us."

Seriously? Was that really necessary? She's such a bitch. Sometimes I forget how much I hate her. This was a good reminder. Given that she's married to my dad, you'd think she'd at least try to get along with me.

"Just tell me how he's doing."

"He's at home now, recovering."

My grandparents have four houses in different locations so 'home' could be anywhere.

"Which home? The one in Connecticut?"

"Yes. Why do you ask? Are you coming for a visit?"

"No. I just wondered."

"Even if you did show up, he'd send you away. He doesn't want to see you. And he definitely doesn't want to see that cheap tramp you married."

I clench my fist in an attempt to control my anger. "Where's Grandmother? Is she with him?"

"I believe she's attending an event in Greenwich this afternoon. Why do you care where Eleanor is?"

"Because I've called her and haven't been able to get a hold of her."

"She doesn't want to talk to you, Garret. Nobody does. You're an embarrassment to the family and your antics last spring nearly destroyed the Kensington name. I still haven't recovered from that."

"Recovered? What are you talking about?"

"My social engagements have been cut in half since you pulled those stunts. We weren't even invited to the Hamilton Christmas party this year. All because of you. The Kensington name is useless now."

"Then get a divorce." I know she can't but I want to see what she says. "Marry someone with a better name."

She's silent.

"Katherine? Are you still there?"

"This conversation has taken up far too much of my time. Stop calling here, Garret. I won't pick up next time. If you want to talk to your father, call his cell."

She hangs up. That was strange. She seemed to be on a roll insulting me and putting me down and then she just got quiet and hung up. Whatever. It's Katherine. I'll never understand her.

It's four-thirty and I decide to just get this over with. My grandfather's home and my grandmother isn't there so now's probably the best time to talk to him. I grab my keys and go out to the rental car. It's freezing cold and windy and a light sleet is falling. I definitely don't miss this weather.

I turn the heat up to high as I drive out of the parking lot. The hotel is a half hour away from my house, which is why I picked it. I didn't want to risk running into my family. But I have to drive by the house on the way to my grandparents' house, which is another 20 minutes away.

When I arrive there, I'm surprised the security guard lets me in. I thought he'd call my grandfather first to make sure it's okay. I know the guard. He's worked here forever. But I wasn't sure if Katherine was right and my grandfather told his staff to keep me out if I ever tried to visit.

I'm greeted at the door by the maid. She's French and doesn't speak much English. I tell her in French that I'm here to see my grandfather. She smiles and nods and walks away.

The house is quiet. I expected to see doctors and nurses, but maybe they're in his room. I walk down the hall to the back of the house where the master bedroom is located. It's huge and overlooks the back gardens and the pool. I open the door but he's not in there. He must be staying in one of the upstairs rooms until he gets better. I go up the winding staircase and down the long hallway, passing several empty bedrooms until I reach a door that's mostly closed. I open it and see him there in bed, hooked up to an IV. He's reading a newspaper and doesn't notice me.

"Hello, Grandfather." I use a flat tone. I don't want to show any emotion around him. Whatever he says, I can't let him get to me.

He slowly lowers his newspaper, his face displaying a smug grin, like my showing up here means he won.

"Hello, Garret."

He doesn't even act surprised that I'm here. He must've expected this. I hate that I did exactly what he thought I'd do. Now I feel like I should've done this differently. I wanted him to be surprised by my visit. I didn't want to just play into his hands. Let him think I'm predictable. Like he knows my every move.

He motions to the chair next to his bed. "Come sit down. Would you like some tea? I can have some brought up."

"No. I don't want anything." My voice sounded rushed, almost breathless, because my heart's beating so fast. I need to calm down.

I take my coat off and sit in the chair. I get a good look at him. He doesn't look sick. Maybe a little thinner in the face, but not sick. His legs are covered with the blanket, but on top he's wearing a long-sleeve, white cotton button-up pajama shirt with a gold swirling emblem on the right pocket. His shirt is freshly pressed, with not a single wrinkle. His dark gray hair is neatly trimmed and set in place with whatever old man hair product he uses. And his face is smooth, like he just shaved. If he had a suit on instead of pajamas, he'd look like he normally does. Like he'd never even been in a coma.

"So what did the doctors say?" I ask him. "Are you getting better?"

His expression turns grim, almost threatening, as his silvery-blue eyes lock on mine. "You were hoping I'd die, weren't you?" When I don't answer, he lets out a single laugh, then says, "That's far too easy. If you want me dead, you need to do it yourself. You need to be a man. A Kensington. Take action. But instead, you wait for something to happen. You're weak, Garret. Just like your father."

I clench both my hands, then slowly release them. I won't let him get to me. "I'm here to discuss your offer."

His smug smile returns. "I'm listening."

I stare back at him. "I'll agree to go to Yale and work at Kensington Chemical if you leave Jade alone."

The smile drops from his face and his eyes narrow. "That was not the offer I made. This isn't a negotiation. I gave you the terms and conditions. The only decision that's yours is whether she lives or dies."

His lips turn up again. He's loving this way too much. The power. The control. The idea of taking Jade's life and destroying me in the process.

I want to strangle him. Kill him with my bare hands. I have this uncontrollable rage building inside me and I might just do it. I might just kill him.

"Garret." He's looking at me like he knows exactly what I'm thinking. It's almost like he's challenging me to do it. "Do you have something you'd like to say?"

I get up from the chair and stand next to his bed, blood rushing to my hands as I clench and unclench my fists. He's just a foot away. I could do this and end it. He'd fight me, but

I'd win. I'm stronger than him. I could end this right now. What do I do?

He's watching me. Waiting.

I step closer, my heart pounding, my hands slowly rising. "Mr. Kensington."

I drop my hands and step back from the bed as an older woman in a nurse's uniform walks in.

"Your wife called and said she's running late. She'll be here around six." The nurse goes up to his bed and checks the IV bag.

I try to breathe, my thoughts still on those moments before she walked in. I almost killed my grandfather. With my bare hands. Holy shit!

"Is this your grandson?" the nurse asks my grandfather, as she checks his pulse.

"Yes. This is Garret."

She smiles at me. "You look just like your grandfather. And your father. The Kensington men are very handsome." She goes over near the closet where a small silver cart is sitting. She wheels it over to the bed. "Do you have a girlfriend, Garret?"

I look at my grandfather. "I'm married."

"That's wonderful," the nurse says in a light cheery tone that makes my grandfather cringe. "What's her name?"

"Jade." I keep my eyes on my grandfather. "She's the best thing that's ever happened to me. I love her with all my heart. With everything I am. I'd do anything for her. *Anything.*" I emphasize the last word, then finally take my eyes off him and look back at the nurse.

She has her hand over her heart and is staring at me. "That was beautiful. I've never heard a man actually come out and say how much he loves his wife. At least not to other people. Especially a man as young as you. How long have you—"

"Are you going to do your damn job or do I need to find someone else?" my grandfather barks at her. "I don't pay you to stand around and talk."

"Yes, sir." She turns back to the cart. "I need to draw some blood. It won't take long, and then you can go back to visiting with your grandson."

"Actually, I have to leave." I put my coat on. "It was nice meeting you," I say to the nurse.

"You as well. Tell your wife she's a very lucky lady." She winks at me.

"Will you be back for another visit?" my grandfather asks as I'm walking out.

"I don't know," I say, casually. "Maybe."

I take off down the hall and the stairs and go straight out to my car. I should've known he wouldn't accept my offer. I gave him two of the main things he wanted and it still wasn't enough.

I never should've even made that offer. Why would I give him what he wants? Why would I change my whole life just for him? Because I'm desperate. That's why. I'm desperate to stop him. He's determined to kill Jade. I think he's even looking forward to it. Knowing him, he wouldn't even hire someone. He'd do it himself. Sick bastard.

I get some dinner and take it back to the hotel and call Jade.

"How'd it go?" She sounds worried.

"Not well. He wasn't interested in what I had to say."

"So now what?"

"I guess I'll go to my house and talk to my dad. See if we can come up with something else."

"How did Holton look?"

"Like he always does. If it weren't for the IV you wouldn't even know he'd been sick. Are you at home now?"

"Yeah. The security guys are outside. I feel weird having them out there. I feel like I should invite them in for dinner or something."

"Jade, they're not your friends. They're only there to protect you."

"So what else did Holton say?"

"I didn't talk to him very long. A nurse came in so I left." I smile. "The nurse asked about you."

"She did?"

"She asked if I had a girlfriend. I told her I have a wife named Jade who I love more anything in the world. And I told her you're the best thing that's ever happened to me."

"You said all that?" By her tone, I know she's smiling. "To a stranger?"

"Why wouldn't I? It's true. I love you and I'm not afraid to tell people. And my grandfather needed to hear it."

"It won't change his mind."

"I know, but I still said it. I don't want to talk about him anymore. Tell me about your day."

We remain on the phone for hours. I don't want to hang up and neither does she. We find a movie on TV and watch it together, but she doesn't fall asleep like she normally does during movies. She only does that when I'm there and we're snuggled up on the couch together. She said she won't sleep at all tonight, with me gone and two strange guys just outside the door. I won't sleep either. I'll be awake, worrying about her and missing her and trying to find a way to fix this.

Around eleven, we say goodbye and hang up. I lie on the bed staring up at the ceiling, replaying that conversation I had with my grandfather. I can still see that look on his face, challenging me to do something. I hear him telling me I'm weak. Part of me feels like I am. I'm lying here, not doing anything, knowing he's going to kill Jade. My wife. The person I love more than anything. So why aren't I doing something?

*Kill or be killed.* William said those words when we were at Grace's house and I haven't forgotten them. Before we left that day, I asked him why he hired someone like Walt to work for him. I knew Walt freelanced for the organization, which means he's killed people, probably lots of people. William explained that he has lots of enemies and that's why he needs someone like Walt. Someone who isn't afraid to take out the enemy. William said that for people like him and my dad, sometimes it's kill or be killed.

*Kill or be killed.* Sometimes that's your only choice. I feel like it's the only one I have left. I kill my grandfather. Or he kills Jade.

This only ends when one of them dies. And it sure as hell isn't going to be Jade.

# Chapter 18

**GARRET**

*I* bolt up from the bed, put my coat on, grab my keys, and burst out the door. I get in the car and speed down the road, not stopping until I reach my house. My dad changed the code on the gate but the security guy knows me and lets me in. He must assume my dad knew I was coming because he doesn't act surprised. But he does make a comment about my getting there so late. I tell him my plane was delayed.

I go in the house, which is dimly lit by the sconces that line the halls. We always keep them on at night, as well as the small lamp that sits on the table in the foyer.

I walk up the stairs and sneak down the hall to my room. I go to my closet and take out the small metal safe. I punch in the code and open the safe and pull out my gun. I take the bullets and load the gun, my hand shaking a little.

I look at the loaded gun in my hand. I don't know if I can do this. But I have to. If I don't, he'll kill Jade.

I make sure I clicked the safety on the gun, then quietly walk out of my room, back down the hall, and down the stairs.

"Garret?" It's my dad. I turn my head and see him walking toward me from the living room. He's still in his suit pants and white dress shirt, the sleeves rolled up a little. He has on a tie, but it's loosened a bit.

"I have to go." I walk to the foyer, heading to the door, but my dad steps in front of me.

"What are you doing here?"

I don't answer him. I can't come up with a lie. I'm too out of it to think. And I'm shaking. Why am I shaking? Shit. My grandfather's right. I *am* weak. I should be able to do this. I should storm past my dad, get in the car, and go shoot the man who plans to kill my wife.

My dad glances down at my hand and sees the gun.

"Garret, what the hell do you think you're doing?"

I can't answer him. I can't look at him. So I stand there, my gaze on the tile floor.

He reaches down and slowly takes the gun from my hand.

"Son, this isn't you." He says it softly.

I hear him move beside me and set the gun down on the table.

He comes back in front of me and places his hands on my shoulders. "Garret, look at me."

I lift my head and see his face. He doesn't look angry. He looks concerned.

"Dad, I didn't know what else to do."

He pulls me into him, his arms wrapped around me. "I know. I understand."

And he does. This is like him and my mom all over again. I don't know all that happened back then, but I know my dad always worried my grandfather might do something to hurt my mom. And in the end, he did.

My dad grips my shoulders, his eyes on mine. "Listen to me. I know you're desperate to do something, but this isn't the answer. This is not you, Garret. You're not a murderer. You don't hurt people. I may not have been the best father to you, but I did everything in my power to keep you from becoming me. Or him. And I will not let you do it now."

"He challenged me to do it. I went there and I almost attacked him with my bare hands. And he waited for me to do it. And when I didn't, he said I was weak."

"Killing someone does NOT make you strong. It does NOT make you a man. It makes you a monster, like my father." He glances at the gun, then back at me. "It changes you. Once you take someone's life, you can't go back to how you used to be. You'll never be the same. That's why my father challenged you to do this. He wants you to change. To be just like him. Even if doing so results in his own death. He'd be happy dying, knowing he did that to you. But I won't let that happen. I won't let my father take away the person that you are. You're a good man, Garret. A good son. A good husband. You're better than my father or I will ever be." He pauses. "You have no idea what I've done over the years. And I don't want you to know. I try to think of that side of me as someone else. The person my father created, not the real me. But I have to live with that part of myself every day, and believe me, you don't want to live this way." He looks down at the floor, then up at me again. "I know you don't want to lose Jade and I don't either. I love her like she was my own daughter. That's why I told you I'd take care of this. You just need to trust me."

"I did, but nothing happened. And I couldn't just sit and wait for you to do something."

"Things have happened. You're just not aware of them. This is being taken care of."

"Are you the one who drugged him?"

He sighs. "Garret, it's late. Go upstairs. Get some rest and we'll talk about this in the morning."

"No. I'm sorry, Dad, but I have to end this." I grab the gun from the table and run out the door before he can stop me.

"Garret, get back here!" He follows me to the driveway. "You don't need to do this!"

I get in the car and take off, heading toward my grandparents' mansion. It's now almost midnight and I have no idea what I'm going to do when I get there. My dad's right. Shooting my grandfather will change me. And once I do it, I can't go back. But it has to be done. He has to die.

When I get to the mansion, I punch in the code the security guy gave me earlier. The gate opens and I turn off my headlights as I approach the house. I don't want to wake up my grandmother. Shit. What's my grandmother going to do? I'm killing her husband. And what about Lilly? I'm killing her grandpa.

I park the car and sit there a moment, the gun in my hand. What the fuck am I doing? My dad's right. I'm not a murderer.

I get out of the car, leaving the gun behind. I walk up to the door with no plan for what I'm going to do when I get to his room. Then I realize I don't have a key to the house. I can't get in. I turn the door handle and it opens. What the hell? Don't they lock their doors? And where are the security guards? There should be at least one outside watching the gate. This is odd. Something doesn't feel right.

I go inside. The house is quiet, but not completely dark. They always keep a few lights on downstairs. I slowly walk up to his room. I'm now convinced I've lost my mind, showing up at my grandfather's house in the middle of the night, not even sure what I'm going to do.

The room he's in is at the far end of the hall, and as I'm walking there I hear voices. It sounds like a man and a woman. Maybe his doctor and nurse? I'm not sure, but if his medical team is in there, I need to leave. As I'm about to turn back, I hear the woman speaking. The voice sounds familiar. I step closer to the door.

"Are you sure he's out?" she asks.

It's Katherine. What the hell is she doing here in the middle of the night?

"He's out," the man says. "Sleeping like a baby. Go ahead." The man sounds familiar, too, but I'm not sure who it is.

I remain outside the door.

"There. It's done," Katherine says. "Straight to the blood-stream this time. Double the dose. It's nice to have friends in the pharmaceutical industry."

Pharmaceutical industry? Was she talking to…no, that can't be right.

I hear the man's voice again. "Now we just wait."

Holy shit! That's William's voice. William's in there with Katherine. What the fuck?

I walk into the room. "What are you two doing here?"

Katherine is standing by my grandfather's bed, right next to the IV pole, a syringe in her hand. William is across from her.

"Garret!" Katherine drops the syringe, a look of horror and shock on her face. "Get out of here! Right now!"

When I don't move, William says, "Garret, you need to leave."

I look down at my grandfather. His eyes are closed and his skin is getting paler by the second.

"What's going on here?" I ask William.

"Nothing," Katherine snaps. "Now get out!"

"What did you do to him?" I ask her. "What did you put in his IV?"

William answers in a calm, even tone, his eyes on Katherine. "She injected a drug that is now seeping through his veins, slowly killing him."

My eyes shift back to my grandfather. His breathing is getting slower, more labored. The color continues to drain from his face. My grandfather's dying. Right now. Before my eyes. And I'm not doing anything. I'm just standing here, watching him die.

"Why the hell would you tell him that?" Katherine spits out at William.

"Garret wants him dead as much as we do."

*We?* Why does William want my grandfather dead? And why does Katherine?

Katherine turns to me. "Why would you want to kill your own grandfather?"

"Because he was going to kill Jade." I'm not even sure if I said the words out loud as I try to figure out if this is really happening.

"So you came all the way out here to kill him?"

"I wasn't going to—I mean, I just needed to talk to him. Get him to back down. Leave Jade alone."

Katherine smiles and looks at William. "Do you want to tell him or should I?"

"Katherine, don't. He doesn't need to know."

"Know what?" I ask her.

"Jade is dead," she says bluntly.

I reach over and grab her arm. "Why the fuck would you say something like that?"

"Because it's true. She's dead. That piece of trash is finally out of our lives."

"You're lying." I let go of her and turn to William. "Why would she say that about Jade?"

He clears his throat. "Jade's not one of us. We can't let people like her marry into families like ours."

"People like *her*? She's a fucking Sinclair!"

"You knew she was a Sinclair?" Katherine says to William.

I ignore her and go up to William and shove him back against the wall. "What the fuck did you do?"

"Garret, just calm down."

"Calm down? Katherine just told me Jade's dead! And you want me to calm down?" I'm so filled with rage I could kill him, right here, right now. "You better tell me this is some kind of sick joke or I swear to God I'll kill you."

"William ordered his security guards to shoot her," Katherine says. "Left a nice suicide note as well."

"No." I back away from him and wait for him to deny it.

But he doesn't. He just stands there, showing zero emotion.

My mind is racing, refusing to believe this, trying to find an explanation. Why would William hurt Jade? Did he want revenge for Royce's death? Was that his plan all along? Get close to Jade and then kill her? But William cares about her. He was trying to protect her. He kept telling me to protect her.

"No!" I remain in front of him, my hands clenched, my heart thumping hard against my chest. "You wouldn't do that! I fucking trusted you! You promised me you'd protect her! Katherine's lying. Tell me she's lying!"

He says nothing. I get my phone out and call Jade. It goes straight to voicemail. I call again. Same thing. Why the hell isn't she answering?

I hear Katherine again. "She's dead, Garret."

"Tell me she's lying!" I yell it at William. "Tell me she's fucking lying!"

He shakes his head. "I'm sorry, Garret. It had to be done."

"No!" I drop my phone and lunge at him.

"Garret!" My dad races into the room, grabbing me and yanking me away, holding me back.

"He killed Jade!" I fight against my dad, my eyes on William, who's now texting someone on his phone. "He admitted it! He—"

"Garret, stop!" My dad yanks me back even more. As I continue to fight him, he says by my ear, "It's not real. I'll explain later."

What? What's not real? This whole scene is so fucked up I don't know if any of this is real.

He lets me go and I turn to see his face. He nods slightly, then his eyes dart to Katherine, then back at me. He's telling me something. What is he telling me?

"Pearce!" Katherine cries out as she runs over to him. "I don't know what's going on here, but I came to see your father and found William putting something into Holton's IV. I was going to call the ambulance but then you showed up and—"

"Katherine!" he says to her. "That's enough!"

I hear someone in the hall. Dr. Cunningham comes in, wearing his white lab coat. He goes over to my grandfather and checks his pulse, then listens to his heart. Then he walks over to Katherine. "He's gone. Do you still want Eleanor to find him in the morning? Or should I go wake her?"

"Please give us a moment," William says to the doctor.

He nods and leaves the room.

Katherine looks up at my dad. "Pearce, I didn't do this. I promise you. It was William. I saw him do it. The syringe is still on the floor. The drugs he used were from Sinclair Pharmaceuticals."

My dad stares down at her. "And how would you know that, Katherine?"

She inhales sharply. "I, I didn't. I just assumed."

"You killed him," my dad says to her. "And William and I will attest to that when we report this to the organization. I imagine the punishment for killing someone at the high-level ranking my father was at will be quite severe. Granted you aren't a member, but your father is and will be punished accordingly. And you will be as well."

She shakes her head. "No. You can't do that. And William..." She looks at him. "William would never accuse me of that. He knows I didn't—"

"The game's over, Katherine," he says, coming over to her. "We played you. Got you to do what needed to be done and kept our hands clean."

"But in the end, you'll get what you want," my dad says to her. "With my father gone, our divorce will be approved. But you won't be marrying the senator. They'll find someone else for him. Someone of a higher social standing. You won't be allowed in our world anymore. They'll make sure of that."

"Pearce, how could you do this to me? I'm your wife! The mother of your child!"

"Yes, about that. I'm getting full custody of Lilly in the divorce."

She narrows her eyes at him. "You can't raise our daughter. You're never even home."

"And yet I see her more than you do. You're in the same house with her all day and instead of spending time with her, you ignore her and force her to stay in her room. I'm not arguing about this Katherine. She's staying with me. If you'd like to fight that, I'd be happy to expose even more of your sins to the members."

Her eyes bounce between my dad and William. "What are you going to do now? Have me arrested?"

"We'd prefer to avoid the hassle and publicity of an arrest," William says. "The punishment handed down from the organization should suffice."

"No. This isn't right. Pearce, you can't—"

"Leave," my dad says to her. "Get what you need from the house and go stay in a hotel." When she doesn't move, he yells, "Get out!"

She hurries out of the room.

I storm over to William. "What the fuck did you do to Jade?"

"Nothing," he says. "I just texted my men and they confirmed that she's safe and in the house watching TV."

I pick up my phone and call her. This time she answers.

"Garret, why are you calling so late?"

I finally breathe when I hear her voice. I feel like I've been holding my breath this entire time.

"Are you okay?"

"Yeah, I'm fine. Why? Is something wrong?"

"No. I mean, as long as you're okay, then everything's good."

"Where are you right now?"

"It's a long story. I'll call you when I get back to the hotel. It might be a while."

"That's okay. Call me as soon as you can. I'll wait up. I miss you."

"I miss you, too. Jade. You have no idea how much I want to see you right now."

"Garret, you don't sound like yourself. What happened?"

"I'll explain later."

"I'm worried about you."

"Don't be. I'm fine. Just relax. Turn on all the Christmas lights and watch a movie. I'll call you soon. I love you."

"I love you, too. Bye."

I put my phone away. William is now standing next to my dad, the two of them talking quietly by the door.

I go up to William. "Why did you let me believe Jade was dead? Why would you do that to me?"

"Because I had to keep this going until I knew Holton was gone. When we started this plan, I needed Katherine to trust me. I told her I was disgusted by the fact that a Kensington would marry someone like Jade and that I had no problem getting rid of her. And to prove it, I told Katherine I took care of Jade tonight. Then I had my men disrupt the cell signal around your house in case Katherine called to see if Jade was really gone. It was all just to gain her trust, Garret. Your father and I needed her to do this for us. Neither one of us could do it. The rules forbid a member from harming another member. And *killing* a fellow member is punishable by death. We had to find another way."

That doesn't make sense. My dad killed Royce and yet my dad's still alive.

My dad sees my confusion and says, "It's a new rule, established by your grandfather as soon as he got the promotion. He knew he had enemies within the organization who wanted him dead."

"I don't get it," I say to William. "Why did you want to kill my grandfather?"

"Holton killed my father. He slipped a drug in his drink to induce the heart attack that killed him."

My dad explains. "Last spring, the organization was preparing to promote Arlin to the highest level. Your grandfather was furious because he wanted that position. And he got it by killing Arlin. I didn't know this until just recently. When your grandfather was promoted a few months ago, he made a comment about how the position should've been his all along, and that Arlin never should've even been considered. I didn't think anything of it at the time. I thought he was just making a comment. My father has been friends with Arlin for many years, so I never considered that he might've played a role in Arlin's death. But when you told me what your grandfather had done to your mother, and what he planned to do to Jade, I remembered that comment he made about Arlin. On Thanksgiving, I asked him if he did something to Arlin and he admitted that he killed Arlin and had no regrets about it."

"This is simply payback," William says. "An eye for an eye. And we weren't going to let Holton kill again. After your father told me what Holton had done, and what he planned to do to Jade, I agreed to help him with his plan. We needed Katherine to do it, and your father couldn't be the one to get her involved. He needed me to do it."

"Why would Katherine agree to it? Why would she want to kill my grandfather?"

My dad answers. "Because she wants a divorce."

"A divorce? She knows you two can't get divorced."

"Actually, we've been planning our divorce for months now. I didn't want to tell you until it was approved. A few weeks ago, the other members voted to allow it, but your grandfather forbid it. He overrode their decision. He wanted to maintain the benefits that come with being related to Katherine's family, specifically MDX Aerodynamics."

That's the corporation Katherine's family owns. They make plane engines and parts and their biggest client is the military. After my dad married Katherine, her father used his connections with the military to get Kensington Chemical some very large contracts worth billions of dollars. If Katherine and my dad divorced, we'd probably lose those contracts.

"Why would the members agree to a divorce?" I ask.

"Because the senator Katherine has been dating needs a wife, and Katherine convinced the members she'd be perfect for the role. She needed the divorce so she can marry him. He's slated to be vice president in the next election and Katherine wants the power and prestige of being the vice president's wife. And her family wanted her to marry him because he's chairman of the Senate Committee on Armed Services and can steer billions of dollars to MDX Aerodynamics by way of government contracts."

"Is the senator a member?"

"No, but he's been working with us behind the scenes for years."

The organization has people within the government helping them get away with stuff. Get confidential information. Destroy files. Whatever they need. And in exchange, the person gets rewards. For politicians, like this senator, the reward is a promise of more power, such as a higher position. I learned this last spring when I was at one of the organization's meetings.

My dad continues. "Katherine also wanted your grandfather gone because her father was one of the men being considered for Arlin's position. But instead, it was given to your grandfather. By getting rid of him, Katherine was hoping her father would take his place, but now, he'll most likely be demoted and forced to do the jobs no one wants to do."

"But how can you prove she did this?" I ask him.

"We can't. It's our word against hers, but they'll believe William and me long before they'll ever believe Katherine. And she had motive. The members know how much she wanted the divorce. When my father stopped it from happening, she had to find another way. She needed to get rid of him. But I knew she wouldn't attempt to do it herself. She'd need someone to help. So I purposely told her what my father had done to Arlin because I knew she'd run to William, assuming he'd want revenge. He played along, but told her he couldn't kill him because of the new rule forbidding it. So Katherine agreed to do it."

"But the drug she gave him will be traced back to you," I say to William.

He shakes his head. "No. The drug is nothing special. It's one he's already getting in his IV, but in large doses it can be lethal. That syringe contained ten times what his body can tolerate."

"So what are you going to tell the organization?" I ask William.

"I'll tell them that Katherine came to me and was asking about various drugs and their effects. I'll tell them how I answered her questions, but became suspicious of why she was asking, concerned that maybe she planned to drug and kill Pearce so that she'd be free to marry the senator. I'll explain

Always Us

that I immediately called and warned Pearce, telling him to be careful. And then your father will tell the members that he wasn't the intended victim. Holton was. He'll say he found Katherine here, injecting Holton with a lethal dose of drugs, but that it was too late to save him."

I stand there, trying to sort this all out in my head.

"Pearce, we need to leave," William says. "Do you want your mother to find out in the morning?"

"No. She needs to find out now. I don't want the maid to find him here in the morning. Then we'd just have more witnesses to deal with. We need to get him out of here. I'll make the necessary calls. You speak with Dr. Cunningham. Have him wake my mother. Tell him to go with the story we talked about."

William leaves and I'm left with my dad. He gets his phone out, but I stop him before he makes his call.

"Dad. You killed him." I say it quietly.

"No. Katherine did."

"But you arranged for it to happen."

"My father taught me how to make the hard decisions. He taught me to make sacrifices for the greater good. I simply did what my father taught me."

He says it without the slightest hint of emotion. This isn't the dad I saw earlier at the house. Now I'm seeing the other side of him, the one he pretends isn't his real self. The dad I'm used to seeing couldn't do this. He couldn't plot his own father's murder. But he knew he had to, so he used the other side of himself, the dark side, to do it.

"Garret, go back to the house. Get some rest."

"I don't think I can after this."

"Then call Jade. Tell her this is over."

"Is it? Or is someone else going to follow through on his plan?"

191

My dad sighs. "Let's not get into this right now. One problem at a time."

"What does that mean? Who else is in on this?"

"Garret, you need to leave. Cunningham will be waking up my mother soon and you can't be here."

"It's Roth, isn't it?"

He doesn't answer. He just looks at his phone.

"Dad, tell me."

He sighs again. "William and I suspect Roth might've been in on it, but not for the same reasons as your grandfather. Roth has no interest in you taking over the company or going to Yale. But he does want you back at the organization, mainly to prove to the other members that you didn't defeat him last spring."

"So this isn't over. He'll threaten to go after Jade if I don't agree to be a member."

"No. That won't happen."

"How do you know that?"

"The other members don't want you back. They only went along with it because Roth and your grandfather insisted on it, and given their high-level positions, the other members wouldn't dare challenge them."

"So why are you telling me not to worry? Grandfather is gone, but with Roth still in power, nothing changes."

"It does if the person who takes over your grandfather's position disagrees with Roth."

"Yeah, like that's gonna happen."

My dad lowers his voice. "William believes he'll be offered the position."

"Are you serious? Why would they pick him?"

"I can't share that information. But having him at that level will give you protection, Garret. And protection for Jade. He'll be able to stop Roth and anyone else who shows interest in you."

"Is William really getting promoted? Do you know this for sure?"

"No, but we will soon." He glances at my grandfather. "Now get out of here. I mean it. You can't be here. I'll see you in the morning."

"I got a hotel room so—"

"Garret, I need you at the house. I'm going to have a lot to deal with tomorrow and I need you to help me handle Lilly. She won't understand. She's never had to deal with death before."

"Shit. She's alone at the house right now. She can't be—"

"She's not alone. Before I left, I had Charles come over and stay in one of the guest rooms just in case she wakes up. But Lilly needs family, now, Garret. You need to be there for her."

"Yeah, okay."

I walk out into the dark hall, down the dimly lit stairs, and out the front door. This is so surreal. My grandfather is dead. I watched him die. I witnessed the set-up. And now, as I leave, the cover-up begins.

# Chapter 19

**GARRET**

*I* drive back to the hotel, get my things, and take them to the house. When I get to my room, I collapse on the bed. I'm so exhausted. I got up early this morning to fly here and now it's 2 a.m. and I'm still awake. It's like this day will never end.

I call Jade. "Hey, it's me."

"Hey. You sound tired."

"I am." I pause, then say, "He's gone, Jade."

She's quiet. She doesn't say she's sorry, but I don't want her to say it. Neither one of us is sorry he's gone. He's a killer. A murderer. And he didn't give a damn about me or anyone else.

"I'll tell you more when I get home." I don't want to tell her what happened over the phone in case someone's listening. I don't think they are, but I can't take the risk.

"Okay." Jade knows not to ask questions. She can tell by my tone that I can't talk about it. "So are you staying out there for the funeral?"

"It'll probably be next week, so no, I'm flying home Sunday, like I planned."

"But you're going to the funeral, right?"

"No. I don't want to. And even if I wanted to, I couldn't. They'll all be there. I don't want to be around them." I'm referring to the members. Again, she gets it and doesn't ask me more about it.

"Garret, you should get some sleep."

"Yeah." I want to talk to her but I'm so out of it I don't have anything to say. I'm still in shock over what just happened. "Goodnight. I love you."

"I love you, too."

I fall asleep shortly after we hang up. I wake up at eight when I hear my dad in the hall. It sounds like he went into Lilly's room. I don't know how she's going to react to the news. My grandfather pretty much ignored her. He wasn't comfortable around kids. So maybe she won't be that upset.

I turn on the TV in my room and flip through until I see his photo. It's on one of the cable news channels. I up the volume. "…believed to have suffered complications from the stroke he had last week. Kensington had been in a coma following the stroke and never regained consciousness. Holton Kensington was 78 and is survived by his wife, Eleanor, his son, Pearce, and two grandchildren."

I click through to another channel and see the news of his death scrolling on the bottom of the screen with all the other news of the day. It's just like when Royce was killed. The world is led to believe whatever the organization tells them to. Whatever story they feed the media.

"Garret?" I hear my dad's voice at my door.

"Yeah, come in."

He walks in looking like he's going to work. He's in a dark suit, crisp white shirt, and blue tie. His eyes are heavy and his face looks tired. I'm sure he didn't sleep last night. He had too much to do. Take care of the body. Get the fake story to the media. Deal with my grandmother.

He comes over and sits at the end of the bed. "I just spoke with Lilly and told her the news. I need you to spend some time with her. She wasn't close to her grandfather but she's still sad. She doesn't understand death and I don't have time to answer all her questions. I'm meeting with reporters in an hour and I need to get to the office to prepare. I don't know what time I'll be back, so if you could just make sure she's not alone."

"Yeah, I'll stay with her. Is Katherine coming back?"

"Unfortunately, yes. Technically, we have to continue to live as a married couple until the members finalize the approval of our divorce."

"When's that going to happen?"

"Probably in a week or two. But I spoke with Katherine this morning and we agreed, for Lilly's sake, it would be best if Katherine lived here until the end of the year. Lilly needs to deal with her grandfather's death before we tell her about the divorce."

"How is Grandmother?"

"I'm not sure. It's hard to tell with her. She didn't say much when she found out. She and my father had a difficult marriage, but she was with him for many years so it'll be an adjustment for her to live on her own."

"Do you know when the funeral's going to be?"

"Next Thursday. But you can't be there, Garret."

"I know."

"The public already knows you've been estranged from your grandfather since last spring so it shouldn't be that surprising if you don't show up at his funeral. I'm sure the media will spin it that way and that's fine. Actually it's good. People will be angry that you didn't show up, which will spur negative comments about you online. We need that after that PR company pulled that stunt trying to fix your image." He stands up. "I need to go."

"Dad, wait." I meet him at the door. "Thank you. For what you did."

He slowly nods. He looks so tired, so stressed, so beaten down. God, I feel bad for him. I knew he had a shitty life, growing up with my grandfather, but I never really knew how bad it was until I saw for myself how horrible a man my grandfather was.

I hug him. "I love you, Dad."

He gives me a tight squeeze. "I love you, too, son."

After he leaves, I go down to Lilly's room. She's curled up on her bed, holding her stuffed panda bear.

I sit next to her. "Lilly, I'm here."

She sits up and climbs on my lap and hugs me.

"Grandpa's gone." Her voice is sad and quiet.

"I know. I'm sorry."

She was crying when I came in, but she wipes her eyes, trying to hide it. She knows her mom's rule. No crying allowed. Stupid Katherine. She's such a bitch.

"Lilly, it's okay to cry. That's what people do when someone they love goes away."

"Mom said not to."

"When did you talk to her? This morning?"

"Yeah. She called me."

"Don't listen to her. If you want to cry, then cry. It'll make you feel better."

"Daddy said Grandpa got sick and that's why he went away. But he was here on Thanksgiving. He wasn't sick."

"It's a different type of sick. It's not like a cold." I can't explain this to her. I have to go with the stroke and coma story, but how do you explain that to a kid? Why didn't my dad talk to her about this? Or maybe he did but she wants to hear it from me. She trusts me more than she trusts my dad, although I think that's changing now that he's spending more time with her.

"Will you stay here, Garret? Please?"

"I have to go home tomorrow, but I'll spend all of today with you."

She lays her head on my shoulder. "Garret?"

"What?"

"Grandpa's in heaven, right?"

That's an odd question and I don't know where she came up with it because my family is not religious at all. And to answer Lilly's question, I honestly think I'll have to lie. Knowing the truth about my grandfather, he might just be in hell.

"Yes, Lilly. He's in heaven."

"Do you think he'll meet your mom?"

These questions just keep getting weirder. He basically killed my mom, so if he's up there, I sure hope they don't meet. And if they do, I hope she kicks his ass straight down to hell.

"I don't know, Lilly. I don't know how that works. Heaven's a big place so they may not see each other."

She hugs me really tight. "I love you. I hope you never die."

"I love you, too."

I don't know how she stays so sweet living with Katherine. I thought when I moved out, Katherine might turn Lilly into a mini version of herself, but luckily, that didn't happen.

We have breakfast and then I watch cartoons with her in the game room. Katherine shows up at noon. She calls me out into the hall. I go out there while Lilly remains in front of the TV.

Katherine's wearing a beige suit, her hair styled like she just had it done. She doesn't look like someone who just committed murder. She isn't showing the slightest sign of guilt or anxiety. The only emotion she's displaying is anger, which is typical for her.

She points to the game room. "Why is Lilly still in her pajamas?"

"Seriously? That's your biggest worry right now? Are you kidding me?"

"Last night is an issue between your father and me. It doesn't concern you."

"You killed my grandfather. That doesn't concern me? Really?"

She steps closer. "Don't you EVER speak of that again. If anyone heard—"

"Just stop. You're done treating me like shit. And I'm done dealing with you. William and my father are taking you down, Katherine. Your life is over."

"Let them try to get to me. They won't succeed. I have my own secrets to share."

"Like what?"

"You'll see." She smirks and walks away.

I don't bother asking her what she means. It doesn't matter. My dad and William will tell the members what she did. And when they're done with her, she'll have nothing left.

I spend the rest of the day with Lilly. Katherine left in the afternoon but came back after dinner. I'm glad she wasn't here all day. That would've been awkward. I don't know how my dad and her are going to live in the same house. It's just for a few weeks, but still. It's going to be a long few weeks.

Sunday I fly back to California. As soon as I get home, I send the security guys away. Then I hug Jade for a really long time. After that, I tell her what happened.

"I can't believe it," she says when I'm done.

"I know. It doesn't even seem real. I mean, I saw it with my own eyes and I still can't believe it."

"He killed Arlin." As Jade says it, tears well up in her eyes.

"I'm so sorry, Jade." We're lying in bed and she's tucked in my arms. "My grandfather was evil. I think I always knew that but I didn't want to believe it."

"They're all evil." She pushes off me. "Every one of them. They kill people and they don't care."

"That's not true. My dad hates being part of this. So does William. But they can't get out of it."

"Carson could get them out. He said he would. That guy he works for, Hanniford, is rich and powerful. He could help your dad get out. Maybe they could work together to take down the organization."

"That's not going to happen. The organization is too powerful and too many people are involved. They have people planted inside the government and law enforcement. If Hanniford had evidence and took it to the authorities, the evidence would disappear."

I shouldn't be telling her this, but I feel like I have to so she'll understand.

"They're not going away, Jade. They'll *never* go away."

"So they just get to control everything and do all these horrible things?"

"The only way things will change is if the change comes from the inside. And actually, that might happen."

She sits up. "What do you mean?"

I tell her what my dad said about how William might be promoted. "If that happens, Jade, he could make changes. He might be able to stop some of the bad stuff they do."

"But he's just one person. There are lots of other men at that high-up level, right?"

"Yes, but William is very influential. People listen to him. He's a good leader and can be very persuasive. That's why he was able to get Katherine to go along with his plan. If anyone can create change in the organization, it's him. And having him in that role will give us protection. He'll make sure they leave us alone."

"When does William find out if he's getting promoted?"

"My dad thinks it'll be voted on at the end of the year meeting. It's the week after Christmas. It's a big meeting where they make a lot of decisions. They'll decide then if William gets the position."

Jade lies down again, facing me. "I guess that's good if he gets promoted, but I wish he could just get out of it instead. I wish your dad could, too."

"Let's not worry about it." I hug her closer and kiss her cheek. "Let's just go to sleep. I'm so tired. I'm so freaking tired."

She snuggles into my chest and we fall asleep. I don't wake up until morning. Jade assumed I'd stay home from class today, but I don't need to. I'm not grieving his death. I'm not sad or depressed that he's gone. I feel guilty for not feeling that way, but the man was evil. He was truly evil and I can't seem to feel sad that he's gone. I can't forgive him for what he did to my mom, or my dad and me. And I will never forgive him for trying to kill Jade. I honestly don't know how I was able to contain my rage enough to not kill him myself when I stood over his bed last Friday.

After my morning class, I check my messages and see one from my grandmother. She called last night when I was sleeping. Shit. I should've checked this sooner. She never calls me and now she probably thinks I'm avoiding her.

I call her back. "Grandmother, it's Garret," I say when she answers. "I'm sorry I missed your call."

"It's fine, Garret." She doesn't sound tired or sad. She just sounds like she always does. "I was calling to tell you that we're having a private gathering at the house on Friday and I need you to be here. I understand your reluctance to attend the funeral, but Holton was your grandfather and you should pay your respects. This will allow you to do so."

My grandmother pretends she doesn't know what's going on with the organization, but she does. That's why she made that comment about the funeral. She knows I don't want to be around all the members who will be there. She knows I was picked to be president and she didn't want that for me. Unlike my grandfather, she didn't want my life ruined by the organization's plans for me.

She may not be a warm-and-fuzzy type of grandmother, but deep down I know she cares about me and wants me to be happy. She wants my dad to be happy, too. But she's from an era where women do whatever their husbands say, which is why she allowed my grandfather to control my dad and try to control me. But that didn't keep her from speaking her mind. I know she argued with my grandfather about the way he treated my dad and me. It didn't do any good, but she still let him know her opinion on the matter.

"Did you talk to Dad about this?" I ask her.

"Yes. And your father agrees you should attend."

"Who will be there?"

"Just some friends of the family."

"Like who?"

"Some friends of mine that you probably don't know. And your father invited some people from the company. Some of the executives who worked with your grandfather. He also invited the Sinclairs. They've been friends of ours for years, and as you know, your father has been checking in on Grace since Arlin died."

"So Grace and William are coming?"

"Yes. And Victoria."

"Why Victoria?"

"It's proper social etiquette, Garret. We attended Royce's funeral. Therefore, Victoria will attend Holton's funeral and will be at the gathering on Friday."

"If I go, I'm bringing Jade."

She sighs, then says, "Do you really think that's a good idea?"

"She's my wife. I'm not going without her."

"Very well. Then I'll see you both on Friday. The gathering begins at six but you should arrive in the afternoon."

"Grandmother, can I ask you something?"

"What is it?"

"Do you feel the same way about Jade as Grandfather did?"

"Your relationship is none of my business. You're a grown man, Garret."

"Just answer me."

"I don't know her, so perhaps it's not right for me to say, but she is not the girl I would've chosen for you. That said, I can see that she makes you happy."

That's good enough for me. I don't need my grandmother to like Jade. I just need her to accept Jade as my wife, and it sounds like she does.

"I don't know about Friday, Grandmother. Finals are in a week and Jade and I need to—"

"Garret, I'm not asking you. I'm telling you. You will be there. Family needs to be together at a time like this. You will do this for *me* and you will do this for your *father*. Goodbye."

She hangs up. Yeah. Warm and fuzzy is not how I'd describe her. At all. But she's my grandmother and I feel like I should do this for her.

I meet Jade for lunch at the coffee shop and tell her about the call. "So I guess we have to go to Connecticut on Friday."

"For the funeral?"

"No, the funeral is Thursday. We're going to a private ceremony at the house on Friday. My grandmother called it a gathering, but I think it's more like a private memorial service."

"You talked to your grandmother?"

"She called me and asked me to go."

"Is she okay?"

I shrug. "You can never tell with her. She hides her emotions. But she seemed okay."

"Did she say I could come? Because I don't want to cause any arguing or—"

"Jade, you're my wife. You're going. And yes, she said you're invited."

It's not really true, but whatever. She didn't say no.

"Who else will be there?"

"Friends of the family. Grace and William are coming. And Victoria. Have you heard anything from Grace?"

"She left me a voicemail but I haven't called her back. She said she called you but didn't leave a message because she wants to give you her condolences directly. You know how she is. She's all about proper etiquette. She said she sent you a card."

Our lunch arrives and as I'm eating, I notice Jade hasn't touched her food.

"Jade, are you gonna eat?"

She glances at her plate. "Yeah. I was spacing out for a minute."

I place my hand over hers. "You're nervous aren't you?"

"A little. Your grandmother doesn't like me. And I know she didn't invite me. She doesn't want me there."

"She doesn't have to like you. But at least she accepts you and that's good enough."

"How long are we staying?"

"We can fly home Friday night."

"I think we should stay for the weekend."

"Jade, you don't have to do that for me. We'll just leave after it's over."

"No, I think you should spend time with your dad. And I'd like to spend some time with Lilly. Unless Katherine won't let me."

"My dad will take care of Katherine. If you're willing to stay the weekend, that's what we'll do. I know Lilly would like that. She's not doing so well right now. But what about finals? Don't you need to study this weekend?"

"I don't have to. I've been studying for weeks. What about you?"

"I can study on the plane."

"Do you want me to get the tickets?"

"No, I'll get them." I lean over and kiss her cheek. "Thank you. I know you don't want to do this."

"I'll do whatever you need me to do." She hugs my side.

Damn, I love her. She's completely selfless. If I were her, there's no freaking way I'd go to that memorial service. But she's not thinking about herself. She's doing what's best for Lilly and she wants to be there for my dad.

After lunch, I buy our plane tickets, then go to my afternoon class. I can't concentrate. My mind keeps wandering to my future with Jade, because I finally feel like we have a future. With my grandfather gone, I feel like we're finally safe. Maybe it's too soon to believe that, but I need to. These past few weeks I've been so damn stressed and I can't take it anymore. I just need to get through this week and then I can relax. The memorial service will be closure. The final end to this nightmare I've been living. My final goodbye to my grandfather.

# Chapter 20

**JADE**

Garret just told me we're going to see his family on Friday and I'm already getting nervous. I'm sure Garret was just being nice when he said his grandmother invited me. She wasn't exactly friendly the last time I saw her, so I'm guessing she doesn't want me at the memorial service.

What if people from the organization are there? I don't want to be anywhere near those people. I wish we could skip the memorial on Friday and just go to Garret's house for the weekend and spend time with Lilly and Pearce. But Garret promised his grandmother we'd go. At least Grace will be there. And William. I feel a little better knowing that.

I'm dreading seeing Katherine. She always makes me uncomfortable, but now that I know she killed Holton I'll be even more nervous around her. I can't believe she just gets away with murder. Well, I guess she'll be punished, but not by the actual justice system. She won't have to spend her life in prison, like any other murderer would.

Then again, Katherine wasn't alone in killing Holton. Pearce and William also played a role and they aren't being punished either. Not that I'd want them to be. Holton deserved to die. I know I shouldn't say that and I never would out loud, but I still think it.

This is so crazy. The three people who killed Holton will be at his memorial service. And nobody knows that except Garret and me.

I'm still at the coffee shop, but Garret left for class. I call Grace because she left a message and I haven't had a chance to return her call until now.

"Hi, Grace."

"Jade, how is Garret doing?"

"He's okay. He got back yesterday and finally got some sleep. This morning his grandmother called and asked us to come out there on Friday for a memorial they're doing at the house. She said you'll be there."

"Yes. I'm staying with William so we'll be arriving together. Meredith is out of the country and won't be able to attend. Victoria will be there, but not the girls."

"Well, I'm glad you're coming. It'll be good to see you again."

"Jade, remember that we have to pretend we're not related. People there don't know you're a Sinclair."

"Yeah, that's right." I know that, and yet it hadn't occurred to me until now.

"Be especially careful around Victoria. She'll be keeping an eye on you and she'll probably ask you and Garret some questions."

"Why is she so interested in us?"

"She knows Pearce has been checking in on me after Arlin died and she knows I attended your wedding. She's been asking me why I'm spending so much time with the Kensingtons. I explained that we've been friends with them for years, and she knows that, but that didn't seem to appease her. She's a very nosy, gossipy woman, much like Katherine."

I smile. I like that Grace hates Katherine almost as much as I do.

"I'm sure she won't be friendly to you," Grace continues. "Victoria always wanted Garret to be with Sadie, so she's not happy he ended up with you. She's not at all fond of Evan, although she approves of his relationship with Sadie, knowing what's in store for him. She just wishes it had been Garret instead."

"Why doesn't she like Evan?'

"He drinks heavily, uses drugs, has multiple girls on the side." Grace sighs. "And yet Sadie still chooses to be with him. It's sad that she feels she needs to do this, but it's her life. Jade, I didn't realize it was so late. I have an appointment I need to leave for. Could we talk tomorrow?"

I smile. "I call you every day, Grace."

"Yes, I know, honey. It's very sweet of you. We'll talk soon."

As I'm hanging up, Harper calls.

"Hi, Harper."

"Hey, I heard about Holton. How's Garret?"

"He's okay."

I'm not going to tell her Garret was just out there with him. That would just lead to questions.

"When are you leaving for the funeral?"

"We're not going. Garret doesn't want to."

"He *has* to go. It's his grandfather."

"I know, but they didn't get along."

"Yeah, but—"

"Harper, he's not going. I can't change his mind and I don't want to. This is his decision to make. But we're still going out there. There's a private memorial at Garret's house on Friday so we're going to that instead of the funeral. It's just for family and close friends."

"My parents are going to the funeral. They're flying out Wednesday."

I sigh inside my head. Of course they're going, because they're part of the inner circle now. Part of the organization. Or if they're not *yet*, they will be soon.

"So are you just going for the memorial?" she asks. "Or are you staying a few days?"

"We're staying for the weekend."

"Do you think we could get together? Just for an hour or so?"

"Yeah. Of course. If I'm out there, you know I have to see you."

Harper and I make plans to meet for coffee on Saturday. I'd love to spend more time with her, but I need to be with Garret and his family.

The next few days we return to our normal routine. Garret doesn't mention his grandfather so I don't either. Pearce calls on Wednesday just to confirm what time we'll be there on Friday, but other than that, we don't hear from him. Garret's been calling Lilly every day to check on her. She's still sad, and with so much to be done for the funeral, I'm sure Pearce hasn't had much time to spend with her. She's probably all alone in her room.

Now it's Thursday and Garret and I are having breakfast at the coffee shop before class. I just checked my phone and noticed it's eleven-thirty on the East Coast, which means the funeral for Holton is about to begin. Garret hasn't said anything about it, but it was all over the financial news channels this morning.

"Garret, it's almost time for the funeral."

"I know." He reaches in his pocket and takes out his phone, swiping through the screen. "Shit, there must be 500 people there."

He shows me a photo from a news website. It's taken from outside of a large church and shows a long line of people filing in. I don't know who all those people are. I can't imagine Holton having that many friends, unless they're evil like him.

Garret puts his phone away, then gives me a kiss. "I need to get to class."

209

"Yeah, I'll see you later."

He grabs his backpack and takes off. I hope he's okay. Even if he's not sad about Holton's death, I feel like he's still on edge from all the stuff that went on the past few weeks. He's still not sleeping well or eating much. I'm hoping he'll feel better after the memorial, when all of this is finally over.

The next day we leave for Connecticut early in the morning and arrive there late afternoon. A car service picks us up at the airport. Eleanor hired them. Maybe she thought we wouldn't show up if we weren't driven there.

When we get to the house, luxury vehicles are lined up out front. All black. The black car thing freaks me out. It seems ominous, like the owners are all members of the organization.

Eleanor told Garret she invited friends of the family but she didn't say who. I'm guessing at least some of them are members. I don't know if I trust Eleanor. She doesn't seem to be like Holton, but they were married for more than 50 years so they couldn't be that different, could they?

The front door is unlocked so Garret and I let ourselves in. A woman in a maid's uniform walks up to me, waiting for my coat. I give it to her and Garret hands her his and she walks away.

The caterers are running around with trays topped with glasses and tiny plates. As we walk farther into the house, I see that they're setting up drink and appetizer stations, like it's some kind of party. I guess you have to serve *something*, but it seems weird to stand around eating fancy appetizers after someone died.

I have almost no experience with funerals or memorials. My mom was cremated and her funeral was nothing more than Frank, Ryan, and me standing in a church while a minister said a few words. Nobody else came because my mom had no friends and no other family. It was depressing. I didn't even want to go but Frank made me.

Garret and I make our way to the living room. There's an easel with a large framed photo of Holton on it. I shudder as I see his stern face looking back at me. He's not smiling in the photo. Not even a tiny bit. I don't think I ever saw him smile. Next to the easel are two huge floral arrangements coming out of a tall stand.

"Garret." I hear Pearce and look over and see him giving Garret a hug. "Thank you for coming."

"Jade." He gives me a tight hug, almost like Garret's hugs have been the past couple weeks.

"Hi." I don't know what to say. I'm so bad with death and grief and all that type of stuff. So I just say the words that I seem to be saying a lot lately. "I'm really sorry."

He nods as he steps back. He's wearing a black suit with a white shirt and silvery-blue tie. He looks handsome as he always does, but his face looks like he hasn't slept for days.

"How are you doing, Dad?" Garret asks.

"It's been a rough week, but things are starting to settle down. After tonight, we'll finally get some time together as a family. It's good to have you two home."

Katherine walks by and completely ignores us. I tense up seeing her, knowing she wanted me dead. I'm sure she's disappointed I'm alive. That's probably why she's ignoring me. She's choosing to pretend I'm dead.

I haven't seen Katherine since last spring. Her hair looks even blonder than I remember. She's wearing a long-sleeve black dress that has a thin belt around the middle. I think she might've had something done to her lips. They look fuller, like maybe she had those injections that plump them up. She used to have really thin lips.

"Why don't you two go upstairs and get settled?" Pearce says. "People will start arriving in a half hour or so."

"Can we see Lilly?" I ask him.

"Yes, of course. She's in her room. My mother is up there with her. She's staying here at the house for a few days."

"Come on." Garret takes my hand and we go up the stairs.

The maid already took our luggage up to his room. I always forget that Garret's family has all this hired help. People are always doing stuff for you.

Garret stops at Lilly's room but I pull on him to continue down the hall. "Let's just see her later."

"Don't you want to say hi?"

"Your grandmother's with her. We should leave them alone."

He turns me toward him, his hands on my upper arms, his eyes on mine. "Jade. She's not like him. I swear."

I notice I'm shaking a little, probably from seeing Katherine and that photo of Holton. I'm feeling anxious and nervous and a little sick to my stomach. And now that I know Eleanor is staying here, I'm even more nervous.

Garret hugs me and says quietly, "She's not going to hurt you. She had nothing to do with it."

He lets me go and knocks on Lilly's door. It opens and I smile when I see Lilly standing there. She's in a black dress and little black shoes, her long blond hair held back with a headband that matches her dress. The headband reminds me of Harper. It wouldn't surprise me if that's why she's wearing it. Lilly loves Harper and is probably trying to dress like her now.

"Hi, Lilly." I bend down and give her a hug. I'm still in the hallway but I need to hug her. She's hurting and could use a hug. And hugging her helps me relax.

"Hi." Her voice is soft and tiny and sad.

She needs her brother. I stand up and Garret picks her up.

"Hey, Lilly." He smooths her hair as she lays her head on his shoulder. She hugs him really tight, her arms and legs attached to him like she'll never let him go.

"I'm sad," she whispers.

"I know." He kisses her head.

Whenever I see those two together, it makes me want to cry. Lilly's doing better now that she goes to school and has some friends, but she still really misses Garret. They have a special bond that Lilly doesn't have with anyone else. She trusts him and listens to him and loves him, probably more than she loves her own parents.

"Hello, Garret." Eleanor appears in the doorway to Lilly's room. She's wearing a black dress that almost matches Katherine's dress but without the belt. And she's wearing a pearl necklace with matching earrings, her short hair framing her face.

"Hello, Grandmother." Garret walks past her into Lilly's bedroom.

I remain at the door, frozen in place, my heart thumping fast.

Eleanor gives me a slight smile. "Jade. Thank you for coming."

"I'm sorry for your loss." I sound like a greeting card, but I didn't know what else to say.

She steps aside and I walk into the room and stand next to Garret, who still has Lilly glued to him.

"How was the flight?" Eleanor asks. "I haven't flown commercial for years. I've heard it's even more unpleasant than it used to be."

"It's not that bad," Garret says.

There's silence. None of us knows what to say. Eleanor hasn't talked to Garret since last summer, other than to call him and tell him to come here today.

Katherine appears at the door. "Lilly, I need you to come downstairs."

Lilly doesn't move or say anything. The room is quiet as we all wait for Katherine's reaction. She straightens up and her lips purse as she stares at Lilly.

Katherine goes and stands next to Garret. "Did you hear me, Lilly? I need you to come downstairs. Right now."

"I want to stay with Garret."

Garret smiles a little, which makes Katherine even more furious.

"He's here all weekend. You'll see him later. Now hurry up."

She doesn't move. I guess Lilly's developing a rebellious streak. Good for her.

"Garret." Katherine's tone has an edge, like she's warning him.

"Katherine." He says it back the same way, staring at her.

More silence as this standoff continues. Then Garret turns and kisses Lilly's head, which is still on his shoulder. His gaze returns to Katherine as he says, "I have to go get ready, Lilly, but later we'll watch a movie, okay?"

"She's not allowed to—"

"She's not what?" Garret cuts Katherine off. He gives her a look which she seems to understand.

She clears her throat. "Very well. But for now, she needs to be downstairs."

He lowers her down to the floor. "Lilly, let go."

She reluctantly releases him. "We'll watch a movie later? You promise?"

"I promise."

Lilly follows Katherine out of the room. The woman still hasn't even acknowledged me.

Eleanor steps in front of Garret. "I should say a proper hello."

He leans over for her usual faraway hug, but she moves in and gives him a full hug. A real hug. Arms all the way around. I see his face. He's completely shocked, but he hugs her back.

"Go get yourself ready." She pats his back, then steps away. "And please shave, Garret. A five o'clock shadow is so unsightly on a man."

"I will. We'll see you downstairs."

Actually, I like Garret's five o'clock shadow. I think it's sexy.

We go down to his room. Katherine still hasn't touched it. I keep waiting for her to tear it apart and redecorate it, painting the walls beige or white instead of the dark blue he picked out.

"Damn, I'm tired." He collapses on the bed and so do I.

"Me too. Maybe we should've left yesterday so we wouldn't have had to get up so early today."

"I guess, but too late now. I'm sure we can find some caffeine to keep us awake. Charles always has coffee going."

"I want to go see Charles. Let's go to the kitchen."

"We'll see him later. We need to get ready. It's getting late." He gets up and pulls me to standing. "You can shower first. I'll shave."

I follow him into the bathroom. "What's going on with you and Katherine?"

"What do you mean?" He turns the shower on for me.

"You gave her a look and she just backed down."

He smiles as he goes back to the sink. "Yeah, we kind of have an agreement when it comes to Lilly."

"What's the agreement?" I strip my clothes off and grab a towel.

"A few years ago I made some videos of Katherine, and just recently I told her about them and threatened to release them to the media."

"Videos of what?"

215

"Her gossiping on the phone about her rich friends. Saying all this bad shit about them." He rinses his razor in the sink.

"Why would the media care about that?"

"The gossip pages would care. Society pages. Whatever they call it. They'd eat that shit up. And Katherine's reputation would be destroyed."

I step in the shower. "So you're blackmailing her?"

"Yeah, but it's not like I need to anymore. The organization will make sure she never attends another charity ball or any other high society gathering. And once my dad divorces her, she won't be able to keep me away from Lilly."

"You think they'll still be allowed to get divorced?"

"I don't know why they wouldn't. My grandfather was the only one who forbid it and he's gone now."

"That'd be great for your dad if he could finally get rid of her."

"It'd be great for *all* of us."

We finish getting ready. Garret puts on a black suit and I wear a black dress. We walk down the hallway and I look over the banister and see at least 30 people downstairs. Everyone is wearing black. It's so somber and depressing.

As we go down the staircase, I spot Victoria. She's looking right at me and she's not smiling. In fact she looks angry.

I can't wait for this night to be over.

# Chapter 21

**GARRET**

Jade and I come down the stairs and the first person to greet us is Victoria. I can't stand the woman. She's almost as bad as Katherine.

"Garret." She puts her long skinny fingers on my shoulders and leans in to hug me. Not a real hug, thank God, but a distant hug, which I expect to get a lot of tonight. "My deepest sympathies to you and your family."

"Thank you, Victoria." Her perfume is filling the air around me and making me feel like I have to cough. I step back.

She smooths the side of her hair which is pulled back into some type of twisted knot. She probably paid someone hundreds of dollars to style it that way. When I was dating Sadie, she'd pay $200 to $300 to have her hair styled for the ritzy parties she made me go to in DC.

"It's such a tragedy when death is sudden like that," Victoria says, referring to my grandfather but also probably to her husband.

"Yes. It is." It's eerie that Royce was killed by my father just steps away from where we're standing and yet Victoria has no idea.

"It's a shame you couldn't attend the funeral." She makes sure to only look at me, like Jade doesn't exist.

"The timing of it just didn't work out." I glance over at Jade. "I believe you've met Jade, my wife."

"Yes, we've met." Her eyes do a quick scan of Jade, then dart back to me.

"Hi," Jade says, but Victoria pretends not to hear her.

"Thank you for coming, Victoria." I walk away before I do what I want to do, which is to call her out on her rudeness.

I'm trying to stay calm and get through this night without any drama. Yeah, like that'll happen. Wishful thinking.

"You okay?" I ask Jade as I lead her down the hall to the kitchen.

"Yes. But let's try to avoid her the rest of the night."

Being around Victoria made Jade as nervous as she was around my grandmother. It makes sense. Both of their husbands tried to kill her. Shit. What the hell was I thinking? I shouldn't have brought Jade here. This is way too stressful for her.

I take her to the kitchen because I know she'll relax if she sees a friendly face.

"Charles," I say to get his attention. He's at the sink, washing a pan. "Someone wanted to see you."

He turns around and smiles. "Jade. Garret. Welcome home." He dries his hands on a dishtowel and comes around the island to shake my hand. "Congratulations on the marriage." He turns to Jade and hugs her. "Is this guy treating you well?"

"Extremely well." Jade smiles. She loves Charles. "And Garret does all the cooking."

"Not even close to as good as you could do, Charles, but I try."

Charles winks at Jade. "I taught him everything he knows. Don't let him tell you otherwise."

"I give you credit all the time," I tell him.

"He does," Jade agrees. "And he uses your recipes, too. He cooks almost every night."

Jade takes a seat on one of the stools by the island. So I guess we're staying a while. She'd stay here all night if I let her.

"I tried cooking, but it didn't work out so well," she says. "I ruined Garret's birthday dinner."

I stand behind her and rub her shoulders. "You didn't ruin it."

"I ruined it," she says to Charles.

He laughs. "Not everything turns out. That's just part of cooking."

Jade points to a tray of cheese-filled tarts that's sitting on the counter. "Those look really good."

"They're all yours." Charles goes back around the island and slides the tray over to her. "Katherine decided she didn't like them so I was getting ready to throw them out."

Jade tastes one. "These are delicious. You can't throw these out. Garret, try one."

She hands me one and I taste it. "Yeah, they're good. Why didn't Katherine like them?"

"She didn't like the way they looked on the tray," Charles says. "It was an appearance issue, not a taste issue."

"That's crazy," Jade says. She doesn't understand how it works when you're rich. She grew up with barely enough food to eat, and here my wicked stepmother throws perfectly good food away because it isn't pretty enough.

I agree it's a waste, but it's how I grew up. For years I watched people toss shit aside because it wasn't pretty enough or good enough or didn't fit with the rest. And yeah, I'm talking about more than just appetizers.

"Charles, we're running out of shrimp." Katherine comes storming into the kitchen. She stops when she sees us. "What are you doing in here, Garret? You need to go out there and mingle with the guests."

"It's not a party, Katherine."

"It is a social gathering and you need to represent the Kensingtons to the best of your ability. And besides that, your father is looking for you."

219

"Let's go." I help Jade off the stool. "We'll see you later, Charles."

"Bye, Charles." Jade waves at him, then says to Katherine, "Those cheese appetizers are the best. You should try one."

As we walk back down the hall to the main part of the house, I put my arm around Jade. "Look at you, trying to rile up Katherine."

"I just think she should serve those appetizers. I'm sure she wasn't listening. She won't even talk to me."

"You're better off not having her talk to you."

"Garret, look. Harper's parents are here."

I follow Jade's gaze to the side of the living room where Kiefer is talking to my dad. Kelly is next to him. Kiefer sees us and motions us to come over.

"There you are." My dad puts his hand on my shoulder. "I was looking for you. In a few minutes I'm going to say a few words about your grandfather and I wanted you to stand up there with me."

Is he serious? I don't even want to *be* here. I can't believe my dad can even find anything good to say about his father.

My dad is much better than me at putting on an act, pretending to be something he's not. Tonight he's playing the role of the grieving son who loved his father and is hosting this event to pay tribute to this wonderful man. Fucking ridiculous. Why not just tell the truth? Tell everyone how he killed my mom and tried to kill Jade. That's the man he was and that's how he should be remembered.

"Yeah, okay," I say, agreeing to stand next to him. But I'm not happy about it. I'm only doing this for my dad.

"Garret, we're very sorry about your grandfather." Kelly sounds sincere when she says it. I think she's a nice person, so I don't know why she's going along with her husband's plan to join the organization. She has to know it'll destroy her family. It already has. Harper's not even talking to her parents anymore.

Kiefer gives his condolences as well, then both of them say hello to Jade.

"How is Harper doing?" Jade asks. "Is her shoulder better? I haven't talked to her for days."

There goes Jade, stirring up trouble. She keeps hoping she can fix this thing with Harper and Sean, and now she wants to fix Harper's relationship with her parents. I know she means well, but she can't keep interfering like this.

"It's a long recovery for that type of injury," Kelly says. "But she's getting better each day."

"That's good." Jade's eyes keep darting over to Kiefer. He seems uncomfortable. He keeps swishing his liquor around in his glass, the ice cubes clinking against the sides.

"If you'll excuse us," my dad says, "I'm going to go say a few words."

Kiefer nods at him. "Of course. Go ahead."

My dad's hand remains on my shoulder as we go and stand by the easel that holds the photo of my grandfather.

My dad lowers his voice and speaks by my ear. "You know how this works. Be serious when I'm serious and smile when I smile."

"Yeah, I got it."

"Do you want to say anything?"

I huff. "You're kidding me, right?"

"We do what we need to do, Garret."

"Well, I'm not doing that. This is all you."

"May I have your attention, please?" My dad's voice quiets the chattering in the room and it becomes silent. "Thank you all for coming. It's been a very sad and difficult week for myself and my family and we appreciate you taking the time to be with us here tonight as we celebrate my father's life and his many accomplishments."

I almost roll my eyes. I actually felt myself starting to but forced myself to stop. My dad rambles on about how great my grandfather was and all the wonderful things he did. I tune it out. I can't listen to the lies. Instead I peer out at the crowd of people gathered in front of me. I spot Grace and William in the back. Victoria isn't with them. She's standing next to a man I recognize from one of the financial news shows I watch. He works on Wall Street but that's all I know about him. Victoria's likely trying to assess his worth to decide if she should date him.

Kiefer and Kelly are standing next to Jade. Kiefer is rubbing his chin, then he rubs the rest of his face. Then he takes a swig of his alcohol. And another after that. He's very fidgety tonight. Not the laid-back, relaxed Kiefer I'm used to.

I scan the rest of the room. I don't know half of these people. Lilly isn't around, which is good. She doesn't need to hear my dad's speech. It would just make her sadder.

"...and we can take comfort in knowing that he is now in a more peaceful place." My dad finally stops talking.

I hear Katherine's voice behind me. I didn't even know she was there. "Before we continue, Garret would like to say a few words."

I turn and see the smirk on her face and almost punch her. She knows I don't want to say anything.

I glance at my dad, who has no expression at all, which is typical for him. Another Kensington rule. Don't show emotion if it will reflect poorly on the family. Use it only as needed, when it works to your advantage.

"Garret, go ahead," Katherine says.

Have I said how much I hate Katherine? After this little stunt, I might just have to release one of those videos.

I face the crowd of people. "Although I had hoped to say a few words about my grandfather tonight, the tragedy of his passing is still too fresh in my mind. Therefore I am unable to do so. I'm sure you understand."

"Of course, son." My dad nods at me, then turns toward the guests. "Again, I would like to thank everyone for coming. Please continue as you were. We ask that you say your final goodbyes at eight tonight so that we may spend time together as a family."

Katherine races off to talk to someone before I can yell at her. I wouldn't anyway. I'm done fighting with her. She'll be out of my life soon enough.

Everyone goes back to their conversations, the noise level in the room slowly rising.

My dad takes me aside. "Thank you, Garret. I'm sorry about Katherine. I didn't know she was planning that."

"It's Katherine. It's not that surprising." I check that no one's around us, then say, "I need to talk to you about something. It's important. It can't wait."

I should've told him this last weekend when I was here, but with everything going on I wasn't even thinking about it.

My dad lowers his voice. "What is this about?"

"Aston Hanniford."

He smiles, but only to cover up the fact that we're talking about something we shouldn't be. "Smile, Garret."

I smile, but I'm sure it looks fake.

"I already know about it," he says. "We'll discuss it later."

He walks off and I go over to Jade, who's talking with Kelly. Kiefer got whisked away by some older man I've never seen before. Kelly doesn't know most of the people here so we stay there and keep her company.

A half hour later I hear some commotion in the foyer. Jade and Kelly are talking and don't notice.

"I'll be right back," I say to Jade.

She nods.

I pass by the other guests, who have now migrated to the appetizer tables and the bar. As I approach the foyer I hear my dad say, "I most certainly did not invite you! You need to leave."

I go around the corner and see my dad standing there with Roth. The foyer is empty except for the two of them.

"Garret." Roth saw me. Shit. I was just getting ready to turn around.

"Garret, go upstairs," my dad orders.

"Pearce, I came to express my condolences," Roth says. "That would extend to your son as well." He comes up to me. "I'm sorry for your loss. Your grandfather was an extraordinary man. He'll be greatly missed."

I glance at my dad. "As my father said, I need to go upstairs and check on Lilly. I was just heading up there now."

"Very well, then." Roth grins. "We'll be seeing you soon, Garret."

What the fuck does that mean?

My dad comes up behind Roth and grabs his arm. "In my office! Now!"

They go in my dad's office and he slams the door.

I can't believe my dad just talked to Roth that way. And grabbed his arm. Roth could have my dad killed for that. He could be dead tomorrow. Shit!

I turn around and see Jade coming toward me. She whispers in my ear, "I want to talk to Grace, so we're going in one of the rooms down the hall so Victoria won't bother us."

"Yeah. Okay." I'd go with her but I need to keep an eye on Roth and my dad.

When she's gone, I approach the door to my dad's office. I hear loud talking but I can't make out the words.

I feel a hand on my shoulder and turn around and see Kiefer standing there.

"Garret, I need to speak with you when we're back in California. What's your schedule?"

He reeks of hard liquor and I back away. "Are you drunk?"

"No. Of course not." He takes off his glasses and rubs his eyes. He's drunk, but also seems anxious and tense.

"What's wrong with you?"

He looks side to side, checking to make sure we're alone. "Just say you'll meet with me when we get back. I'll make a trip up to see you."

"Um, yeah, okay." I agree to it just to get him to go away. "You have my number. Just call me and let me know when you're coming."

"Good. Very good." He puts his glasses on and walks away.

What the hell was *that* about? And why was he acting so strange?

"Garret." Lilly runs down the stairs. "Can we watch a movie now?"

I glance at my dad's office. "It's not a good time right now. Maybe later."

"Please." She grabs my hand. "You promised."

"I know, but I can't right now. I'm busy."

She lets go of my hand and her head drops down as she turns back toward the stairs. I see her shoulders creep up, then down, like she's crying. Dammit. Why is everything happening at once? First my dad and Roth, then Kiefer, now Lilly.

"Lilly, wait." I meet her halfway up the stairs.

"It's okay. You're busy." She wipes her tears with her tiny hand and I feel like the worst brother in the world.

"I didn't mean that. I'm not busy. Come on." I walk her up the rest of the stairs and to her room. "I'll start the movie but I can't watch all of it right now. I have to go downstairs and talk to people, but when I'm done I'll come back, okay?"

She nods.

"What movie should we watch?" I'm standing in front of her TV. Below it is a white basket filled with movies, all of which have pink boxes. Princess cartoons.

"You pick," she says.

I grab one from the middle. It has a princess and a snowman on it. Good enough. I put it in the machine and turn the TV on.

"I got your spot ready." Lilly has pillows lined up against the headboard, the same way I used to arrange them whenever I'd watch TV in her room. Her headboard is made of wood and has a design carved in it that digs into your back when you lean on it, so I always had to pile up pillows behind me.

"I can only watch for a few minutes." I sit next to her as the movie starts.

She leans against my shoulder, holding her stuffed panda bear in her arms.

"Garret?"

"What?"

"Is Daddy going to die?"

"What? No. He's not going to die."

Actually, he *might* if Roth kills him, which could happen if I don't get them away from each other, or at least get my dad to calm down.

"Grandma said everyone dies." Lilly pets her panda bear as she says it.

"Usually just when they're old. Dad's not old."

"Grandma's old. Is she going to die?"

Seriously? She has to ask these questions *now*? I don't have time to explain death to her. And I shouldn't be doing it at all. Her parents need to do that, not me.

"Lilly, you need to talk to Dad about this. Let's just watch the movie."

"I can't talk to Dad. I can only talk to you." She looks up at me with her teary blue eyes. "Why do people have to die?"

Shit. I can't explain this to her. I don't even have the answers. What do I know about death?

I don't have time for this. I need to get downstairs.

# Chapter 22

**JADE**

*G*race and I are sitting in a room I've never been in before. The only things in the room are a grand piano and a long white sofa. Nobody in Garret's family plays the piano so I don't know why they have a room with a piano.

Grace and I came in here to talk. If we didn't, Victoria would be watching us and wondering why I'm talking to Grace. We left William out there to keep an eye on her. Victoria seems to like William, as in more than just a brother-in-law way. All night I've noticed her hanging on him and talking really close. William's wife didn't come with him tonight and Victoria seems to want to take her place.

"Maybe I shouldn't be asking this, but does Victoria have a thing for William?" I ask Grace.

"Yes," she says, matter-of-factly. "She always has, but then again her eyes wander to a lot of men. She was never faithful to Royce. But as you know, he wasn't faithful to her either. William, on the other hand, has no interest in other women. His heart belongs to Meredith. Always will." She smiles and smooths her skirt. "Pearce did a lovely job tonight. Don't you think?"

"You mean when he talked about his father?"

"Yes. I thought his words were very heartfelt. I know the two of them didn't always get along, but it's nice to hear Pearce speak of his father that way."

If Grace knew the truth about Holton and what he did to Arlin, she would've hated Pearce's speech. She wouldn't have even shown up here tonight to hear it. But Garret said I can't tell her the truth. He said it's best if she doesn't know, and he's probably right.

I couldn't stand listening to Pearce's speech, hearing him go on and on about how Holton was a great man and did all these great things. Pearce was doing what he was expected to do, but it was hard to listen to. And then when Katherine tried to get Garret to speak, I almost went up and strangled her.

"Jade, honey, are you okay?" Grace rubs my arm.

"Yes. Sorry. I'm just tired from getting up so early."

"So how is your friend, Harper, doing? Will you be seeing her while you're in town?"

"Yeah. I'll see her tomorrow. She's going through a rough time. She just had shoulder surgery and she broke up with her boyfriend."

"Sean. The chef."

"That's right. I forgot that you met him at the wedding."

"It's too bad they couldn't have ended things sooner. Waiting makes it so much more difficult."

"Waiting for what?"

"Jade, you know the rules. And Kiefer has known them for months. He just hasn't taken action until now."

"How do you know about Kiefer?"

"I've been around long enough to know what's going on. And when I found out he was meeting with Roth last July, I assumed they changed the rules."

We shouldn't be talking about this. And yet I want to know more.

"Is there any way Harper can be with Sean?"

"Honey, you already know the answer to that."

"Who will she end up with?"

229

"She'll be given some choices."

"They won't just pick someone for her?"

"They used to, but it's not that way anymore. At least not for everyone."

I don't know what that means. Why do some people get to choose and some don't? Why wouldn't the rules be the same for everyone? I know she can't tell me so I don't ask her about it.

"So they picked Arlin for you?"

"Actually, his *father* picked me and got the other members to agree to it. Back then, parents had more influence on the decision. I actually had several parents wanting to set me up with their sons." She laughs. "I was a real catch back in the day. Not to be boastful, but I was a very pretty young woman. And I come from an excellent family."

"Did Arlin like you right away?"

"He liked me before we were even set up together. Arlin wanted to date me for years and his father knew it. So he purposely told Arlin he was picking a different girl, just to see how much Arlin would fight for me. And he did. Arlin argued with his father until his father finally told him that he'd picked me. His father even planned our first date. He got us reservations at a very nice restaurant in Manhattan and theater tickets for a Broadway show. It was quite an evening."

"And you liked Arlin?"

She smiles. "I always did. Even when he was younger, Arlin was a gentleman, much like Garret. That's hard to find, Jade. You're very lucky." She checks her watch. "We should be getting back before Victoria starts asking William where I went. Oh, before I forget, the taxes on the land I gave you will be due shortly. I wasn't sure if you received a notice in the mail so I wanted to mention it to you."

"I'll tell Garret. We'll look into it and make sure they get paid. I can't thank you enough for giving us that land. It's the perfect spot for our house. It's exactly what we wanted. But Garret and I still feel like we should pay you for it."

"Jade, don't be silly. You're my granddaughter and the land was a gift." She pats my leg. "Now let's go before people start looking for us."

"Too late," a voice says from behind us.

The couch is facing the piano, and with our backs to the door, Grace and I didn't see anyone come in. We both stand up and turn around to see someone standing in the doorway. Someone my age. With long brown hair. Who looks a lot like me.

"Sadie, honey, what are you doing here?" Grace walks over to her but I stay where I am.

"What did you just call her?" Sadie's eyes are on me.

"That's Jade," Grace says. "You've met her before. She's married to Garret."

"I know who she is. But I heard you call her something." Sadie looks at Grace. Actually, it's more like a glare. "What did you call her?"

"Sadie, calm down. There's no need to get upset. Jade and I were just talking."

"You called her your granddaughter. Why would you call her that?"

Grace looks back at me, like she wants *me* to answer instead of her. My heart is pumping so hard I feel breathless. How did this happen? Where did Sadie come from? She lives in DC. She doesn't transfer to Yale until the spring. What is she doing in Connecticut?

"Why, Grandmother?" Sadie yells it. "Why would you call her that? Tell me!"

I can't stand watching Sadie yell at Grace that way.

But Grace remains perfectly calm and says, "Jade. It's up to you."

She's asking if I want to tell Sadie the truth. Do I? I don't know. She kind of already knows the truth. She heard Grace say it. But Sadie doesn't know the whole truth and I don't know if I want her to. No daughter wants to hear that her father is a rapist and a murderer.

I walk over and stand next to Grace. "I'm her granddaughter."

"No, you're not." Sadie's eyes move over my dress, inspect my shoes, then go back up to my hair and finally my face. "That's impossible."

"It's true. I'm not lying."

"William never had a child." She stands up straighter, crossing her arms over her chest.

"William isn't my father." I pause and let her figure it out.

She stares at me, and the only sound in the room is the sound of her breathing, which keeps getting faster. Finally, she looks at Grace. "Grandmother, don't let her say these things about our family. Say something!"

"Royce was Jade's father," Grace says. "Jade is your half sister."

Sadie huffs. "If she told you that, she's lying."

"Honey." Grace tries to hold Sadie's hand but she pulls it away. "She's not lying. Your father had proof that he was Jade's father. He had a file in the safe in his office. That's how we learned about Jade. We found out shortly after your father passed away."

"He didn't pass away! Would you stop saying that? He killed himself!" Sadie takes a deep breath to regain her composure. She narrows her eyes at me. "Why are you doing this?"

"Doing what?"

"Is it to get money? The Kensington fortune isn't enough for you? Now you have to come after the Sinclairs?"

"Sadie, that's enough!" Now Grace is yelling. I've never heard her yell. "Jade is not after anyone's money. She is a

Sinclair, just like you and me. Your father had no contact with her when she was growing up. She was raised by her mother."

"And who's your mother?" Sadie gets right up in my face. "Some whore who forced herself on my father? Some stripper who got my father drunk, then used him to get pregnant so she could get his money? I'd love to meet this whore! Tell her what I think of her."

"Sadie! Stop it right now!" Grace says from beside me.

I haven't backed away. Sadie and I remain face-to-face, my eyes locked on hers. "My mother is dead. And she wasn't a whore. She wasn't any of those things you said. Your father—" I stop because I don't know if I should tell her.

"My father what?"

Sadie would never believe the truth, so I say, "He met my mom when he was in Iowa for the caucus. He was working on a political campaign and he was there for a speech. My mom didn't know he was married. He asked her out for dinner. And that's it. It was one night. She never heard from him again."

Sadie takes a step back. "How old are you?"

"Twenty."

"So you're saying he did this while my mother was pregnant? He wouldn't do that. He'd never do that."

"Sadie, your father wasn't perfect," Grace says. "Nobody is. He had his faults like everyone else does."

"Does Mother know?"

"Not that I'm aware of. If she *does* know, she hasn't told anyone. Jade just found out about this last year, but she hasn't told your mother."

"Who else knows?"

"Your Uncle William knows. And your grandfather knew. He's the one who found the file."

"Don't tell Mother this," Sadie orders. "Or my sisters."

"We don't have to tell them," I say.

"Maybe we should sit down," Grace says.

"No." Sadie scowls at me. An actual angry scowl, as if what her father did to my mom is somehow my fault. "We're done here."

# Chapter 23

**GARRET**

*A*fter I talk to Lilly I go downstairs to my dad's office but he isn't there. Roth isn't either. I ask Katherine where my dad went and she says she doesn't know.

The house is still full of people, including Victoria, who waves at me when she sees me, like she wants me to come over and talk to her. She's standing next to William, who gives me an eye roll as Victoria latches onto his arm. It's clear William doesn't like her. I'm guessing he's on Victoria-watch while Grace talks to Jade. I smile at William and give him a head nod, letting him know I feel his pain.

I need to find Jade. She and Grace have been gone too long and people will start to notice, mainly Victoria who's scanning the room like she's searching for Grace. The woman just can't mind her own business. She's always watching people, gossiping, making up stories that aren't true.

Jade said she was going to find a place to talk to Grace. I saw her go down a hallway filled with rooms we never use. We even have a piano room down there, which I've only been in one time. Nobody in my family plays the piano, but since rich people tend to have grand pianos, Katherine thought we needed one, so it sits there collecting dust in an empty room.

I go down the hall, checking each room. I hear talking and notice light coming out of the piano room. I walk down there and see Jade standing just inside the door.

"There you are." I walk in and stand in front of her. "You should get back down there before—"

"Does Garret know?" A voice behind me cuts me off. I know that voice. I turn and see Sadie there, her arms crossed tightly over her chest. Grace is next to her.

"Yes," Jade says to Sadie.

"Know what? What is she talking about?" I look at Jade to answer.

"I told Sadie I'm her half-sister."

I'm not sure what to do with that information, so I turn to Sadie and say, "Sadie, what are you doing here?"

"I'm picking my mother up to take her to the hotel. I was visiting Evan at Yale and since Mother is also here in Connecticut, we decided to meet up and go shopping in the city tomorrow."

"But your mother came here with William and me," Grace says.

"Yes, but she called and asked me to come get her. She was bored."

Who the hell admits to being bored at a memorial service? Only people like Victoria.

Grace sighs. "Your mother should show some respect. If she's that bored, then go get her and leave."

Grace is pissed. I've never seen her angry before. Something must've happened before I got here. Was Sadie being a bitch to Jade? Or was she just being a bitch in general? Having dated Sadie, I know either is a possibility, but she better not have been a bitch to Jade.

"I've decided I'd like to speak with Jade some more," Sadie says. "You can go, Grandmother."

I give Grace a look, letting her know I'll handle this.

"Watch what you say to her, Sadie," Grace says. "My will can easily be changed."

Sadie's mouth drops open as Grace exits the room. So Sadie *was* a bitch to Jade. Yeah, I'm not putting up with that.

I step in front of Sadie. "What did you say to her?"

Sadie's about two feet in front of me and all I smell is her perfume. It's way too strong and the same perfume Victoria wears. I always hated that perfume.

"*I* didn't say anything. She's the one who accused my father of cheating."

"Your father had sex with another woman while he was married to your mom. That's the definition of cheating, Sadie. Doesn't get any clearer than that."

"Whatever." She twists her hair around her finger. "I know her slut mom tricked my dad into it. Jade can deny it all she wants, but she doesn't know the truth. She wasn't around when it happened. She's relying on what her whore of a mother said."

"Stop saying that about her!" Jade moves to my side. "She wasn't a whore!"

I inch closer to Sadie, my temper rising. "Is that what you call a woman who's been raped? A whore? That's a pretty fucking sexist comment there, Sadie. Are you seriously one of those people who think women asked to be raped? Because of what they wear or how they act?"

"Garret, no." Jade grabs my arm and pulls me back a little. "She doesn't know that part."

Shit. I didn't know that. Whatever. She needs to be told.

Sadie huffs. "Now you're saying he raped her?" She narrows her eyes at Jade. "I thought you were nice when I first met you. But you're a bitch. And probably a whore just like your mom."

"Don't you dare speak to her that way." I walk forward, forcing Sadie against the wall. "I swear to God, Sadie."

"What? You'll hit me?" She rolls her eyes. "Please, Garret. You'd never hurt a girl." She glances behind me at Jade, then looks back at me. "Why would you marry someone like her? She's lying, Garret. To all of us. She's—"

"Your father raped Jade's mother." I lock my eyes on Sadie. "I don't give a shit if you don't believe me. Just keep thinking Royce was a saint if that's what you need to do. But the facts don't change. He did that to her mother. There's a police report and hospital records to prove it."

"You're disgusting. Both of you." She shoves on my chest but I don't move. "Just get away from me."

"Apologize to Jade." I say it loud, right in her face.

"She makes up lies about my father and you expect me to apologize?" She moves her head so she can see around me to Jade. "Never."

I remain in front of her. "Apologize. Now."

"If you don't back away, I'll scream. I'll cause a scene."

"What are you, six? You're going to throw a tantrum? We're not leaving here until you apologize to Jade."

"Then I guess we'll be here all night."

I hear Jade behind me. "Garret, she doesn't have to apologize. Just forget it."

"She called you a whore. She called your mother a whore. She needs to apologize."

"She's just upset." Jade stands beside me and speaks to Sadie. "I'm sorry, Sadie. I didn't want you to ever know the truth about your dad. I know it's hard to hear. And I know you don't want anything to do with me, and it's fine. I understand."

Jade just keeps amazing me. Just when I think she can't do it again, she does. Sadie attacked her, said horrible things to her, acted like a spoiled child. And Jade just let it go, acted like an adult, kept control of herself.

Sadie has spent years in etiquette classes, being coached on how to act and what to say, and yet Jade, who had none of that, is the only one with class.

I'm still in front of Sadie. "Jade may not need you to apologize, but I do."

I wait for Sadie to say something. She doesn't.

I take a step back. "Sadie, what the hell happened to you? You didn't used to be like this. Back when we were friends, you didn't used to be like this. What changed?"

A smirk crosses her face. "Nothing changed. I've always been ambitious. I've always been driven to succeed. You just didn't acknowledge those traits in me because you like your women weak. Submissive. You like to control them."

"That's a fucking lie and you know it. If anyone's that way, it's Evan. He has zero respect for you and he treats you like shit."

"Evan's going to be president someday. And you? What will you be doing, Garret? Hanging out on the beach every day? Living off your father's money? Doing nothing with your life?"

I put my arm around Jade, my eyes still on Sadie. "Just go. I've wasted enough of my time on you. I wish you and Evan the best. Have a great life."

She turns to leave, then whips back around and sets her eyes on Jade. "If you EVER tell anyone those lies you just told me about my father, you will pay."

I let go of Jade and storm over to Sadie. I take her arm and walk her into the hall and down a little so Jade won't hear me. "You will NOT threaten her and you will not even THINK about harming her. Do you understand?"

Sadie laughs. "I see you got a little rougher since we dated. I like it."

"Just shut the fuck up and listen to me. Jade is your sister and she has done nothing wrong. She found out about Royce last year and she told no one. She could've gone to the press, destroyed his campaign, but she kept silent. You should be thanking her. She saved your father's reputation." I grip her arm a little tighter. "I'm not that nice. I'd be more than happy to destroy his reputation. And I'm pretty sure nobody wants the daughter of a rapist to be first lady. You mess with Jade? I'll make it my own personal mission to make sure you never step foot in the White House." I let go of her arm. "Did I make myself clear? Or do we need to go over this again?"

She hesitates, then says, "Fine. But tell her to stay away from me. I don't want to see either of you ever again." She scurries away, her heels clicking on the tile.

Victoria appears at the end of the hall. "Sadie, where are on Earth have you been? I've looked everywhere for you."

"I'm coming, Mother."

I go back in the room.

Jade's sitting on the piano bench, staring at the keys. "I didn't think she'd react that way. I didn't think she'd hate me that much."

"Forget about her." I sit next to Jade, my arm around her middle, sliding her closer to me on the bench.

"She's my sister. I thought we could be friends or at least talk once in a while."

"You don't have to be friends with the people you're related to. You don't even have to like them. And sometimes a relative turns out to be your worst enemy. Like my grandfather."

Jade runs her hand over the piano keys, but doesn't press down on them.

I pick up her other hand and hold it in mine. "I always wanted a grandfather like you see on TV. The kind that brings you candy and takes you fishing or to baseball games. But I never had that. I kept waiting for my grandfather to become that person, but he never was and I knew he never would be. But it took me years to accept that. I kept hoping he'd stop over some day with a couple fishing poles and a tackle box and take me to the lake." I laugh just picturing that. "It's funny how you get these crazy ideas in your head as a kid. My family doesn't fish. My grandfather didn't even like being outside. And yet I kept thinking he'd take me fishing. My point is that you can't change people into what you want them to be. And hoping and waiting for that to happen just leads to disappointment."

Jade leans her head on my shoulder. "So you're saying Sadie will always hate me?"

"She's not going to change. If anything, she'll only get worse the more involved she gets with Evan and the plan they have for him." I turn Jade toward me and cup her cheek, looking into her eyes. "It's Sadie's loss. She's passing up the chance to get to know the most amazing person I've ever met. And the most beautiful, both inside and out."

Jade smiles. "I wish you'd had a grandpa to take you fishing."

"It's okay. I'd rather go to a baseball game than fishing. And at least my dad took me to those."

"I guess we should go back out there. I'm sure Sadie's gone by now."

We leave and go back to the living room. Only a few people are left and they're all people I don't recognize. My grandmother is talking to them so they must be friends of hers. I still don't see my dad anywhere.

Katherine walks by and I stop her. "Have you seen my dad?"

"I already told you I didn't know where he was, so stop asking me. I'm not his babysitter." She continues on to wherever she was going.

Grace and William come up to us and Grace gives Jade a hug. "I'm so sorry about Sadie."

"It's okay," Jade says. "I kind of thought she might react that way."

William hugs Jade and says quietly, "For the record, you're my favorite niece."

She laughs and whispers back, "And you're my favorite uncle."

"William and I need to get going," Grace says. "It's a bit of a drive back to New York."

We walk them to the foyer. "Have a safe trip," I tell them as they leave.

I check my dad's office again but he's not in there. Where did he go?

"Is something wrong?" Jade asks.

"I need to talk to my dad but I can't find him anywhere."

"Is this about Carson?"

"Yeah. But I'll just talk to him tomorrow."

I don't want to tell Jade about Roth. Not yet. Not until I find out why he was here and what he wanted.

I need to know where he went, and if he left alone or with my dad. I hope their argument didn't escalate beyond where it was when I left to go upstairs with Lilly. Because if it did, there's a good chance one of them is dead, or will be soon.

# Chapter 24

**JADE**

*G*arret and I go upstairs. It's too early to go to bed but I want to change out of this dress. On the way to Garret's room, we stop at Lilly's door.

Garret knocks once before going inside. "Hey, Lilly. I'm back. Is the movie over?"

*Back?* Was Garret in here earlier? When did he have time to watch a movie with Lilly?

I walk into her room. She's sitting on her bed, hugging her stuffed panda. I see her red eyes and tear-stained cheeks and feel horrible that she was left up here all alone.

Garret sits down next to her. "Hey, come over here."

She scoots over to where he's sitting. He picks her up and holds her as he leans back into a stack of pillows arranged against the headboard. She sets her panda down and hugs his chest.

I'm not sure if I should stay or leave. Garret's the only one who can help Lilly right now and I feel like I need to give them time alone.

"Jade, why don't you go change clothes?" Garret says. "Wear something comfortable. It's going to be a long movie night. It's a princess marathon."

Lilly lifts her head up and smiles. "It is?"

"That's right. A whole night of princess fun. Just you, Jade, and me."

She wiggles away from him and hops off the bed. "I'll get Jade a doll. You can have my panda, Garret."

I try not to laugh as I watch Lilly pick from her assortment of dolls. I still have the doll she gave me last year. Garret told me I could get rid of it, but I can't do it. It's special because Lilly wanted me to have it.

"I'll be right back." I go down to Garret's room and change into jeans and a t-shirt. I'm kind of excited about this movie marathon. I know it sounds strange because princesses aren't my thing, but it's not about the movies. After the night I've had, I just like the idea of being with Garret and Lilly, in her bright pink room, all three of us squished together on her tiny twin bed watching cartoons.

When I get back to her room she's got fluffy pink throw pillows lined up on one side of the headboard. I guess that's *my* side and Garret gets the other, with Lilly's spot in between us. She has a doll with brown hair and a purple dress sitting on my side of the bed.

"I'll be right back." Garret heads down to his room to change.

I take my place on Lilly's bed, holding the doll in my lap. "Who's this?"

"That's Lexi. She looks like you and she has a purple dress like you had when I met you."

"She *does* look like me." I hold up the doll, inspecting her dress.

Lilly sits next to me, holding a doll with long blond hair and a light green dress. She leans against me, brushing her doll's hair with a tiny hairbrush. "Jade?"

"Yeah?"

"Were you sad when your mom died?"

"Um, yeah. I was sad."

"And then it went away?"

"Eventually, yeah." I hope she ends this line of questioning quickly because I'm not good at talking about death. I don't even like to think about it.

"How long did it take?"

"I don't remember. It was years ago."

She stops brushing her doll's hair. "It takes years to feel better?"

"No. That's not what I meant. My mom died years ago. I felt better in a few weeks." It's not true, but I'm trying to be positive for Lilly. I can't say exactly when the sadness went away after my mom died. Honestly, I think some of it's still there.

"Is your dad going to die?"

*My dad?* What is she talking about? My dad is dead. And then I realize she means Frank. I forgot I told her he's my dad.

"No. He won't die for a long time."

"Because he's not old enough?"

So many questions. And why is she asking *me* and not her parents?

"Yeah. He's not old enough."

"Is your dad the same age as my dad?"

"Almost the same. They're just a few years apart."

"Okay." She returns to brushing her doll's hair. Whatever I said must've made her feel better because now she's smiling.

Garret comes in wearing a white t-shirt and blue striped pajama pants. Damn, I should've worn pajama pants. They're way more comfortable than jeans. He's carrying one of those reusable grocery bags.

He sets it on the bed. "Look what I got."

Lilly looks in the bag. "Licorice! And soda!"

"And bags of popcorn. Charles made us some snacks but don't tell your mom."

"I won't." She grabs a string of licorice.

Katherine doesn't allow Lilly to have candy, so if she catches us, she'll be mad. But I think she left. When I was coming back to Lilly's room, I looked down the stairs and saw Katherine with her coat on, heading out the door.

So much for the comment Pearce made earlier. Family time after eight? Yeah, right. Katherine's gone. We can't find Pearce. And who knows where Grandma Kensington went? At least Garret, Lilly, and I are having family time.

Lilly has some candy and soda and falls asleep, all within a half hour. Garret and I stay on her bed and finish watching the princess cartoon. Garret sneaks his arm above Lilly's head and around my shoulder, his hand dangling down. I thread our fingers together and use my other hand to eat my licorice.

To an outsider, tonight would've seemed completely crazy. Nonstop drama. Secrets revealed. And it all ends with a princess cartoon. But now that I'm part of this family, it doesn't seem strange at all. Just a typical Friday night at the Kensington mansion.

The next morning at eight, I leave to pick up Harper at Moorhurst. Garret had planned to go with me, but then decided to stay home and talk to his dad, who we still haven't seen since last night.

Harper can't drive yet because of her shoulder so I'm picking her up, which means I had to borrow one of Pearce's Mercedes. I'm afraid to drive it because I'm afraid I'll get in an accident. Pearce has so much money he wouldn't care, but I'm still nervous driving his car.

As I approach the Moorhurst sign, I get an anxious, queasy feeling in my stomach, like I had when I first arrived on campus last year. I don't know why I keep feeling this way whenever I come back here.

Before I left this morning, Garret reminded me to think of all the good things that happened at Moorhurst and forget all the bad. So that's what I'm trying to do. I see the big stone buildings where I used to have class and it makes me think of going to English class with Garret and the notebooks we shared. Then I see some girls running toward the trail I ran on a million times last year. I remember racing Garret on that trail the weekend before classes started. He told me he liked me and I thought he was going to kiss me. He didn't, but I really wanted him to.

As I drive into the parking lot in front of my old dorm, someone pulls out and I take the spot, then realize it's the same spot where Ryan parked on the night I arrived here and met Garret for the very first time. I was so mean to him. I couldn't figure out why some guy I just met would want to help me move into my room.

I get out of the car and see Jasmine coming out of the dorm. Her hair is longer, but other than that, she looks the same.

"Jade, is that you?" She comes over as I lock the car.

"Yeah. I came by to get Harper."

"You look great!" She smiles really wide, staring at my face. "Something's different. You look more mature or something."

"Really? I don't feel any different." The wind blows hair in my face and I secure it behind my ear.

"Oh my God!" She grabs the hand I was using to fix my hair. "Did you get engaged?"

"I got married. Last summer."

"You did not!" She keeps hold of my hand.

"I did."

"Why didn't Harper tell me?"

"I don't know. I guess she didn't think about it."

The truth is I told Harper not to tell anyone at Moorhurst because I don't want them to know. I don't want the people here gossiping about Garret and me or trying to find out stuff about us. I just want them to forget about us.

Jasmine's attention quickly switches to my ring. "This ring is gorgeous! And it's huge." She drops my hand. "Wait. Who did you marry?"

"Garret."

"Garret Kensington? After he did all that stuff? Trashing hotel rooms and the drugs and crashing all those cars?"

I shrug. "He's changed since then. And I love him so I had to marry him."

"I get it." She grins. "You like a bad boy, huh? I do, too. Only usually you can't get one to marry you."

"I gotta go, but it was good seeing you, Jasmine."

"You, too. Say hi to Garret for me." She gets into her car, which is in the parking spot next to mine.

Walking in the dorm, I instantly smell whatever odor I could never identify but didn't like. It's like a mix of dust and old building smell combined with nail polish remover and assorted perfumes. Not a pleasant smell, but it's better than the guy's floor, which smells like beer and sweat.

As I knock on Harper's door I see a girl coming out of my old room. She has black hair with neon green stripes in it and piercings on her face. She's dressed in all black; black cargo pants, black tank top, and a black hoodie. She doesn't at all look like the typical rich, preppy Moorhurst student.

"Jade, you're early." Harper pulls me into her room and hugs me. "I feel like I haven't seen you forever."

"I know. It's been too long." I stand back and look at her. She looks pretty, as always, wearing skinny jeans and a white sweater, her hair straight and slightly longer than when I saw her last. Her arm's in a sling, tucked against her side.

"How's your shoulder?" I ask her.

"It's fine, but I can't really move it so it's hard to do anything, like get dressed or do my hair. I used to have Sean—" She stops herself.

Before she broke up with him, Sean would help her get ready every morning. He even helped her with her hair.

"Anyway, I have to get the girls on the floor to help me now." She fakes a smile but I can see how much she's hurting. She can't hide it from me.

"So who's the girl who has my room now?"

"Sydney. She's a freshman. She's the Kensington scholarship winner this year. Didn't Pearce tell you about her?"

"No. I didn't even think to ask. I'm kind of surprised he picked her."

"I know. She's got the whole goth thing going, but she's really nice. And super smart. Like genius smart."

"How do you know she's smart?"

"She has a really high IQ and she's good with computers. She can hack into most any system. She told me she hacked into the FBI servers when she was 15. Can you believe that? The FBI! How is that even possible?"

"Did she get in trouble?"

"Since she was a minor they let her go, but she had to promise never to do it again. She said she didn't look at anything on the server. She just did it to prove that she could."

Maybe I'm thinking too much like Carson with his conspiracy theories, but I find it suspicious that Pearce would pick this girl for the scholarship. Is he thinking he might be able to use her skills? Having her hack into government servers, or any server, could be advantageous, both for his business and for the organization. He could find out information or delete files he needs to have disappear.

"Where is she from?"

Harper rifles through her dresser drawer and takes out some earrings. "Somewhere in Montana. She was raised by her dad. Her mom died a long time ago." She hands me the earrings, big gold hoops. "Can you put these on me?"

"Sure." I carefully fit the earring through the hole in her ear. "I talked to your parents last night."

"I don't want to talk about them. They stopped by here to take me to breakfast this morning and I wouldn't go so they left. They're flying home later today."

"Harper, you can't ignore them forever." I slip the other hoop in her ear. "It's almost Christmas break. When you're home, you'll have to talk to them."

"I'm staying with a friend from high school who lives in Pasadena. I'm not going back to my parents' house."

"Not even for Christmas?"

She sighs. "I don't know. I have to think about it. They want me there, but right now I'm too mad at them to agree to it. If I was still dating Sean they wouldn't have let me come home for Christmas, so going there is almost like letting them win." She loops her healthy arm in mine. "Let's get out of here and go to my favorite coffee shop. Remember how I used to make you go there all the time?"

"At least now I can afford a coffee." We walk to the parking lot and I point to the car as I unlock it. "It's this one."

"Nice car. Pearce loaned you his Mercedes, huh?"

"It's just one of many. I think he has five of them and they're all black."

On our drive to the coffee shop I tell her about Lilly and how sad she was and how she kept asking me about death.

"I think Katherine's lost interest in her," Harper says as I park in front of the small brick building. The place has a new sign that's shaped like a coffee cup.

"Lost interest in who?"

"Lilly. It's like she doesn't care about being a mom anymore. She spends all her time with her boyfriend. She's never home, and when she is, she ignores Lilly."

I shouldn't be talking about Katherine with Harper. I don't want to accidentally spill what I know. It's another huge secret that I'll never be able to tell Harper, or anyone else.

I hold open the door to the coffee shop. "Looks like they got new tables."

"Yeah, they did some renovations over the summer."

We order our coffees and find a booth to sit in. That nervous feeling I had earlier is gone now that I'm with Harper. Being with her at this coffee shop is a good memory. We had a lot of good talks here.

"Oh, I forgot to tell you." She sets her coffee on the table. "I saw that guy, Carson, on campus the other day."

And the nervous feeling is back. "At Moorhurst?"

"He was on my floor. I think he was looking for someone. Maybe he's dating one of the girls."

"That doesn't make sense. He doesn't live here anymore."

"How do you know where he lives?"

"I don't." I say it too fast. I smile and calmly say, "I just thought he might've moved."

"He could still be here in Connecticut. There are a lot of colleges here."

"So you didn't talk to him?"

"No. I just saw him in the hallway."

That's strange. Why would Carson be at Moorhurst? And why would he be on Harper's floor? Is he spying on the students he thinks have ties to the organization? Or maybe he's interested in Pearce's latest scholarship winner. Sydney, the computer genius. Maybe he wants to use her hacking skills to get into Pearce's computer.

Harper's talking and I'm not listening so I shove Carson out of my brain and focus on what she's saying. We stay there for almost two hours, but it goes really fast. That's how it always is with her. Once we start talking, we lose track of time. It shows what good friends we are, even now, living on opposite coasts.

Last summer we both worried that our friendship would end, but it's the same as always. No matter where we live, Harper will always be my friend.

# Chapter 25

**GARRET**

*I*'ve been calling my dad ever since he left last night. Now it's ten-thirty in the morning and he's still not home. He hasn't called me back and I'm getting really worried. I call him again just as he walks in the front door.

"Where were you?" I ask him.

He takes off his coat and gloves and hands them to the maid. He's wearing the same suit he had on last night but his tie is undone and his shirt is wrinkled. "Garret, I just walked in the door. Meet me in my office in an hour or so."

"We need to talk. This can't wait."

He sighs, heavily, and rubs his forehead. "All right." He notices the maid walking away. "Marta."

"Yes, sir."

"I need some coffee. Could you bring some to my office, please?"

"Of course, sir."

I follow him into his office. "Where have you been all night?"

He takes a seat at his desk. "I had some things to take care of at work."

"What happened with Roth?" I sit in the chair opposite his.

He checks his phone. "Nothing. I simply asked him to leave. He wasn't invited."

"Why did he say he'd see me soon? When would he see me?"

"Garret, why do you let that man get to you? Stop worrying about him. I'll deal with him." He checks his phone again. "Now what do you need to tell me?"

"This guy who went to Moorhurst last year showed up at our place last week. He's the guy I told you about that kept bothering Jade last semester, telling her all this stuff about our family."

My dad nods. "Yes. Justin. I know who he is."

"How did you know his real name?"

"Because I've been investigating him ever since he started following me a few months ago."

"Last semester he said his name was Carson. He pretended to be a student but he's really 24 and—"

"A reporter in Chicago. Yes, I know all this. Get to the point."

My dad is really on edge today. Usually he isn't this impatient. And why does he keep checking his phone? He did it again just now.

"He said that he knows you're part of the organization but that he can't prove it. He said his sister had evidence of election fraud but that she was killed before she could show it to anyone."

There's a knock on the door, then the maid comes in with a mug filled with coffee. She hands it to my dad.

"Thank you, Marta."

"Would you like something?" she asks me.

"No, thank you."

The maid leaves, closing the door behind her.

"Justin's sister was also a reporter." My dad swipes through the screen on his phone as he talks. "And she was indeed killed. She was killed by your grandfather."

"What?" I move to the edge of my chair. "Are you serious? Why did he kill her?"

"*He* didn't do it. He hired someone, like we always do. The girl knew too much. She had to go."

"Dad, what the hell? You act like she deserved it."

"Of course she didn't deserve it, but that's the business we're in, Garret. Well, not you, but the rest of us. Knowing too much can get you killed. That's why I keep telling you to stay out of things like this. And that goes for Jade as well."

Normally my dad wouldn't tell me all this. He's never come out and actually admitted to having people killed. But maybe now that I know what he did to his father, he feels less of a need to keep secrets from me.

"Do you think Carson, I mean Justin, knows it was Grandfather who arranged to have her killed?"

"I'm almost certain he does. I think he somehow traced her murder back to my father and that's what led Justin to investigate our family and become involved with Aston Hanniford."

"Shit." I sit back in my chair. "No wonder the guy hates me."

"Your grandfather was careless when it came to these things. He was arrogant and took too many risks. And because of that, I now have Hanniford to deal with, along with the FBI."

"The FBI is after you?"

"Aston has friends in high places. He knows an FBI agent who agreed to look into this for him. There's no open case against me. The agent is doing this on his own as a favor to Aston. But I'm sure he's using the FBI's resources to get it done. And if finds any conclusive evidence, he'll tell his fellow agents and they'll open an official case and start an investigation."

"So what are you going to do?"

"I'm not doing anything. I'm supposed to keep my distance. The other members are taking care of it."

"Meaning they'll kill the FBI guy?"

"Even with him gone we'll still have to get rid of whatever files he had on me," my dad says, glossing over my question. "We'll also need to destroy any files Justin may have on me."

"You're not going to kill Justin, are you?"

"It's not up to me. It's out of my hands. I told the members the situation and now it's up to them to decide what to do. If Justin shows up at your house again, or harasses either you or Jade, let me know. We'll take care of it."

"I don't want you to kill him. Just let me handle it. If he shows up again, I'll find a way to make him leave. Beating him up would be better than killing him."

My dad picks up the remote and turns on the TV that's on the wall behind me.

"Dad, what are you doing? We're in the middle of a conversation."

"I just want to check the weather. I heard we might get snow later tonight."

My dad never checks the weather. He doesn't care about the weather.

I turn to see the TV. A news station is on and an older man is talking. "In other news, we've just learned that billionaire Cecil Roth was killed in a car explosion near his home in Westchester County, New York. Reports are still coming in, but it's believed he was speeding and lost control of his vehicle. He hit a telephone pole and a fire started, which likely sparked the explosion."

"Holy shit." I look back at my dad. "He's dead? Roth is dead? What the hell?"

My dad sighs. "That's a shame. Another funeral to go to. That's two in one week."

"Dad, did you—" I can't accuse him of that. It was a car crash. Roth was speeding. It had nothing to do with my dad.

He flips to a weather channel. "You see? A winter storm is on the way. I hope it doesn't affect your flight home."

His phone rings and he answers it. "Yes, William. I saw the news." He listens. "Let me know how it goes." He sets the phone down.

"Was that William Sinclair?"

"Yes. He's been asked to attend a meeting tomorrow."

"A meeting about what? Do you think they're going to offer him the promotion?"

"Perhaps, although it has to be voted on by the members and that won't happen until the meeting at the end of this month."

"With Roth gone and Grandfather gone, there are two spots open. Who will get the other one?"

"I don't know. It doesn't matter. We really shouldn't talk about it."

I sit there, my mind coming up with all kinds of scenarios that probably aren't true. Or maybe they are.

"Doesn't William live near there?" I ask.

"Near where?"

"Near the crash site. Westchester County."

My dad turns on his computer. "I'm so behind at the office, I'll never even begin to catch up. This past week, with planning the funeral and the memorial, I've barely had time to return phone calls."

He's avoiding my questions. But why? Did he do that to Roth? We own a chemical company and chemicals cause explosions. So did he rig Roth's car? Was William in on it? He had just as much motivation to get rid of Roth as my dad did. Maybe more. William wants Jade and me to be safe, but he also wants to be promoted. Having two open spots gives him an even better chance of getting that promotion. So maybe my dad provided the chemicals and William rigged the car.

257

My dad's typing something into the computer.

"Where were you last night?" I ask him.

"I told you, I had to go into the office. There was an issue with one of the plants and it couldn't wait until morning."

I examine his face, his expression, his tone. But there's nothing there. No emotion. No expression. No change in body language. His voice is even. He's completely calm.

"What would you like for dinner tonight?" He sips his coffee. "We could go out if you'd like."

I sit back in my chair. "So you're really going to Roth's funeral? I thought you hated the guy."

"He was a friend of my father's, therefore I must set aside my personal feelings for the man and pay my respects."

"What did Roth say to you last night that made you so angry?"

"I was angry because he showed up here uninvited."

"It was more than that. You wouldn't normally show your anger to someone like Roth. It's disrespectful for someone at his level." The organization is all about hierarchy, and the members must honor that hierarchy, and last night, my dad didn't do that. "Just tell me what he said. It was about me, wasn't it?"

"Charles makes excellent coffee." He drinks the last of it and sets the cup down. "Your grandfather said he never liked Charles' coffee. He said it tasted like tar. And yet one day I saw him in the kitchen pouring himself a cup of it. He never knew I saw him do it."

"Dad, I need to know the truth. Was Roth trying to get me back in the organization?"

"Yes," he says casually.

"Why didn't you tell me?"

"I just recently found out. My father and I discussed it the night we had dinner, before he suffered the stroke."

I stare at him. He's completely serious, like he truly believes the fake story about my grandfather having a stroke. I don't know how he does it. I don't know how my dad is able to pretend the truth doesn't exist and act like the fake story is what really happened. It's just like he said. Like he lives his life as two different people. The dad I know is the one who chooses to believe he didn't plot to kill his own father and that my grandfather died of complications from a stroke. The other side of him knows the truth. I guess that's the only way my dad can live with himself and still do the bad things he does.

"Dad, I need to know more than that. What exactly did Grandfather tell you?"

He sighs. "Roth and my father were both trying to get you back in the organization. Both men had too much pride and too much arrogance to allow you to just walk away from the plans they had for you."

"You're saying Grandfather was in on Roth's plan to make me president?"

"Your grandfather claimed it was his idea. He said he came up with it years ago and convinced Roth to use his power and influence to make it happen."

"Why would Roth do that for him?"

"I don't know. I may never know. It doesn't matter. The point is that Roth looked like a fool when the plan fell through. And he blamed my father for that and wanted him to fix it. My father told Roth it wasn't possible unless Roth got him promoted to the top level at the organization. That way they could used their combined power to force the other members to give you a second chance. And it worked. My father used Roth to get the promotion, and together they were able to convince— or rather bully—the other members to reinstate you, given you met certain conditions, of which you already know about."

"But even if I was a member again, their plan for me is over. I destroyed my reputation and the members voted. Like you said, they can't go back on their decision."

"Roth still wanted you back, just to prove that he's the one in charge. And to punish you for your behavior last spring."

"Does he know it was fake?"

"Luckily, your grandfather didn't share his theory on that, probably because he couldn't prove it. But Roth knew about your grandfather's plan to kill Jade and he was prepared to follow through on it."

"How do you know someone else won't?"

"There's nobody left in the organization who cares about you anymore. You were being talked about the past few months because of this rumor about Roth trying to get you back. But only he and my father wanted that. As I've told you before, the other members are tired of dealing with you after the trouble you caused last spring."

I hesitate, then just come out and say it. "You killed him, didn't you?"

He looks directly at me, his eyes dark, his face serious. "Why would you ask me something like that?"

I feel like he's daring me to say what I'm really thinking. But he knows I won't, because he knows I don't really want the answer. I don't like the world he lives in, and I don't want to be part of it or know what goes on there. I've seen more than enough already.

"I just—"

"Accidents happen, Garret. Cars crash every day. Roth shouldn't have been speeding." He gets up from his desk. "I need to get more coffee and then I'm going to check on Lilly."

"She needs to talk to you about some stuff. She was asking me all these questions about death."

"Yes, I'll spend some time with her." He opens his office door. "Where's Jade?"

"She's with Harper." I get up and follow him into the foyer. "Oh, I wanted to ask you about Kiefer. Last night he said he wanted to talk to me about something. He wants to talk in person so he said he's driving up to see me when we get back to California. Do you know what this is about?"

My dad turns back to face me. "Don't talk to him."

"I already told him I would."

"Then call him and tell him you won't. You need to stay out of this."

"Stay out of what? Is this about—"

"Garret." He grips my shoulder. "I can't protect you forever. You need to start seeing things for what they are and taking the necessary precautions."

My dad's telling me this is about the organization. Kiefer wants to talk to me about it, but why?

"Okay. I'll tell him I can't meet with him."

"Good. And make sure Jade knows that her friendship with Harper needs to end. Soon."

"She's not going to like that."

"What did I just tell you?"

"That I need to take precautions. I know. I'll tell her about Harper. When is this thing with Kiefer official?"

"January first."

"Daddy, you're home." Lilly comes running down the stairs.

"Yes, honey." He picks her up. "Let's go in the kitchen. Daddy really needs some coffee."

He leaves me standing there in the foyer. My conversation with him left me with more questions than answers. Did he kill Roth? He had the motive to, which makes me think he did.

My dad is all about rules. So maybe I already have the answer.

Rule number two. Protect your family above all else.

# Chapter 26

**JADE**

*I* get back to the Kensington mansion and open the door to find Garret standing in the foyer with nobody else around.

"What are you doing?" I hug him. "Waiting by the door for me?"

"Yeah." He sounds a little out of it. He must still be tired from yesterday. "How was Harper?"

"She's okay. I thought she'd talk about Sean the whole time but she didn't talk about him at all. Oh, and when I picked her up at Moorhurst I ran into Jasmine. She couldn't believe I was married. She was shocked when she found out I married you after your bad boy behavior last year."

"Did you see anyone else while you were there?"

"No. We left as soon as I got there." I notice Pearce's office door is open. I peek inside. "Where's your dad? Did you talk to him?"

"Yes, and he already knows about Carson. He's been investigating him for months. My dad knows about Hanniford, too."

"So what's he doing about it?"

"He told the organization and I guess they're dealing with it."

"They're not going to hurt Carson, are they?"

"He doesn't know. It's not up to him. Jade, this isn't our problem so we need to stop talking about it."

"What if Carson shows up at our place again?"

"We'll tell him to leave and then we'll tell my dad and he'll take care of it."

"I don't like this, Garret. They're going to—"

"Jade. It's not our problem." He pauses. "I have some other news. Roth is dead."

"Roth, as in the guy who showed up before our wedding?"

"Yeah. He died in a car explosion not far from his home."

"Someone blew up his car?"

"He was speeding and crashed into a telephone pole. It sparked a fire and the car exploded. This just happened so the news didn't have many details yet."

"Does your dad know?"

"Yeah, he had the TV on in his office and that's when we found out."

"Maybe I shouldn't say this, but I'm glad he's gone."

"Yeah, me, too." Garret hugs me as he says it, and again, his hug is a little too tight.

"Garret, is something wrong?"

He pulls back. "No. Why?"

"Nothing. I just—never mind."

I need a moment to process this. Roth and Holton are dead. The two men who were trying to control Garret, trying to take over his life, are gone. They're really gone. I feel like we should celebrate. That's wrong, I know. I shouldn't celebrate people dying, but feeling safer and more secure is something to celebrate.

"Let's go out," I say to Garret.

"Where do you want to go?"

"I don't know. Anywhere. Go get your coat."

Garret gets his jacket from the closet. "I know it's early, but do you want to go out for lunch?"

"What about your dad and Lilly? Should we invite them to come with us?"

"I don't think so. My dad wants to spend some time with her since he hasn't been around much, so it's probably better if we leave. We'll see them this afternoon." He opens the door. "You driving?"

"No." I hand him the keys. "Driving your dad's car makes me nervous."

He goes over to it and opens my door. "Why does it make you nervous?"

"Because if I get in an accident, he'll yell at me."

Garret laughs as I get in the car. "He would never yell at you, Jade, especially about wrecking his car. He'd just fix it or buy another one." He gets in the driver's side and pulls out of the circular driveway. "So what did you decide about lunch? Yes? No?"

"Yes. I'm starving. Where should we go?"

"You'll see."

"You're not going to tell me?"

"It's a surprise." He smiles. "Because I know how much you love surprises."

He drives out of the fancy rich neighborhood his dad lives in and goes down some winding roads for about five minutes, then turns off onto another small road. I recognize the area and know exactly where we're going.

"The Mexican place?" I ask him as I see the sign for it just a few feet ahead. It's the place he took me to on our first official date.

"I know you're dying to hear that guy sing again." He pulls into the lot and parks. "And no laughing this time."

"That's impossible," I say, already laughing. "You know that, right? Because I'm telling you right now, there will be laughing."

He takes my hand as we walk to the entrance. A man with a huge sombrero opens the door. "Welcome, amigos!"

I burst out laughing. I don't know what my problem is, but this whole place makes me laugh. For some reason, I find everything funny here.

"Jade, stop." Garret's laughing, too, but at me, not the sombrero guy.

"Two for lunch?" the hostess asks. At least she's not wearing a funny hat.

She takes us to a table that's three down from where we sat on our first date.

"Can we have that one?" Garret points to the other table.

"Sure." She leads us to the table and hands us our menus. "Your server will be here shortly."

There's hardly anyone in the restaurant because it's just after eleven and they just opened.

"I don't see your singer," Garret says, glancing around. "I bet he only works at night. You wouldn't want to waste a talent like that on the lunch crowd. You need to save it for the more serious dinner patrons."

"Yeah, I'm sure that's it." I peruse the menu. "He's so good he probably got a better job, like in Vegas or something."

"I'm getting the burrito platter." Garret sets his menu down. "What are you getting?"

"Nachos." I set my menu on top of his.

"Why don't we get that as an appetizer and you can get something else?"

"Nope. I just want nachos. And I want the whole platter all for myself."

"You're going to eat the whole thing?" He smiles. "Have you seen how big the nacho platter is here?"

"No. But I can eat it."

"I bet you can't finish it."

"I bet I can." I lean back, folding my arms over my chest.

"So are we really betting here?"

I shrug. "We can, but I already know I'm going to win."

"Pretty sure of yourself, huh?" He cocks his head. "What do you wanna bet?"

"Hmm. Okay, I got it. If I eat the whole platter, which I will, you owe me a massage every day for a week."

"Jade, I'd do that anyway if you asked me to."

"Doesn't matter. That's the deal. Now what's yours?"

"If you can't finish it, you have to wear the cheerleader costume every day for a week."

I smile and hold my hand out. "Deal."

We shake on it. I wouldn't mind losing the bet. I like the cheerleader costume and I love the effect it has on Garret.

The waiter appears at our table. "Have you decided, my dos amigos?"

The way he says 'dos amigos' makes me laugh but I try really hard to suppress it.

"Jade, go ahead." Garret's smiling at me. He knows I can't speak when I'm all giggly like this.

"What would you like, Seniorita?" The waiter grins really wide and I see that there's a shiny gold cap on his front tooth. His dental work should not be funny, but to me it is. What is wrong with me? A laugh sneaks out but I pretend it's a cough.

"She'll have the nachos," Garret says, handing him the menus. "And I'll have the burrito platter."

"Gracias." He walks away.

"Is there a problem over there?" Garret takes a drink of water.

"I think they pump laughing gas into this place. I swear they do. There's something about this place that—" I stop as the familiar voice rings out from the side of the room. He's back. And still off tune.

"Jade, look who's here," Garret says.

My laughter bursts out again. There's no stopping it now.

"He's coming over." Garret's smiling. He's loving every minute of this.

"Make him go away." My stomach hurts I'm laughing so hard. "I'm begging you, Garret. Wave him away."

Instead, he waves the guy over to us. The singer nods and smiles. When he gets to the table, I clamp my mouth shut and try to smile. About a minute later, his song ends, but he remains there, looking at us.

"I know you two." He points at Garret and me. "You come here last year. I sing at your wedding."

"Actually, we already got married," Garret says. "But the wedding was in California. We didn't think you'd want to travel that far."

"Si." He nods. "You have babies?"

"No," Garret says. "No babies."

"I sing for you. Very romantic." He grins. "You have babies. Lots of babies."

Garret just smiles but, of course, I'm laughing. I try to suppress it, but once the guy starts singing, I lose it. He's so loud and so off key. I cover my mouth, pretending to cough. Garret holds my hand and gazes at me, like he did last year when this guy sang to us. The song ends just as four people are seated at the table across from ours. Thankfully, the singer goes over to them.

"He needs to come back," Garret says. "I have to give him a tip."

"No. Please don't tell him to come back."

"The guy is giving us babies, Jade. He deserves a tip for that."

"Yeah, I don't think so." My laughter goes away as I think about the baby comment. I've finally come to a decision about that and I need to talk to Garret about it when we get back.

Garret squeezes my hand. "What happened?"

"What do you mean?"

"You stopped laughing and the guy's still singing."

"I must be getting used to it now."

More customers arrive and the mariachi band greets them as they're seated. The singer doesn't come over to our table again, but he's so loud his voice fills the entire restaurant.

Our food arrives and Garret's right. The nacho platter is huge.

"Dig in," he says, eyeing the platter.

Ten minutes later I'm stuffed, but half a platter of nachos remains.

"You done?" A smug smile crosses Garret's face.

I don't answer. I just push the platter away.

"Looks like I'll be having sex with a cheerleader when I get home."

"I said I'd wear the costume. Sex wasn't part of the deal."

"It's implied." He gets some money out and sets it on the check.

"Actually, it's not, but I'll throw it in as a bonus."

"You ready to go? Or would you like to stay and listen to the music?"

"I think I've heard enough. Let's go."

As we walk out, Garret hands some money to our waiter, telling him to give it to the singer.

When we get outside, Garret draws me into him and kisses me. It's a sweet, gentle kiss that reminds me of the kiss we had in this same parking lot last year.

"Are you recreating our kiss?" I ask him.

"I am. Was it the same?"

"It was better. Because now I love you."

He pulls back. "You didn't love me back then?"

"I'd just met you."

"We'd been going out for months." His cocky grin appears. "You totally loved me."

I roll my eyes. "I don't think so."

"Yeah, because you *know* so."

"Fine." My lips turn up. "Maybe I loved you. Just a little."

"And when that mariachi singer said he'd sing at our wedding, it made you think of us getting married. And you liked the idea of that."

"Now you're just being ridiculous. I did not think about our wedding. And technically, it was only our first date. That's way too soon to think about marriage."

"You thought about it," he says confidently as he walks me to the car.

Damn, how did he know that? Was I that obvious?

He stops and gives me another kiss, then says, "Jade." He points up at the sky. Tiny snowflakes are falling. "Must be something about this restaurant. It snows whenever we come here."

"It's beautiful." I watch it fall as he opens my door.

As we're driving back, the snow gets heavier, covering the road and the trees.

"We should go for a walk in the woods behind your house. I love seeing the white snow on the dark trees."

Garret glances over at me, smiling. "Are you trying to recreate Thanksgiving last year?"

"I guess I am. Which means you have to kiss me again in the snow."

"Kissing you is not something I *have* to do. I *want* to kiss you. And if we're recreating that weekend, we'll be doing more than kissing."

"Garret, you know I don't like doing it in your dad's house."

He laughs. "And yet we always do."

"Well, not this time. Your grandmother is staying two bedrooms down from yours. She might hear something."

"Then you'll have to tone down your moaning. And be a little quieter when you yell out my name."

I swat his arm. "I do not moan. And I do not yell out your name."

"You do both those things, Jade." He smiles at me. "I guess you're just so consumed with passion you don't even realize the sounds you're making."

It's embarrassing, but true. I get so caught up in the moment, I don't know what's coming out of my mouth. And I do get kind of loud.

"That's just all the more reason not to do it," I tell him.

We're back now and Garret parks in front of the house. He comes around the car and takes my hand and walks to the door, opening it for me. The foyer is empty and there's nobody in the living room.

"Where is everyone?" I ask him. "You think they're having lunch?"

"Probably." He slides my coat off, then hangs it on the coat rack, along with his own.

"I thought we were going outside. I want to walk through the woods."

"Later." He takes my hand and leads me up the stairs and we go down the hall to his room. He kisses me as he shuts the door and locks it without looking.

"If we're recreating our first time together," I say, walking backward to the bed, "it should be the middle of the night. And I should be sneaking in here."

"I didn't say we were recreating our first time." He eases me on the bed and hovers over me. "I said I wanted to do what we did that weekend, which was have sex."

"We did it a lot that weekend, didn't we?" I smile as he inches my sweater up, leaving soft kisses along my stomach.

He doesn't answer. He's too busy undressing me, kissing me, touching me. He gets up and takes his shirt off. I reach out for him and he smiles.

"You miss me?"

"Yeah, so hurry up."

He gets the rest of himself naked, then hovers over me again, his mouth dipping down to my breast.

I moan a little too loud, then whisper, "Sorry."

"Nobody heard you, Jade." He kisses his way over to my other breast. "Except me. And I love that sound so do it again."

"No. I can't. I'll be quiet now."

I swear he takes that as a challenge because he teases my breast with his tongue in a way he knows gets me all fired up inside. I moan even louder.

He covers my mouth with his lips, then says, "Thought you weren't going to do that again."

"I wasn't, but then you do things to me that make me forget where I am."

"Which I will do again right now." His cocky smile appears as he thrusts inside me.

I suck in a breath, then smile. "Forget it. I can't be quiet."

Although it's not like I don't try. It's just that Garret's really good at this and sometimes being quiet is not an option. When we reach the point where I tend to yell, he kisses me before I can, and keeps his lips just over mine until my body comes down from its high. And it was a definite high. I'm glad we skipped the walk in the woods. This was way more fun.

"Not exactly like our first time, huh?" I say as we lie there, still out of breath.

"Did you want it to be?"

"No. That time was good. But this time was even better."

# Chapter 27

**GARRET**

*I* remember every detail of the first time Jade and I had sex. She came in my room in the middle of the night and crawled into my bed. I assumed she didn't like being alone in her room and just wanted to sleep next to me. I had no idea she wanted to have sex. I didn't think she was ready for that. I knew she wasn't a virgin, but I also knew she'd only done it one time. We hadn't officially dated that long so I figured she'd want to wait a few more weeks. Or months.

But that night, she started kissing me and rubbing up against me and finally I just came out and asked her what she was doing. How far she wanted to go. She made it clear she wanted sex, but at first I didn't believe her. I thought maybe she was kidding around or maybe she was tired and didn't realize what she was saying. So I asked her again just to be sure and the answer was the same. She was ready.

As for me? I was *more* than ready. I'd never waited that long with a girl. Usually I'd do it after a couple dates—a week, max—and I'd had my share of one-night stands. But I didn't want that with Jade. I didn't want to rush her. I was willing to wait as long as she wanted, even though it was killing me. She's so freaking hot. I'd never been that attracted to a girl. I wanted to have sex with Jade from the moment I met her. So all those times we kissed, or did more than kiss? Shit. It wasn't easy to hold back.

That first time with her, I tried to take it slow. I wanted her to love every second of it, which meant teasing her, exciting her, getting her ready for me. Then once we moved on to the actual sex part I, again, tried to slow down for her. She felt so freaking good it was nearly impossible, but I had to make sure she was taken care of before I took care of myself. I was determined to make it good for her, or amazing if I did my job right. And I did. She was a very happy girl when I was done. So happy she wanted to do it again later that morning. We did it a lot that weekend.

"Garret." Jade kisses my chest. "We should get dressed and spend some time with your family."

"Do we have to?" I smooth her hair. "Because I'm kind of liking it right here."

"We're leaving tomorrow. We should go see them."

"We'll be back here in a week for Christmas."

She pushes off me. "Come on. Let's go."

"If I go, you have to promise me a shower later." I pull her back down and kiss her.

"Definitely." She rakes her fingers through my hair. "Tonight. After everyone's asleep." She gives me a kiss, then gets up and walks over to the window. I watch her, keeping my eyes on her naked ass.

"It's still snowing. Let's go outside." As she turns around, she pulls her hair up which raises her breasts and flattens her stomach even more.

"We're not going anywhere if you keep showing off your body like that." My eyes trail over her curves.

"Then I better cover up." She comes over and picks her clothes up and starts dressing.

There's a faint knock on the door. "Garret?"

I bolt from the bed. "It's Lilly." I say it quietly to Jade as I gather my clothes from the floor. Jade already has her jeans and sweater back on. "You talk to her. I'll go in the bathroom and get dressed."

When I'm in the bathroom, I hear Jade talking. "Garret's in the bathroom. He'll be out soon. Did you see the snow?"

"Daddy said it's going to be a blizzard."

"We should go sledding!" Jade sounds so excited. I love that about her. She has all this money now and she still gets excited about stuff like snow.

"Really?" Lilly sounds as excited as Jade. "Will Garret go?"

"I'll go," I say, coming out of the bathroom. I have on jeans and a t-shirt. I go to the closet to grab a sweatshirt.

Lilly follows me. "Can we go right now?"

"Did you have lunch yet?" I ask her.

"Daddy and I had grilled cheese."

Katherine must not be around. If she was, Lilly wouldn't have had grilled cheese for lunch. That's one of those poor people foods Katherine doesn't allow.

I pull my gray sweatshirt over my head. "Where's your mom?"

Lilly shrugs. "I don't know. But Daddy's downstairs."

"Where's Grandma?"

"She left this morning."

Left? As in moved back to her house? My dad said she was staying here for a few days. Did she leave because Jade and I are here? Or did she just want to go home? Either way, she could've at least said goodbye.

"Are we going sledding now?" Lilly asks.

"Yeah. Let's go." I take her hand and we meet Jade by the door.

"Do you still have the sled?" Jade asks as we walk down the stairs.

"I'll have to ask my dad. Why don't you two go out in the snow and I'll find the sled and meet you out there."

"Yay! We're going sledding!" Lilly jumps around in circles.

Jade smiles at her. "Let's get our coats on. We'll build a snowman while we wait for Garret."

They go down the hall toward the back patio. Jade is so great with Lilly. I wish she could see how good she is with kids so she'd stop worrying so much about being a mom. I know it's different caring for a baby. The constant crying might get to Jade and make her nervous and stressed, but I'd be there to help her out. If the kid's screaming, I'd take over and let her have a break. I'm more patient with stuff like that than she is.

I walk into the foyer and see my dad's office door open. He's in there working on his laptop.

He notices me in the doorway. "Come on in. Lilly was looking for you."

"Yeah, Jade and I are taking her sledding but I don't know where the sled is. You didn't throw it out, did you?"

"No, it's in the shed out back where the gardeners keep their supplies."

"Good. I thought Katherine might've gotten rid of it. Speaking of Katherine, where is she today?"

He types something, his eyes on his laptop. "She's staying with her parents this weekend. She left last night."

"So what's going to happen to her? Do you know yet?"

He types some more, then turns to me. "She won't be allowed to continue her relationship with Lyndon Tate, the senator she's been dating. As I mentioned before, he's slated to be the next vice president, which was very appealing to Katherine. But given her recent actions, she's no longer allowed to be with him. Being the wife of a vice president is a role that comes with many benefits and Katherine is no longer deserving of those benefits."

"Does Tate know he can't see her anymore?"

"Yes, but we can't tell him what she did because he's not one of us. But given what we're doing for him in the next election, we basically own him now and he needs to follow orders. He knows this, and he's agreed to stop seeing her."

"What about the divorce? It's still going to happen, right?"

"She killed my father, so yes, it'll be approved. They wouldn't make me stay with her after what she did. And they don't want her benefitting from my money."

"How do you think Lilly will take the news?"

"I think she's already expecting it. She knows her mother and I don't get along. And I think Lilly will be okay with the fact that her mother isn't getting custody. Katherine has never been a decent mother."

"You're being too nice, Dad. Katherine's a horrible mother. Thank God you're getting custody. Even though you're at work all the time, you're still a better parent than Katherine."

"Yes, well, I'm not going to be spending so much time at work. I need to establish more normal work hours so I can be here with Lilly in the evenings and weekends."

"So is Katherine planning to buy a house around here?"

"No. She's thinking of moving to France for a few months and living with her sister. After that, she might get a place in Manhattan. Or she might stay in France. She hasn't decided yet."

"She doesn't want to see Lilly?"

"She'll see her. Just not very often. And frankly, I'm glad she won't be around. I don't want Lilly turning into Katherine the way Sadie turned into Victoria. By the way, I had no idea Sadie would be here last night."

"Yeah, that didn't go well. Sadie found out about Jade."

"How did *that* happen?" He leans back in his chair. "Did Jade tell her?"

"No, Sadie overheard Grace calling Jade her granddaughter. Instead of being nice to Jade, Sadie was a total bitch. She called Jade's mom a whore. It was bad."

"How much of the story does Sadie know?"

"She knows about the rape, but she doesn't know Royce tried to kill Jade. And of course, Sadie didn't believe us about the rape. She blamed Jade's mom for the whole thing. Before she left, she told Jade not to tell anyone about this, and that she never wanted to see Jade again. So yeah, Sadie has pretty much become Victoria. Total bitch."

"I never understood why you dated Sadie."

"She didn't used to be that way. Plus, she's hot. The problem is, she knows it."

My dad shakes his head. "I'm glad you didn't end up choosing a woman based solely on looks."

"Jade's way hotter than Sadie. So I got lucky. I found someone I love who's also the most beautiful woman I've ever seen."

He nods, smiling. "I felt the same way about your mother."

"Maybe I shouldn't ask, but are you still seeing that woman from DC?"

"No. That ended a long time ago. I'm not seeing anyone right now. I'm trying to spend my free time with Lilly, especially now that her mother's never around."

My phone rings. It's Jade.

"Yeah, I'm coming," I tell her. "The sled is in the gardening shed. I'll be there soon." I put my phone away as I stand up. "You want to go sledding, Dad?"

"Sure." He closes his laptop. "Although I probably won't fit on the sled."

"You're seriously going sledding? I was kidding. I didn't expect you to say yes."

"I want to spend time with my children." He hangs his arm off my shoulder as we walk out of the office. "I haven't been sledding since you were a kid. Remember when I took you to that hill by our old house? That was a steep hill. I didn't think you'd go down it."

"I loved that hill. You could really get some speed going on that thing."

We get our coats and head out back. Jade and Lilly have a small snowman already built. I check it out while my dad gets the sled. Lilly's shocked when she sees my dad out there. I'm a little shocked myself. He keeps surprising me with this stuff. I keep thinking that one day he'll return to the cold, uncaring father he was during my teen years. But instead, he's becoming more and more like the dad I knew as a kid. And if Katherine's out of the picture, I think he'll become even more like that dad.

The four of us go out to the small hill that Jade and I took Lilly sledding on last year, but my dad thinks it's lame. He's right. It sucks. So we take the sled and pile into his SUV and head to a real sledding hill. Jade keeps giving me this look like she can't figure my dad out. I just smile and kiss her and tell her to go with it.

On the way to the sledding hill, my dad stops at the store and gets three more sleds so we each have one. We go to the same park Jade and I went to last year. It has a big, steep hill that's great for sledding. Lilly's too scared to go down it by herself so my dad goes with her. It's good he's doing this. It helps take her mind off her grandfather being gone. She's smiling and laughing as the sled hits some bumps on the hill. It reminds me of myself at her age, out sledding with my dad.

We stay there all afternoon, then go home and change into dry clothes. My dad orders pizza and asks Charles to join us for dinner. After Lilly goes to bed, my dad, Jade, Charles, and I play poker at the kitchen table.

I hate to admit it, but I almost forgot the reason why I'm here. We're all having such a good time that we're not even thinking about my grandfather. Is that bad? Maybe. But like I told Jade after Sadie left the other night, you can't choose your relatives, and just because you're related doesn't mean you have to like them. And I didn't like my grandfather. And after I found out what he'd done, and what he planned to do, I hated him.

My dad and I tried for years to please him, hoping that one day he might actually give a shit about us, but he never did. He wanted us to suffer. He didn't want us to be happy. So I don't feel guilty about having fun today instead of mourning his death. I don't think my dad does either.

I don't bother asking my dad about my grandmother. She knows I'm leaving tomorrow and apparently has no interest in saying goodbye to her grandson. I don't understand her. Sometimes, she's warm and caring, like she is with Lilly, and sometimes she's cold and distant.

"Maybe we could shower in the morning," Jade says as she closes the door to my room and locks it. We just came upstairs after finishing our last poker game.

"It already *is* morning." I unbutton her shirt as I kiss her. Playing poker with her got me turned on. I don't know if it's because she's so competitive, or that she's good at it, or just the fact that I find it sexy when a girl plays poker. But I'm all fired up and not the least bit tired.

"It's one-fifteen. We should get to sleep."

"Or we could take a shower." I slip her shirt down over her arms, letting it drop to the floor. "Hot steam." I kiss her neck. "Wet skin. My warm hands all over your body." She tilts her head to the side and closes her eyes as my lips move up her neck to her ear. "You sure you wanna wait?"

She smiles. "I swear, someday I'll say no to you. Just not tonight."

I strip the rest of her and haul her off to the shower.

And then, a half hour later, we finally go to sleep.

In the morning, as we're packing up to leave, Sean calls. I haven't talked to him for days. Every time I call him his phone goes straight to voicemail. He's in LA now and working at his new job.

"Hey, stranger," I say when I answer.

"Yeah, I know. I've been working a lot. I wasn't able to call you back. Sorry."

"I'm just giving you a hard time. So do you like the job?"

"Yeah, it's great. Way better than my last one."

"How's your new place?"

"Good. It's small, but it's clean and in a decent area. I have to work this afternoon, but I wanted to give you a quick call. Let you know I'm still alive."

He shouldn't joke about that. With the organization after him, I feel like I *do* need to check that he's alive.

"How was the funeral?" he asks. "I mean, not like it was good or anything, but are you okay?"

"Yeah, I'm fine. We didn't go to the funeral. Just a memorial service here at my house. We're leaving today."

"Will you guys be around during Christmas?"

"We'll be back here for a week, but after that we'll be home. Why?"

"Just wondering if you guys wanted to come to LA for a few days. You could come to the restaurant. I'll cook you something."

"Sure, we can do that. We have four weeks off for winter break."

"What about the photographers? You think they'll leave you alone?"

I always forget about that. Where we live, nobody bothers me, but if I go to LA, I risk being recognized.

"I'm not worried about it. I'll disguise myself. Maybe I'll grow a beard."

He laughs. "There are so many famous people around here, chances are nobody will notice you. I've already seen three movie stars and I've only been here a week."

"Get used it. They're everywhere out there."

"I gotta go, but I'll call you later. Have a safe trip back."

"Thanks. See ya."

"Was that Sean?" Jade asks as she zips up the suitcase.

"Yeah. He wants us to go see him in LA over winter break."

"What about the photographers?"

I shrug. "I'll wear a hat and won't shave for a week. Nobody will recognize me."

"I wonder if Harper will try to see him when she's home."

"She better not. She needs to stay away from him."

Jade sets the suitcase upright. "It's ready to go."

As we walk down the stairs, part of me is hoping to see my grandmother there, waiting to say goodbye. But she's not there. It's just my dad and Lilly waiting to take Jade and me to the airport.

As we're on the plane heading home, I keep thinking about how much has changed the past year. Not just with me, but with my family. And with my grandfather gone, and my dad and Katherine getting divorced, things will continue to change. It makes me wonder what life will be like a year from now. A lot can change in a year.

# Chapter 28

**JADE**

$\mathcal{E}$ ver since Garret and I got married, I've done a lot of thinking about being a mom. I've talked to my counselor about my fears and I've started to address those fears. And I've made a decision about having kids. I've decided that it's definitely something I want. Not right now, but in the future.

Even though I've made this decision, sometimes my fears creep back in my head when I think about my childhood and hear my mom yelling at me. But like I told the women I gave that speech to, life is full of choices and those choices determine what path you end up on. When I said those words, I was describing my past, but those words also apply to my future. I can make the choice to be a good mom. To be completely different than my own mom.

The past doesn't have to dictate the future. And I have examples of that right in front of me. Like my friend, Sara. She grew up with a bad mom and yet Sara is one of the greatest moms I know.

Then I think of Pearce. Holton was a terrible father and yet Pearce isn't like that. Despite his dad's influence on him, Pearce tries really hard to be a good father. In fact, this past weekend, seeing Pearce being such a great dad to Garret and Lilly just reaffirmed my decision to have kids. I don't know what Holton was like when Pearce was a kid, but I'm guessing he was abusive to his son. Maybe not physically, but emotionally. And Pearce had to put up with that for years. So if he can be a good dad, despite having Holton as a father, then I can be a good mom.

"Jade, we're getting ready to land." Garret's voice wakes me from my thoughts. I'm resting on his shoulder with my eyes closed.

"That was fast." I sit up and stretch a little.

"Fast? We've been flying all day."

"I slept for most of the flight so it seemed fast to me."

"I wish I could sleep on planes, but I just can't get comfortable."

"What have you been doing all this time?"

"Studying for finals. And then I was reading this." He holds up a business magazine. "There was an article in here about the guy who owns WaveField Sports. The guy who offered to be my mentor."

"Yeah, what did it say?"

"They interviewed him and he said he wants to start a new company. He didn't say what it would be, but he said he'll need to put all his efforts into the new company, which means he'll probably be selling WaveField."

"That's too bad. You think he'll still be your mentor?"

"Well, yeah. It doesn't matter what company he owns. He can still teach me stuff. It's just that I was really interested in the sporting goods company, but I'm sure he won't sell it right away. He'll probably wait a couple years."

The speaker above me blares as the pilot announces we're about to land.

Garret holds my hand, like he always does during takeoffs and landings.

"Hey." He says it quickly, and when I look at him, he gives me a kiss just as the wheels touch down, and he keeps kissing me until the plane comes to a stop. "Thought I'd distract you this time."

"Thanks. You should do that every time."

"It's a deal." He gives my hand a squeeze, then gets up and stands in the aisle. "My legs are killing me. Too much sitting. I need to walk around."

"Let's take a walk on the beach when we get home."

He agrees and we exit the plane, then get our luggage and head to the car. It's warm and sunny outside, a complete contrast to the winter wonderland we left back in Connecticut. That storm dumped eight inches of snow on the ground, making it seem a lot more like December than it does here. I kind of miss not having the four seasons anymore, but the warm weather is a lot better than the bitterly cold weather we just left.

Garret and I have a quick dinner, then go out on the beach and stroll along the sand. We walk for about a mile, then turn around.

"Kiefer wants to drive up here and talk to me," Garret announces when we're almost back at the house.

"Why does he want to talk to you?"

"I think he wants to ask me questions about the organization."

"Why you? If he has questions, he can ask your dad."

"My dad will just tell him what he wants to hear. That being a member is great and wonderful and a privilege and whatever other bullshit lies they tell their members, or future members in Kiefer's case. My dad can't tell him the truth. He'd get in trouble if he did."

"You think Kiefer's having second thoughts?"

He shrugs. "I have no idea. But I'm going to call him and tell him I can't talk to him. I told him I would that night of the memorial, but I only said it to get him away from me. He was drunk and he wouldn't go away unless I agreed to meet with him. He didn't say what he wanted to talk about, but it has to be the organization. Anything else he could've just asked me that night or later over the phone."

"We keep getting sucked into this, Garret. When will it end?"

He stops and faces me, holding both my hands. "It already has. And I'm not just saying that to make you feel better. My grandfather is gone. Roth is dead. The members have no interest in me. The only connection we have to them now is my dad and your uncle."

"That's a pretty close connection."

"Yes, but it's not a direct connection. And the organization doesn't want to deal with me anymore. Last spring, I caused them too much trouble. I wasted too much of their time. They're not going to spend even more time coming after me. I'm telling you, Jade. The only people who wanted me back are Roth and my grandfather and now they're both dead."

"Do you think someone killed Roth?"

"Maybe. He has a lot of enemies so it wouldn't surprise me if someone rigged his car to blow up. I'm surprised it hasn't happened sooner."

"Who are his enemies? Like other members?"

"Not members, but people he's screwed over. Like men he hired to do his shit and then didn't pay because he didn't want anything being linked back to him. Or people he made deals with, but then he didn't do his side of the deal. Guys like Roth are arrogant. They think they can get away with shit, but they can't. At least not always."

I don't want to tell Garret this, but there were thoughts floating around my head that maybe his dad killed Roth, or hired someone to do it. Ever since Roth showed up last July, I had this feeling he'd try to get Garret back in the organization. I think Garret and Pearce thought so, too. They just wouldn't admit it. So in the back of my mind, I wondered if Pearce would do something to get Roth out of our lives, but it sounds like someone else did that for us. Or maybe it really was just a car accident.

"So it's over?" I smile really wide. "It's really over?"

"We'll always have to be careful, Jade. That's just part of being a Kensington. But as for the organization? It's over. They're done with me, which means we can stop worrying about them and start living our lives."

"And build our house?"

"You want to build the house? Like now?"

"I guess not, but I want to go visit our land. We haven't been there for a while and I miss it."

"Do you want to go tomorrow? There aren't any classes and neither one of us has a final tomorrow."

"Don't you have to study?"

He shrugs. "I need a break from it. My brain can't hold any more information."

"Okay, then we'll go tomorrow."

"Let's pack a lunch and have a picnic there." He kisses me and talks over my lips. "And for dessert I'm bringing the Halloween candy."

"I can't wait." I kiss him back, then take his hand and we walk back to the house.

On Monday, Garret and I drive to the land where we're building our house. It's sunny but cool, so I brought a sweatshirt and some extra blankets. While Garret sets up our picnic area, I stand at the edge of the cliff, gazing out at the waves and feeling the cool breeze. Every time I come here, I can't believe this is ours.

"Jade, get away from the edge," Garret yells.

I run over to him. "You worry too much."

"You about give me a heart attack when you stand so close to the edge. I'm gonna have to put up a six foot fence just to keep you away from it."

"You can't do that. I wouldn't be able to see the ocean."

"I will, if you don't stop standing on the edge like that."

"Fine." I kiss him. "I'll make sure to stand at least a foot away from it."

"More like three feet. Or six."

I pull on him to sit down with me. He has a blanket spread out over the ground with the picnic basket and cooler holding it down. The other blankets I brought are stacked up next to us. I take one and put it over my legs because the breeze is chilly on my bare skin. I probably should've worn jeans instead of shorts.

"Garret, what are you going to do when we have kids? They'll want to run to the edge just like me."

He doesn't react to the kid comment. I make these comments all the time now. I have for the past month so he's used it. He doesn't read anything into it because he assumes I'm just saying it hypothetically.

"If we had kids," he says, "I'd have to build a ten foot fence. Actually, a fence isn't sturdy enough. I'd need a solid wall."

I laugh. "That would ruin the view, which is the whole purpose of living here."

"I don't care. I'm not gonna risk having our kid fall off the edge of a cliff. There would have to be a solid wall all along there." He points to the edge, moving his hand left to right.

I sit cross-legged and hold his hand and look at him. "Then I guess you better add that to the house plan."

He doesn't react. I'm sure he thinks I'm just talking hypothetically again.

"It can wait. We don't need to build it when we build the house. Like you said, we don't want to ruin the view."

"We need to put *something* there. Maybe not a solid wall, but something to keep our kids safe." I hold his other hand and wait for him to look me in the eye. "Because we're having kids, Garret. Not now, but someday."

He looks like he doesn't believe me, like he thinks I'm joking. But when he sees the serious expression on my face, he says, "Jade, what are you saying?"

"I'm saying that I made a decision. I want us to have kids. Well, I'd like to start with just one and see how it goes."

His cautiously smiles. "Are you serious?"

I nod. "Yeah. I've thought about this a lot. And I've decided this is what I want." I smile. "I think you want that too, right?"

A huge smile fills his face. "You know I do. Get over here." He pulls me into his arms.

"I know I still have issues to work through and I'm not saying I'll be a perfect mom, but I'll be the best mom I possibly can."

"You'll be a great mom, Jade. I know you will."

"I'm still scared. But you'll help, right? I mean, you won't be one of those dads who's never around, right?"

"Of course not. I promise, I will do as much as I can to help."

"Good, because I'm going to need it. I'm already feeling overwhelmed just thinking about having kids, even though it's still a ways off in the future."

He pulls back a little to look at me. "How far in the future? Do you have a timeline in mind?"

"Well, I thought we should talk about that together. But I don't want to be too old. I was thinking maybe when we're 25? Is that too soon?"

"No, it's perfect." His huge smile remains. "That's what I was thinking too. We'll be done with school, our careers will be somewhat started, and the house will be built by then."

"But I think we should start trying when we're 24 so that we have it when we're 25. It could take a while to get pregnant and then you have to wait nine months, so we may not even have one until we're 26."

He brings me in for a kiss. "Then we'll start working on it the night of my 24th birthday."

I smile. "I didn't mean we had to do *that*, but—"

"I know what you meant." He kisses me again and lays me down on the blanket, his hand slipping under my shirt.

I break from the kiss and laugh. "We're not starting right now, Garret. I said 24, not 20."

"I'm just practicing," he says, still kissing me. "Gotta keep my skills up in this area."

I laugh again and push him back. "We'll practice later. I'm not done talking yet."

He props himself next to me on his side. "Go ahead."

"I can't promise you three kids. I know you want three, but I can only agree to one, at least for now."

"We don't have to have three. I'll be happy with whatever we have." His hand brushes over my cheek. "I love you."

"I love you, too." I smile up at him. "We're going to be parents someday."

He glances back at the cliff. "I'm definitely gonna have to put up a ten foot wall."

"No, you're not." I yank him over me and kiss him and keep kissing him, stopping just briefly to say, "We can practice now if you want."

"Finally." He grabs the blankets and covers us up and we have outdoor sex. I was hoping for the Halloween sex but he was in too much of a hurry to grab the candy. And so was I. But we can do it later. We have all afternoon.

This is celebration sex. We're celebrating that I finally made a decision. A decision that's made Garret very happy. And more importantly, a decision that makes us *both* happy.

# Chapter 29

**GARRET**

*J*ade just told me she wants to have kids, which kind of shocked me. It's not that I didn't think that would be her answer. I knew it was a possibility after she made that comment about wanting kids when we were at Frank's house. But she said she needed more time to think about it, so I thought she'd need a year or two. I didn't think she'd decide this soon. I hope this really is what she wants and she's not going to change her mind later. But I don't think she will. I know she's given this a lot of thought and talked to her counselor about it.

All I can say is she's made me a very happy man with that decision. And if she only wants one kid, that's fine with me. It's better to have one than none. Her timing is perfect, too. I thought she'd want to wait until she was 30 or even later than that, so when she said 25, I was relieved. To me, that's the perfect age. Before I met Jade I would've said that's way too young, but I've matured a lot the past year and by 25, Jade and I will have been married six years, so it seems like a good time to have a baby. That gives us plenty of time to just be a couple. Just the two of us, doing things like we're doing today, spending the afternoon hanging out on our own private land.

"Garret, when should we build the house?" Jade's gazing up at the sky, a blanket wrapped around her naked body.

We just had outdoor sex, one of my favorite kinds. Who am I kidding? They're all my favorite kinds. But doing it outside in the cool fresh air is up there at the top of my favorites list.

"I thought you wanted to build it this spring." I sit up and grab a bottle of water from the cooler, a blanket covering my lower half. "We should probably put clothes on in case someone drives by."

I start getting dressed, but Jade remains under the blanket. "I'd only build it this spring if we planned to live here this summer. But we don't have to do that. We could find another beach house to rent. We talked about doing that anyway."

"That was when we thought Sean and Harper would be living next door. But now they're not together, so would you still want to rent a place?"

"I think so. I'd like more time to plan the house. I don't want to rush into building it and then wish we'd done something different. And now that we've added a kid to the equation, we need to plan for another room."

"It's just one room, Jade. It's not that big a deal." I hand her my water and she sits up just enough to take a sip, then hands it back to me.

"We should plan for more than one, even if we're not sure yet. It's too hard to add bedrooms later."

"How many rooms would you like?" I set my water down.

"We should probably have three, for the three kids you might end up talking me into."

Holy shit. She's actually considering three? How'd we go from one to three? She seemed pretty adamant about only having one kid, but hey, if she's open to three, all the better. I've always wanted three. I don't really know why.

"Then three for the kids and a big master bedroom for us. What about the guests?"

"I'm not sure. What do you think?"

"A couple guest rooms should be plenty."

"That's only enough for Frank and Ryan. What if your dad was here, too? We wouldn't have room."

"My dad can stay at a hotel."

"No, that's no good. I want him here with us." She sounds so determined it makes me laugh. "What's so funny?"

"You. Worrying about having room for everyone. They don't have to all stay at our house, Jade."

"But I like having everyone around. And I don't want your dad to not feel welcome."

She's so sweet. I don't know how she ever forgave my dad for the way he treated her last year, but she has, and now she cares about him and worries about him almost as much as she worries about me.

"Then we'll add another guest room for my dad. That's six bedrooms plus the master. That's plenty. If we add any more, the house will get too big and we agreed we didn't want a huge house."

"But what about Grace? What if all the rooms are full? She'll have no place to stay."

I laugh and lean down to kiss her. "Jade, chances are these people will never all be at our house at the same time. And if they are, then my dad can sleep on the couch. Or he can sleep in the same room as his grandkid. We'll put an extra bed in there. Same with Lilly. She can bunk with one of her nieces or nephews."

Jade bolts up. "I forgot about Lilly! We don't have enough rooms."

"Seven rooms. That's it. No more." I toss her bra and shirt at her. "Now get dressed in case someone drives by."

She starts putting her clothes on under the blanket. "As long as we're out this way, we should drive down to Santa Barbara and see Grace. I know we just saw her, but we've only been to her house once since she moved here."

"Call her up and see if she's around. Tell her we could be there later today."

Jade finishes getting dressed, then calls Grace and makes plans to have dinner with her. I set up our lunch while she's talking.

When she's done on the phone, she says, "Too bad Grace doesn't live closer to here. When we finally move here, I want to have her over a lot, especially since she loves this location so much."

I hand Jade her sandwich and grab us each a soda. "You know what we should do?"

"What?" She takes the soda from me.

"Never mind. She'd never go for it." I take the potato chip bag and set it between us.

"Go for what? Tell me what you were going to say."

"A while back we talked about building a guest house here and I was just thinking it might be good to have Grace live in it, so she wouldn't be living alone. I mean, she'd have her own place so technically she'd be living alone, but she'd have us right next door in the main house." I take a bite of my sandwich.

Jade grabs my arm. "Garret, are you serious? Would you really do that?"

"Sure, why not? Grace gave us the land and she said she always wanted to live here. She could make a flower garden with that map she drew up."

"That's a great idea! I could have my grandma right next door." Jade drops her sandwich and reaches over and hugs me. "I love you! You're the best husband ever!"

I set my sandwich down and hug her back. "Guess I should've suggested this sooner. But do you think Grace would go for it? She likes being independent."

"Which is why the guest house idea is perfect. She'll have her own separate living space. She can spend time alone or she can hang out with us. But if she needs us, we'll be right next door. I know she's in good health now, but in a few years, she may not be. She needs to have family close by." Jade sits back on her knees. "Before I say anything to her, are you sure you're okay with this?"

"Jade, I suggested it, so yes. Grace is more like a grand-mother to me than my own grandmother. I'd be happy to have her live here with us."

Jade hugs me again. "I'll say it again. You're the best hus-band ever! I love you."

"I love you, too. Let's finish lunch." I whisper by her ear, "And then let's have dessert."

We do exactly that, except we wait an hour before having that dessert. We just lie there and enjoy the sun and then move on to dessert, which is code for Halloween sex. It's not as hot out today as it was last time, so I put the chocolate bar on her bare stomach and then warm it with my mouth before licking it off. She likes that. A lot. I think we need to have Halloween sex more often. We'll do it at home next time and I'll have her wear her cheerleader costume.

Later, we drive down to Grace's house. We probably should've given her more notice before coming over, but I knew she wouldn't say no. She loves having us visit.

She takes us to dinner, and as we're having dessert, Jade brings up the idea we discussed. "So, Grace, I wanted to ask you something. You don't have to answer right away but I hope your answer is yes."

Grace was eating her ice cream, but she sets her spoon down. "Go ahead, dear."

Jade looks at me, then back at Grace. "As you know, Garret and I are going to build a house on that land you gave us and we've been talking about what the house would look like, how many bedrooms it would have—stuff like that. Anyway, we decided to also build a separate smaller house next to the main house."

"Like a guest house?"

"Yes. Except the person living there wouldn't just be a guest. It would be more of a permanent residence if this person agrees to it." Jade smiles. "We want you to live there, Grace. We want to build you your own house next to ours. You can plant a flower garden, a vegetable garden, whatever you want."

She pats Jade's hand. "Oh, honey, I can't live there. I have my own house. Several houses."

"Those can be your vacation homes. You can visit them whenever you want. Grace, you said that you and Arlin always wanted to live on that land."

"Well, yes, but that was different. That was when Arlin was alive. We had our dream for what we'd do with that land, and now that dream belongs to you and Garret. It's part of your new life together. If I lived there, I'd just be in the way."

"You wouldn't be in the way," Jade says. "If anything, *I'll* be the one getting in *your* way. If you live that close, you know I'll be stopping over all the time."

"We have four acres, Grace," I say. "We have plenty of room. If you want more privacy, we'll put the guest house farther over on the property. It doesn't have to be right next to ours."

"It's very kind of both of you to offer this to me, but I don't feel right about it. I gave that land to the two of you. I don't want to take up space on it. You should use it however you see fit."

"This is how we want to use it," Jade says. "We're still going to build the guest house, so if you don't want to live there, it'll just have to sit empty. But you at least have to come stay for a few weeks throughout the year or spend the summers with us."

Grace smiles, then sips her coffee. "Give me some time to think about it. You're not building right away, are you?"

"No, probably in a year or two."

"Then I have plenty of time to decide." She goes back to eating her ice cream.

"There's another reason I'd like you to live there. It's kind of a selfish one but I'll say it anyway." Jade hesitates. I can tell she's nervous so I reach over and hold her hand. "I was hoping maybe you could help out when Garret and I have a baby."

Grace's eyes widen. "Jade, are you—"

"I'm not pregnant. But maybe in a few years." Jade glances at me and smiles, then looks back at Grace. "And I'll need help when the baby comes. Since you're a mom, I was hoping you could teach me some things."

"Of course I will." She rubs Jade's arm. "I'll stay as long as you need me to."

"I'm going to need you for a really long time. I'm not very good with babies."

"She thinks she's not, but she is," I say to Grace. "She's really good with Sara's baby."

Jade turns to me. "No, I'm not. You're the one who's good with him." She turns back to Grace. "You should see Garret with Caleb. He always makes Caleb laugh. The kid never cries when Garret's around."

Grace smiles at us. "You two will make wonderful parents. And you will be a wonderful mother, Jade."

Jade looks down at her plate. I know she's uncomfortable talking about this, so I'm surprised she even brought it up. But if she's telling other people about us having kids, then I know she's committed to this, which makes me even happier.

We head home after dinner because it's getting late and we have a long drive back. Grace seemed better than the last time we saw her, but she still seems lonely. I hope she decides to live on our property. It'd be good for her and it would mean a lot to Jade to have her there. I'd like it, too. Grace is becoming more and more like a grandmother to me. She's so different than my own grandmother. She's warm and caring and actually listens when I talk. And I can tell her stuff and not have her judge or criticize me the way my own grandmother does.

When we get home, I check the house like I always do. I look for signs of a break-in, like an open window, misplaced furniture, a pillow that isn't where we left it, and any other signs that someone might've been in the house. I don't need to do this anymore, but I still do. I probably always will.

Tuesday morning I go to my first final. Jade stayed home because her first final isn't until this afternoon. When I left, she was putting up more Christmas lights. Our whole place is covered in them. Every window, the bedroom ceiling, the two Christmas trees, the potted plants, the top of the dresser. Jade puts them everywhere and I love it. It gives the place a warm festive glow, and best of all, it makes Jade happy.

We won't have much time to enjoy the lights because this Saturday we go back to Connecticut, this time for Christmas. We're staying for a week. We considered staying a little longer than that but we wanted to leave before the big meeting started. Every year, the organization has their big end-of-the-year meeting. It lasts for the entire week between Christmas and New Year's. Members fly in from all over. Even though I supposedly don't have to worry about them anymore, I don't want to stick around and risk running into them.

When we return from the holiday, Jade and I plan to stay home and relax for the rest of the winter break. We need some time to de-stress after all the shit that happened this past semester. But we did make plans for New Year's. We're driving down to LA to see Sean. We'll see Harper, too, but we haven't figured out when. With the two of them broken up, we have to split our time between them.

My morning final turns out to be easier than I thought it would be. Afterward, I go to the library to study, then eat lunch and take another final in the afternoon. I have five finals and they're all crammed into Tuesday, Wednesday, and Thursday. Jade's last final is Thursday, too. On Friday, I'm sure we'll collapse from exhaustion. It's only Tuesday and I'm already exhausted.

After my afternoon final, I walk to my car, feeling like my brain's fried. I hate finals.

"Garret." I turn and see Kiefer standing next to me. He must've snuck out from behind a tree or something. His hair's a mess and it looks like he hasn't shaved for a few days.

"What are you doing here, Kiefer? I told you I couldn't meet with you." I keep walking, heading to the parking lot.

He grabs my arm. "Please, Garret. I'm begging you. I just need a few minutes."

I yank my arm back. "I can't. I'm sorry."

"It's important." He jumps in front of me. "You know what this is about, right?"

"Yes. And you know I can't talk about it. Nobody can."

"I know that. It's just that I don't know what to do. I don't know who to turn to. I got myself into this and now I don't know if I can get out."

I stop walking. "You're already in it? I thought—"

"No, I'm not officially a member yet. That's why I need to talk to you."

"What do you mean when you say you want to get out? Like not become a member?"

"Yes. I don't think I can do it." He scratches his head, which messes up his hair even more. "I didn't know what I was getting involved in, and now I'm in so deep I fear what they would do to me if I told them no."

A couple guys walk past us, staring because Kiefer's freaking out here. Or maybe they're spies for the organization, watching us, listening to our conversation.

"Kiefer, I can't do this." I walk around him. "You'll have to figure this out on your own."

He follows me. "I need to know the truth. If I'm going to risk everything to try to get out of this, I need to know that my suspicions are correct and that this group isn't who I thought they were."

He keeps pace with me. We shouldn't be out in the open like this. We're at the parking lot now where anyone could see us.

"Garret, if you don't help me, Harper's life will be over. They already have someone picked for her."

He needs to stop talking. I don't want to know any of this. I just want to be left out of it. I spot my car and click the remote and quickly get inside.

Kiefer grabs hold of the car door before I can close it. "I just found out who it is. I don't want my daughter with this man. They told me it would just be a sham marriage. Just for appearances. That she wouldn't even have to live with him. But they lied. This man has had his eyes on Harper for months. He saw a photo of her and decided he wanted her. I think Harper was one of the reasons I was offered membership. I knew Roth never liked me, so I was surprised when he came out here last summer and officially asked me to join. Now I know why."

"What does Roth have to do with this?"

"The man who wants Harper is Roth's son, Andrew. He's 40 and rich and spoiled. He doesn't work. He just lives extravagantly and gambles away his father's money. He uses women, then tosses them aside. He'll never be faithful to Harper and—" He pauses, closing his eyes as a few tears run down his face. "He has a history of being abusive to women."

Shit. Why did he have to tell me that?

*I can't get involved. I can't involved.* I repeat it in my head because getting involved could put Jade and me at risk. Doing so could get us on the organization's radar again. It sounds like they really want Kiefer as a member and if they found out I was helping him get out, or even just talking to him about it, I could get in big trouble.

"Just tell them no," I say, trying to close the door.

He steps in front of the door so I can't close it. "If I do, they might kill me."

I shake my head. "They won't kill you. You have skills that they need."

"They've already made it clear that any new recruit who tries to back out at this stage will be punished. But I don't know what that means."

New recruits? How many new people are they adding? I thought it was just Kiefer.

"Garret, I know you and Jade care about Harper. If you can just give me some advice."

Shit! I hate this. What do I do? Save Harper? Even if it means risking Jade and me? I scan the parking lot. Nobody's around.

"Get in. Back seat." I click open the door. "Hurry up."

My back windows are tinted so Kiefer won't be seen. I start the car and drive onto the street, then turn and go down a side street and park. Hardly anyone goes down this street, but in case they do, I get my phone out and pretend I'm just sitting here making a call.

"Why did you want to be part of it?" I ask him.

"Because they offered me a lot of money. I'm talking hundreds of millions. And they offered me access to a medical clinic that is supposed to have advanced treatments that the public isn't allowed to have. Kelly has a family history of breast cancer. There's a good chance that she or one of my daughters could get cancer, and if they did, I was told this clinic would be able to help. Maybe even cure them."

"I don't know if that's true. I don't think they have a cure for cancer. So the money and the clinic? That's why you wanted to join?"

"They also promised me even greater success as a director. Not just money, but prestige. They even promised me an Academy Award."

"But now you want out because of Harper."

"Yes. But also because I found out this group is violent. I knew about the election fraud, but it didn't bother me. I always assumed those things were rigged, so I had no problem making the fake videos and fake recordings. But I didn't realize these people were criminals."

"How do you know they are?"

"I did a video a few months ago to help boost poll numbers for Kent Gleason. You probably saw it on the news. It was a scene with Gleason saving a little boy on the beach. Anyway, the actress in the video figured out what was going on and threatened to tell the press. A member was there on the shoot that day and heard her say it. And just last week, I found out she was killed while jogging in the park. I know they did it. They had to get rid of her, just in case she decided to tell her story. Then a few weeks ago, when I told them I was having trouble getting Sean out of Harper's life, they—"

"They what?" My anger keeps rising the more he talks.

"They sent some guys after him. They told Sean they'd kill him if he didn't leave Harper alone. They beat him up and probably would've killed him that night if the police hadn't driven by and stopped to see what was going on. Garret, I had no idea they took things this far. You have to tell me, are they always like this? Or were these just isolated incidents?"

I'm silent. He can figure out what that means. And he does.

301

He starts talking really fast. "I can't be part of this. I need to get out. I need you to help me."

"What do you expect *me* to do?"

"You got out. How did you do it?"

Does he really not know? You'd think he would've put the pieces together and figured it out. He made the videos that ruined my reputation. Did he really think that was all because of the reality show? To make me less popular with the fans?

"I was never in it," I tell him. "I didn't need to get out."

"I thought you were born into it."

"The rules have changed. That's why they're letting you in."

"Could you talk to your father for me? I've tried, but he just keeps giving me the sales speech, telling me it's a privilege and an honor to be part of it."

"He won't listen to me. I'm sorry, Kiefer. I can't do anything. And frankly, I'm pissed that you're even here. You're putting me at risk and you're putting Jade at risk. You never should've come here. You need to get out of my car."

"But what about Harper? And what if they go after Sean again?"

"Why do you care about Sean? I thought you hated the guy."

"No, not at all. I think he's a nice young man and I don't want to see him get hurt."

"So if you get out of this, you'll let Harper date Sean again?"

"I would do more than *let* her. I'd encourage it. Since being with Sean, she's never been happier."

"Then why the hell did you go and fuck everything up?" I'm so angry I didn't filter my words. "Sorry. I didn't mean to—"

"No. You're right. You're absolutely right. I got caught up in the money and the prestige and I fucked everything up." He opens the car door just slightly. "I'm sorry that I just showed up like this. I'll leave you alone. I don't know what I was thinking coming here. I was just desperate. I sincerely hope I didn't put you in any kind of danger. I won't bother you again." He quickly gets out of the car, then shoots over to the sidewalk and starts walking down the street.

I take off and turn down some side streets to make sure I'm not being followed. I'm not, so I head home.

Just when I told Jade this was over for good, Kiefer shows up and brings it all back to us. Shit.

# Chapter 30

**JADE**

"*I* need to talk to you," Garret says as he walks in the door. He has that serious look on his face that I don't like.

"What's wrong?" I watch as he checks out the window. "What are you looking for?"

"I'm trying to make sure I wasn't followed."

"Garret, do not say stuff like that." I go over and turn him away from the window. "What's going on? Why would someone be following you?"

"They're not. I'm just making sure." He lets out a heavy sigh. "Kiefer came to see me today. He showed up on campus wanting to talk."

"About the organization?" I feel the tightness in my chest that forms every time this topic comes up.

"Let's sit down." He takes me over to the couch.

"Did you talk to him?"

"I didn't want to, and I tried to get rid of him, but he wouldn't go away. He was desperate to talk to me. You should've seen him. He looked like he hadn't slept for weeks."

"He didn't look so great when we saw him at your dad's house either."

"He looks a lot worse now."

"So what did he say?"

"That he doesn't want to do this. He doesn't want to be part of the organization, but now he feels trapped, like he can't get out of it. He got lured in by the money and the power and the clinic. He has no problem supporting the rigged elections, but he had no idea about the other things the organization does. The things they do in order to keep their secrets. Now he wants no part of it."

"Why does he think *you* can help?"

"Because he thinks I got out and he wanted to know how I did it."

"So he doesn't know what happened? How could he not know? He was part of it."

"He believed the story about the reality show being the reason we made those videos. So I didn't tell him the truth. I just told him I was never a member."

"Did you tell him we can't be involved in this?"

"Yes. Which is why I got in my car and told him he had to leave but then—"

"Then what?" My stomach knots and my chest tightens even more.

Garret holds my hands. "Promise me you'll stay out of this if I tell you."

"Tell me first."

"No. This is bad and I probably shouldn't even tell you but—just forget it. You don't need to know this. I'm pissed that he even told me."

"Garret, you can't say something like that and then not finish. Tell me what he said. Is it about Harper?"

He doesn't answer. Dammit. I hate it when he does this.

"I swear, if you don't tell me, I'll call Kiefer myself."

"Jade, I'm serious. Do not get in the middle of this. If I have to, I'll talk to my dad, but that's it. Kiefer got himself into this and he has to get himself out. And he better do it damn quick because the initiation is early January. And once he's in, he's never getting out."

"Garret, please. Just tell me. I promise I won't get involved."

"You say that now, but after you hear this…" He drops his head, his gaze on our hands.

"You have to tell me. You can't leave me guessing."

He nods. "They found someone for Harper. Actually, someone requested her. He saw her and decided he wants her."

"Wants her to what? Marry him?"

"Yes." Garret lifts his head and his eyes meet up with mine. "It's Andrew Roth."

"Roth, as in—"

"Yes. The son of Cecil Roth. Apparently he saw photos of Harper sometime last year and told his dad he wanted her. Kiefer thinks that's why he was offered membership. It sounds like Roth had to give the final approval to let Kiefer in. And he did, but Kiefer thinks it's only because of Harper."

"I think Harper met this guy. A few months ago when your grandfather had that party at his house and Harper was baby-sitting Lilly, she said some rich guy kept trying to get her to go out with him. She said his name was Andrew and that he was like 40 years old."

"That was him. He probably wanted to see her in person to make sure he still wanted her."

"And Kiefer didn't know this?"

"He just found out and now he's panicking. He doesn't want Harper with this guy. Andrew sleeps with a lot of women and can't stay faithful to any of them."

"So they're setting Harper up with a guy who's twice her age and cheats?"

"That's not the worst part. I don't know how Kiefer found this out, because if it's true, the organization would make sure it stays hidden, but maybe one of the members told him."

"Told him what?"

"Andrew has a history of abusing women."

"No." I shake my head, tears welling up in my eyes. "They can't do that. They can't make her be with him. Why would Kiefer let them do that?"

Garret brings me into his arms as tears roll down my face. "He didn't know about this until just recently. He doesn't want this, Jade. He didn't know it would be this way when he agreed to be a member."

"But he knew they'd make his daughters marry whoever they picked."

"Maybe they told him she'd be able to pick who she wanted. They do that sometimes. They give you options and you get to pick. But this guy saw Harper and said he wanted her. And since he's Roth's son, he gets whatever he wants."

"But Roth is gone now."

"It doesn't matter. The deal was made when Roth was still alive."

"Did Kiefer say anything about Sean? Did he admit to threatening Sean if he didn't leave Harper alone?"

"He said he had nothing to do with that. He said the organization sent some guys to go after Sean and that they attacked him and might've even killed him if the cops hadn't shown up. Kiefer didn't want Sean getting hurt. He claims that he likes Sean and that if all this wasn't going on, he'd want Harper to be with Sean."

"Are you serious? Then why did he go and mess everything up?"

Garret laughs.

I shove away from him. "Why are you laughing? This isn't funny."

"Because I said the same thing to Kiefer except I used worse language. It's good my cursing hasn't rubbed off on you." He kisses my cheek.

"So what is Kiefer going to do?"

"He's trying to get out, but I don't know how he's going to do it. He knows too much, so even if they let him go, he'll always be tied to them. They'll make him do all their shit for free. And they'll punish him for backing out of his commitment."

"You think they'd hurt him? Or…kill him?"

"No. They need to keep him around. They'll find some other way to punish him. But honestly, Jade, I don't think he can get out of this."

"He has to. Harper can't end up with that man. He'll hurt her."

Tears stream down my cheeks and Garret wipes them away. "I knew I shouldn't have told you. It's no use knowing this when we can't do anything about it."

"But you'll talk to your dad? Please say you'll talk to him."

"I will, but what's he gonna do? He can't get on the organization's bad side. Then *he'll* be the one getting punished, and they've already done enough to ruin his life. Kiefer will just have to tell them no and deal with the consequences."

"What am I supposed to do when I talk to Harper? I won't be able to just pretend everything's fine. She'll be able to tell something's wrong, so what do I say to her?"

"Jade." Garret gently rubs my hand. "You need to know something else."

"No. I can't hear any more bad news."

"You have to."

"Fine. Just hurry up and get it over with."

"If Kiefer becomes a member, you can no longer be friends with Harper. You can't have any contact with her. No phone calls. No texts. Nothing."

"What? No!" I yank my hand back. "Harper's my best friend! I'm not letting them take Harper like they tried to take you." I'm crying again and Garret forces me into his arms.

# Always Us

"I'm sorry, Jade. But this is how it has to be. Deep down, I know you realize that. You're just not ready to accept it."

"I hate these people! Why do they have to be this way? Why do they have to destroy lives and hurt people? I don't understand how they can be so evil."

"Money and power can do that to people. It takes away their humanity, their compassion. And the members who *aren't* like that, like my dad, have to pretend it's someone else doing this stuff. My dad has two sides, but we only see one of them. You wouldn't want to see his other side. I think William's the same way. And as for the other members, I think they just get numb to it. They stop feeling and caring and just go along with whatever they're told to do."

My phone rings and I stare at it, not sure if I should answer it. I don't want to talk to anyone right now, especially Harper. How can I just pretend nothing's wrong when I know she's in danger? When I know that she'll soon be forced to marry a man who has a history of abusing women?

I let the phone go to voicemail, but a few minutes later it rings again. I go over and pick it up. It's not Harper. It's Sara.

"Hey, Sara, can I call you back later?"

"Oh. Are you busy?"

"Kind of. Why?"

"I know it's finals week so I hate to ask you this, but I wondered if you could watch Caleb for an hour, maybe not even that long. I just got a call for a job interview at a law firm and the guy asked if I could meet right now. He's going out of town tomorrow and wants to do a quick interview before he leaves. His office is really short-staffed and they need to hire someone to answer the phone and file paperwork. The job would just be two days a week for now, but he said it might become full-time in a few months."

309

I don't feel like babysitting right now, but I have to help her out. Sara really needs a better job.

"Um, sure, I'll come over. I need your address." I've never been to Sara's apartment before. I think she's avoided having me over there because it's really small and run-down and she's embarrassed by it. I wish she wouldn't worry about stuff like that. I'd never judge her for living in a crappy place. It can't be any worse than the house I grew up in.

"Thanks, Jade. I really appreciate this." She gives me her address and I jot it down.

"I'll be there soon." I hang up and grab my keys. "I have to go watch Caleb for an hour."

Garret gets up. "I'll go with you."

"You don't have to."

"I want to." He opens the door for me. "I miss the little guy. I haven't seen him for a while. And like you said, if I'm there, he won't cry."

I'm glad Garret offered to come with me. I've never babysat before. I keep offering to, but then it never happens. I've spent a lot of time with Sara when she has Caleb with her, but I've never been alone with him for more than a few minutes.

We drive to the address she gave me. It's in an area of town I've never been to before. It's full of abandoned buildings with the windows broken out. There are some guys hanging out on the street and they eye Garret's black BMW and watch as he parks it along the curb. It'll probably be gone when we come back out.

The entrance to Sara's apartment building is locked. I look up her apartment number so she can buzz us in. But then someone walks past us and holds the door open, making the locked door basically useless for security purposes.

There's no elevator and Sara's on the third floor. So she has to carry Caleb and all her stuff up three flights of stairs? If she had groceries, she'd have to make three or four trips.

The staircase up to her apartment is dark and narrow and the paint's peeling off the walls. It also smells really bad, like a musty, moldy smell.

When Sara answers the door, she doesn't act surprised that we didn't buzz first. I guess the people in her building just let everyone in. Again, not safe.

She hugs me. "I can't thank you enough. And Garret came, too." She smiles at him. "Thank you. Both of you. Come inside." We walk in and I see Caleb in his crib. "I just put Caleb down for his nap. He might sleep the whole time you're here, unless my neighbors come home. They can get kind of loud and it always wakes Caleb up."

She grabs her purse and her keys. "I'm sorry I asked you guys to do this on such short notice. It's just that this could be a really good job and Alex is out of town at a conference. I didn't have anyone else to watch Caleb."

"Sara, don't worry about it." Garret walks her to the door. "We got this. Go meet your new boss."

She laughs. "You're way more confident in me than I am. I'm sure he won't hire me."

"You can't think that way. You have to go in there thinking you'll get the job."

"Okay. I'll try. Bye!" She closes the door and Garret locks it behind her. Then he turns around and inspects her apartment.

I can tell he's thinking the same thing I am. It's bad. Really bad. I see why she didn't want me coming over here. It's not like it's messy or dirty. She tries to keep it clean. But the walls are cracked and the paint is peeling. The electrical outlets are exposed, meaning they don't even have those covers that get screwed into the wall. There's some kind of wire hanging from the ceiling. And the ceiling has water spots all over it and black mold growing on it.

This place is not safe, for Caleb or for Sara. It's even worse than where I grew up.

It's a studio apartment so it's just one room with a twin mattress on the floor and Caleb's crib next to it. There isn't room for any other furniture. There's a tiny TV in the corner sitting on a yellow milk crate and a few boxes of clothes lined up against the wall.

I go over and look in the bathroom. There's a toilet, a tiny sink, and a shower. It's such a small space you can barely close the door.

"Jade, check this out."

I walk out of the bathroom and see Garret in the kitchen. He's at the sink and has the water turned on. Instead of being clear, the water is a yellowish-brown color. "I hope she doesn't drink this shit or give it to Caleb."

I meet him over there. "I don't think she does." I hold up a gallon jug of bottled water that was sitting on the floor. "But she has to shower in that water."

There's a rusty stove next to the sink but I doubt it works. An old microwave sits next to it on the counter.

"She can't live here." Garret shuts the water off.

"I know. It's horrible, but where is she supposed to go?"

"We'll get her a place. It doesn't have to be fancy. It just needs to be safe."

"She won't take our money."

"Then we'll give it to her anonymously." He takes a few steps, which puts him in the living room. Yeah, it's that small of a place.

"She'll use the money for food and bottled water and diapers. She won't use it for an apartment."

"We'll give her enough money so she can get that stuff *and* a new apartment." He scans the walls and the wire hanging down from the ceiling. "This is fucked up. Nobody should live like this. Guys in prison live better than this. I'm going to find out who owns this building and report him. He's gotta be breaking some kind of laws. You can't even drink the water. And I'm sure there's a law saying he has to fix shit like that." He points to the hanging wire.

"How are we going to give her money without her knowing it's from us?"

"I don't know. I'll figure it out." He shakes his head. "Why the hell isn't Alex letting her stay at his place?"

"Alex has tried to convince her to stay at his place but she won't do it. She said she doesn't want Alex thinking she's trying to move in, or that she's using him for a free place to stay."

"No wonder you two are friends. She's just as stubborn as you." Garret goes to the window and tries to close it but it won't shut. It's broken. "Jade, you can't even close this thing. Some guy could climb the fire escape and come right in through the window."

"She doesn't have anything to steal."

"She's got a baby. People want babies, Jade."

A chill runs through me. "Don't say stuff like that. Nobody's taking Caleb."

"It's a shitty world. And bad guys have no problem stealing a baby and selling it to couples who desperately want one. And even if they leave Caleb alone, a guy could sneak in here at night and attack Sara. Rape her. Beat her up. Whatever."

"What are we going to do?"

He rubs his jaw as he looks around the room. "They can stay at our place tonight."

"We can't get Caleb's crib in our car."

"We'll go buy one of those portable ones."

"Sara won't agree to stay with us. You know she won't. "

"Then we'll talk her into it. She won't have to stay there for very long. We'll find her a new apartment this week. We'll put it in her name and pay for a few month's rent so she can save up some money."

"How are we going to explain that?"

"We'll make up a fake foundation and tell her she was picked to receive assistance."

"Do you think she'll buy that?"

"She's gonna have to because she's not living here anymore. I had no idea she was living like this, did you?"

"If I did, I would've got her out of here. This is worse than my mom's house. At least *there* we could drink the water. And we didn't have mold growing everywhere. That black mold is really dangerous. It can make you sick, especially Caleb, since he's so small."

There's noise in the hallway. People are stomping up the stairs, yelling at each other. Then a door slams as they go in the apartment next door. The walls are thin and we can hear them fighting. They're cursing and screaming and then there's a loud bang on the wall by Caleb's crib. He instantly wakes up and starts crying as the neighbors continue to yell and curse and throw things at the wall.

"Shit." Garret goes and picks up Caleb, holding him against his chest and covering his ears. He bounces him a little, which usually soothes him, but this time it doesn't. The neighbors are too loud. "Do you think we can take him somewhere?"

"No. Sara will freak out if she gets home and we're not here. Besides, I don't want to walk around in this neighborhood, and we don't have a car seat so we can't drive anywhere."

Garret glares at the wall that the neighbors keep banging on. "I need to go over there and tell them to shut the hell up."

"No, don't. They probably have a gun or a knife."

"Can you grab his blanket?" Garret nods at the crib.

I pick up the blue blanket and hand it to him. He wraps it around Caleb, who's dressed in shorts and a t-shirt.

"His arms and legs are freezing," Garret says. "It's too cold in here for him. You know why? Because you can't close the damn window."

"Shh. Don't swear in front of Caleb."

"Trust me. He's heard worse living next to those two." He motions to the wall, where the F-bombs are flying as the neighbors continue to fight. "See if you can find Caleb some warmer clothes."

I check the cardboard boxes along the wall. Inside one of them are some baby clothes. I take out a navy sweatshirt and some gray sweatpants and bring them over to Garret.

He kneels down and sets Caleb on the twin mattress. Caleb squirms and cries.

"I'm just going to change your clothes, okay?" Garret tickles him a little, trying to distract him from the noise. It works. Caleb stops crying and giggles and grabs his toes.

"Hey. I can't put these pants on you if you do that." Garret tickles him some more and Caleb giggles so much he drops his toes.

Garret tries to put the sweatpants on Caleb, but they're too small. "Jade, can you find some other pants? He's outgrown these."

I go back to the box as Garret puts the sweatshirt on Caleb.

"I need a different sweatshirt, too. This one barely fits him."

"He doesn't have anything. The pants are all the same size as the ones I gave you. Same with the shirts. That's probably why Sara's got him in the clothes he's wearing. They're the only things that fit him."

Garret picks Caleb up off the bed. "Guess we're going shopping for baby clothes. How can she not have any clothes that fit him?"

"She doesn't have money for clothes. Her car breaks down every week. She's always paying to get that thing fixed. And then rent and food and day care."

The fighting next door is getting even louder and making Caleb cry.

"It's okay, buddy." Garret holds Caleb against his chest, trying to soothe him. "I swear I'm going to kill those people."

"I think they're going to kill each other in a few minutes."

A half hour later, Garret's still trying to calm Caleb down. The neighbors are still loud, except now they're having sex, so it's a whole different kind of loud.

"Check your phone," Garret says. "See if Sara left you any messages."

I check, and see that she sent me a text. "She says she'll be back in about 10 minutes. What are we going to do?"

"We're telling her she's staying at our place tonight."

I agree with Garret, but I know Sara won't go for it. She always thinks she's in the way or bothering people. I used to think that way, too, and sometimes I still do. So I understand where she's coming from, but she needs to accept our help because this involves her safety and Caleb's safety. She can't live here. It's too dangerous. She's just lucky nothing bad has happened yet. Or maybe it has and she didn't tell me.

I smile as I watch Garret with Caleb. The way he's holding him, talking to him, rubbing his back, trying to calm him down? It melts my heart. It's not even his kid and yet he's so sweet and caring with him.

Now I'm starting to think one kid isn't enough. I might just have to have two with this man. And they're going to be the luckiest kids in the world.

# Chapter 31

**GARRET**

$\mathcal{I}$ don't usually get into other people's business, but I feel I
have to intervene when it comes to Sara's living conditions.
It's not safe for her and Caleb to live this way. I know she likes
to be independent and able to support herself, and I respect
that, but there's a point where you have to admit you need
help. You can't let your pride get in the way of your safety.

I hear someone trying to open the door so I go over and
say, "Who is it?" because there isn't even a peephole to check.

"It's Sara. I'm having trouble with my key."

I open the door, still holding Caleb. I finally calmed him
down. The poor kid was scared to death when the neighbors
got home and went fucking nuts. I don't even want to know
what was going on over there. They've quieted down now.

"How'd it go?" Sara sets her purse down on the kitchen
counter. "I see Caleb woke up. Sorry about that. I was hoping
he'd stay asleep. He wasn't too much trouble, was he?"

I wish she wouldn't say stuff like that. A baby isn't trouble.
Yeah, the crying sucked, but shit, if I were him, I'd cry to. He's
trying to sleep and all hell break's loose next door. And then
he wakes up and finds two strangers here instead of his mom.
Plus, he's freezing because he doesn't have warm clothes that
fit. Of course he's going to cry.

"He wasn't any trouble." I hand him to Sara. "He's a great
kid."

"How was the job interview?" Jade asks.

"It went really well. I think he's going to offer me the job. Like I said, it's just two days a week but it pays way more than I get now." Sara bounces Caleb on her hip. "The guy said he'll call me tomorrow and let me know if I got it. If so, I can start next week. And I can still work at the coffee shop. I'll just have to change my schedule. Anyway, thanks again for watching Caleb. You guys can go. I'm sure you have to study."

Jade looks at me. I guess she wants me to be the one to talk to Sara about this. How do I say it without hurting her feelings?

"Sara, we were thinking you should stay at our place tonight."

She looks at Jade, then back at me. She knows what we think of her place and I can tell she's embarrassed and ashamed. She doesn't say anything but her eyes are watery like she's about to cry. Shit. So much for not hurting her feelings.

I try to explain. "It's just that we saw a cockroach and where there's one there's hundreds and Jade said you hate bugs."

A little white lie never hurt anyone, right? And in this case, I'd say it's justified.

"Yeah, I hate bugs," Sara says. "Where did you see it?"

"Right over there." I point to the corner by Caleb's crib. "Your landlord will have to get an exterminator. But for now, you shouldn't stay here."

"That's okay. I don't want to inconvenience you guys. I'll just stay awake all night and keep them away from Caleb."

"You need your sleep," I tell her. "You've gotta work tomorrow. You're staying with us."

She hesitates, so I say, "Pack up what you need. I'll hold Caleb." I use the take-charge tone I use with Jade and it works on Sara, too. She hands Caleb to me and goes to a box in the corner where she keeps her clothes.

318

Sara and Jade are both so stubborn about taking help from people that you can't give them a choice. You just have to tell them you're helping them, not ask if they want it.

"This is just for one night," Sara says, holding her box of stuff as we go down the stairs. "I'll meet you guys at your place."

"We need to stop at the store first and get some stuff," Jade says to Sara as we walk to Sara's car. "We need to get a portable crib for Caleb to sleep in. Are you okay sleeping on the couch? If not, we could get a blow-up mattress, although our couch is probably more comfortable."

"The couch is fine. And Caleb can just sleep with me."

"He's a big boy," I say, handing him to her. "He can't sleep with his mom. He needs room to stretch out. We're getting him a crib."

"Really, you don't have to do that." Sara puts Caleb in the car seat.

"Too late. We're doing it. Just follow us." I head to my car, which surprisingly hasn't been vandalized or stolen by the guys who were checking it out when we pulled in.

"Do you think she's mad at us?" Jade asks as we get in the car.

"She didn't seem mad. She seemed relieved."

"Yeah, she did." Jade reaches over and holds my hand as I drive off. "I love you."

"I love you, too." I glance over and see her smiling at me.

"I think I'm going to have to add another kid to the one I already promised you."

"Oh, yeah?" I give her hand a squeeze. "You sure you don't want to think about that some more? You just doubled the number of kids we're having."

"I know, but one just doesn't seem like enough."

"Well, if we're having two, we might as well have three. It's just one more."

She laughs. "Don't push it."

I don't think Jade's serious about having two kids. She's just saying that because she saw me with Caleb. By tomorrow she'll be back to wanting just one kid, which is fine. Like I said, one is better than none.

We stop at the store and I grab a cart and start tossing stuff in. Baby wipes, baby powder, baby shampoo.

"Garret, what are you doing?" Sara's freaking out, as I knew she would. "I can't afford all that."

"You're not paying for it. So load up."

She grabs my arm. "No. I don't want you guys buying me stuff. I have a job. I just don't make enough to afford all this." She picks up the baby shampoo. "And I never buy name brand. It costs way more than generic."

I feel like I'm reliving scenes from when I met Jade last year. Jade's standing there, not saying anything, but she's smiling at me because this money argument is so familiar. It reminds me of the first day I spent with her. She got mad at me for buying her groceries and she insisted on only buying generic brands, just like Sara's doing.

I take the baby shampoo from her and toss it back in the cart. "We're getting this one. What else do you want? Some shampoo for yourself?" I grab a bottle. "This is what Jade uses. Do you want this one or a different one?"

Jade takes it from me and opens the cap, holding it up to Sara. "Smell it. It's flowery but not too strong. And it makes your hair really soft."

She smells it. "Yeah, it smells nice, but I don't need it."

She's lying. I went in her bathroom and she had no shampoo. Just a bar of white soap that she must use on her hair.

"We'll get it anyway." I grab it and toss it in the cart. "If you don't like it, Jade will use it." I push the cart over to the diaper aisle and say to Sara, "I don't know what size he is, so go ahead and pick some out."

She puts her hands on her hips. "Okay, you guys. Stop it. This is enough. You're not buying me any more stuff. I mean it."

I look at Jade. "Should we tell her?"

Jade doesn't know what I'm going to say, but she goes along with it. "Yeah, go ahead."

I turn toward Sara, crossing my arms over my chest. "So a few weeks ago a friend of mine started a foundation to help people out with expenses. Just until they can get a good job, go to school, whatever."

Sara keeps her eyes on me. "Is this a friend from high school?"

"No. He's like five years older than me. He's a swimmer, so I'd see him at the pool and that's how we got to be friends. Anyway, he's like a computer genius and he's made all these software programs and sold them for millions of dollars. That's why he started the foundation. He's not a materialistic guy. He doesn't want all that money. He just likes developing software, and doing so makes him a lot of money."

"And he just likes to give it away?"

"Pretty much. But he likes to give money to people who deserve it. People who are working hard but just need a little help making ends meet. The other day he called and asked if I knew anyone who could be one of the first people to benefit from his foundation. So what do you think? Are you willing to take his money? Because he would really appreciate it."

Sara laughs. "You're kidding, right? Some rich guy wants to give me money?"

Jade leans in closer to her and says, "I know this guy and I'm telling you, he's got more money than he'll ever spend. And he makes more every day. He doesn't know what to do with it all."

She smiles. "Um, okay. So what do I do?"

I point to the cart. "Fill this thing up. Get whatever you want."

"But he doesn't even know me."

"I hope you're not mad, but I kind of already told him about you. And he was really impressed that you work full-time and take care of Caleb all by yourself."

"Really?"

"Yeah. He was very impressed. And then he asked if you needed help with housing and I told him I'd have to ask you first. But I think you should take him up on the offer. You could get a new apartment. You don't want to live at your current place now that you know about the cockroaches."

"He'd really do that for me? Help me with rent? Because if I got a better place, I could pay some of the rent. I just can't afford all of it."

"Then you're the perfect candidate. So should I tell him yes? You'll help him get rid of some of his money?"

She nods, tears running down her face. "Yes. Tell him thank you."

Jade hugs her. "Don't cry, Sara. This is a *good* thing."

"I can't believe a stranger would help me like this."

"He's not a total stranger." Jade smiles at me. "He's Garret's friend."

Sara looks at me, sniffling, her eyes all red. "I have to meet him or call him, so I can tell him thank you."

"He wants to remain anonymous. He's a computer nerd. You know how those guys are. He's quiet, likes to be left alone."

"Maybe I could write him a thank you letter?"

"Sure. You could do that. Just give it to me and I'll make sure he gets it." I motion to the shelves. "Now would you pick out some diapers? I'm getting hungry. We need to eat dinner, then get this guy to bed." I point to Caleb, who's sitting in the cart, yawning.

"Okay." She picks up a box of generic diapers.

"Name brand, Sara," I tell her. "We'll never spend the guy's money buying the generic."

She smiles and puts the box back. "Those generic ones always leak. I'll try these." She puts a box in the cart.

"Seriously?" I shake my head at her. "One box?"

"Sorry." She giggles and adds another box.

I sigh and grab three more boxes and throw them in the cart. Jade's laughing.

We make our way through the store, filling the cart with baby clothes, baby food, a few toys, the portable crib, and some food and clothes for Sara. I fill the trunk of her car with as much as I can fit in there and put the rest of the stuff in my car. Then we get a pizza and go back to our place.

I really needed to study for finals tonight, but this was more important. We had to get Sara and Caleb out of that place. And as for that fake foundation I told Sara about? I've decided to make it real. I'm going to give money anonymously to people like Sara, who work hard but still need a little help to pay their bills. It felt good to do that for her and Caleb, and I know there are a lot more people out there who are just like her.

The next morning, Sara leaves early for work and takes Caleb to day care. Jade left, too, because she has a final this morning at eight.

Jade's picking Sara up during Sara's lunch break and they're going to see if they can find an apartment. They went online last night and found one that looks decent and is in a better part of town and doesn't cost too much. It's the middle of the month so I'm not sure if they'll let her move in right away, but there's no way she's staying at her current apartment over Christmas. I'm sure Alex would let her stay with him or she can stay here. She'd have the place to herself while Jade and I are gone.

My next final isn't for an hour so I call my dad to see if he's around.

"Yes, Garret." He sounds rushed.

"Can you talk? It's important."

"Just a minute." I hear him telling someone to leave and the door closing. "Okay, go ahead."

"Kiefer showed up on campus yesterday. I tried to get him to leave but he wouldn't. He followed me all the way to the parking lot."

"Garret, if someone was following him and saw him talking to you—"

"There was nobody around. I checked."

"They don't stand out in plain sight. You wouldn't know if they were there."

"Well, what was I supposed to do? Kiefer wouldn't leave me alone. And then he told me this stuff about Harper and—"

"Garret, I know Harper is your friend but you can't let your feelings get in the way of your safety."

"Yeah, I got it. I'll stay out of it."

"So what was the purpose of Kiefer's visit?"

"He told me he doesn't want to join. He wanted me to ask you for help. He thinks you can get him out of this."

"I can't. It's too late now."

"I thought the initiation isn't until January."

"Yes, but this process started months ago and Kiefer's been given information only members are allowed to have. He doesn't know everything, but he knows more than he should as an outsider."

"If he doesn't agree to be a member, what do you think they'll do to him?"

"I don't know. This is all new territory for us, accepting outsiders like this. He'll face punishment of some kind. But that's not your concern, so I don't want you asking about it and I don't want you talking to Kiefer. If he shows up there again, just walk away." He pauses and I hear him typing on his computer. "Oh, I wanted to tell you that I just signed the paperwork for the divorce."

"Really? I thought you two would spend months fighting over everything."

"We'd already discussed the terms, so there was nothing left to fight over."

"What about Lilly?"

"I'm getting full custody."

"Did Katherine sign the papers?"

"Yes, so we're officially divorced."

"Shit, that's awesome. I never thought this would happen."

"Don't mention it to Lilly. We aren't going to tell her until after the holidays. Katherine will be staying at the house until the end of the year. Garret, I have people waiting outside my door for a meeting so I need to hang up. Good luck with your finals."

"Thanks. Bye."

I slide my phone in my pocket and grab my backpack and keys. I need to go to the library and study. I have two more finals today, and with everything going on I feel like I haven't studied enough. I'm doing well in my classes, so it's not like I have to get all A's on my finals but a mix of A's and B's would be good.

When I get to campus, my phone rings as I'm walking to the library. I stop when I see it's Kiefer calling. What the hell? I told him to leave me alone. I consider not answering, but I do because I don't want him to keep calling.

"You can't call me," I say when I answer. "If they found out—"

"I'm telling them no," he says, his voice frantic. "I can't do it. I can't be part of this. And there's no way that man's getting my daughter."

I move off to the side, away from the people that were around me. "Did you tell them yet?"

"No. I'm going to as soon as we hang up. Did you talk to your father?"

"Yeah, but he can't help you."

"Did he say what the punishment would be?"

"He doesn't know. It's not up to him."

"Oh, God, they're going to kill me."

I don't deny it, because truthfully, they might actually kill them. I thought they might keep him around for his movie-making skills, but like my dad said, Kiefer knows more than he should. He's been given information he can't have as an outsider.

"I have to go," I tell him. "I need to study for my final."

"Of course. I'm sorry I bothered you." He pauses. "I just wanted you to know, because I know how much you and Jade love Harper." His voice cracks. "She'll be safe if I do this, right?"

Shit. Why is he asking me this? How the hell would I know the answer to that? The organization does what they want. They make up their own rules.

"I really need to go," I say.

"Tell me she'll be safe!" He yells it. "Please. Just tell me she'll be safe." His voice cracks again. I think he might be crying.

"I can't," I say quietly. "I don't know what's going to happen. You need to fix this, Kiefer, and leave me out of it. And you need to stop calling me. I can't help you. I'm sorry."

I hang up and he doesn't call back. I wasn't trying to be mean to the guy, but he can't keep calling me or showing up here. He's putting me in danger and it pisses me off. What if they're tracking his calls? I don't want them knowing I've been talking to him.

I go to the library and open my laptop and the Internet pops up with an ad for Kiefer's next movie. Like I need yet another reminder about Kiefer. I'm trying to get him out of my head so I can study. But now, all I can think about is how they're going to punish him. If he agrees to never tell their secrets, maybe they'll leave him alone. Yeah, that won't happen. They love to punish people to show how powerful they are. I just hope they only punish Kiefer and not the rest of his family.

# Chapter 32

## JADE

"So what do you think?" I spread my arms out, showing off the apartment. Sara and I just got here and the landlady stepped out in the hall to make a phone call.

"I love it." Sara smiles really wide as her eyes dart around the room. "It's so big. I'm not used to all this space."

The apartment has two bedrooms so Sara and Caleb can each have their own room. The place looks kind of dated, but it's clean and there aren't any loose wires anywhere. I don't see any mold, and the water coming out of the faucet is clear, not brown.

"It's in a great neighborhood," I say. "And it seems really quiet. Plus, when we drove in I saw some playground equipment next to the building."

"This place is perfect. And like you said, it's a great location. But do you really think I should get it? I still feel weird letting Garret's friend pay for part of the rent."

"Why? He wants to do it. Garret called him last night and told him and he said he's happy he could help."

"Okay, I'll do it." She squeals and hugs me. "I'm so excited about this!"

"Let's go fill out the paperwork and find out when you can move in."

After Sara fills out the forms, the landlady reviews them. Sara has a nearly empty bank account and her job pays next to nothing so I'm worried the lady won't rent her the apartment. And from the look on her face, I can tell she's about to turn Sara down. So before she can say anything, I introduce myself to the lady, making sure to say my last name and that I'm Pearce Kensington's daughter-in-law. When I tell her I'm really good friends with Sara, she's suddenly much more receptive to Sara living there.

I've never dropped the Kensington name before to get people to do stuff because it seems really lame to do that. But in this case I needed to or she wouldn't have rented to Sara. Then I wrote a check for the first six month's rent and the woman agreed to let Sara move in today. So I've now seen firsthand how money and a powerful last name can get things done.

I didn't let Sara see the check I wrote. I told her it was a signed check from the foundation and I just filled in the amount. Then I told her Garret's friend insisted on paying all the rent for the first six months and that she could help pay for the rent later on. She was thrilled about that, because even paying just half of the first month's rent would've cleared out her bank account.

We get the keys to her apartment, then bring in all the stuff we packed in her trunk last night. She has to get back to work, so she'll put everything away later.

"Jade, I can't even tell you how happy this makes me," she says as we're driving to the coffee shop. "If it were just me, I wouldn't care where I lived, but with Caleb, I..." Her voice trails off and a tear sneaks down her cheek.

"I know, Sara." I smile at her. "But now you both have a safe and quiet place to live. And Caleb's going to love it."

She nods and wipes her cheek. "He will. Now he'll be able to crawl on the floor. I didn't let him do that at the other place and he'd get really mad at me. The boy just wants to crawl." She laughs.

"I can help you move when you get off work. Garret has to study, so I don't how much time he'll have to help but—"

"Don't worry about it. Alex gets back in town later today so he's going to help me. You and Garret have done enough and you both need to study for finals."

"What's Alex think about you moving?"

"He's so relieved. He hated my old place. He said it was too dangerous, but he didn't have enough money to help me get a different place. And even if he did, I didn't want him paying my rent. But he did offer to buy me a new bed as a Christmas present."

"A bed, huh?" I tease. "Like maybe one you could both fit in?"

"No!" She jabs my arm. "He's buying it because he thinks I need one."

"You do. You need to replace that twin mattress."

"We're going shopping for a new one tonight. He's getting me a queen mattress with a frame so it doesn't have to sit on the floor."

"That's sweet of him."

"I know. I really love—" She catches herself and her cheeks blush. "I have to go."

We're parked in front of the coffee shop now and she opens the car door to leave.

I grab her arm. "Wait. Did you just say you love Alex?"

"I have to go or I'll be late." She steps out of the car.

"Sara. *Do* you?"

She smiles really wide and nods, then shuts the door and hurries into the coffee shop.

I'm so happy for her. She found a guy she loves, and from the things she says about him, I think he loves her, too. And now she'll be living in a better apartment and has plenty of diapers and baby clothes and other baby supplies.

I love Garret so much for finding a way to help out Sara like that. He was desperate to do something after he saw how she was living. I felt the same way, but I didn't know how to get her to accept our help. But his made-up foundation was perfect. And I've been thinking that maybe we should make his fake foundation real, to help out people like Sara.

Garret gets home at four-thirty. Before I can tell him about Sara, he says, "The divorce is final. My dad's finally rid of Katherine."

"Are you serious? Did they sign the papers?"

"Yes. It's official. He is no longer married to Katherine. But they're not going to tell Lilly until after the holidays, so unfortunately Katherine will be living at the house through the end of the year."

"That sucks."

"I know, but it's probably best for Lilly." He pulls me down to sit on the couch with him. "I have some other news." His face has that serious expression I don't like.

I sigh. "What now? More bad news?"

"I'm not sure yet."

I roll my eyes. "You need to explain what that means. And hurry up. You're freaking me out here."

"Kiefer called. He's going to tell them he's not accepting their membership offer. Actually, he's probably already told them. He called me earlier today and was going to tell them right after he hung up with me."

"You haven't heard back from him?"

"No. I told him to stop calling me."

"So what does this mean? Harper won't have to marry that guy?"

"I don't know. I mean, if Harper was part of the deal and now Kiefer broke the deal, then she should be safe. But…"

"But what? You think that guy will still try to take her? He can't do that."

331

"If they abide by the rules of the deal, then no. But I get the feeling this Andrew guy doesn't like following rules." Garret sees the worry on my face and brings me in for a hug. "For now, let's just go with the idea that she's safe."

As much as I'd like to believe that, I won't until I know for sure. But I feel some relief knowing Kiefer's not going to be part of the organization.

I sit back. "If he's not going to be a member, then I can still be friends with Harper." I wait for Garret to respond. He doesn't, so I say it again. "I can still be friends with her, right?"

"I don't want to say you can until we know for sure. And we won't know that until we know Andrew's going to leave her alone. For now, you should just try to act normal around her so she doesn't suspect something's wrong."

"How long do you think it'll be until we know about Andrew?"

"I have no idea. But, Jade, we're not going to spend time worrying about it. We have to focus on finals and then it's Christmas, and we're not letting this ruin the holidays."

My shoulders slump. "But I'm really worried about Harper."

"We can't do anything about it, Jade."

"I know, but—" I can't finish because he starts tickling my sides, pushing me back on the couch. I squirm, trying to get away from him. "What are you doing?"

"Distracting you from thinking about Harper. I'm going to keep tickling you until you stop worrying."

"Okay, stop!" I'm laughing so hard my stomach hurts.

He stops, but keeps his hands close to the tickle zone. "Are you still worrying?"

"Nope." I tense up, preparing for more tickling.

But instead he kisses me. "You're lying, but I'll let you rest a minute." He sits back. "So how'd it go with Sara?"

"Great. That place was perfect for her." I tell him about the apartment and about how excited she was and that Alex is getting her a bed.

"Oh—and get this! Sara loves Alex!" I say it in a higher-than-normal voice.

Garret laughs at me. "Are you taking credit for that?"

I laugh. "I should, shouldn't I? I totally pushed her to go out with him. They're really happy together. Just like us." I kiss him. "Hey, I had another idea."

"You want to turn my fake foundation into a real one?" He smiles.

I huff. "How did you know that?"

"I had the same idea."

"Then let's do it. Except I don't know how to set up a foundation."

"I'll do it. Maybe I'll set it up after the holidays."

"Speaking of the holidays, you know what we should do?" I don't wait for him to answer. "We should get Sara a Christmas tree. We'll tell her it's a present from us since she doesn't know we gave her that other stuff."

"Okay, but I can't get it tonight. I really need to study. Maybe we could get it on Friday. Actually, I might be too tired to get out of bed on Friday. We'll just order her one and have it delivered."

"Sounds good." I get up but he grabs my hand.

"Where are you going?"

"I'm leaving you alone so you can study."

"I need to spend time with my wife first."

"What would you like to do?" I straddle his lap, smiling.

He grasps the back of my neck and brings me in for a kiss. His fingers tangle in my hair as his kiss goes deeper. I grind my hips into him and feel him against me and it gets me all hot inside. His other hand goes between us and he unbuttons my shirt. When he's done, I take it off, then lift up on my knees, my breasts level with his face. I bury my hands in his soft hair as he leaves kisses along the outline of my bra, but he doesn't take it off. Instead, he keeps gently kissing the outline of it, his hands grasping my waist, keeping me firmly in place. The tension inside me keeps building and I know that's why he's doing it. His teasing kills me. I love it, but it kills me.

Finally, he hoists me up in his arms and takes me to the bedroom, laying me down on the bed. I finish undressing, watching as he strips his clothes off. He lies over me, but I push on his chest, stopping him. "Let me be on top."

"Are you sure?" He's surprised because I usually don't like being on top.

"Yeah." I sit up and he pulls me over him as he lowers himself down on his back. I straddle him and guide him inside me. He grabs my hips pulling me into him as he pushes up. I close my eyes and focus on how he feels. I keep my hips moving as his hands roam over my backside, then up my front and along my breasts. I open my eyes and trace his gaze over my body. I don't like being on top because one, I don't know what I'm doing, and two, Garret always looks at my body like this and I get self-conscious.

"Okay, your turn," I tell him, getting that self-conscious feeling.

"You're not going anywhere." He holds my hips in place. "I'm loving this way too much." He flashes his sexy smile, then his eyes follow the path of his hand as it glides over my breast and down the side of my hip. "Damn, you're hot. Every part of you is so fucking beautiful."

I swear he knows exactly what to say. It's like he senses the moment I feel self-conscious and says what I need to hear to make those feelings go away.

His words boost my confidence and I move a little faster, positioning myself to feel him deeper. I usually don't get much pleasure out of this position because I'm too worried about *him*, but this time I focus on myself instead, grinding into him in a rhythm that makes the sensations inside me build and build and then finally release.

I stop and feel Garret's hands gripping my hips, urging me to keep going, and I do until he releases as well. Then I lie over him, my head on his chest.

He kisses my forehead and strokes my hair. "We should do that more often."

"Have sex? I think we do it enough already."

"I mean, do it like that. With you on top. I love being able to look at you. All of you. And being able to touch you."

"I'm not very good at it."

"Jade, you always say that and it's not true. You're good at it. And I think you actually liked it that time."

I lift my head up to look at him. "What do you mean? I liked it before."

"No. Whenever we do it like that, you're never satisfied. You worry too much about me."

I sigh. "How do you know all this? Do you read my mind or something?"

He kisses me. "I know you better than anyone."

"You don't know if I'm satisfied or not. And for the record, I am."

"*Now* you are, but in the past when you're the one on top, you haven't been. I can tell."

"You can?" I drop my head on his shoulder. "That's so embarrassing."

He laughs. "Why do you get so embarrassed around me? Especially now, after we've been together all this time?"

"I don't know," I mumble. "I just do."

"Jade." He waits for me to look at him. "I'm your husband. You never have to be embarrassed around me. You can say or do anything around me and I'll still love you and think you're sweet and adorable and beautiful and the perfect woman."

"Thank you." I smile. "But I'll still get embarrassed."

"Then we'll just have to keep working on that." He swats my butt. "Now get off me. I gotta study."

"No cuddle time?" I'm just kidding, but I try to sound really sad.

He sees my sad face. "Okay. But not all night. I really need to study."

"I was kidding." I hit his arm. "I don't want to cuddle. I need to get away from you so I can cool off. I'm dripping sweat after you made me do all your work."

"You're the one who wanted to be on top. Now get up." He tickles my sides until I move off him.

As he's getting dressed, I say, "Shouldn't we take a shower? We're both sweaty."

He holds his shirt, not putting it on. "Jade. Stop tempting me with sex. I need to study."

"Who said anything about sex?" I stand in front of him, letting my hands roam over his lower abs.

He sighs. "Let's go."

I laugh as he drags me to the shower.

And after that, I leave him alone so he can study. I study, too, because I have another final tomorrow.

Finals week turned out to be not so bad, at least not for me. I only had to take three finals. Garret had five and he tends to wait until the last minute to study so he hasn't slept much all week.

We haven't heard anything more from Kiefer, but Garret called his dad, and although Pearce couldn't say much, he did confirm that Kiefer turned down the membership offer. So now Kiefer awaits his punishment.

As for Andrew, we still don't know anything. I've been trying to do as Garret says and not think about it, but I still do. Harper's my best friend. Of course I'm going to think about it. But I'm trying to keep my thoughts positive. If Kiefer isn't a member, Harper should be free to be with whoever she wants. Maybe if I just keep thinking that, it'll be true.

Now it's Friday and finals are over. We slept in this morning, then spent the day packing because tomorrow we leave for Connecticut.

Garret and I are really tired, but I promised Sara we'd go out for dinner with her and Alex tonight. We keep saying we will and we never do, so I can't cancel on her now that we finally made plans. Her Christmas tree was delivered this afternoon so she called me and thanked me like a million times. She was so excited. She and Alex are going to decorate it this weekend.

At six, we all meet at a restaurant that specializes in different types of burgers with crazy toppings. They also brew beer, so it's a hangout for college students, but families with kids come here, too.

We're sitting in a booth, with Caleb at the end of the table in a high chair, chewing on his toys. He's funny. He chews on anything he can get his hands on.

"So when are you guys leaving for Christmas?" I ask Sara. She and Caleb are going with Alex to his parents' house for the holiday.

"Next Thursday. I have to work in the morning, so we'll leave in the afternoon. Alex's mom wants us there for Christmas Eve. She makes a big brunch in the morning and then everyone hangs out there all day."

"Holidays at my house are insane," Alex says, smiling. "I don't know if Sara told you, but my family is huge and they

337

all come to my parents' house for the holidays. The place will be packed. It's the same way at Thanksgiving."

"I can't wait," Sara says to me. "We had so much fun at Thanksgiving. Everyone in his family is awesome."

Alex hugs her into his side and kisses her cheek. "You need to spend more time with them before you decide that."

I haven't seen these two together for months, and back then they weren't dating. Now that they are, I can see how much they like each other. They're across the table from us and Sara's tucked under Alex's arm. She's so short and small that she makes Alex look like a big guy even though he's not. He's about 5'8 and on the thin side. Not skinny, but he's not a muscular guy. He's into art and movies and music, not working out. But he does like sports, which gives him something to talk about with Garret, who could literally talk about sports for hours. In fact, he's done that with Sean. I don't know how anyone can talk that long about sports. Harper loves sports and even she can't talk about it for hours.

"Alex's nieces are so cute," Sara says.

"Cute?" Alex gives Sara a funny look. "On Thanksgiving, they took Caleb and we couldn't find him. And then they put some girly headband on him and almost painted his nails."

She laughs. "They were just playing."

"You need to have him hang out with your nephews," Garret says to Alex.

"They don't want to be around a baby. They want to be outside playing ball. But my nieces go crazy whenever someone brings a baby over."

"Can I get you something to drink?" The waitress stands next to Caleb at the end of the table. She's a cute blonde, wearing black, very tight shorts and a white cotton shirt with the sleeves rolled up and unbuttoned to the point that it shows a lot of cleavage. It's a revealing uniform, which means she probably gets good tips from the college guys hoping to get a date with her.

Sara and I order soda and Alex orders a beer. Then Garret orders a soda and the waitress says, "You sure you don't want a beer? They're on special tonight."

"No, thanks." He looks at his menu.

"Have you ever tried one of our craft beers? If not, I can bring you some samples so you can see which one you like."

"Thanks, but I'm not quite 21 yet."

"Oh, sorry." She points to my hand. "I saw her ring and thought you two were married."

"We *are* married, but we're only 20."

She gives us that confused look people always give us whenever we tell them we're married. But then Caleb distracts her by pulling on her shirt and smiling at her.

"Hi, sweetie." She leans down and her cleavage is practically in his face. He stares at her boobs, which is kind of funny. She looks at me and says, "He's so sweet. What's his name?"

"Caleb. But he's not mine. He's hers." I point to Sara.

"He's really cute," the waitress says to Sara.

"Thank you."

The girl seems flustered as she straightens up and turns to Garret. "Did you decide what you want to drink?"

"I think I ordered a Coke."

"Yeah, that's right. Sorry. I'll be right back."

She leaves and Sara laughs. "I told you being a waitress isn't easy. You have to be friendly, but you can't make assumptions about people. It always gets you in trouble."

"I forgot you guys are only 20," Alex says. "You seem older. Maybe because you're married."

"Yeah, we're old married people now," I say, looping my arm with Garret's. "It's almost our six month anniversary. We're not even newlyweds anymore."

"Yes, we are." Garret leans down and gives me a kiss.

Caleb squeals and we all look over at him. He's pumping his arms up and down and staring at the floor, where his toy fell.

"I got it." Alex gives it back to him, then tickles Caleb's belly. "I saw you checking out that girl. I think she's a little old for you."

"He was totally checking her out," I say, laughing.

"I know, right?" Sara laughs, too. "He couldn't stop staring at her boobs. I thought he was going to reach out and grab one, like he does to me all the time. I would've been so embarrassed if he did that."

"You might want to work on being a little more discreet next time," Garret tells Caleb. "You can get away with staring like that when you're nine months old, but later, if you look at a girl like that, she'll slap you."

We all laugh.

The waitress returns with the drinks and Caleb stares at her cleavage again as she leans over to set our drinks down. Sara and I start laughing. I don't want the waitress to think we're laughing at her so I try to stop, but Caleb won't look away from her chest and it's just too funny.

When she leaves, Sara says, "Maybe he thinks they're balloons. Or some kind of toy."

The guys laugh.

"I think guys a lot older than him also think they're toys," Alex says.

Sara rolls her eyes as her cheeks turn pink. "We need to change the subject. And if he does that again, you need to distract him."

"It's nature, Sara," Garret says. "You can't stop it."

"Boys." I roll my eyes and she laughs.

Sara and I ignore the guys and she tells me more about Alex's family, while the guys talk about football. Of course. What else would they talk about?

Our food arrives and we continue our separate conversations. During dinner, I notice Alex bringing out a jar of baby food and some finger foods for Caleb to eat. He feeds Caleb in between eating his own meal. It's like Caleb is his own kid. Sara glances over at them now and then, but otherwise just keeps talking.

It's nice seeing Alex helping out with Caleb like that. It makes me think that maybe Alex might consider marrying Sara someday. I think she'd like that. I guess I don't know. She's never shared her opinion on marriage.

We order dessert, and as we're waiting for it, I decide we need to do this double date thing again. We all get along really well.

"Dinner's on me tonight," Alex announces.

"You don't have to do that," Garret says.

"You guys really helped out Sara and Caleb and I want to show my appreciation. I tried to get her out of that apartment for months and she wouldn't accept my help, but you finally convinced her to move, so I owe you."

"Thanks," I tell him. "That's really nice of you."

Caleb starts fussing and Sara nudges Alex. "Can you take him out of the high chair? He's been in there too long."

Alex lifts him up and hands him to Sara. The three of them already look like a family. Sara and Alex look like they go together and Caleb could easily pass for Alex's kid.

Dessert arrives and halfway through eating it, I'm stuffed.

"I can't finish that." I push my brownie sundae away.

"Their desserts are huge," Sara says. "We should've split one." She holds Caleb up to Alex. "Could you take him? I need to wipe his sticky face."

He takes Caleb, whose chubby cheeks are covered in chocolate ice cream. As Sara's cleaning up Caleb's face, a guy stops by our table.

"Sara," he says, trying to get her attention.

She looks up at the guy. Her expression is a mix of shock and panic.

"Brandon. What are you doing here?"

He nods toward the bar. "I'm getting a beer with Kyle. I came down to see him for a couple days."

"Okay. Well, have fun." Her eyes shift down to the table.

She seems really uncomfortable. Maybe she used to date this guy. He's not much taller than Alex, maybe 5'10, but he's much wider, with a muscular, stocky build. He's got short, medium-brown hair and dark brown eyes and stubble along his face. He's wearing khaki shorts and a bright green polo shirt that looks too tight on his arms.

"So how've you been, Sara?" He directs his body toward her, crossing his arms over his chest.

"You should get back to the bar." She tosses her scrunched-up napkin on the table. "We were just leaving."

He peers down at Alex. "Aren't you going to introduce me?"

Sara glares at Brandon but he doesn't notice. His eyes are still on Alex. She says really fast, "This is Alex and those are my friends, Jade and Garret."

Brandon points to Caleb, who's still on Alex's lap. "Is that our kid?"

"Yes." Sara takes Caleb and holds him against her chest.

Holy crap! That's Caleb's dad? Sara never told me his name. She hardly ever talks about him.

Before I even knew who this guy was, I could tell he was an ass, just by the way he came over here and acted like we should all stop what we're doing and pay attention to him.

"Let me see him," Brandon says.

Sara slowly turns Caleb around and sits him on her lap. "His name's Caleb."

"Who came up with that stupid name?"

342

I see both Garret and Alex tense up.

"Obviously, *I* named him since you weren't around for his birth." Sara sounds pissed. Good for her.

"You're the one who wanted it. I gave you the money to take care of it."

"You need to leave," Alex says to him.

"Who are *you?* The new boyfriend?"

"Brandon, just leave," Sara says. "Go back to the bar."

He leans down in front of Alex, placing his palms on the table. "Are you trying to play dad to my kid?"

Alex looks him in the eye. "You're clearly not interested in the job."

Sara holds Alex's arm. "Alex, just ignore him. He'll go away."

"I'm not going anywhere," Brandon says, a big smirk on his face.

Alex keeps quiet. I can almost see the wheels spinning in his head as he tries to figure out what to do. Sara doesn't want him to get in a fight, but Alex wants to stand up for her. And I'm sure he'd love to beat up Brandon for leaving Sara alone with a baby and no money. The problem is, Alex isn't a fighter.

"Just leave," Alex says, staring at Brandon.

"Make me, tough guy."

Even if Alex wanted to fight him, there's no way he would win a fight with this guy. Brandon may not be much taller than Alex, but he's way bigger.

"You gonna just sit there, or are you gonna do something?" Brandon says, trying to provoke him.

Alex doesn't answer. He seems nervous, his eyes darting everywhere but at Brandon.

"Alex." Garret waits for Alex to look at him. "You mind if I step in?"

"Go ahead."

Great. Just what I need. My husband getting into a fight.

"Garret, don't," I say quietly to him.

He gets out of the booth and stands next to Brandon. He looks like a giant next to Brandon. Garret's a lot taller and he's been working out constantly to get his shoulder back in shape, so he's really muscular. Way bigger than when I met him.

Garret holds his hand out. "Garret Kensington."

Brandon looks confused. He wasn't expecting the handshake, but he shakes Garret's hand. "Brandon Lintz."

"That's lesson number one. When you're introduced to someone, you look them in the eye, you shake their hand, you smile. Basic manners."

"What the hell does—"

"Lesson number two." Garret glances over at Sara. "Cover his ears."

"What?" Sara's confused.

"Cover Caleb's ears."

She does, and Garret continues talking to Brandon. "Lesson number two. You treat the mother of your child with respect. I don't give a shit if you don't like her, don't want to date her, don't want to marry her. The woman gave birth to your child. By herself. With no support. And you're going to treat her with respect."

"I didn't even want the fucking kid. I told her to get rid of it."

Garret checks to make sure Caleb's ears are still covered. "You think she didn't deserve a say in that?"

He waves his hand at Sara. "The bitch got her way. The kid's right there."

"Already forgot lesson number two, huh? You're clearly too fucking dumb to comprehend any more of my lessons, so we're done for today. Now do as Sara asked, and Alex asked, and get the fuck out of here."

"I get it." Brandon laughs. "You and Sara. Makes sense." He looks at Alex. "I didn't think she'd go out with that loser."

"Alex is her boyfriend. Not me. And before you open your mouth again to show us how fucking stupid you are, turn around and walk your ass out the door."

"I'm not leaving. I still got a full beer left at the bar."

Garret sighs. "I'm not going to say it again."

"I don't give a fuck how many times you say it. I'm not leaving."

Caleb starts crying.

"Get that thing to shut up," Brandon says to Sara.

Garret gets in Brandon's face. "I didn't want to hurt you, but what the hell? I love beating up assholes like you."

"Garret, no!" I scoot to the end of the booth. "You'll get arrested again."

Brandon steps back. "You got arrested for fighting?"

Garret slowly smiles. "Yeah. I did. Arrested and thrown in jail. For beating up an asshole just like you. The guy had no manners. Treated women like shit. I started punching him and I couldn't stop. I have a bad temper and my rage just took over. I broke his nose, bruised every square inch of his body, and pounded his face in the wall so hard he went unconscious."

Brandon looks scared. Like seriously scared. He takes another step back. "And you only got jail time? You should be locked in prison for something like that."

Garret shrugs. "I've got friends in high places. And friends in places you'd never want to go, unless you had a death wish."

Brandon's staring at Garret, breathing fast. I think I even see his forehead sweating. That story about Garret beating up Blake really freaked Brandon out. Hearing Garret describe it, it did sound pretty bad and yet that's exactly what happened. Damn, my husband's a real badass. Not that I like him beating people up, but Blake deserved it.

"This is bullshit," Brandon says, walking backward, away from Garret. "I'm outta here."

Garret watches him. "Hey. Before you go, I need you to apologize to Sara."

"For what?"

"Breaking up with her when she got pregnant. Leaving her with nothing. Not paying child support. I could go on all day."

Brandon looks at Sara, then back at Garret. But he doesn't apologize.

Garret crosses his arms over his chest, which makes his biceps appear even bigger. He keeps his eyes on Brandon, giving him a look of warning.

Brandon lets out an annoyed sigh and looks at Sara again. "I'm sorry, Sara."

Sara's too speechless to answer.

"See? That wasn't so hard." Garret nods toward the exit. "You can go now."

Brandon turns and walks out the door.

A guy from the bar yells, "Brandon, where are you going?"

Garret checks who it is, then sits back down in the booth. "You've gotta be kidding me."

"What?" I ask him.

"Brandon's friend is Kyle, the guy who keeps calling me, trying to get me to introduce him to my dad."

"Brandon used to be on the football team with Kyle," Sara says. "They're good friends."

"I knew I hated that guy." Garret takes a drink of his water.

"Did you really get arrested for fighting?" Alex asks Garret.

"Yeah, but it was back in high school. I made it sound worse than it was."

I'm glad Garret didn't tell him the truth. I don't want Sara or Alex thinking Garret's violent.

The waitress stops by and drops off the check. "Did Brandon leave?"

"Yeah. Why?" Sara says, as she rubs Caleb's back. He's falling asleep now.

"I hate that guy. Last year he was always in here grabbing my ass and trying to get me to go out with him." She shudders. "I was so happy when he left town. He didn't move back here, did he?"

"No, he's in San Francisco now."

"They can have him." She smiles. "You guys can pay whenever you want. No rush."

Alex drops some cash on the check. "It's all set."

She picks up the money. "Thanks. Have a good night."

"We should go," Alex says to Sara.

"Yeah, I need to get Caleb to bed." She reaches under the table for her purse.

We all get out of the booth and Garret goes up to Alex. "Hey. Are we good? I didn't mean to step in like that but—"

"No, I'm glad you did. If you want to come over and watch a game when you guys get back from your trip, just let me know."

"You guys are watching a game?" Sara asks. "Why can't us girls come over?"

Alex kisses her cheek. "You can. I just didn't think you'd want to watch the game."

"Jade and I could still come over. You want to, Jade?"

"Sure. We'll talk when I get back and figure it out."

"Have a good trip." Sara gives me a hug. "See you guys later."

On the drive home, I say to Garret, "I can't believe Caleb's dad showed up tonight."

"*I* can't believe Sara dated that guy."

"She doesn't have good self-esteem so she puts up with stuff she shouldn't."

He holds my hand. "If we have a daughter someday, we're gonna make damn sure she feels good about herself so she doesn't put up with guys like that."

"With you as her dad, every guy she dates is going to seem like a loser. She'll never be able to go out with anyone."

"Good. Just the way I want it."

He's not joking. If we have a daughter, no guy will ever be good enough for her.

# Chapter 33

**GARRET**

When we get home from the restaurant I turn on the TV, and the horror movie Jade made me take her to last year for her birthday is on.

"Jade, remember this one? It's that shit movie you made us go to last year."

"Yeah, I didn't like that one." She sits on my lap and slips her sweater off. Then she reaches behind her back and unhooks her bra and tosses it on the floor.

"Are we watching TV naked tonight?" My eyes go right to her breasts. It reminds me of Caleb staring at the waitress. Doesn't matter what age we are, we can't help ourselves. Our eyes just go there.

"I'm not really in the mood for TV."

"I'm not either anymore." I click the TV off. "So what brought *this* on?"

"What do you mean?" She stands up and turns around, her ass facing me as she takes her jeans off, leaving her in just her black string bikinis.

"You usually don't want to have sex the second we get home." I grab hold of her hips and pull her down on my lap.

"I do tonight." She reaches back and strokes my face, her fingers landing on my lips.

"Any reason why?" I kiss each of her fingers as I cup her breast with my hand and slide my other hand down her stomach and under her bikinis.

She arches back at my touch. "I just got really turned on watching you tonight."

"Watching me what?"

"Take down Brandon. You were a total badass. I liked it."

"I was far worse in high school."

"I like this version better." She grinds her ass into me as I touch her, her arched back displaying her breasts right under my face. Fucking hot.

"We need to move to the bedroom," I tell her.

She smiles, tilting her head to the side. "But I like it right here."

"So do I." I talk next to her ear. "But I've got too many clothes on for what I'd like to do to you."

"You're such a bad boy." She pushes off me and stands up.

"You love it." I swat her ass. "Now get in there."

We have sex a couple times before finally going to sleep. I didn't know Jade would get so turned on by me yelling at Brandon. I thought she might get mad about it and we'd have to talk about it when we got home. But instead we had sex. Yeah, I love my wife.

The next morning we get up early and head to the airport for our flight to Connecticut. I almost wish we weren't going. This is our first Christmas as a married couple and I really wanted it to be special. But instead it's going to be tense and uncomfortable because of Katherine. I know she has to be there for Lilly's sake, but I still don't want her around.

We'll also have to deal with my grandmother, who will be judging everything I do and say, and ignoring Jade. When I was there for the memorial, I thought my grandmother might be starting to change now that my grandfather is gone. She gave me a hug, a real hug, not one of her distant hugs. I took that as a sign she was changing. But then after that, she hardly talked to me. And when I left, she didn't even call or stop by the house to say goodbye. So I don't know what to expect at Christmas. I'm assuming she'll be back to her old self.

Christmas is a week from today and we're not leaving until the following Monday, which means we have eight days with my family. That'd be great if it were just Lilly and my dad, but adding Katherine to the mix will make those eight days go by excruciatingly slow.

The wheels of the plane touch down and Jade stirs a little in her seat. She's been asleep the entire flight. She usually wakes up when the flight staff makes all those announcements about the plane preparing to land. This time she didn't wake up, so I let her sleep until the plane comes to a stop.

Her face is against my shoulder. I kiss her forehead. "Time to get up, sleepy girl."

"Are we almost there?" she mumbles.

"We just landed."

She sits up. "But I just fell asleep."

"You fell asleep hours ago." I unfasten my seatbelt and grab our carry-on bags.

She hangs onto the back of my shirt as we exit the plane. She's still groggy, yawning as we walk through the terminal.

"Ready for a week with my family?" I ask her.

She perks up. "Yeah, I can't wait."

"You do know Katherine will be there, right?"

She laughs and loops her arm in mine. "Yes, Garret. You've reminded me a million times and I told you, I'm not letting her ruin Christmas. I'll just ignore her."

"Maybe we should've gone to Frank's house."

"He wants to be with his girlfriend. He doesn't want us hanging around."

Frank is still dating Karen and they're spending the holiday together. It sounds like they're getting pretty serious. He'll probably marry Karen before Ryan marries Chloe.

Ryan and Chloe are spending Christmas in Florida with her sister, who lives in Tampa. Her parents will be there, too. Then the day after Christmas, Ryan and Chloe are driving down to the Florida Keys for vacation. It'll be the first time Ryan's had a real vacation.

"We could've stayed home," I say to Jade. "Had our own Christmas. Just the two of us."

"Why are you acting like this? I thought you *wanted* to be here for Christmas."

"I do. I just don't want our Christmas ruined by Katherine."

"We had a great Christmas last year even though she was there, so we'll have a great one this year, too."

I love that Jade has such a good attitude about this. My grandmother ignores her. Katherine's mean to her. And yet Jade still wants to be here for Christmas.

We go past the security checkpoint area and I stop and give her a kiss. "I love you."

She smiles. "I love you, too."

"Garret! Jade!" Lilly comes running up to us, slamming into our legs. "Merry Christmas!"

"Merry Christmas." Jade hugs her.

Lilly holds her arms out to me. I pick her up. "Where's Dad?"

"Over there." She points to him as he walks toward us.

"She ran ahead of me." He goes up and hugs Jade. "Welcome back."

She laughs. "I know. We were just here. You're going to be sick of us by the end of the week."

"Not at all. I wish you two lived closer so I could see you every day." He smiles at me. "Garret."

"Hey, Dad." I half hug him since Lilly's attached to me.

I set Lilly down and she grabs my hand as we walk to the baggage area. "Daddy said we can watch a movie tonight."

I can't imagine Katherine going along with that. She'll be doing everything she can to keep Lilly busy so Jade and I can't spend time with her.

"Is your mom going to watch the movie with us?"

"Mom isn't home." She swings our arms back and forth as we walk.

"Where is she?"

Lilly shrugs. "I don't know. Dad said she had to go somewhere. She won't be back till after Christmas."

Katherine's gone? For the entire week? That can't be right. Lilly must be confused.

I look back and see Jade and my dad talking.

"Dad." I wait until I have his attention. "Did Katherine go somewhere?"

"Yes. I was just telling Jade that Katherine and her parents went to see Katherine's sister in Paris. They'll be having Christmas there this year."

Jade smiles at me.

My dad nods toward Lilly. "We'll talk about it later."

"Yeah. Okay." I look down at Lilly.

She's still holding my hand and skipping a little as she walks. "We're gonna swim in the pool and watch movies and make cookies and play the race car game."

I smile at her. "Sounds like a busy week."

Now I'm glad we came. Lilly needs us here. Her mom left her on Christmas, and even though she doesn't act upset, I know it hurts her. Lilly's good at hiding her feelings, but what kid her age wouldn't feel sad when her mom just takes off like that at the holidays?

"Don't forget sledding," I say as we arrive at the baggage claim area.

"Sledding!" She jumps around. "Daddy, can we go to the big hill again?"

"Yes, honey." He takes her hand. He has to keep a close watch on her, especially in a crowded airport. Even if he wasn't part of the organization, he'd still have to watch her. That's just what you have to do when you have his kind of money and people know who you are. You always have to be extra cautious.

As we're driving to the house, I hear Jade talking to Lilly in the back seat.

"So how are your swim lessons going?" Jade asks her.

"Good." She pauses, then says, "Mom and Dad are getting divorced."

The car goes silent. My dad glances back at Lilly, who's sitting behind me. I don't think he told her about the divorce yet. I think she just knew.

Jade breaks the silence. "I'm sorry, Lilly."

"It's okay." She says it softly. "They didn't like each other."

"Lilly, why don't we talk about this at home?" my dad says.

"I don't want to talk about it," she says.

I turn back and see her looking down at her shoes. Jade's holding her hand.

The car goes silent again. It's awkward, but luckily, a few minutes later we're at the house. As Jade helps Lilly out of the car, my dad comes up to me, lowering his voice. "Go ahead and get settled. I need to talk to her."

"Yeah. We're fine. Take all the time you need."

I get our luggage from the car while he takes Lilly inside. Jade and I go up to my room.

"Did he already tell Lilly about the divorce?" Jade asks.

"I don't think so. I think she just guessed." I set the suitcase on the floor by the closet. "I think Katherine might've already moved out."

"And she didn't say goodbye to Lilly?"

"It doesn't sound like it."

"How could Katherine just leave like that without even telling Lilly goodbye? And she does this at Christmas? How could she do that?"

"It's just the way she is. She doesn't care about anyone but herself. Her parents are like that, so it's how she was raised." I open the suitcase and start hanging stuff up in the closet.

"Garret?"

"Yeah?" I turn around and see Jade sitting on the bed.

"Do you think Lilly could stay with us this summer?"

"Maybe. We'd have to ask my dad." I go and sit next to her. "Do you want her to stay for a couple weeks, or what?"

"She could stay as long as she wants. Maybe even the whole summer. Your dad works all the time and I don't want Lilly to be all alone in this big house."

I smile and hug her into my side. "How long have you been thinking about this?"

"For a while." She puts her head on my shoulder. "I feel really bad for her, Garret. She's always alone and she gets ignored and then she tries to pretend everything's okay. It sounds like me growing up. But it shouldn't be like that for her. And she shouldn't have to spend the summer all by herself in her room."

"I don't know if my dad would agree to the entire summer, but I'm sure he'd let her stay with us for a few weeks."

She nods.

"Hey." I lift her face off my shoulder so I can kiss her. "I love you. And I love that you care about Lilly so much." I stand up

355

and pull her up from the bed. "Let's go downstairs and watch TV. I think my dad will be talking to Lilly for a while."

Jade and I go in the game room and watch the last half of a movie that's playing. An hour later my dad comes and finds us and we follow him to his office.

"How did Lilly take the news?" I ask him.

"She knew it was coming, but she acted like it didn't bother her. I told her it's okay to be upset or cry but she still didn't react. Katherine has forced Lilly to hide her emotions for so long that it'll take a while for her to open up. Maybe you two could help with that. She opens up to you, Garret, more than anyone else."

"I know. I'll talk to her. What did she say when you told her you got custody?"

"That's the only time she showed any emotion." My dad smiles. "She was happy. She hugged me, then asked if we could move to California and live next door to the two of you."

"Speaking of that." Jade glances at me. "Do you think Lilly could come stay with us this summer? Just for a few weeks?"

My dad nods. "I think that's a good idea. She would love that."

"Do you have to ask Katherine?"

"I don't think she'll have much involvement in Lilly's life anymore. Katherine has her own issues to deal with now. She has no time for Lilly."

"Is the organization going to do anything else to punish Katherine for what she did to Grandfather?" I ask. "They have to do more than just ban her from marrying the senator."

"They'll be taking away the money she receives from the divorce settlement and giving it back to me. They don't want her getting any benefits from the organization. And they'll likely put a limit on how much money her parents can give her."

I smile. "She's gonna hate that. She won't survive without money."

"She'll still have money. It just won't be the type of wealth she had before."

"She must've been pissed when she found out."

"Actually, she doesn't know about the money yet. They'll tell her later this week. Her other punishment affects her ranking in society. Her social standing is being destroyed as we speak. The organization planted some rumors about her, which have already started circulating among her friends. Damaging stories and photos of her will follow in the society pages. She'll never be allowed back in our world."

"Does she know this is going on?"

"Yes. They didn't tell her, but she quickly figured it out when none of her friends would return her calls. She was furious. That's why she left. She took off to stay with her sister in France and didn't say when she's coming back." He stands up. "One of you go get Lilly. We're going out for dinner. It's the holidays and I don't want to spend it talking about Katherine. I'd like us all to enjoy this week together as a family and try to relax and have a good time. Lilly needs that, and I'm sure you two would like that as well."

As he picks his phone up from the desk, Jade says, "Before we go, can I ask you something?"

"Go ahead." He sits back down.

"I know we're not supposed to talk about it, but I have to know. What's going to happen to Harper?"

He sighs. "Jade, you know that's confidential."

She scoots to the edge of her chair, pleading with him. "I'm not asking you about Kiefer. I just need to know about Harper. Please. If you could just tell me something. Anything."

"I'm sorry, Jade, but I can't—"

"Dad," I say, interrupting him. "Just tell us. You know we won't tell anyone. Or if you can't say anything, just nod if she's okay."

He doesn't nod, but he says, "I only know about Kiefer, not Andrew. And I can't tell you anything about Kiefer."

Jade's eyes shift to me, then back to my dad. "But he can't try to take Harper, right? It's against the rules. They had a deal. Andrew can't just—"

"Jade." My dad uses his warning tone, the one I've become quite familiar with over the years. "I'm not discussing this. You're part of this family now and you know the rules."

She slumps back in the chair and nods. "Yeah."

"Dad, she was just asking."

"You both know the rules." Now it sounds like he's scolding us, which annoys me.

I roll my eyes. "Don't ask questions. Yeah, we've got it. But we can't exactly enjoy the holiday knowing our friend might be in danger."

He rubs his jaw, his eyes on Jade, who's now staring at her hands, avoiding his gaze.

"Jade." He waits for her to look at him. "If I knew for sure he wouldn't bother her, I would tell you. But I honestly don't know. I've heard nothing. All I know is that he's currently in Europe and will be spending the holidays there."

"But you'll see him at the meeting next week," I say.

"Perhaps. Although, knowing him, he'll continue his partying across Europe all next week and end up staying there for New Year's. It wouldn't be the first time he's skipped out on the meetings."

"And he didn't get in trouble?"

"As Cecil Roth's son, Andrew was able to do whatever he wanted. But now that Cecil is gone, I think Andrew will have to start playing by the rules."

"Maybe he's found someone else by now," Jade says quietly.

I take her hand. "He probably has. I'm sure he's not interested in her anymore."

My dad shoots me a look, not wanting me to give Jade false hope. But I'm not going to ruin her holiday with this. And who knows? Maybe Andrew really will lose interest in Harper.

My dad gets up. "It's getting late. We should head out for dinner." He goes around us and out the door, leaving Jade and me there.

"You okay?" I ask her.

She shrugs. "I guess."

I rub her hand. "Jade, he wasn't trying to be mean. And I don't think he's lying. I think he really doesn't know." I lean over and kiss her. "Let's just try to have a good holiday, okay?"

She gives me a weak smile. "Okay."

Her smile gets bigger when Lilly runs into the room and jumps on her lap. "You wanna have a tea party? Or watch a movie?"

Jade perks up, seeing Lilly so excited. She gives her a hug. "We're going to dinner and then we'll watch one."

Lilly seems to be feeling better now that my dad talked to her. Or maybe she's just happy having Jade and me here.

My dad pokes his head in the room. "Ready to go?"

Lilly hops off Jade's lap and runs up to him. "Daddy, can we make Christmas cookies?"

"Not tonight. But maybe tomorrow."

Jade and I meet them out in the foyer.

Lilly's twirling around. "We're going to go sledding and play games and go swimming."

My dad laughs. "Yes, we'll do all those things."

We go out for dinner, then go home and watch a movie. And for the rest of the week, we do just as Lilly said. We swim, watch movies, play video games, make Christmas cookies, and go sledding. My dad works from home all week, but takes lots of breaks to do stuff with us. And he shuts his computer down every night at five so we can spend the evenings together. Even Charles joins in on the activities.

It snowed on Monday and again on Thursday. With the piles of snow outside, and the lights and decorations inside, the house has a real Christmasy feel. I don't even mind the white lights. Instead of reminding me of Katherine, they remind me of being here with Jade last year. And my dad made sure to have the decorators put colored lights in the game room just for me. There's a small tree with colored lights in my bedroom as well.

With Lilly as a distraction, Jade gets into the holiday spirit, setting aside her concerns about Harper, or at least acting like she has. But we both still think about it, especially since Kiefer's been in the news all week.

Last Monday, the news reported that Kiefer is currently being investigated for stealing funds from the movies he's worked on. The story's been everywhere; national news, the newspaper, gossip shows, talk shows. It's a huge scandal. The story is that Kiefer made up fake expenses, then took the money for himself. They say he's stolen millions over the years. Earlier this week he was fired from the studio, and some are saying he'll never work in Hollywood again. Right after he was fired, Kiefer released a statement admitting his wrongdoing and saying he'll give all the money back, which I'm guessing won't leave him with much.

I asked my dad about this but he wouldn't tell me anything. But he *did* nod when I asked him if this was Kiefer's punishment. Kiefer should be thankful. Instead of being killed, his punishment is this made-up scandal. They ruined his reputation, he lost his job, and now they'll take his money.

I don't feel that bad for him. He got himself into this by being greedy and selfish. And in the process, he destroyed his relationship with Harper. He might've also destroyed his relationship with Kelly. The rumor is that Kelly and Kiefer are separating and Kiefer's moving out after the holidays. I don't know if Kelly knew the whole story about the organization or just part of it, but I know she wasn't happy with her husband. Last fall, Harper kept saying that her parents weren't getting along and weren't spending as much time together. It wouldn't surprise me if Kiefer and Kelly end up getting divorced.

Harper's been calling Jade all week but she hasn't said much about her dad. She used to be really close to him and it's devastating for her to think of him as a criminal. And Kiefer will never be able to tell her, or anyone else, the truth. He has to accept his punishment as given and be happy the organization didn't do something even worse to him.

Harper hasn't spoken to her dad since this happened. She said she's waiting for him to call her and explain what's going on, but so far he hasn't. Her sisters moved into a hotel. They didn't want to be around their dad. They're angry with him as well, because of what he did, but also because his scandal could negatively affect their careers, especially Kylie's. Movie studios won't want to hire her for acting roles, knowing her dad stole from them.

So that leaves Kiefer and his wife alone at Christmas, assuming Kelly is still there. She might've gone to stay at the hotel with Kylie and Caitlyn. I'm sure she'd rather spend the holiday with her daughters than her husband.

Kiefer really screwed up. His whole life is destroyed, which I'm sure is exactly what the organization wanted as punishment for him rejecting their offer. And I assume they'll still make him work for them. That's probably part of the deal. He has to do whatever they say or he'll face additional punishment. He'll never be free.

# Chapter 34

**GARRET**

The past week has gone way too fast. It's already Saturday, Christmas Day. This morning, my grandmother finally showed up. She only lives a half hour away but didn't bother coming over until now. She's been here all day, and it's not like she's mean or says anything rude to Jade or me, but she's being very cold and distant.

Katherine called Lilly earlier, but they didn't talk long. Katherine's flying home tomorrow morning and going to stay at her parents' house. My dad assumed she'd want Lilly there, but she doesn't, which means he has nobody to watch her while he's in his meetings next week. Luckily, Charles offered to take care of her. Charles is great with kids and Lilly loves spending time with him. I have no idea why Katherine refused to take Lilly. She hasn't seen her for over a week. She's such a horrible mother. I'm so glad she isn't here for Christmas. She would've ruined it for everyone.

We opened presents this morning and had Christmas dinner this afternoon. Now my grandmother is upstairs with Lilly, my dad's playing cards with Charles in the kitchen, and Jade and I are watching TV in the game room. We're both stuffed from eating too much. We're lying on the couch in front of the TV, cuddled up under a blanket. We turned the main lights off so we could see the sparkling Christmas lights. We agreed that we would suspend any discussion of the Harper issue until tomorrow. It's Christmas and we want to spend the day being happy.

"Did you have a good Christmas?" I kiss Jade's head because it's all I can reach. She's got her face on my chest, the blanket pulled up to her chin.

"It was a *great* Christmas." She scoots up so I can see her face.

"Was it better than last year?"

"Well, yeah. Katherine isn't here and you aren't recovering from being shot. This year is way better. Plus, now I'm married to you."

"You like that, huh?"

"I love it." She kisses me and I kiss her back, my hand touching her under the blanket.

"Garret, not here." She pulls my hand away. "We need to go upstairs for that."

"Then let's go upstairs."

"Can we go later? I'm really full right now."

"Do you want me to put a movie in?"

"You can watch one. I'm going to take a nap. I'm really sleepy."

"Then I'm going to call Sean."

Sean wasn't able to fly home for Christmas, so he's in LA, spending the holidays by himself. I hope he at least went out for Christmas dinner. He's still not over his breakup with Harper. He doesn't talk about her as much as he used to, but I know he really misses having her in his life. The guy was totally in love with her. I think he still is. Actually, I *know* he is, but he's trying to move on the best he can without her.

Harper's back in LA for winter break, but she's avoiding her family. She's staying with one of her friends from high school. She's still mad at her parents for forcing her to break up with Sean. She tried to get back together with him a few weeks ago, but when he wouldn't return her calls, she gave up. Sean would love to get back together with her, but he's still worried people will come after him if he does. Obviously he hasn't told me this, but I know that's the reason. And I can't say anything because I'm not supposed to know about any of this. Plus, I don't know if he's safe. If Andrew still wants Harper, he'll make sure Sean stays away.

I call Sean. It's early afternoon out there. He should be around unless he went out to eat.

"Hey, Garret." Sean sounds happier than normal. Must be because it's Christmas. It's good to hear him sounding happy again. He's been so depressed the past few weeks. "How's your Christmas going?"

"Great. We just had dinner and Jade and I are so full we can't move." I look down and see her smiling. "What did you do for dinner?"

"I haven't eaten yet."

Shit. I hope that doesn't mean he ran out of money for food. He makes more money at his new job, but LA is really expensive so maybe he's still broke.

"You should've brought home leftovers from the restaurant."

"I did. The fridge is full of stuff. I just haven't had time to eat." When he says it, I hear a girl giggling in the background. Sean hasn't mentioned dating anyone. I didn't think he was ready to start dating again. But I guess he is. It's kind of odd that he'd bring a girl he just met over to his place on Christmas.

"You got some company there, Sean?"

"Yeah." He laughs. "My company arrived this morning, wrapped up in a bow."

"Sean, don't tell him that part," the girl says. I think I recognize the voice but I'm not sure.

"Who was that?" I ask him.

"It's me." I hear Harper's voice on the phone. "Hi, Garret."

"Hi." That's all I say because I'm not sure if this is a good thing. If Andrew still wants Harper, then she should not be over at Sean's. Andrew could have someone watching her. And why is Sean allowing her to be there? If he thinks his life is in danger by being with her, then why is he doing this?

"Garret, are you there?" Sean asks.

"Yeah. So Harper got there this morning?"

Jade bolts up. "Harper's there?"

I nod. "Sean, can I put you on speaker? Jade wants to say hi."

"Sure. You're on speaker, too."

"Hi, Sean," Jade says. "Merry Christmas."

"Merry Christmas, Jade." Harper giggles.

Jade grabs the phone from me. "Okay, what's going on there? Are one of you guys going to explain?"

"I showed up at Sean's door this morning," she says.

"In a red dress and a green bow," Sean says. "Best present I ever got."

We hear them kissing. Jade and I look at each other, confused.

"So you're back together?" Jade asks.

"Yes," Harper says, followed by more kissing sounds. "And I'm not leaving."

"I wouldn't let you even if you tried," Sean says. More kissing sounds.

Jade looks even more confused. "You mean you're staying at Sean's place until you go back to school?"

"I mean I'm staying *here*. In California. And I'm moving in with Sean."

"I don't understand. What about school?"

"I was waiting to tell you guys because I wanted to tell Sean first."

"Tell us what?"

"I'm transferring to UCLA. I applied a few months ago when I was feeling homesick, just to see if I could get in. And I did, but I wasn't sure if I wanted to transfer. But I decided it's a better fit for me. I miss California. And I really miss Sean." More kissing sounds.

"You're seriously moving to California?" Jade jumps off me, taking the phone with her. "I can't believe you kept this from me!"

"I had to know for sure before I told you. And then I wanted to tell Sean."

I hear Sean again. "I didn't even know she applied."

"I didn't tell anyone," Harper says. "Not even my parents."

"We're gonna come see you guys all the time." Jade's so cute when she gets this excited. I pull her down on my lap and kiss her.

"We'll drive up and see you guys, too," Harper says. "Oh, and Sean's boss wants him to work at his Santa Barbara restaurant this summer, so we'll be even closer to you guys."

"We could get a place there on the beach," Jade says. "It'll be just like last summer. We could be neighbors again!"

Jade and Harper start planning it out. I don't know what Jade's thinking. She knows this thing with Andrew isn't settled yet, so she shouldn't be making plans like this. I think she's caught up in the moment or maybe she thinks this means the issue with Andrew is over. Maybe it is.

"I'll be right back," I whisper to Jade as I get up off the couch. She nods as she continues to talk to Harper.

I search for my dad and find him in his office. He has the TV on, turned to a news channel. Updates are scrolling on the bottom of the screen. I catch Andrew's name scrolling by, but I didn't see what it said.

I point to the TV. "Did that just say Andrew Roth?"

"Yes." He turns the TV off. "Sit down."

I take a seat across from him. "Did something happen?"

"Andrew was found in a hotel room in Amsterdam early this morning. He was taken to the hospital for a drug overdose.

They found cocaine, heroine, and several prescription pain-killers in his hotel room."

"So he's in the hospital?"

"He was, but they just reported that he passed away."

I get this big ass grin on my face. That's bad, I know. I shouldn't be happy someone's dead, but shit, the guy beat on women and acted like he owned them. And besides, he did this to himself. He overdosed on drugs and killed himself. At least I think he did.

"Did they do this?" I ask my dad.

"No, this was all Andrew. Honestly, I'm surprised it didn't happen sooner. He's had a drug problem since college." He smiles a little. "You should go tell Jade the news."

"Yeah. I will." I get up to leave, then stop. I know he won't answer my question, so I phrase it differently. "So I was just talking to Sean. Harper's over at his place. The two of them are back together and Harper's moving in with him. She's going to UCLA."

My dad nods. "Good for them. I'm sure they'll be very happy."

I watch my dad's response. And his response, although sub-tle, confirms that it's okay they're together. Even with Andrew gone, I still thought maybe the organization might try to do something to Harper or Sean to get back at Kiefer. But my dad's response is telling me they won't. But how did Sean know he could be with Harper? I wonder if my dad had something to do with that. I wonder if he had someone pay a visit to Sean, or give him an anonymous message telling him he was safe. My dad knows Sean is one of the few real friends I've ever had, and he knows how much Harper means to Jade. But how did he get Sean the message so fast? He just found out about Andrew, and yet it sounds like Sean's been with Harper since this morning. So was Andrew's death really his own doing? Or was he killed?

"Garret, go talk to Jade." My dad motions me to the door.

"Yeah, okay," I say, shaking those thoughts from my head. I don't care how Andrew died. I'm just happy he's gone and Sean can be with Harper.

When I get back to the game room, Jade and Harper are still planning out our summer. I sit next to her, and when there's finally a break, I say, "It's good you two are back together. Sean was really starting to depress me, moping around all the time."

"How do you know if I was moping?" Sean asks. "You never see me."

"We know you were moping because Harper was, too," Jade says. "You two are happiest when you're together."

"We totally are," Harper says, followed by more kissing sounds. "Hey, guys, let's talk later. Sean and I have some catching up to do."

Jade rolls her eyes, but smiles. "Enjoy the rest of your Christmas. We'll celebrate when we get there on Wednesday. Hopefully you two will be caught up by then."

Harper laughs. "Probably not, but we'll make time for you. We love you guys. Merry Christmas."

"Merry Christmas." Jade and I say it at the same time.

Jade tosses the phone on the couch and hugs me. "Can you believe it? They're back together! I'm so happy for them."

"Hey, I have to tell you something."

She sits back. "What's wrong? Is this about Andrew?"

"Yeah. He's dead."

She jumps off me. "Are you serious?"

"He died of a drug overdose. Someone found him this morning in a hotel room in Amsterdam."

"And he, um…" She pauses. "He did this to himself?"

Although I can't say for sure, that's the story I'm going with. "Yeah. He did it to himself."

She sits on my lap and hugs me again. "I'm so relieved." She pulls away. "But how did Sean know he could get back together with Harper?"

"Someone must've told him it was okay."

"But who—"

"Jade, it doesn't matter. Let's just be happy those two are back together."

She gets a huge smile on her face. "This is so great! We're going to live next door to them again this summer, but in Santa Barbara, which means I'll be able to see Grace all the time. This is like a Christmas gift!"

"Yeah, it is." I kiss her.

My dad walks up behind us. "I don't mean to interrupt, but Garret, your grandmother is going home and she wanted to say goodbye before she left."

"Yeah, okay."

Jade and I follow my dad to the main part of the house. My grandmother is waiting in the living room. At least she's saying goodbye this time.

"Dad said you were leaving," I say to her.

"Yes, I need to be going." She walks up to me. "Goodbye, Garret."

I hear my dad behind me. "Jade, I want to show you something. Could you come to my office?"

"Um, yeah, okay," she says, realizing he wants to give my grandmother and me a moment alone.

They leave and my grandmother stands there, looking uncomfortable. She keeps glancing at the Christmas tree, then back at me. "It was good seeing you, Garret. Have a safe trip back."

"Grandmother." I pause until she looks at me. "Are things always going to be this way?"

"I don't know what you mean." She stands up straighter and looks at the tree again.

"Are you going to keep treating me like a stranger instead of your grandson?" I can't believe I asked her that, but I did because I really want the answer.

"Garret, don't say such things. I don't treat you like a stranger."

"You barely speak to me. And when I was here a few weeks ago, you didn't even say goodbye."

She doesn't respond.

"Grandmother, I know you don't want to be this way. You didn't treat me like this when I was a kid. And I see you with Lilly. You act like a grandmother to her, but not me. I know you only treat me this way because of him. Because he told you to. But he's gone now. You don't have to be like this anymore."

She nods.

I pull her into a hug, a real hug, and keep her there. "I love you, Grandmother."

I've never said that to her, but it's true. I may not have loved my grandfather, but I love my grandmother. I know deep down she's a loving person. That part of her comes out when she's with Lilly. And I know last Fourth of July, she didn't show up here because she wanted to watch the fireworks. She showed up because she knew I'd be there and she wanted to see me. My dad told me that later.

I feel my grandmother's arms tighten around me. "You're a good young man, Garret. I know you'll do well in life."

She can't do it. She can't tell me she loves me. Those words just aren't said in the Kensington family, at least not by my grandparents. But at least she said something positive to me and gave me a real hug.

She releases her arms and I step back and see her forcing out a smile. She walks around me to the foyer and I follow behind her.

My dad hears her coming and walks out of his office with Jade. "I'll see you after your trip, Mother."

She gives him a quick shoulder hug. "Yes. I'll call you when I get back."

"Where are you going on your trip?" Jade asks her.

"To London. Just for a few days, to see an old friend."

"Have a good time." Jade smiles at her.

"Thank you." My grandmother gives Jade a weak smile. She still doesn't approve of her and probably never will.

Once she's gone, my dad grins like a little kid who's happy his mom finally left so he can do the stuff she doesn't approve of.

He hangs his arm off my shoulder. "Do you want to race?"

For Christmas my dad bought Lilly two new car-racing games. One has cartoon animals, so it's meant for kids. The other one is for adults, so I think my dad really bought it for himself, and for me when I visit.

"You know I'll beat you, right?" I say.

"We'll see about that."

"Dad, you're gonna lose. I'm just preparing you."

"Is he always this overly confident?" my dad asks Jade.

She laughs. "Yes. Always."

"Just like his father." He pats me on the back. "Well, I've been practicing, son, and my skills on the raceway have improved, so you might want to tone down that confidence a little."

"I don't need to. I know I'll beat you."

Jade walks to the stairs. "I'm going to let you two battle it out. I'm going upstairs to play with Lilly."

"After she goes to sleep, are you up for some poker?" my dad asks Jade.

"Definitely. But I'm going to beat you again." She continues up the stairs.

"Who's overly confident now?" I yell at her.

"She's definitely a Kensington," my dad says as we walk away. I look back and see Jade smiling at his comment.

My dad and I play the video game and get so into it that we're still playing it when Jade and Lilly find us two hours later. I play the kid race car game with Lilly and then Jade plays with her. Then Lilly goes to bed and the three of us play poker with Charles until two in the morning.

Sunday, we all sleep in, then have breakfast together. It snowed again, so after breakfast my dad takes everyone sledding at the park that has the big hill. In the afternoon, while Jade's playing with Lilly, my dad and I watch a football game.

Every time I see my dad, I'm amazed at how much he's changed. My relationship with him just keeps getting better. I hope my mom is watching over us, because if she is, she'll be very happy.

# Chapter 35

**JADE**

*M*onday morning we wake up to someone knocking on the bedroom door. I check the clock. It's only nine and our plane doesn't leave until one.

"Garret. Jade. I need you to get up." It's Pearce. He should've left an hour ago for the organization's meeting. He knocks again. "Are you awake?"

Garret shoves the covers back and gets out of bed. "Yeah, I'm coming." He yawns as he opens the door. "What are you doing here? Why aren't you at the meeting?"

"Something came up. It's been delayed until later today."

"Why? What's going on?"

"Katherine told the organization about Jade. She told them Jade is Royce's daughter."

"She what?" I stumble out of bed wearing sleep pants and a t-shirt. I grab my sweatshirt and yank it on as I go to the door. "Why would she do that?"

"She's trying to get back at my dad and William for setting her up," Garret explains, like he's not surprised that this happened. "I assume she told them that you and William knew about Jade?"

Pearce nods. "Yes. She's hoping William and I will be punished for knowing this information and not telling the organization. Katherine is irate over her punishment and she wants revenge. If she's going down, she wants to take William and me with her."

"When did she tell them?" Garret asks.

"Last night. She reported it to one of the high ranking members, knowing the meeting was today. She knew they'd try to take her money and thought if she shared this secret, the organization might reward her by letting her keep it." He checks his watch. "Get dressed and come down to my office. I have more to tell you. And hurry up. We don't have much time."

We take a quick shower and get dressed and meet him in his office.

"So what are they going to do to you and William?" Garret asks.

"Nothing. They called me early this morning and I explained that I had no idea who Jade was until after Royce's death. I talked to William just now and he told them the same thing. According to the rules, we aren't required to disclose secrets we learn about another member after that member is deceased. Katherine wasn't aware of that rule, and now that she is, I'm sure she's furious that William and I will not be punished."

"But Katherine knows the truth," Garret says. "Why didn't she tell them you knew about Jade a long time ago?"

"Because if she did, I'd tell the members that Katherine has known about Jade for as long as I have, and then Katherine would be in even more trouble. She insisted that she just recently found out about Jade, and I didn't refute her story. As long as we both keep this secret, we'll be fine."

"So Katherine's trick didn't work. Nobody's being punished."

"It *did* work, but in Katherine's favor. By sharing this information, Katherine will be allowed to keep some of her money. And as for the punishment, it's being handed down to Victoria, not William or myself."

"Victoria?" I ask, trying to keep up with his story. With all the secrets and cover-ups and blackmail, I can't keep track of it all. "What does Victoria have to do with this?"

"She knew," Pearce says.

"She knew about Jade?" Garret asks. "Royce told her what he'd done?"

"No. Years ago, Victoria got an anonymous letter in the mail, saying that Royce had a daughter with another woman."

"How do you know this?" Garret asks.

"William told me when I talked to him this morning. He said that last week, Sadie called him to complain that the credit card Grace gave her had been canceled. Grace took it away to punish Sadie for treating Jade the way she did when they met that night of the memorial service. Sadie asked William to talk Grace into giving her the card back. William refused and Sadie got angry, yelling and screaming about how Jade has ruined everything. Sadie still didn't believe Jade was her sister and was determined to find out the truth. She searched through some old boxes Royce had stored away, and that's when she found the letter."

I look at Garret, then back at Pearce. "I don't understand. Hardly anyone knew about Royce and my mom, so who wrote the letter?"

"It was anonymous but I assume your mother wrote it. It was postmarked right after you were born. The letter didn't say he raped your mother. It just said he fathered a child, then pleaded for Victoria to convince him to leave the child alone. Your mother obviously thought Royce might come back and harm you. I'm guessing she thought Victoria, being a new mother herself at the time, would keep Royce from doing anything to an innocent child."

"So Victoria didn't know I was that child," I confirm.

"I think she knew when she saw you at the fundraiser I had for Royce last year. You look like Royce, and Victoria knew he had a child out there so I'm guessing she put it together."

"If Sadie has the letter, how can William prove it exists?" Garret asks.

"When Sadie told William about the letter, he told her it might be fake and that she should send it to him so he could have it verified. So she did, and now William has the letter. He scanned it and emailed it to the organization. The ruling council is reviewing it as we speak."

Garret smiles. "Shit, William really wants to get back at Victoria."

Pearce nods. "There's a history there, but I don't know the details. Anyway, now that the members are aware of this, they've decided to punish Victoria. Someone has to be punished for Royce's failure to disclose this, and since Victoria was in on this secret, the organization felt that she should receive the punishment."

"Is anything going to happen to Jade?"

"No, but she does need to do something. That's why I woke you up. You can't go home today. You'll have to leave tomorrow. Don't worry about rescheduling your flight. You can take my jet back to California."

"Why are we staying here?" Garret asks.

"They need to talk to Jade."

"Who?"

"The organization. They've summoned Jade to the meeting."

"Are you serious?" Garret stands up. "And you agreed to this?"

"We don't have a choice," Pearce says.

Garret huffs. "No. Forget it. I'm not letting her get anywhere near them."

"Garret, they know she's a Sinclair. They can't hurt her now. It's against the rules. When your grandfather got his promotion, he instituted a rule forbidding a member from causing physical harm to other members or their families."

"I don't care! They tried to kill her, and you seriously want her around those people?"

"She's already been around them. She's met them. She's seen them at parties. She just didn't know they were members."

"Why do they want me to go to their meeting?" I ask him.

"Technically, it's not a meeting. It's a sentencing. They want you there when they hand down their punishment to Victoria. They ordered the whole Sinclair family to be there. They're probably going to ask you a few questions and then they'll hand over Victoria's punishment."

"What kind of questions?" My stomach knots just thinking about having to talk to these people.

"I don't know for certain, but I'm assuming they'll be questions related to Victoria, such as if she ever showed any signs that she knew you."

"So Victoria will be there? And all of her daughters?"

"Yes. And William will be there. Grace is excused since she was given such short notice and couldn't get here in time."

"Jade's not going," Garret says. "She doesn't need to be there. I'll go in her place."

"They won't accept that. Jade's a Sinclair. She needs to be there. I told them you'd want to accompany her and they agreed to it, so all three of us will be going."

"No. Forget it, Dad. I don't trust them. This is just one of their sick games and I'm not playing it."

"They won't harm her, Garret. I promise you, they won't. And we'll both be there with her. We won't let her out of our sight."

"Garret, it's okay." I pull on him to sit down. "Let's just do it. I don't want to get on their bad side and have them come after us again."

"Jade is right," Pearce says. "If you're cooperative, they'll be more likely to leave you alone in the future. Jade being a

Sinclair changes things. She's considered one of us now. And they don't want to waste time going after their own. They'll stop trying to scare you. They'll let you live your lives. This is a simple request. Do this and you'll be done dealing with them."

"When's the meeting?" I ask him.

"Today at noon. We'll leave here at ten-thirty. It's an hour away and we don't want to be late."

"Do I need to prepare for it? And what am I supposed to wear?"

"You don't need to prepare anything. Their questions will be very basic. You just need to go along with the story I told you about how William and I didn't know about you until after Royce died. And don't tell them about the rape. Go with the story of it being an affair. As for dress code, you need to wear a black dress. Everyone wears black to the hearings and sentencings."

"I don't have a dress. I'll have to go get one."

He gets his phone out. "I'll have one sent over. It'll be here within the hour."

We wait for him to text whoever's buying me a dress and then Garret says, "Dad, you should tell Jade exactly what you told the organization about Royce so she doesn't accidentally say the wrong thing in case they ask her about it."

Pearce agrees and goes over the story he and William told the organization. Then my dress arrives and Garret and I go upstairs to change. We skipped breakfast. I don't feel like eating after hearing I'm being summoned by the organization. I don't know if I can do this. But I need to. If doing this will get them to leave us alone, I'll do it.

I put on my dress and Garret puts on one of the suits he still had in his closet. When we meet downstairs to leave, it looks like we're all going to a funeral. I'm in my black dress and Garret and his dad are both in black suits.

A black car with tinted windows arrives to pick us up. Normally, Pearce would drive himself to the meeting, so I'm not sure why the organization isn't allowing him to now. Is it because of me? I asked Pearce, but he didn't answer, so I assume it's because of me.

The driver is wearing a black suit. I don't know if he's a member or just a driver. Pearce instructed me not to talk on the way there. The car has microphones and cameras inside and he doesn't want the people watching and listening to us getting any kind of information about us, even if it's just normal things, like stuff about school. So we sit there in silence for 55 minutes. I can't tell where we are because I can't see out the windows. They have some kind of covering over them that blurs the view. Some light filters through but I can't see the outside. There's a partition up between the front seat and the back seats so I can't even see out the front window.

The car slows down and the driver's voice booms through the back speakers. "Put the blindfold on the girl."

Pearce picks up a piece of black fabric from the seat. I hadn't even noticed it was there because the seats are black so it blended in.

Garret takes it from him. "Dad, what the hell? She's not wearing this. She's not going to tell anyone."

"Garret, they won't let her in without it. You know the rules."

He sighs. "But she takes it off when we get inside, right?"

"Once we're in the room, she can take it off."

I'm feeling sick to my stomach. I don't like this at all. The black clothes. The black car I can't see out of. The blindfold. I feel like I'm being taken to my execution.

"I don't feel good," I say quietly to Garret.

He holds my hand. "It'll be okay. I'll be with you the whole time."

"I really have to wear that?" I point to the blindfold.

"Not for very long. Just until we get to the room."

"Why aren't *you* wearing one?"

"I've been there before. I've already seen where it is."

I nod and let him put the blindfold on me. As soon as it's on, the car moves again. A few minutes later it comes to a stop.

I hear the driver through the speaker. "Mr. Kensington, your son will go first, followed by the girl and then you. The blindfold must remain on the girl until they tell you otherwise."

I hear the door open. Garret helps me out, then takes my hand and I slowly walk forward, with him ahead of me. I feel Pearce behind me, his hand on my shoulder. I'm shaking now, fearful of what's going to happen. Why do they want me here? I don't understand this.

I hear another door open. It sounds heavy. It makes a loud creaking noise as it opens. We must be walking through it because the air suddenly changes and becomes damp and musty, like we're in an underground tunnel. We keep walking, not saying a word. I'm gripping Garret's hand and he's rubbing mine with his thumb, trying to calm me. Pearce's hand is still on my shoulder, so at least I feel somewhat protected having both of them surrounding me.

We finally reach another door, and as it opens, I feel warm air coming out. We go inside and the wet, musty smell is gone.

"Right this way," I hear a man say. "Pearce, you may go to your seat."

Pearce's hand leaves my shoulder and I suddenly feel exposed, like someone's going to come up behind me and do something. Garret leads me forward, taking several small steps and then stopping.

"Turn her around," a man says.

Garret turns me the other direction, our hands still attached.

"Now go sit by your father," the man says.

"No," Garret says. "I'm not leaving her down here alone."

I hear someone walking and then, "Garret, you need to sit down."

He sighs, then I feel his hands on my face, his breath over my lips as he whispers, "I'll be right behind you, okay?"

I nod, my body still shaking.

He kisses my forehead. "I love you."

As soon as I feel his hands leave my face, I panic. I don't know where I am or what they're going to do to me. Someone's behind me now, taking the blindfold off.

"Don't turn around," a man says. "You must remain facing forward at all times. Do you understand?"

I swallow hard and nod. I squint at the bright light shining down on me. I look up and see three rows of tiered seating ahead of me. It looks like it continues around the room, although I don't dare turn back and check. I keep my eyes forward. The seating area is dark, but there's enough of a glow from the spotlight in the middle of the room that I can see figures in front of me. They're sitting down, wearing black robes with large hoods that cast shadows on their faces so I can't see them. Why are they wearing robes? Are they the judges? Or is everyone wearing robes? I can't look behind me so I don't know.

I'm so nervous I might throw up. I wish they'd just hurry up and start whatever this is so it can end and we can leave.

"Bitch."

I hear someone whisper it and glance to my right and see Sadie standing next to me. I was so focused on what was in front of me, I didn't even see her there. She's staring straight ahead. Did she really just call me a bitch? Maybe I'm imagining things.

"Whore."

I definitely heard that. But it came from my other side. I glance left and see Sadie's sister. Her name's Emily and she's two years younger than Sadie. I've only seen photos of her. She's also staring straight ahead. I glance farther down and see Tamryn and Camille, the other two half-sisters I've never met. They catch me looking at them and glare back at me, but just briefly.

So they all hate me. Not just Sadie and Victoria. All of them. But do they really need to call me a bitch and a whore?

Someone comes through the door. It's Victoria, blind-folded and guided by another man in a black robe. She takes her place next to Sadie and her blindfold is removed.

"We will now begin," the man in front of me says. I can't see him. He's just a dark shadow like the rest of them. "We're here to hand down the punishment for Royce Sinclair not disclosing the fact that he had a child resulting from an extra-marital affair. As you know, failure to disclose an indiscretion from one's past, especially one of this magnitude, is against the rules and cause for punishment. Given our plans for Royce, this violation of the rules is even more serious. Based on our earlier investigations, we've absolved both Pearce Kensington and William Sinclair from punishment, given our belief that neither one of them were aware of Royce's illegitimate child until after Royce's death."

"That's not true!" Victoria calls out. "Pearce knew—"

"Stop!" The man puts his hand out toward Victoria. "You will not speak unless spoken to. Am I clear?"

She nods.

"Given that Royce was deceased at the time, William and Pearce were not required to disclose this information, although it is encouraged since secrets are not to be kept from the group. But technically, they did not break the rules. Royce, of course, did break the rules by not telling us about this, but since he is no longer with us, his punishment must be passed to someone else in his family. Typically, punishment would automatically pass to a brother, but given the many years of dedicated service paid by both William, and his father, Arlin, we have decided against punishing him. Instead, we are here today to pass Royce's punishment to his wife, Victoria Sinclair. We feel Victoria is most deserving of this punishment, given that she knew of her husband's affair and the child that resulted from it. We have proof that she knew about this years ago."

"No!" Victoria raises her hand. "That letter was—"

"Enough!" the man yells. "One more outburst like that and your punishment will become much more severe."

She purses her lips, her eyes narrowed.

"The child who resulted from the affair is here today. Jade Sinclair. Please step forward."

I stand there, noticing the room is silent. And then I realize what he said. *Jade Sinclair.* Shit, that's me! I've never heard myself called that before now. I slowly step forward.

"We have run a DNA test and the test showed that Jade is indeed a Sinclair," he says.

DNA test? What? When did they do that?

He continues. "Which means that she is not to be harmed in any way, given the new rule instituted by Holton Kensington and approved at our meeting last October. If any member is found in violation of this rule, he will be punished. Jade Sinclair, we now have some questions for you."

Oh, God. I'm definitely going to throw up. I take some breaths, trying to calm my nervous stomach.

"Were you aware that Victoria knew of your existence before Royce's death?"

"No," I blurt out.

"When did you first meet Victoria?"

"At a fundraiser for Royce at Mr. Kensington's house."

"And how did she act when you met her?"

I take a deep breath so I can speak. My heart's pounding and it's making me breathless. "She acted like she didn't want me around her husband. She gave me an angry look, like I shouldn't be talking to him. And then she told Royce he had to go give his speech."

"Looking back, and knowing what you know now, do you feel like she knew you were Royce's child during that encounter?"

I'm not sure how to answer. I really have no idea. If I think back, I guess it's possible she knew and that's why she was trying to keep me away from him. I look a lot like Sadie and a little like Royce, so Victoria had to have figured it out.

I'm not protecting that woman. I'm just going to say it.

"I can't say for sure if Victoria knew. But given that I look a little like Royce and a lot like Sadie, I think it's likely that Victoria knew who I was."

There's silence, except for the sound of Sadie whispering 'bitch' just loud enough for me to hear.

"Sadie Sinclair," the man says. "Step forward."

She steps up so that she's even with me. There's some whispering among the members.

"You do look very similar," the man says. "I don't see how it's possible Victoria wouldn't see the similarity and put this together. It just confirms that she knew. And yet even after meeting Royce's daughter that night, Victoria still didn't come forward and disclose this. Her goal was to be first lady and she put her own selfish goals ahead of the organization. She knew Royce would be punished and demoted if this were ever revealed, so she hid it from us."

As he says it, I realize that if Victoria *had* told them, they would've killed me. Back then, they didn't have that rule about not harming a member's family. They would've killed me because I know things I shouldn't know. So although she didn't intend to, Victoria saved me. And now, the members can't hurt me because of the rule Holton made. How crazy is that? Two of my biggest enemies ended up saving me. If Holton knew that, he'd be rolling around in his grave, trying to claw his way out to come back and kill me.

I'm assuming the protection rule only applies to a member's blood relatives. Otherwise, Holton wouldn't have made it. He would've made sure it couldn't apply to me. But he didn't know I was a Sinclair, and since I am, Holton's rule *does* apply to me. As Royce's daughter and William's niece, I'm now protected from ever being harmed.

The man in front of me slams his gavel on the table. "Punishment will now be given. If there are any objections to the punishment discussed earlier, speak now."

The room is silent, so he continues. "Jade, please step back."

I do as he says. Sadie starts to step back as well but the man stops her.

"Sadie, remain where you are," he says.

"What? Why? What did I—"

"Quiet! You will not ask questions." The man's getting very impatient. "Victoria, step forward."

He waits until she does, then continues speaking. "Victoria Sinclair, the benefits you and your husband received because of his membership in this organization are now rescinded, and any such benefits received in the past will need to be repaid. We've already begun siphoning money from your personal bank accounts and if it's not enough to cover his debt, we'll be withdrawing money from your investment accounts. You will not be allowed to take money from your parents or Royce's family, given that they, too, receive financial rewards from the organization. You will also no longer have access to the clinic. Should you choose to seek revenge via blackmail or selling secrets about us to outsiders, you will be terminated. You are no longer under the newly instituted protection rule. As for your four children, they may continue to receive money from either side of the family, but if we find that any of that money has been given to you, they will no longer be allowed to receive that money. Do you understand?"

Victoria clears her throat. "Yes."

"Sadie Sinclair. Because of your parents' actions, we are no longer considering you one of our options for Evan's future wife."

"But—" She stops when he puts his hand up.

"Your relationship with him has now ended and he will be notified. You are not to contact him in any way from this point forward. If we find out you disobeyed, there will be consequences." He pounds his gavel. "This ends the sentencing. They may now be escorted out, except for Jade Sinclair."

What? I can't leave? Why can't I leave? I answered their questions. I'm done.

Two robed men appear with blindfolds. They place them on Victoria, Sadie, and her sisters, and lead them out of the room. I remain standing there under the hot lights. I close my eyes a moment to escape the harsh glare.

"Yes, Pearce." I open my eyes when I hear the man talking again. I didn't hear Pearce say anything. Maybe he raised his hand.

"Jade has answered your questions regarding Victoria," Pearce says from somewhere behind me. "I request that she be allowed to leave now."

"We have other questions for her. Please sit down." He pauses, probably waiting for Pearce to sit, then says, "Jade, the members would like to know why it is you re-entered into a relationship with Garret Kensington after his actions and behaviors last spring?"

Shit. What kind of question is that? I'm not prepared for this. I don't know what to say. I feel like I have to craft each word perfectly for these people or I'll screw up and get myself in trouble.

"Ms. Sinclair?" he says, waiting for my response.

"It's Kensington. Jade Kensington. Garret and I are married."

Dammit. I shouldn't have corrected him like that. Now I'm going to get in trouble.

"We know your name is Kensington. We used Sinclair just to avoid any confusion while discussing this case. Now, please answer the question."

"I um—" I'm so hot under these lights I feel dizzy. Or maybe it's just because I'm nervous. "I love him." I take a breath. "I love Garret and I forgave him for what he did. He's young, and people tend to do stupid things when they're young. He needed to do all that stuff and get it out of his system."

"And is it out of his system? Is he no longer doing those things?"

I hesitate. If they think Garret's a new man who doesn't do anything bad, they might try to get him back.

"Garret isn't perfect," I say. "He still has some issues to work through."

"What kind of issues?"

"You've asked her enough," Pearce says. "She doesn't have to answer your questions. Garret is no longer a member. His issues are no longer your concern."

"That may be true," the man says. "But *you're* still a member, Pearce. And what your son does could affect us. We don't want more images of him on the news, crashing cars and destroying hotel rooms."

"He's not doing that," Pearce says. "And if he does, I will stop it before the media gets word of it."

"Jade." The man pauses. "I trust that Garret and Pearce have informed you that any and all information you know about this group must be kept confidential, and that if you ever share this information with others, your protection under the newly instituted rule will no longer be valid, putting you at risk."

"Yes. I understand."

The man nods at someone on the side of the room. "Jade and Garret may leave now."

I look to my right and see a robed man walking toward me, holding a blindfold.

"Oh, and Jade." The man with the gavel is speaking again.

"Yes?"

Beneath the hood, on his dark shadowy face, I see his mouth curve up just slightly. "Welcome to the family."

An icy chill runs down my spine as the blindfold is wrapped around my eyes. Why did he say that? What does that mean? Is it good or bad? I need to get out of here. I know they said I'm safe, but I don't feel safe and I want out of here as fast as possible.

I feel Garret's hand around mine. He leads me out of the room into the cold, damp hallway and back outside. Garret helps me into the car and I feel it drive away. After we've been driving a while, Garret takes the blindfold off me.

We still can't talk because of the microphones in the car. So I just lay against him and close my eyes and try to calm down. That whole experience totally freaked me out. The only good thing that came out of it was that Victoria got punished. Making her poor doesn't seem like that big of a punishment, but I guess to her it is. And now Sadie won't be first lady.

I smile at that. I used to want to try to be friends with my half sisters but not anymore. I'm done trying. Like Garret told me before, you don't have to be friends with your family. And after today's events, I know for sure that Sadie and I will never be friends.

# Chapter 36

**GARRET**

*I* hated being back there. Back in that underground dungeon where they have their meetings. It's not really a dungeon. It's just a room with tiered seating. But when they dim the lights and do that spotlight thing, it looks like a damn dungeon. Then they add the black robes with the hoods and you feel like you're in a medieval torture chamber, preparing to be beheaded.

Their usual meetings aren't like that, but this was a sentencing, so they have to make it dark and ominous. Jade was shaking the whole time. I knew she'd be scared, standing there all by herself. And I wouldn't have left her side, but then I found out I'd be sitting right behind her so I went along with it. My dad was seated next to me. Across from us, in front of Jade, was the ruling council. They give out the punishments. I don't know who's on the council. I couldn't see their faces.

I never wanted Jade to be anywhere near those people. Not just the ruling council, but any of the members. But she insisted we do this, thinking they'd leave us alone if we did. And although I think it was good the members saw her in person and were told that she can never be harmed, I still didn't like having her so close to them.

When we're back at the house, we go up to my room and Jade collapses on the bed.

"Jade, get up."

"I just need to rest a minute after all that stress."

"Take your clothes off."

She sits up. "What? Garret, I don't want to have sex right now."

I start undressing. "We're not having sex. We're checking for microphones."

"On our clothes?"

"Yes. They could've planted them on us while we were there. So take everything off."

She takes off her dress and we change into different clothes. Then I bring her dress and my suit downstairs and leave them in the study. My dad will check the clothes later when he checks his suit. He has one of those wand things to check for hidden microphones but I don't know where he keeps it.

"Okay, now we can talk," I say when I get back upstairs. Jade is lying on my bed. I lie next to her.

"Are all the meetings like that?"

"No, but I can't tell you what they're like so let's not talk about it."

"Do you think Victoria's going to try to do something to me now that she's been punished?"

"No. If she did, she'd be punished again. The members see you as one of us now, and Victoria no longer is. She knows if she messes with you, she'll get in trouble."

"Maybe she doesn't care. She's already been punished so she has nothing to lose."

"She has a lot more to lose. They went easy on her."

"What about Sadie? Do you think she'll do something to me?"

"If she does, I'll go after her myself. You didn't do anything wrong, Jade. This is all happening because of what Royce did. Did Sadie say something to you while you were standing there? I saw her turn her head and it looked like she said something."

"She called me a bitch." Jade says it softly.

I sigh. "What the fuck is Sadie's problem? You've never said or done anything bad to her and she still acts like that."

"Her sister called me a whore." Jade's eyes are tearing up. She really wanted sisters, but I think she's finally getting that having the Sinclair girls as sisters is not a good thing. "Emily doesn't even know me and she still called me that."

God, I hate those girls so bad.

"Jade, come here." I hug her into my chest. "Just forget about them. You don't need them in your life."

"I know. But I wanted them in my life. I wanted more family."

"You *have* family. You have my dad and Lilly, Frank and Ryan. Grace and William and Meredith. You don't need Sadie and her sisters."

Jade's phone rings. She gets up to check it. "It's Harper. I'm surprised she's taking a break from Sean long enough to call me."

I leave, so the two of them can talk. As I'm going downstairs, I see Lilly walking toward me from the living room. She has her head down, her shoulders slumped.

"Hey." I meet her at the bottom of the stairs and pick her up. "You want to play a video game?"

She shakes her head, then rests it on my shoulder. I think it's finally hitting her that her parents are divorced and her mom isn't going to live here anymore. Last week, she was distracted by all the holiday activities, but now Christmas is over and my dad will be at his meeting all week and Jade and I are leaving. This will be a hard week for her as reality sets in and she realizes that things aren't going to be the same anymore.

I go in the living room and sit down, setting Lilly on my lap. "Do you want to talk about it?"

She shrugs.

"Tell me what's wrong."

"Why did Mom leave me?" She keeps her head down and picks up the drawstring on my hooded sweatshirt, wrapping it around her finger.

"She didn't leave you. She just had some things to care of. She'll be back."

"No, she won't. She's never coming back. She doesn't want me anymore."

"Lilly, that's not true. Why would you say that?"

"She gave me to Dad because she doesn't want me."

Unfortunately, it *is* kind of true. Katherine doesn't seem to want Lilly. She didn't even fight my dad for her. But that has nothing to do with Lilly. I think Katherine's just done being a mom. She's moved on, but I can't tell Lilly that.

"Lilly, your mom wants you. It's just that it's easier if you live most of the time with one parent instead spending half the time with your mom and half with Dad, especially if they don't live close to each other. Are you saying you don't want to live with Dad? You'd rather live with your mom?"

"No. I'd rather live with Dad."

"Are you sad because your mom didn't say goodbye before she left?"

She nods.

"That doesn't mean she doesn't want you. And it doesn't mean she isn't coming back. She just has a lot going on right now. She'll be back. You'll see her again."

"Can we call her?"

Katherine's the last person I want to talk to, but Lilly wants to, so I get my phone out and call her. But if Katherine sees it's me calling, she probably won't answer.

Surprisingly, she picks up. "What do you want, Garret? Are you calling to congratulate me?"

"For what?"

"Haven't you seen the news?"

Lilly takes the phone from me. "Hi, Mom!" Lilly perks up, a big smile on her face. "Are you coming home soon?" She listens, her smile slowly fading as she nods. "Yeah. Okay. Bye." She gives me the phone back.

"Katherine?" I listen, but nobody's there so I end the call. "What did she say?"

Lilly shrugs. "She's busy, just like you said."

"Where is she?"

"In New York. With her boyfriend."

Boyfriend? The senator? I didn't think Lilly knew about him. Katherine's not even supposed to be dating that guy anymore.

"She said she's with her boyfriend?"

"Yeah." Lilly lays her head on my shoulder. "She said they're busy and she can't come back here for a while. They have stuff to do."

"What kind of stuff?"

"Stuff for the baby."

"Baby?" I sit up straighter. "What baby? Who's having a baby?"

"Mom."

"She just told you this? Like just now?"

Lilly nods. "I told you she doesn't want me. She only wants the new baby."

"Maybe you heard her wrong. Maybe someone else is having a baby."

"She said she's having a baby."

Katherine's having a baby? It sure as hell better not be my dad's. It can't be. Given how much he hates her, I can't imagine him having sex with her. It's gotta be the senator's baby. So that's why Katherine told me to congratulate her. And she acted like it was on the news.

I slide Lilly off my lap and stand up. "Why don't you go in the kitchen and see what Charles is making?"

"He's making cookies. Chocolate chip."

"Let's go have some. But first I have to go upstairs and get Jade. Wait for me in the kitchen."

"Okay." She walks off while I sprint up the stairs. I pass Jade in the hall on the way to my room.

She follows me in there. "What are you doing?"

"Katherine's pregnant with the senator's baby." I turn the TV on and flip through to a news channel. I see her name scrolling at the bottom of the screen, with the words, 'Katherine Kensington, recently divorced from Pearce Kensington, admits to having an affair with Senator Lyndon Tate of New York.'

I flip to a different channel and see the senator's photo in the corner. The news guy is talking, "...major scandal for Senator Tate, who currently serves as the chairman of the Senate Committee on Armed Services, a very prestigious and powerful role. News of this scandal will not likely harm his position as chairman, but it could affect him when it comes time for re-election, given his conservative base. Katherine Kensington, the woman he had the affair with, broke the news to the media just this morning, adding that she recently found out she's pregnant with the senator's baby. No word yet on whether the two of them plan to get married. This will be the senator's first child. We'll update you later as more details come in."

"Holy crap!" Jade sits on the bed. "Katherine's pregnant? She hates kids. Why would she want another one?"

"This isn't about wanting a kid. This is about making the senator marry her."

"Maybe he won't do it."

"His campaign was all about family values. If he wants his constituents to vote for him again, he needs to marry her. Katherine knows that. She also knows that making this public means she's protected."

"Protected from what?"

"The organization. If the pregnant wife or girlfriend of a well-known senator ends up dead, reporters will be all over that. The members don't want to deal with that."

"You think they were going to kill her? I thought they couldn't hurt her now that they have that new rule."

"She lost her protection under that rule when she killed my grandfather. She knew she wasn't safe. Let's go downstairs. I told Lilly we'd have cookies with her and Charles."

My dad's there when we get downstairs. He's already changed into different clothes.

"They dismissed us early because of everything that's going on," he says.

"So you heard the news?" I ask him. "About Katherine?"

"Yes. It was discussed at the meeting."

"She did it to save herself, didn't she?"

"I don't know how far along her pregnancy is, so I can't say for sure. She might've been pregnant before your grandfather's death. But I do think the pregnancy was her way of making sure the senator would marry her. He has no choice in the matter. He wouldn't be re-elected if he didn't. But he's out as VP. Katherine thought she was being clever. She thought getting pregnant would secure her both a husband and a place as the vice president's wife. But the VP part isn't going to happen. They're going to find someone else. In fact, they're not even going to support Tate when he's up for re-election. Now that he's forever tied to Katherine, the organization wants nothing to do with him."

"Speaking of Katherine," I say, "Lilly's really upset that Katherine just left without saying goodbye. She thinks her mom doesn't want her anymore. Lilly wanted to call her, so she did, and Katherine told her about the baby."

He sighs. "What is wrong with her? That's not something you tell a child over the phone."

"Daddy." Lilly runs down the hall and up to him. "You want a cookie?"

He picks her up. "I would love a cookie. How's my favorite girl?"

"Good." She smiles really wide. "Where'd you go? This morning I woke up and you weren't here."

"I had a meeting to go to."

"I missed you." She hugs him.

"I missed you, too."

She looks surprised. "You did?"

"Yes, and I have the rest of the day off so I thought we could go do something. But let's go have some cookies first." He sets her down.

She smiles. "Okay!"

My dad's so much better with her than he used to be. Thank God that he is, because it sounds like he's going to be the only parent she has left.

As we're walking to the kitchen, my phone rings. "Go ahead," I tell Jade. "I'll be right there."

I go in the living room to answer it. I don't recognize the number. "Hello?"

"Garret?"

"Yeah. Who is this?"

"It's Justin. Let's just go with Carson since that's how you know me."

"How did you get this number?"

"It's not that hard to get a phone number. I have resources, remember? Hanniford. The FBI."

"What do you want?"

"I followed you this morning."

"What are you talking about?"

"I'm here in Connecticut and I saw you and Jade leaving this morning with Pearce. I tried following you, but I lost track of the car when I got stopped at a light."

"You have nothing better to do than follow us around?"

"You were going to a meeting, weren't you? A meeting for the secret society."

"I'm done listening to your fucked-up conspiracy theories, Carson. I'm hanging up."

"We've been following your father for months now. We know he's part of this. And he's going to lead us to the others."

"There are no others. There's no secret group. You need to stop obsessing over this."

"My sister's dead, Garret. They killed her. You really think I'm going to just give up?"

"Why are you calling me?"

"I want you to convince your father to talk to Hanniford. Just talk. He's not asking for names or to make any kind of deal. He just wants to talk to him."

"Then he can call him himself."

"He knows your father won't answer the call. Besides, it's impossible to get through to Pearce. His assistant won't let anyone talk to him."

I smile. "You couldn't find his cell number?"

"No. Even the FBI guy we're working with couldn't get it."

"That should tell you he wants to be left alone. Tell Hanniford my dad's not going to meet with him. That guy needs to get over the fact that he didn't win the election and stop making up stories to explain why he lost. He's just as crazy as you are."

"Garret, please. Just listen to me. You have a sister. I know she's a half sister, but I'm sure you still care about her. If she were murdered simply for knowing something she shouldn't, wouldn't you want to find the people who did that to her? Take them down before they did that to someone else?"

He's right. I'd want to do exactly that, but I can't help him. Besides, the man who murdered his sister is dead. Carson couldn't get his revenge even if I told him who did it.

"What are you saying, Carson? You want to find her killer and then kill that person? Doesn't that make you just as bad as her killer?"

"I didn't say I was killing anyone. I'm just trying to expose them. Let their actions be known so they can't keep doing these things."

"You really think that's how this works?"

"What do you mean?"

I can't say this over the phone. He's probably recording this conversation.

"Where are you right now?"

"I'm sitting outside your house."

"You're kidding me, right?"

"I'm parked on the street."

I sigh. "Get out of your car and go stand at the gate. I'm going out there, and after this, we're done talking. I don't want to hear from you ever again."

I end the call and grab my coat from the closet, then go in the study and get the wand-like device that checks for listening devices. My dad left it in there after he checked our clothes.

I go outside and down to the gate. Carson's standing there, wearing jeans, a black coat, and a baseball cap. He does look young for his age. He's a big guy, but his face looks young, which is why he could pass for a college freshman.

"Where's your phone?" I ask him.

He holds it up.

"Go put it in your car."

"I'm not recording you, Garret."

"Yeah, like I'm really going to trust you."

He goes back to his car and tosses the phone on the front seat, then comes back.

"Now stand right next to the gate."

He does, and I run the wand over him. It doesn't go off.

"And you think *I'm* the one who's paranoid?" he asks.

"You've made it clear you have an agenda. I'm not letting you record me so you can twist my words to fit whatever story you plan to tell the media."

"So why did you come out here? Why are you even talking to me?"

"Because I want this to end. My family doesn't need this stress. My dad just got divorced and my sister, Lilly, isn't handling it well. It's a rough time for both of them and they don't need you and Hanniford and whoever else you're working with causing them even more stress."

"I'm sorry about your dad's divorce but this issue is larger than that. I can't give up on this, Garret. I need justice for my sister."

"You're not getting justice. Harassing my family and following us around won't bring your sister back."

"No, but I'll feel good knowing I took down the people who did that to her."

"You don't know who did it to her. You're just guessing. Making up theories with no evidence to support them."

"It's not just a theory. She had proof the last election was rigged. And I know it's some type of secret society that's behind it."

I pause, trying to figure out how to say this without giving too much away. "Let's just say, hypothetically, that some secret group existed and that they were able to somehow control things."

"Like elections."

"Doesn't matter what it is. Let's just say they had enough power to make certain things happen. Do you really think exposing them would take them down?"

"Why wouldn't it?"

I roll my eyes. "Seriously? You really think that would work? This is real life, Carson. This isn't a movie where the bad guys get taken down at the end and the good guys walk off into the sunset. In real life, the bad guys get together with other bad guys and they usually win."

"And you're saying your dad and this group are the bad guys."

I sigh. "No. That's not what I'm saying. I'm not talking about my dad. I'm talking about how bad people don't just go away. And if you go after them, you could be putting yourself in danger. It's like when you're a kid and some bully starts bothering you on the playground. What happens when you go tell the teacher?"

"She tells him to stop."

"Yeah, and then he gets pissed that you told on him and he beats you up even more. Do you get what I'm saying?"

"This isn't elementary school. And I'm not telling the teacher. I'm telling the FBI."

"And what if the bully had friends in the FBI?"

He looks down, his eyes darting to the side. I don't think he thought about that. Shit, he's really naive. He has no idea what he's getting himself into.

He looks back at me. "Do they?"

"This is hypothetical. There's no secret group. What I'm saying is that bad guys almost always have people on the inside. That's why they don't get caught."

"If this group had people on the inside, the agent we're working with would know."

"Maybe. Maybe not. The point I'm trying to make is that if this was really going on, you wouldn't be able to stop it. And if you keep making allegations against people, especially rich, important people, you're going to piss them off. They could destroy your reputation. Prevent you from ever getting a job. Are you really willing to risk that?"

"Yeah, I am."

"And you think if you got rid of these so-called bad guys, new ones wouldn't show up in their place?"

"Not if the government did their job and made sure groups like this couldn't control the system."

"The government is run by politicians. People who get into office by lying, cheating, and making promises they have no intention of ever keeping. People who will do most anything to make sure they win, even if those things are illegal. And you're trusting these people to keep the bad guys away?" I laugh. "Sorry, I don't mean to laugh, but I can't believe you really think that way."

"So what's your solution? Just let the bad guys win? Do nothing?"

"I don't have a solution. I just know that things aren't always what they seem. Just because someone has a lot of money doesn't mean they're doing bad things or that they belong to some secret group. Sometimes the people you think are good are the ones you need to watch out for the most. Like this FBI guy you're working with. Are you really sure you can trust him?"

"He's doing this on the side, not as part of his regular job. There's no open case."

"And why would he do that? What's he getting out of this?"

"He wants justice. He wants to bring these people down."

"That's it? He's spending his free time helping Hanniford just because he wants justice? I don't believe that."

"Why else would he be doing it?"

"I'm not going to stand here all day and analyze his motives. You need to think this through yourself. I need to go inside. I want you to leave now and I want you to stop coming over and stop following my family around."

The speaker attached to the gate comes on. "Garret, do you need assistance down there?"

It's the security guy. I waved at him when I came out here so he'd know I didn't need him. But he's probably wondering why this is taking so long.

"No, I don't need any assistance." I look at Carson as I say it. "Carson was just leaving."

The speaker clicks off.

"You need to leave now, Carson. I'm not joking around here. I don't want to see you again."

As he walks away, he says, "I'm not giving up on this, Garret."

He needs to give up. He's wasting his time. The organization can't be brought down. And even if they could, another group just like them would take their place.

I tried to warn him but he wouldn't listen. There isn't anything else I can do. He's determined to pursue this, and in doing so, he might get killed.

# Chapter 37

**JADE**

*G*arret never came to the kitchen, so I went looking for him and found him coming in from outside. He's holding that device that tests for hidden microphones.

"Where were you?" I ask him.

"Out talking to Carson." He takes his coat off and hangs it in the closet.

"Carson was here?"

"He followed us this morning and he's been sitting out there on the street for who knows how long."

"Why do you have that wand thing?"

Garret sets it in the study, then comes back out into the foyer. "I had to make sure Carson wasn't recording me."

"What did he say?"

"That he's not giving up. That he's determined to find out who the other members are."

"So he still thinks your dad is one?"

"Yeah. That's why he's following him. Carson's convinced that my dad will lead him to the other members."

"You need to tell your dad this."

Pearce appears just as I say it. He's talking to Lilly. "Go up and change and then we'll go." She runs up the stairs. "We're going out for an early dinner," he says to Garret. "I gave Charles the night off."

"Dad, Carson was just here."

"Who's Carson?"

"That guy, Justin. Jade and I know him as Carson. Anyway, he followed us this morning."

"Yes, I know."

"And you're okay with this?"

"I wanted him following us. I was recording him. I have it all on video. And I told the driver to lose him before we got there so Justin wouldn't find out our location."

"Why were you recording him?"

"I'm collecting evidence to prove that Hanniford's not giving up in his mission to expose the organization. Justin will keep following me until he finds what he's looking for. If I'm able to show the members how determined he is, I might be able to distance myself from the organization."

"You think they'd let you out?" Garret asks.

"Not completely, but they might be forced to release me from some of my commitments. If I'm constantly being followed, it puts the other members at risk. They don't want to have to worry about their identities being revealed or the group being exposed. It would be easier if they kept me at a distance, meaning I would no longer attend the meetings or be involved in their activities. I'd continue to run the company and give them access to whatever they need there, but that would be it."

"How long have you been planning this?" I ask.

"For several months now. I've already shared my concerns about Hanniford with the members, and at the meeting this afternoon, the topic came up again. I explained how I'm being followed everywhere I go and that there's a good chance Hanniford will eventually discover the identities of some of the other members. Everyone agreed that it would be best if I step away for a while."

"But they could easily end this," Garret says. "They could just kill Carson."

"He's not the only one who's been following me. There are others, including that FBI agent. Getting rid of Carson, I mean, Justin, won't make this end."

"So they're not going to kill him, right?" I ask Pearce.

"I can't control what they do. What Justin is doing is dangerous and he's putting himself at risk."

I get a sick feeling in my stomach. Carson annoys me, but I don't want him getting hurt. Or killed.

Pearce continues. "The members aren't worried about Justin right now. He's young and a nobody, so if he told his theories to the press, it's unlikely they'd take it seriously. Hanniford is the one they're concerned about. He'll be the one they'll go after. He's been voicing his theories to anyone who will listen. So far, his theories haven't gotten much traction. People aren't taking him seriously. But if he was able to provide evidence to support his theories, it could cause problems."

"Problems, as in it could destroy the organization?" I ask.

Pearce laughs a little. "No. That would never happen. And even if it did, nothing would change. Hanniford doesn't understand that we aren't the only group trying to manage how things are run in this country. If we weren't in charge, one of those other groups would be. And as much as you don't like the organization and what they do, those other groups are far worse. It's better us than them. And at least now you're on the inside. You're protected."

"That doesn't make me feel any better."

Pearce puts his arm around me. "You and Garret need to go on with your lives and stop worrying about this."

"What are they going to do to Hanniford?"

He smiles. "Jade, I just told you to stop worrying about this. Focus on school and your future with Garret."

"I just don't like people getting hurt. I don't want Carson to end up like his sister."

"I'll see what I can do." Pearce lets me go as Lilly comes back down the stairs.

We leave for dinner, and when we get back we play a board game with Lilly. There's no more talk about Carson or Hanniford or the organization. I ask Garret about it later when we're in bed and he repeats what his dad says. I'm not to worry about it. We're done with this. We're not looking back. We're staying out of it and focusing on the future. It's exactly what I want to do, but I think it'll take a while for me to put this behind me and accept that this is over. That the organization will finally leave us alone.

The next morning, Pearce drives us to the private airport where he keeps his jet. I'm not thrilled about getting on a small plane, but all the regular flights were booked with people flying home after Christmas. If we wanted to fly commercial, we'd have to wait until later this week and we can't. We need to get home. We promised Sean and Harper we'd meet them in LA tomorrow.

On the drive to the airport, Lilly's sitting next to me in the back seat. When we're almost there, she says, "Do you have to go?"

"Yeah. Garret and I are going to see Sean and Harper tomorrow in LA. We're spending New Year's with them."

Lilly tugs on my arm. I lean down and she says, "Sean is cute."

I laugh. "He *is* cute, isn't he?"

Garret's in the front seat, but he heard us talking. He whips around and says to Lilly, "Did you just say Sean is cute?"

She nods, a shy smile on her face.

"Since when do you think boys are cute?"

She shrugs. "I don't know."

He sighs and turns back around. I swear, he will not survive if we have girls.

I feel Lilly staring at me, specifically my stomach. "Are you having a baby?"

"Baby? No, I'm not having a baby." I look down at my stomach. I don't look pregnant, so why would she say that? "Why would you think I'm having a baby?"

"Mom's having a baby. Why aren't you?"

Pearce turns the radio down. He must've heard Lilly.

"I'm kind of young to have a baby. Usually you wait until you're a little older. I have to finish college first."

"And then you'll have a baby?"

Garret looks back at me and smiles.

"Um, probably. Or maybe a few years after college."

I see Pearce eyeing me in the rear view mirror. "I have to wait that long to be a grandfather?" He smiles.

This is awkward. I've never talked about this with Garret's family. I just recently talked to Garret about it.

Before I can answer Pearce, Lilly says, "You should have it now. Then I'd have another sister to play with."

"The baby would be your niece, not your sister," Garret says. "You'd be an aunt."

"Like your Aunt Caroline," Pearce says. "Remember her? She came for Christmas one year."

Caroline is Katherine's sister who lives in France. Garret never mentions her. I think he's only met her that one time at Christmas.

"I didn't like Aunt Caroline," Lilly says.

"I'm not a fan of her either," Pearce says quietly to Garret.

"Max said babies don't come from storks," Lilly says.

That's just great. Garret already doesn't like Lilly's friend, Max, also known as bow tie boy. Now Garret will hate him even more, knowing he's telling Lilly the truth about babies.

Garret turns back to look at Lilly. "Where did he say they came from?"

"He didn't say. The bell rang and we had to go inside."

"Don't listen to him." Garret faces forward again. "He doesn't know what he's talking about. The stork brings babies. That's all you need to know."

"Garret, don't confuse—"

"Dad, she's seven. It's not time yet."

Lilly holds my hand. "I hope you have 10 babies and they're all girls and they all wear pink and have long blond hair."

Garret laughs. "So you basically want 10 copies of yourself."

"I just want someone to play with," she says quietly.

I smile at her. "I'll see what I can do, okay? But 10 is kind of a lot."

We arrive at the airport, which is just a big square building. It doesn't really look like an airport. A man comes out and takes our luggage. As we approach the door to the building, it swings open and Victoria storms out, wearing sunglasses and a long black coat with fur around the neckline.

She sees me and abruptly stops right in front of me. "You! How dare you and your whore of a mother destroy my family like this!" She reaches up like she's going to slap me, but Garret and Pearce both grab her arm before she does it.

"Get away from her!" Garret's in front of me now, still holding Victoria's arm.

"Garret, let me handle this," Pearce says. "Take Jade and Lilly inside."

Lilly's behind me, holding on to my coat. I'm sure she's scared after hearing Victoria yell at me like that and seeing her almost hit me.

Garret picks Lilly up and takes my hand. "Let's go."

We go inside, but I can still hear Pearce talking. "You come near my family again and I'll make sure you—"

I can't hear the rest of what he says because Garret's pulling me away from the door. He doesn't want Lilly hearing any of that.

We go and sit down on one of the couches. The airport is an open space that has couches and chairs. Some TVs hang down from the ceiling. There are windows all along the back wall where you can see the private planes lined up. Lilly runs off to look out the window while Garret and I remain seated and wait for Pearce. He comes in about a minute later and sits across from us.

"Why was she here?" Garret asks him.

"She wanted to use the Sinclair jet, but the pilot told her she's not allowed on it. William banned her from using it. She'll have to fly commercial."

I laugh, then cover my mouth. "Sorry. I guess it's not really funny."

Garret laughs. "Are you kidding? It's fucking hilarious. Can you imagine Victoria on a regular plane? I'm sure she'll fly first class, but still. She's gonna hate it."

Pearce nods toward the windows. "You two need to go. They're loading your luggage." We stand up and Pearce gives Garret a hug. "It was good having you home." He lets Garret go and gives me a hug. "Come back any time. I miss having you two close by."

I smile at him. "We miss you, too. Maybe you could come out for spring break."

"Yes, I'll try to clear my schedule." He walks us over to the windows where Lilly is standing, looking out at the planes. "Honey, say goodbye."

She turns around and hugs me. "Please don't go."

I kneel down and hug her back. "We'll come back soon and see you. And your dad will take you to California, so we'll see each other a lot."

My words don't seem to help. Her eyes are tearing up. She hugs Garret as he picks her up.

He kisses her cheek. "Hey, don't be sad. You can call me whenever you want, okay?"

She nods. "I love you, Garret."

"I love you, too." He hugs her tight once more, then sets her down.

"Have a good New Year's," Pearce says.

"Yeah, you too," Garret says. "Got any plans?"

Pearce picks up Lilly and says to her, "What do you think? Are you going to celebrate New Year's with me?"

She nods. "Okay."

He smiles at us. "I guess I have plans."

Garret laughs. "Those plans will probably involve a tea party."

Pearce laughs as well. "I imagine they will." He walks us to the door. "Have a good trip."

We wave goodbye, then go outside and walk toward the line of planes.

"It's that one right over there," Garret says, pointing out his dad's plane.

"I don't think I can go on that," I say as we approach it. "It's really small."

Garret holds my hand. "It's not that small. For a private jet, it's actually large. You can't compare it to a commercial jet."

We get on and take the seats in the back. There are 10 seats and they're all much larger than the seats on a normal plane. They look comfortable and luxurious, covered in a soft beige leather.

"Have you been on this before?" I ask Garret as I buckle my seatbelt.

He smiles at me. "Jade, I only flew private until I met you."

"You'd never been on a regular plane before?"

"I had, but it was when I was a kid."

He means back when his mom was alive. His mom hated small planes because she thought they were dangerous. And she was right. She ended up dying on one. Shit! What if Garret and I die on this thing?

I feel my palms sweating as the plane moves.

"I can't do this." I undo my seatbelt. "Let's get off."

"Relax." He fastens my seatbelt again. "Everything's going to be fine."

I take some deep breaths and squeeze his hand as the plane goes down the runway. My stupid brain keeps imagining it crashing and going up in flames.

"Think about something else," Garret says, as if he can read my mind.

"Like what?"

He kisses my cheek. "Our house."

I'm clutching Garret with one hand and gripping the seat with the other. "We're not going to have a house because we're going to die when this thing takes off."

"It already took off. It was so smooth you didn't even notice."

I lean over to look out the window. All I see are clouds. Wow, that really was a smooth takeoff.

"We could die during landing," I tell him.

"We can't die," he says. "We have to be here for our kids."

"We don't have kids."

"Not yet. But we already put in our order, so they're coming, which means we need to be around for them when they arrive."

I don't know how Garret does it, but he always makes me laugh when I don't at all feel like laughing. "Are you still thinking the stork brings babies, Garret?"

"Just because you haven't seen him doesn't mean he doesn't exist."

Garret's so serious, it makes me laugh even more. "And who put this order in? Because I know I didn't."

"*I* did. You have to get on his list years in advance."

"And how many did you order?"

"Two. That's what you wanted, right?"

"Yeah, two's good. You didn't tell him to bring them both at once, did you? Because I don't think I could handle twins."

"We could handle it." He kisses me. "But no, I told him to space them apart."

"How much apart?"

"I didn't specify. Did you have a timeline in mind?"

"I haven't really thought about it. Maybe a couple years apart?"

"That works. I'll send him a note and let him know."

I laugh again. "You have his address? Where exactly does he live?"

He shrugs. "Somewhere in Florida. He likes warm weather and hanging out on the beach."

"You're funny." I smile and rest my head on his shoulder. "I love you."

He kisses my head. "I love you, too."

And just like that, he's calmed me down. I was a nervous wreck just a few minutes ago and now I'm relaxed and imagining a big white bird sunbathing on the beach in Florida. I love that he can calm me down like that. It's like he senses what I need and knows just what to do.

Garret rests his head back and reclines a little. The armrest between us is up and I let go of his hand and he instantly raises his arm so I can sneak in my spot against his chest. He lowers his arm over me and it relaxes me even more. I close my eyes and imagine those kids the stork is bringing us. Now that I know I want kids, I get really happy when I think about having them.

I fall asleep, and when I wake up, we're back in California. Garret's leaning over, looking out the window.

"We're almost there." He rubs my hand. "See? It wasn't so bad, was it?"

"The plane? No, it was good. But isn't this against the rules? I mean, isn't taking your dad's plane like taking his money?"

"He's not giving it to us. He's just letting us use it."

"I know, but still."

"If it wasn't okay, he wouldn't have let us use it. Besides, I get the feeling they won't be as strict on the rules now that they know who you are."

I smile. "I thought we weren't talking about them anymore."

"You're right. We're not. Talk about something else."

I glance out the window and see nothing but tree tops. "I'm getting nervous."

"Don't be. The landing is as smooth as the takeoff. My dad has really good pilots."

I feel the plane starting its descent. I sit back and close my eyes and feel Garret's lips on mine. He's distracting me so I relax during the landing. And it works. I get so into his kiss, I barely notice the wheels touching down.

When the plane comes to a stop, I open my eyes and see Garret smiling at me. "We're home. You ready to go?"

"Yeah." I smile back, realizing that we really are home. This is our home. We're going to stay here in California and build a house and have a family.

After all the obstacles that have been thrown at us, I was starting to think that our dream would never happen. But now I feel like it finally will. Garret and I are going to have what we always wanted. A life together. Without any more interference.

"Jade, are you coming?" Garret's standing in the aisle of the plane, looking down at me in my seat.

I stand up and hug him. "I love you."

"I love you, too." He kisses me. "Let's go home."

*Home.* Garret and I have a home. Together. And I finally feel like nobody's going to take it away from us.

# Chapter 38

**GARRET**

Wednesday morning, Jade and I drive to LA and check into the hotel we got downtown. I wore a baseball cap and sunglasses and so far nobody's recognized me. I don't think anyone will, but Jade's all worried about it.

We meet up with Sean and Harper at Sean's apartment. It's a small one bedroom, not much different than the one he had in Connecticut. As soon as we get there, Harper takes Jade out to the patio and tells Sean and me to stay away so they can have girl talk. Whenever she says that, it always makes me wonder what this 'girl talk' *is* exactly. I'm guessing they're talking about Sean and me.

"So how's it going?" I ask Sean, taking a seat on his couch.

"Couldn't be any better." He's got this huge grin on his face, showing off his dimples. "I got my girl back. And now she's living with me."

"What's going on with her and her parents?"

"She's talking to her mom and her sisters, but not her dad. She's waiting for him to call, but so far, she hasn't heard anything. Her mom and sisters moved back to the house and Kiefer moved out. I think Kelly's going to divorce him."

"Have you seen her family since you guys got back together?"

"Yeah, we went to her house last night and picked up some of her stuff. Kelly was really nice to me. She apologized for how she acted before, so I guess it's just Harper's dad who hates me."

Sean never did tell me that he was threatened and attacked in the park that day. But he must assume Kiefer was behind it, which is the only explanation that would make sense, since Sean doesn't know about the organization.

"So are you and Harper back to the place you were before you broke up?"

His grin gets even wider. "Better than that. I finally feel like we're in the same place. Like we want the same thing."

"That's great."

"Hey, for New Year's Eve, do you care if we go to my restaurant for dinner? I know we didn't talk about it, but I really want to take you guys there."

"Sure, that's fine. Whatever you want."

"Good, because I already reserved one of their best tables. It's a really upscale place. It's hard to get reservations."

"Then I'm surprised your boss let you have the table. He must really like you."

"Yeah. Something like that." He's still got that huge freaking grin on his face.

I'm happy for him. He's back to his old self and back with the girl he loves.

We turn the TV on and watch sports news until Harper and Jade finally come inside. Whenever they get together it's like they were never apart. The miles between them the past few months didn't change their friendship at all.

The next day we go to the Santa Monica Pier, walk around Griffith Park, and check out some other tourist spots. Nobody's recognized me, so maybe my fame is over. Or it could be the baseball cap, which Jade keeps insisting I wear.

On Friday, New Year's Eve, Jade and I spend the morning on our own, then meet up with Sean and Harper in the afternoon and hang out at their apartment until dinner.

Sean's been acting strange since we got here. Usually, he and I just sit and talk or watch TV while Jade and Harper do their thing, but today he can't sit still. He keeps getting up, walking around, going to the kitchen and back. It's like he's had too much caffeine.

During dinner, he's still acting that way. We're at the restaurant he works at, seated at a table that's set off on its own with lighted greenery all around it. It's a fancy place and I'm sure it's really expensive. I don't know *how* expensive because they don't list the prices on the menu. That doesn't bother me, but it drives Jade crazy. She can't understand why even rich people wouldn't want to know what they're paying for their meal. But the food was excellent so it's worth whatever it costs.

When the waiter gives us the dessert menus, Sean says, "Forget the menus. I made a special dessert for everyone. I need to go in the kitchen and finish it."

Harper looks at him funny. "When did you make dessert? We've been together all day."

"I made it yesterday when I came into work for a few hours." He gets up from the table.

"What kind of dessert is it?" Harper asks.

He kisses her. "You'll see. I'll be right back."

Jade sets her dessert menu down. "You'd think the chef who's working tonight could just finish the dessert for Sean."

Harper shrugs. "Sean's all about presentation. He probably wants to make sure it looks right on the plate."

A few minutes later, the waiter brings out our dessert. It's a dark chocolate, triple-layer cake with strawberry filling and a dark chocolate frosting.

"This looks really good," Jade says as the waiter sets a piece of cake in front of her. The plate has swirls of chocolate syrup on it that go all around the cake.

"Where's Sean?" Harper asks the waiter.

"He'll be here shortly. Enjoy."

The waiter leaves and Harper scans the dining room, looking for Sean.

Jade's checking out Harper's plate. "Why do you have all those strawberries with yours?"

"Sean probably put them there because he knows I love strawberries with anything chocolate." Harper picks her fork up, still searching for Sean. "We should wait for him. I don't know what's taking him so long."

I'm sitting next to Harper and something on her plate catches my eye. "Harper, you might want to take a look at those strawberries."

"Why?" She looks down at her plate and sees it. She drops her fork. "Oh my God!"

"What?" Jade drops her fork, too. "What's wrong?"

"Harper." Sean appears at our table wearing a tuxedo. He looks really nervous. His body's stiff and he's breathing fast.

Harper turns to him, covering her mouth with her hand, her eyes already wet and ready to spill tears.

"Harper." Sean takes her hand and gets down on one knee. "I know I'm not the richest guy, or the most sophisticated guy, but I'm a guy who loves you more than anything. I love your beautiful smile and your beautiful eyes and your beautiful spirit. Everything about you is beautiful to me. From the first day we met, I knew I'd never be able to get you out of my head. And I was right. Since the first moment I saw you, I've never stopped thinking about you. Even when you're not around, you're always with me, in my mind, and in my heart. I love you, and I would love to spend the rest of my life with you. Harper, will you marry me?"

Harper now has tears streaming down her face. "Yes." She nods. "Yes! I'll marry you!"

He kisses her, then takes the ring from the strawberries and places it on her finger and they kiss again.

My arm's around Jade and I look over and see that she's crying, too.

"Happy tears?" I whisper in her ear.

She nods, sniffling. "Yes."

Sean goes around to the tray stand and comes back with a dozen long-stem red roses and hands them to Harper.

Jade and I stand up, startling Harper. I think she forgot we were here.

We exchange hugs and congratulations, and when everyone calms down, we finally eat our dessert.

"Did you practice that proposal?" Jade asks Sean.

"Only about a million times."

"You did?" Harper kisses him. "That's so sweet." The two of them are sitting so close she's practically on his lap.

"That was an amazing proposal," Jade says.

"Hey." I look at her. "You didn't say *mine* was amazing."

"Yours was more than amazing." She kisses me. Her lips taste like chocolate and it reminds me of all the times chocolate has led to us having sex. My gaze wanders down to her cleavage and the tight red dress she's wearing, then back up to her beautiful jade green eyes, and it makes me wonder how I got a woman this gorgeous and this incredible to say yes to my proposal.

"I love you." She whispers it in my ear, then smiles and goes back to eating her cake.

"This ring is so beautiful." Harper holds her hand out to look at it. "When did you get it?"

Sean smiles at me from across the table. "Right after Christmas."

I smile back. I'll keep his secret. Harper doesn't need to know he bought it months ago. It might freak her out. Back then, she wasn't ready for a proposal. Someday he can tell her the truth.

"It's perfect." She admires her ring again, then hugs him. "I love you."

"I love you, too." They kiss again.

I notice the people at the table across from us pouring champagne. I check my watch. "Only a minute until midnight. Is anyone going to make a toast?"

"I will." Sean ordered us some non-alcoholic champagne. We each stand and hold up our glasses. "To Moorhurst College, for bringing Garret and me the two greatest women in the world."

We laugh as we clink glasses, but it's true. Jade and Harper both showed up at that tiny college in Connecticut, far away from their hometowns. And then I met Jade, and Jade met Harper, and Harper met Sean, and somehow we all ended up together. Jade married me, and now Harper's marrying Sean, and the four of us are best friends.

When I think about that, it amazes me how everything worked out like this. I can't explain it. That's what I like best about the story of Jade and me. It can't be explained. It doesn't make sense. Two people from vastly different backgrounds coming together and becoming best friends and falling in love despite everyone around us trying to keep us apart.

So tonight, on this New Year's Eve, I'd like to toast to those things in life we can't explain, but that end up making our lives fuller and richer and better than we ever imagined.

Life doesn't need to be explained. It just needs to be lived. And appreciated. And spent with those you love.

I turn to Jade, holding up my glass. "To the unexplainable."

"What?" She has no idea what I mean.

"Just go with it." I smile and clink her glass. "Happy New Year, Jade."

# Chapter 39

*Three Years Later*

## JADE

*G*arret gives me a New Year's kiss that melts me from the inside out. I relax into him and feel his arm go around my waist, holding me up.

"Too much champagne?" he asks.

"No. It's your kisses." I smile at him and he gives me another one.

He tugs me closer, getting a firmer grip on my waist. "My kisses make you weak in the knees?"

"They always have and they always will."

He kisses me again. "Happy New Year, Jade."

It's another new year. Another year of this wonderful life that seems to just keep getting better.

Three years ago on this night, Garret and I were watching Sean propose to Harper. She was shocked, but also happier than I'd ever seen her. But she was even happier on her wedding day, which was last year on New Year's Eve. Sean and Harper had a long engagement, which is what Harper wanted, especially after all the stuff going on with her parents.

A few months after Sean and Harper got engaged, Harper's parents got divorced, and for the whole year following, her dad had to go through an investigation regarding his alleged theft of funds from the movie studio. He almost went to prison for it, but his lawyer convinced the judge to just make Kiefer pay back the money, which left him with five million dollars. It sounds like a lot but he was worth way more than that before. Kelly and

Kiefer had to sell their mansion and some of their expensive cars. Kelly moved into a small house in Pasadena and Kiefer moved to New York. He now makes low budget indie films. And he still makes fake videos for the organization.

The story is that Harper's mom divorced her dad because they didn't get along anymore, but I think the truth is that Kelly never wanted Kiefer to join the organization. I don't think she knew everything about it, but she knew enough that she didn't want to be part of it. And despite her objections, Kiefer still wanted to join, at least he did until he found out about their plans for Harper. But by then, I think Kelly had lost respect for her husband and that's what led to their divorce. Kiefer put money before his family and it broke them apart.

Harper said her mom has adjusted to living alone, but she's not really alone. Harper's sisters rented an apartment just down the street from their mom's house, so the three of them always do stuff together. And Sean and Harper, who now live in Santa Barbara, are always down there visiting because Harper's mom and sisters can't get enough of the baby.

Yes, Sean and Harper have a baby. Soon after they got married, Harper found out she was pregnant. She says they weren't planning on that, but I'm not sure if she's telling the truth. I know the two of them didn't want to wait to start a family. They had a baby boy last October. He's super cute. He has bright blond hair just like his mom and dad.

As for their careers, Sean worked his way up to head chef at that restaurant in LA. He stayed there until Harper graduated from college last May. They didn't like the craziness of LA so they moved to a house in Santa Barbara and started a catering and party planning business. The business is already so successful that they can't keep up with all the requests. They're booked through next year. Harper loves planning parties, so this is her dream job. And Sean likes the catering side of things. Plus, by owning their own business, they have control over their schedule, which they both like.

Garret and I also have a lot going on. We graduated last spring. Garret got his business degree and I got a degree in psychology. Garret is now a business owner, or part business owner. He and his dad bought WaveField Sports. The guy who started the company sold it last summer so he could work on his new business, some kind of Internet startup.

Garret didn't have enough money to buy the company himself, so his dad offered to be a partner. By doing this, Pearce isn't giving Garret money so the organization can't say he's violating any rules.

Speaking of the organization, William was promoted to the highest level. It happened three years ago, the same week I was summoned to that sentencing for Victoria. I know it sounds like a bad thing that William was promoted, but it's actually been good. He's changed the way they do things. I can't say exactly what that means because I don't know. I stay out of it. I don't ask questions. But Pearce told Garret that the members can now face punishment for hurting innocent people who happened to see something they shouldn't have, which has caused the members to be much more cautious in how they do things. Pearce said the older members, including his father, were reckless in how they did things and that's what caused people like Carson's sister to end up dead. But the older members are dying off and the younger members want to do things differently. I don't know if they still rig elections. I'm sure they do. But Garret always tells me that if the organization didn't, some other group would. He says that even the local elections in our town are controlled by a small group of people, basically whoever has the most money. I guess that's kind of true. It seems like the candidates with the most money always win.

William comes to visit us a few times a year, but I never ask him about the organization. But I have asked Grace, and like Pearce, she said William's had a positive influence on the group and that Arlin would be proud of him. So I take that to mean that they aren't doing as many bad things. As much as I don't like having my uncle so involved with the organization, the good thing is that with him in such a high-up position, I feel like Garret and I are safe and that they'll leave us alone.

Pearce is no longer actively involved with the organization. He's still a member, but they've asked him to keep his distance until they're sure he's not being followed. Pearce's plan to distance himself from the organization worked. Well, kind of. It didn't go as smoothly as he'd hoped. Carson, also known as Justin, and Hanniford, his billionaire boss, were determined to prove Pearce was a member. And they didn't just follow him. They also tried to hack into his computer, using that girl, Sydney, the one I saw at Moorhurst that day, to do it. It's a long story and I try not to think about it because it turned into this big mess and Garret and I ended up having to get involved. We wouldn't have done it if it was just to help the organization. We only did it to save his dad. If his secrets got out, Pearce would've had enemies lining up to kill him.

Luckily, that didn't happen. Carson, and the rest of the people who were after Pearce, were led to a dead end and they eventually gave up. But they planted their theory in the minds of enough curious reporters that it would be too risky for Pearce to get involved with the organization again anytime soon. Carson is now a reporter overseas so hopefully we'll never see him again. But despite all the headaches Carson caused, he ended up being helpful. His actions allowed Pearce to be temporarily released from his obligations as a member.

So at least for now, Pearce is free from the organization. Pearce is also free on a personal level. After divorcing

Katherine, he wasn't forced to marry someone else, so he's been single for years now. Katherine married that senator, but he's no longer a senator. His conservative voters were angry when they found out he'd been dating a married woman and got her pregnant. He wasn't re-elected so had to go back to his regular life as a Manhattan attorney. He and Katherine had a son, but just like with Lilly, Katherine has no interest in being a mom. A nanny raises the kid while Katherine tries to establish herself again among the social elite. So far, she's been shunned, and last I heard, she was trying to convince her husband to move to France so she could live next to her sister and try to latch on to her sister's high society friends. Even though Katherine lives close to Connecticut, she rarely sees Lilly. It's like Katherine forgot she even has a daughter.

Lilly is 10 now. She still goes to private school and her favorite subject is art. She's a really good artist. She can sketch, paint, sculpt—all that stuff that takes creative skills I don't have. When she used to color me all those pictures, I always thought they were really good for someone her age. I guess she had a talent for art early on. She also still takes swim lessons, and when she gets to middle school, she's going to try out for the swim team. Garret is so proud of her. Every time we go visit her, she races Garret in the pool. She hasn't beat him yet, but someday she might.

Frank is doing well. He has his good days and bad, but mostly good. He married Karen two summers ago. It was a small out-side wedding in Des Moines with just friends and family. And then that fall, Ryan married Chloe. It was sooner than any of us expected, given Ryan's insistence on waiting, but once he no longer had to worry about Frank, he was ready to marry Chloe. Ryan's still in med school, but Chloe graduated and is now in her residency.

Going back to Garret's company, since buying it, he's been working nonstop, trying to learn as much as possible and coming up with strategies to make it grow. He already knows a lot about the company because the guy he bought it from has been Garret's mentor for the past few years. He taught Garret all aspects of the business; the financial side, the sales side, the product side, and more. Pearce has also been mentoring Garret, teaching him all the stuff he's learned after years of running a successful company.

In this company they bought together, Pearce is more of a silent partner. He lets Garret run the show, but is available if Garret needs advice or has a question. Garret has such a great relationship with Pearce now. It's so much different than when I met him.

And I love Pearce. He's like a dad to me. Frank will always be my first dad, but Pearce is definitely my other dad. We talk on the phone all the time. He's still super busy with work, but he never rushes me off the phone. Pearce has helped me be more confident in myself. He tells me to go for stuff and not back down from things I'm afraid to do. Garret tells me the same things, but it's different coming from Pearce. Garret will sometimes tell me I'm good at stuff even when it's not really true. But Pearce isn't afraid to tell me what I need to work on and how to use my strengths to overcome my weaknesses. I find that empowering and I use it in my business.

Yes, I have a business now. I help teens who are at the same dark place I was at years ago, find their way back to the light. I speak at conferences, workshops, summer camps, youth shelters, schools, and more. Ever since I spoke to that group in Des Moines, I started getting requests to speak again. Then word spread and the jobs just kind of found me. I did about five speaking events a year when I was in college, but since then, I've done a lot more. And I love it. I absolutely love my job.

Sometimes it's hard for me to relive what I went through, especially when I see a girl's face in the audience and I can tell she's stuck in that same horrible place I was stuck at for so many years. But I keep giving these speeches, hoping my words will help. I don't always know if they do, but occasionally I get an email telling me how I changed someone's life. The first time I got one of those, I cried for 10 minutes straight. I couldn't believe I had that much of an effect on someone. Even today, those emails make me cry.

While we're on the subject of helping people, I should mention our charities. The summer after our sophomore year, Garret formed Rachel's Swim Club, a non-profit organization that provides free swim lessons to kids. It's named after his mom, who always wanted every kid to know how to swim. Garret convinced his mentor at WaveField Sports to help him out by providing equipment and using his connections to help get the program up and running. It's now in 20 states and is modeled after the program at Camsburg, where members of college swim teams volunteer their time to teach kids how to swim.

Garret and I also started The Taylor Foundation, named in memory of my mom and her parents, who I never got to meet. The foundation gives out money to people like Sara, who need help making ends meet. People can go online and nominate someone they know who needs help. They can either provide the money themselves or they can ask the foundation for the money. But however it's done, the person remains anonymous, just like with our fake foundation. The recipient never knows who nominated them or the source of the money. It could be us, or whoever it was who nominated them. We have a staff of people who review all the nominations and send the money out. So far we've helped a lot of people and it was all inspired by Sara.

I almost forgot about Sara, probably because I never see her anymore and she's too busy to call me, which I totally understand because she and Alex have a new baby girl. Sara and Alex got married two years ago, then moved to Oregon, where Alex got a job as a junior architect. They have a house with a big back yard for Caleb to play in. He's almost four years old now. Sara's been taking classes at the community college, but she's taking this semester off since she just had a baby.

Alex has been a great dad to Caleb. He even adopted him after a long legal battle with Brandon, Caleb's father. When Brandon found out Alex wanted to adopt Caleb, he fought the adoption and tried to get custody of Caleb. Brandon was just being a jerk and everyone knew it, but the law is the law and he *is* Caleb's father so he has rights.

Sara was a mess when this happened. She didn't eat. She didn't sleep. She was totally stressed. She and Alex couldn't afford all the legal fees so Garret's fake rich friend stepped in again and paid for the best lawyer we could get. The lawyer proved to the court that Brandon never wanted Caleb and had no intention of being a father and that he was only doing this to stop the adoption. Eventually it all got settled and Alex was able to adopt Caleb. I'd love to see them again and see how much Caleb's grown. Sara said they'll come visit when the baby is a little older, maybe next summer. I told her she has to stay with us in the house. We have plenty of room and I like having people over.

Our house is now completely done. We built it last year and moved in right after graduation. The pool was put in last May and Grace moved into the guest house in June. I love having her live right next door to us. Garret's been traveling a lot for the business so it's nice to have Grace around so I'm not alone. She doesn't like being alone either so it works out well. She's been planting flowers around her house, using the same flower map she showed me a few years ago. She also started a garden with tomatoes, peppers, cucumbers, and herbs. She's never grown vegetables before so she's excited to see how her garden turns out.

So yeah, a lot has happened the past few years and things are good.

# Chapter 40
## Garret's 24th Birthday

**JADE**

Things are still crazy busy with Garret and me. WaveField Sports has really taken off and we've opened three more stores in California and are looking at expanding into more states. We already have stores in Arizona, Nevada, and Oregon, but are hoping to open a store in Colorado in the next year or so.

I've become a lot more involved with the business. Last spring, Garret asked if I wanted to help expand the women's line of clothing and sporting goods and, of course, I said yes. I love all that stuff, and now I get to check out all the latest items before they come out and decide if we should carry them in our stores.

Owning a sporting goods store has expanded my interest in all kinds of sports. I'm not just running anymore. I'm doing other sports as well. Garret's been teaching me how to surf and I've been swimming in our pool and I've even taken yoga classes. I used to think yoga was boring but I've come to like it. It's helped me build strength and increase my flexibility, which has made me a better runner. I did a marathon last May just to see if I could run that far. I finished it, but I wouldn't do one again. I like to run just to run, not to compete. And I no longer use running to escape my problems. Instead I use it to clear my mind and relax.

I'm still speaking to young women, but have had so many requests that I had to turn some down. It was getting to be too much travel. Plus, I'm trying to get more involved with WaveField and I can't do that if I'm never around. So I cut back to just two or three trips a month, and when I'm home I do video chats with high school students and community groups. I absolutely love what I do. I can't imagine a better job. It doesn't even feel like a job. It just feels like what I was meant to do.

I used to wonder why bad things happened to me. Why I had to grow up in such a bad home with an abusive mother and not enough money for food. I used to wonder what I did to deserve that. Why I had to suffer when other people didn't. But now, I almost feel like I was meant to go through that. Like I had to in order to get to the place I'm at now. And using my experience to help others has helped me get over the pain I felt from the hell I went through as a kid. It's helped me heal and grow and become a stronger person.

"Hey." Garret comes up behind me in the kitchen, his arms circling my waist. "Thanks for dinner."

Tonight was his birthday dinner. I made him lasagna, like I did the first year we were married. Only this time, I didn't actually make it. I ordered it from his favorite Italian place and just heated it in the oven. He didn't want to go out. We love our house so much that we tend to stay in a lot. He cooks or we get takeout and then we eat outside on the patio, which overlooks the ocean. Living here is even better than the dream I had in my head. It's amazing.

I turn to face him, looping my arms around his neck. "You ready for dessert?"

He smiles. "What are we having? Chocolate cake?"

I shake my head. "Nope."

"Ice cream?"

"Try again."

"Hmm. Those are my two favorite desserts. I don't know what else to guess."

I smile and step back until I'm out of his grasp. I'm wearing a strapless white sundress and I tug it down slowly until it's down at my ankles. I step out it, and am left wearing just my lacy white string bikinis.

"This is dessert." I spin around, showing myself off. "But if you don't like it, there's some ice cream in the freezer."

His gaze sweeps over my nearly-naked body. I see the want in his eyes. The need. The desire. He's been traveling the past two weeks and just got back before we had dinner. Two weeks is a long time for us to be apart. It seems like months since we've been together.

He steps forward, his arms enveloping me. "Damn, I've missed you." His lips crash into mine as his arms tighten around me, bringing me closer. Our tongues tangle as our bodies press together. I feel his desire for me and it fires up my core. He lifts me up, our mouths still joined, and I wrap my legs around his waist.

"I can't go this long without you," he says as he carries me to the bedroom. "I missed you way too much."

He lays me on the bed, then strips his clothes off, his eyes on me as he does. He slides my panties off and lies next to me, gazing at my body as his hand drifts over my skin. "I swear you look even hotter now than when I met you. How is that possible?"

I don't usually compliment myself, but he's right. Expanding my workouts beyond running has really reshaped my body. My muscles are more defined, my butt has more shape, and being out in the sun a lot has given my skin a golden glow.

Garret looks better, too. I thought he was hot when I met him, but back then he still had the body of a teen. Now he has the body of a man. He's bigger, more built. And he still has those incredible abs.

He slips his hand between my legs and his mouth moves to my breast. My breath catches, and I close my eyes, savoring the feel of his touch. I've missed him, too. So much that I'm surprised we made it through dinner without ripping each other's clothes off.

I reach down and feel him, stroking him.

"Jade," he breathes out. "I've really fucking missed you."

"I missed you, too."

His hand continues to tease me as his mouth moves back up to my lips. We kiss, and it stirs up more want, more desire between us. But it's more than just physical. It always has been with him. Whenever Garret and I are together like this, I feel the love he has for me. The love we share. I feel it in the way he touches me and kisses me.

His body shifts, covering me, and I feel the tip of him, then all of him as he pushes inside me. He gazes down at me. "I love you. I love you so damn much." He leaves soft kisses along my cheek and my lips as he moves in and out in slow rhythmic movements.

I run my hands through his hair. "I love you, too."

He keeps his pace steady, not wanting to rush this, but I crave the release as the tension winds tight within my core, continuing to build as he moves inside me. I feel his muscles tense, his hand gripping my hip as he drives harder and deeper. My whole body responds, quaking beneath him as my release finally erupts in powerful waves. I grab hold of him as it does, and then I relax, my arms and head falling back on the bed.

Garret softly kisses my forehead and my lips, then his movements speed up again and he continues until I feel his body shudder and come to rest over mine.

We lie there for several minutes. My body is warm, still filled with sensations. That might've been the best sex we've ever had. Or maybe it's just because I haven't been with him for weeks.

"I actually do have a real dessert for you," I tell him.

"I don't need it. That was more than enough. That was amazing." He moves off me to the side.

I take my spot under his arm, looking up at him. "It was even better than normal, wasn't it?"

"Yeah. I mean, it's always amazing but that was—shit, that was beyond amazing."

"Did we do something differently?"

"I don't think so." He runs his warm hand up and down my arm, which is lying over his chest. "Maybe we're just getting better at it. We should practice more so we just keep improving."

"I agree, but to do that, you have to be home more." I say it jokingly, but his traveling *does* bother me. He's been gone way too much.

"Yeah, I need to figure out my schedule. Try to cut back on the travel. But you know, you can always come with me."

"I will. But I like being home. I like this house and being here with Grace. I just wish you could be here, too." I lay my head on his chest. "Garret, I don't want you to become your dad. I mean, I don't want you to get so into your work that I never see you."

"Jade." He waits until I look at him. "If you want me to cut back at work, I will. Just tell me. I'm trying to make this company a success, but sometimes it's hard to stop. I'm competitive and driven to succeed and sometimes that takes over. I need you to stop me from letting that side of me get out of control. The past few months you've been busy, too, so I just kept working. But we need to find the right balance between work and this. Us." He kisses me. "Because us is the most important thing."

"I don't want to tell you what to do."

"When it comes to work, I need you to. I need you to tell me to slow down. Otherwise, I can't stop myself. I'll keep pushing myself to make this company grow."

"But that's what you should be doing. Growing the company. Making it a success."

"It's already a success. It doesn't need to be the world's largest sporting goods company. It doesn't even need to be nationwide. We don't have to keep expanding."

"But isn't that what you want?"

"Not if it means not seeing you. Talking on the phone isn't good enough. I married you so I could see you every day. So you could fall asleep in my arms. So I could wake up every morning and see your beautiful face." He brings my hand to his lips and kisses it. "And make you breakfast. By the way, what exactly do you eat when I'm not around?"

"I kind of skip breakfast when you're not here."

"See? That can't happen." He lays my hand back over his chest and rubs my arm. "What should we do, Jade?"

"I just miss you. I miss you when you're gone, but I also want you to do whatever you need to do for the company."

"I don't care about the company. I mean, I do, but I don't care enough to let it come between us. I can hire people to do what I'm doing. The traveling. The sales calls. I don't need to be the one doing it. In fact, I shouldn't be doing it. That should be someone else's job. I should be doing the higher level stuff."

"If you did, would you be home more?"

"I can be home as much as you want. We own the company. And it's private so we don't have to report to shareholders. We make the rules."

I lie back on my pillow, pulling the sheet over me. "You need to make this decision, Garret. It's *your* company."

He shifts onto his side, gazing down at me. "It's *our* company. Yours and mine."

"I know, and I love the store. And I love being involved in it and seeing it grow. But I also love *you*. And I miss you, Garret. I miss you a lot."

"I miss you, too." His hand cups the side of my face and he leans down to kiss me. "Jade. I'm sorry that I even let it get to this point. I don't know what the hell I was thinking. We worked so hard to be together and now I'm never here with you. We built our dream house and you're living here all alone."

I'm glad he realized this because I didn't want to be the one to say it. I don't want to hold him back from achieving his goals, just like I wouldn't want him holding me back from mine. But this constant traveling he's been doing is getting to be too much. I never see him.

"So here's the deal," he says. "Tomorrow I'll call HR and have them work on getting some people hired. And I'm done traveling without you. If I need to go somewhere, you're coming with me. But there's not going to be much traveling anymore because I'm cutting way back. I want to be here. With you. Not flying to different cities. Staying in hotels."

"Are you sure this is what you want to do?"

"I'm positive. I don't like being apart from you. In fact, I hate it. Like I said, I just got caught up in the drive to succeed. To expand to other states and keep growing the company. But once you start down that path, it never ends. It's never enough. I promised myself that I would never let work take over my life and I'm keeping that promise. We have plenty of money. I don't need to work so hard. I don't need to travel. What I need," he kisses me, "is you."

I kiss him back. "Are you saying I might see you every day now?"

"Every day. And I'm going to try to start working from home. You'll see me so much you'll be sick of me."

"What about your trip tomorrow?"

"I'll send one of my sales guys. I don't need to be there. In fact, I'm taking tomorrow off. Shit, I own the place. I'm taking the whole damn week off."

I smile. "What are you going to do with all this time off?"

He presses his lips to mine as he slips his hand under the sheet and brings me closer. "I have some catching up to do with my gorgeous, hot, beautiful wife. Unless you're busy."

"I could use some time off." I run my hand over his smooth hard chest. "You sure you don't want your birthday dessert? I got you an ice cream cake."

"Later. I like the dessert I've got right here. You feel so damn good I may not leave this bed until tomorrow."

We have 'dessert' again. And again a few hours later.

Tonight was a wake-up call for us. Actually, it was a realization for Garret. He realized how much he'd been working and how his life was becoming what he always said he didn't want. He never wanted to end up like his dad, working all the time and missing out on life. But I think for a moment, he saw himself turning into that, and that's all it took for him to decide to end the long hours and the travel and to start down the path we'd talked about. The one where we're together, in the home that we built.

# Chapter 41
## Jade's 24th Birthday

**JADE**

So today is my 24th birthday and I got a gift I wasn't expecting. It's a good gift, and it's what I wanted, but I didn't think this little present would arrive so soon.

I went off the pill last July. I didn't tell Garret, because for one, he was traveling at the time and I didn't even think to tell him, and two, the doctor said it might take a while for my body to get back on its regular cycle and I wanted to get it on track before we started trying for a baby. According to my doctor, it can take months to get pregnant after going off the pill. But apparently, I'm the exception to the rule.

The past few weeks, I haven't felt so great. I haven't felt sick, just really tired. I hid it from Garret the best I could because if he knew, he'd think I'm sick and he'd make me go to the doctor. And I didn't need to go. I was just tired. I thought maybe I wasn't sleeping well or maybe going off the pill messed up my body. I thought the tired feeling would go away, but it didn't. It just got worse. I could hardly keep my eyes open during the day. I was starting to get worried that maybe I really was sick, so I called the doctor and the only appointment they had open this week was for today. My birthday. Who wants to go to the doctor on their birthday? But I wanted to find out what was wrong with me. I assumed I had to be sick if I was that tired all the time.

Turns out, I'm not sick. I'm pregnant. When the doctor told me, I asked her to test me again to make sure. I didn't believe her. I thought it would take at least six months for this to happen, maybe a year.

But nope. It happened right away. And now I have to tell Garret. I'm a little worried he might be mad at me for not telling him I went off the pill. We said we'd start trying to have a baby when we turned 24, but we said that a long time ago. Since then, we haven't really discussed it. He has so much going on right now with the company that I'm worried he's not ready to have a baby. That maybe he wants to wait. But it's too late now. I'm pregnant. And I'm not sure how he'll react.

## GARRET

It's Jade's birthday and I got stuck going to a meeting for work. It was the only time I could get all the right people in a room to make some decisions that had to be made in order to move forward with some stuff. But there was no way I was going to waste even more hours of Jade's birthday driving down to the company headquarters in LA, so I made my employees drive here. We're meeting in a hotel conference room. I rent out an office in town but it doesn't have enough space to hold meetings.

I made Jade breakfast this morning, then went to my meeting. I scheduled it to end at noon so that I'd be home in time to have lunch with her. She wasn't upset that I had to go to this meeting. In fact, she seemed like she was in a hurry to get rid of me. She acted like she had somewhere to go. Maybe she had errands to run and wanted to get them done before I got home.

As long as she's okay with it, I don't mind going to the meeting. I love my job. The company is a lot of work, but I love it. I've always dreamed of running my own company, and the fact that I ended up with a sporting goods company shoots that dream straight out of the ballpark.

My life is pretty fucking awesome. I have the best wife ever, who I love more than anything. I live in a beautiful house on the ocean. And I own a company that sells sports gear. I mean, shit, it can't get any better than that.

I've got some balance in my life now, too. Last year, I was working way too many hours and traveling too much. It was stressful on both Jade and me and I didn't even realize I'd been working that much until my birthday. I'd been traveling for two weeks straight, which is the longest I'd been away from Jade since we got married. When I finally got home and we were together that night, it hit me that my life had gotten off track. I was becoming my father and that scared the shit out of me. I don't want to work all the time. I want to spend my time with Jade. Enjoy our house. Our life. And I wasn't doing that when I was constantly working. Now my life is more balanced. Less work, more time at home. I like it that way.

When I get home from my meeting, Jade is waiting for me in the living room, which is odd because she's usually in the kitchen. She still doesn't cook much but she likes hanging out there. We have a huge kitchen with a see-through fireplace. On one side of it is a little sitting area where Jade likes to read or drink her coffee in the morning. Or she'll just sit there and gaze out at the ocean. The kitchen is in the back of the house, which is all windows and has a great view of the ocean.

"Hey, birthday girl." I take a seat next to her on the couch. "What are you doing in here? The TV isn't even on."

"I was waiting for you."

"Well, here I am." I kiss her. "I'm taking you out to lunch. You ready to go?"

"Not yet. I want to talk to you about something first."

That doesn't sound good. But she's smiling so it can't be that bad.

"What do you want to talk about?"

"I want to go over some of the new products I think we should stock in the store this spring."

I put Jade in charge of the women's merchandise in our stores. And damn, she's good at it. She seems to know exactly what our customers want. We sell out of the women's clothing and gear way faster than the men's.

"Jade, we can do this later. We don't need to go over it now. I don't want to talk about work on your birthday."

"I know, but I'm excited about this and I wanted to ask your opinion."

She does look excited. She's on the edge of her seat, her face beaming.

"Okay, go ahead."

"I was thinking we should start carrying baby and kid clothes. A lot of parents shop at our stores and I know they'd buy kids' clothes if they were there. We don't have to change the whole store layout around. I was thinking we could just start small, with some displays, maybe in the women's section."

"I think it's a good idea. At the last marketing meeting, we were just talking about this. Someone mentioned that customers were asking why we don't sell stuff for kids. I think we should look into it."

She pulls a small bag out from behind her back. "I got some samples to show you what I'm talking about."

She hands me the bag. I open it up and take out the tiniest pair of board shorts I've ever seen. They're bright green with a white stripe on the side. Then I pull out a tiny white rash guard t-shirt. "Are these for infants?"

"Yeah. Aren't they cute?"

"Yeah, but I don't know if we want to sell clothing for infants. We should probably start with stuff for older kids first. See how it sells."

She takes the board shorts and t-shirt from me and holds them up. "If I was a surfer and saw these in the store, I'd totally buy them. Parents like to dress their kids the same way they dress. So surfers would definitely buy this stuff for their baby. I know they would."

I lean over and kiss her. "Well, you seem to know this stuff so I trust you. If you want to try this in the stores, we'll try it. But we'll need to test it at a few locations first to see how it sells before rolling it out to all the other stores."

"Then I'll start looking for suppliers."

"Talk to Christine. She already knows all the suppliers. It'll save you a lot of time."

"Okay." Jade hands me the clothes again. "Here."

I laugh. "What am I supposed to do with these?" I hold up the tiny shirt that's about the size of my hand. "It's a little small for me, Jade."

She nods, nervously. "Yeah. I know."

I put my hand on her arm. "Jade, what's wrong?"

"Nothing's wrong. I just—" She takes a breath. "I don't want you to be mad at me."

"Why would I be mad at you?" I set the clothes down and hold her hand.

"Because I—" She takes another breath.

"Jade. Just tell me."

"Um, I had something else to show you." She reaches behind her back again and hands me another tiny shirt. Just a plain white t-shirt with some words on it.

I hold it up. It says 'Daddy's Little Surfer' and has a surfboard on it. "Yeah, it's a cute. I'm sure the customers will love it."

Jade's giving me this look and I don't know what it means. I set the shirt down but she gives it right back to me.

"It's not for the customers. It's for you." She pauses. "I mean, not for you specifically, but for—" She stops.

I still don't know what she's trying to tell me or why she's so nervous about it. She's looking down at my hands, which are still holding the tiny 'Daddy's Little Surfer' shirt.

Wait. Is she telling me what I think she's telling me? That can't be right. She's on the pill. We had planned on starting a family this year, but we haven't talked about it for a while. I was thinking Jade wanted to wait a little longer. Maybe she missed her period and just *thinks* she's pregnant, like she did right after we got married. But if that were the case, she would've taken a pregnancy test. Maybe she did.

"Jade, are you telling me you're—"

"Pregnant." Her eyes move up to mine. "For real this time."

"Are you sure?"

"Yes. I went to the doctor this morning."

I cautiously smile, not sure I believe this. "You're not joking here, right? You're really serious?"

She shakes her head. "I'm not joking."

"We're having a baby?" I grab her and pull her into a hug. "We're really having a baby?"

"Yeah," she says softly. "Are you mad at me?"

I let her go just enough to look at her. She looks worried.

"God, no. Why would I be mad at you?"

"Because I went off the pill in July and I didn't tell you. You were out of town and when we talked on the phone, I didn't even think about it. And then you were gone all those weeks in August before your birthday and then after that I—"

"Jade." I kiss her. "You don't have to explain."

"I just never thought this would happen so soon. The doctor said it takes months to get pregnant after you go off the pill. But I guess that's not true for everyone. I'm sorry, Garret. I should've talked to you before I went off the pill."

I hold her face and set my eyes on hers. "Jade. I want this. I've always wanted this with you. I didn't give a shit when it happened."

She smiles. "So you're happy?"

"Are you kidding? I'm more than happy." I hug her, then gently push her back so I can see her face. "Jade, are *you* happy about this?"

She nods, smiling. "Yeah. It's what I want. It's exactly what I want. I just wanted to make sure it's what you wanted, too. I mean, the timing of it."

"You can have as many babies as you want, whenever the hell you want them, and I'd still be happy. I'd have a thousand babies with you."

She laughs. "Let's just have this first one and see how it goes."

I glance down at her stomach. Holy shit! There's a baby in there. *My* baby.

I look back at Jade, holding her hands. "What did the doctor say? Are you okay? Is the baby okay?"

"Everything's fine so far. My next appointment's in a few weeks."

"How do you feel?"

"Okay, except for being really tired. I couldn't figure out why I've been so tired the past few weeks. That's why I went to the doctor. I thought I was sick or something."

"Why didn't you tell me this?"

"Because you worry too much. I was just tired. I didn't feel sick."

"So you haven't been sick? Like morning sickness or anything?"

"No, I didn't have any other symptoms except missing my period, but the doctor said that might happen after going off the pill. That's why I didn't think I was pregnant."

"Do you know your due date?"

She smiles. "May 15th."

I smile back. "The day I proposed."

"And the day you told me you were free from the organization. It was a really good day. And it's going to be even better now. There's something else, too."

"What?"

"The doctor can't say for sure, but she thinks I conceived on August 22$^{nd}$."

"Really?"

"Yeah. Your birthday. So we made the baby on your birthday and found out about it on mine. And our baby will arrive on the day we got engaged. I guess this baby's into celebrations, just like you. She's just like her dad."

"She? You already know—"

"No. I just didn't want to call our baby 'it.'"

"Our baby." I smile as I hug her against my chest. "I like the sound of that. Actually, I fucking love the sound of that. I can't believe we're having a baby."

"I know. I can't either. It hasn't really sunk in yet."

I sit back and look at her. "I love you. I love you so much."

"I love you, too."

"Holy shit. We're having a baby!"

Jade laughs and I hug her again. Then I take her for lunch, then a movie, then out for a nice dinner, followed by a romantic sunset cruise on a sailboat. Jade still loves sailboats.

Later, when we're in bed, Jade thanks me for giving her a great birthday. But the fancy dinner and sunset cruise were nothing compared to the news we got today.

It's Jade's birthday, but we both got a gift. A gift that will make our life together even better.

# Chapter 42

### Another Birthday

**JADE**

"Garret, you cannot be in the room with me," I tell him as I waddle through the kitchen. That's right. Waddle. I no longer walk. In fact, I haven't for months. I miss walking. I can't wait to walk again.

"Jade, every father is in the delivery room. It's normal."

"Not in the old days. Fifty years ago, men sat in the waiting room, smoking cigars. That's what you should do. Get some cigars."

I'm slowly pacing the floor. I'm nervous because I might give birth today and I'm scared to death. I woke up at six this morning, worrying about it. I got out of bed, because even just lying in bed is uncomfortable now.

"I don't smoke cigars, and even if I did, you can't smoke in a hospital. And I'm not sitting in the waiting room. I want to be with you."

"Garret, we've been over this a thousand times. I don't want you in there."

"Jade, I swear. I will stay by your head. I won't even look."

This is why I don't want Garret in the delivery room. I went to the birthing classes. I saw the films. And I don't want Garret seeing any of that stuff. I don't want him down there when the baby comes out. No way. Other women may be fine with it, but not me.

I sigh, because I can't sit down. I'm so big in front, I feel like I'm going to tip over trying to sit in my favorite chair. It's in a little area that's connected to the kitchen and looks out at the ocean. I always sit here in the mornings before I start my day.

"Here." Garret helps me into the chair.

"I can't believe how huge I am," I say, looking down at my belly.

He leans down and kisses me. "You're beautiful."

"I'm huge."

"You're not huge. From the back, people don't even know you're pregnant."

It's true. The rest of me looks normal but my stomach is huge. Like I swallowed a giant beach ball. And all that weight in front throws me completely off balance.

"How can a tiny baby take up so much space?" I ask.

Garret sits on the arm of the chair. "Maybe it's not a tiny baby. Maybe it's a big baby."

"Garret! Don't say that! I'm already freaking out about getting it out of me."

He reaches down and holds my hand. "Don't worry about it. You're gonna do great." He smiles. "Especially since I'll be there coaching you through it."

I smile back. "Fine. You can be in the room. But if you glance down there even once, I swear I'll—"

He kisses me before I can say it. "You know what?"

"What?"

"By tomorrow at this time, we could be holding our baby."

"I don't think so. I think this baby plans to stay in here a while." I rub my belly. "And that's fine with me because I don't think I can do this."

Garret laughs. "It's a little late for that, Jade. The baby's coming and I bet it comes today." He said 'it' because we still don't know if we're having a boy or a girl. We wanted it to be a surprise. "You should've read the books, Jade. If you did, you wouldn't be so freaked out."

When Garret found out I was pregnant, he went out and bought every pregnancy book he could find. And then he read them all. But I wouldn't. It was too much information. I read a few pages of one of the books and all it did was freak me out even more.

"Between you and Harper, I got more than enough information. I didn't need to read the books."

Harper is also pregnant, with baby number two. She's due in a couple weeks. She's having another boy. She thought for sure she was having a girl this time. She even started buying pink baby clothes, but then found out it was a boy. I just laugh because she's such a girly girl and she ends up having boys. But she loves her little boy and she can't wait to have another one. And Sean is a great dad and a great husband. He always has these dad and son days so Harper can get a break and go shopping or get a massage or do the other girly stuff she likes doing.

"You two are up early." Karen walks in the room, with Frank right behind her. "It's only six fifteen."

"I couldn't sleep," I say, as she comes over to me.

Karen and Frank got here a few days ago. I asked them to come stay with us because Karen's the only person who's able to calm me down whenever I panic about the delivery. Karen's been a labor and delivery nurse for more than 30 years, so she's seen pretty much everything. She keeps telling me that giving birth is no big deal. That it's natural and my body will know exactly what to do and that women have been doing it forever. It's all stuff I know, but the way she says it always makes me feel better.

I love Karen. She's awesome. She treats me like the daughter she never had. She and Frank come out and visit all the time. Frank really lucked out when he found Karen. He's so much happier with her in his life. And she takes such great care of him that now he has way more good days than bad.

She smiles and rubs my arm. "All ready for the big day?"

"Not really. I'm kind of freaking out."

Frank leans down and kisses my head. "Relax, honey. You'll be fine."

"You may not deliver today," Karen says. "It could be tomorrow or later this week. How do you feel?"

"I feel okay. But I feel like I should do something. Maybe I'll clean out the refrigerator." I try to get up, but can't.

Garret laughs. "The refrigerator doesn't need to be cleaned, Jade."

"She's still nesting," Karen says to him. "I'm going to go make some coffee." She and Frank walk into the kitchen.

Karen's nesting comment is referring to my need to clean and organize the entire house. I've been doing this for weeks. Apparently it's something pregnant women do before giving birth.

"I'm not nesting," I insist. "I just need to clean."

Garret kisses my cheek. "What you need is breakfast. What do you want?"

"Could I have some donuts? I'm dying for a donut."

Garret's been making food runs for months. My cravings are out of control. My donut cravings, especially.

"Jade, I'm not leaving you on your due date. What if you go into labor and I'm not here?"

"According to your books, labor goes on for hours and the donut shop is only a few minutes from here. Nothing's going to happen while you're gone."

"I don't think it's a good idea. How about some toast instead?"

"But I'm really craving donuts. Please." I give him my sad eyes, which I know he can't say no to.

He sighs, then leans down and talks to my stomach. "Stay in there until I get back."

I laugh. "You're funny. Hey, get me the chocolate ones with chocolate frosting and sprinkles."

He shakes his head. "I hope this doesn't mean our baby's going to be born addicted to donuts."

"There's nothing wrong with donuts." I try to sit up to kiss him but I can't reach him and now I'm stuck in this chair. It's a deep, squishy chair that's hard to get out of.

Garret notices me attempting to move. "You want help getting up?"

I sigh. "No, I'll just stay here. If I need help, Frank or Karen will help me."

He leans down and gives me a kiss. "I'll be back soon. Love you."

"Love you, too."

He leaves.

And a few minutes later, my water breaks.

## GARRET

I'm at the donut place when my phone rings. It's Frank.

"Garret, she's having the baby. Meet us at the hospital."

"Are you serious? I just left the house."

"And as soon as you did, her water broke."

I race back to the car. "I'll be home in a few minutes. I'll take her to the hospital."

"We're already on the way. Karen said things are moving fast. We couldn't wait."

Shit! I whip out of the parking lot and speed off. "Okay, I'll meet you there. Let me talk to Jade."

He gives her the phone.

"Garret?" She sounds out of breath. "Sorry. I didn't know this would happen."

"I'll be right there, okay?"

"I'm scared. I'm not ready for this." When she says it, I know what she means. This time she isn't talking about giving birth. She's talking about being a mom. She was so excited about it for the first eight months of her pregnancy and then the past month, she started panicking, thinking she'll be a bad mom.

"You're ready, Jade. This baby is so lucky to have you as a mom."

I tell her this all the time and it always makes her cry. I hear her sniffle, then moan. "Oh, God, that hurts. Garret, I can't talk. I'll see you at the hospital."

She hangs up and I speed even faster down the road. Then I hit construction and have to slow down. Going to the donut shop took me off the road I would normally take to the hospital and now I'm stuck here, waiting in a line of cars. I honk but it's no use. There's nowhere to go. I call Frank and let him know. He tells me Jade was taken straight to the delivery room. This baby's coming fast. Jade and I both thought she'd be in labor for 15 or 20 hours, like most new moms. But no. This baby's as impatient as Jade is and it wants out.

Ten minutes later, I finally move past the construction zone and speed to the hospital. I park and run inside.

Frank is waiting for me by the nurse's desk. I must look like a nervous wreck because he laughs at me. "Calm down there, Garret. Everything's fine."

I'm out of breath from running. "Where is she?"

"She's in one of the delivery rooms. The nurse will show you."

An older woman dressed like a nurse comes over to me. "First timer, huh?" She smiles.

"Yeah."

"Right this way." She takes off and I follow her, waving good-bye to Frank. This is all happening so fast. This isn't how I pictured it in my head. I read all those books and was all prepared for a long labor, spending hours sitting beside Jade trying to keep her calm.

The nurse takes me to the delivery room. Jade's doing the breathing exercises she learned in birthing class. Karen's next to her, holding her hand. Karen sees me and smiles, then says to Jade, "I'm going to leave now."

"No! Don't leave me!" Jade didn't notice me walk in. "Please! Not until Garret—"

"I'm right here." I take her hand and kiss her forehead, which is all sweaty.

"Garret." She squeezes my hand really hard, then squeezes her eyes shut and bites down on her lip. Must be a contraction.

Karen comes over and talks in my ear. "There was no time for an epidural. The baby's coming fast. Shouldn't be much longer."

I nod, and she leaves.

Natural childbirth? That's gotta hurt. And it's not at all what Jade wanted. She was counting on that epidural.

"Jade, you're doing great." I smile at her as she squeezes my hand again, so hard she might break some bones. At least we're at a hospital.

"Okay, it's time to push," the doctor says.

I glance down at the doctor. It's not Jade's normal doctor. It's some other woman. She's older and very calm, which is just what Jade needs.

After a lot of pushing and breathing and squeezing of my hand, our baby is born.

A baby girl. Eight pounds, two ounces. With dark brown hair.

And all of a sudden it hits me. I have a daughter. I'm a dad!

The nurse wipes the baby off and hands her to Jade. "She was sure in a hurry to meet you."

Jade takes the baby, tears running down her face. Happy tears.

"Hi." She smiles at the baby and lifts her up to kiss her cheek.

I lean down and kiss her, too. "She's beautiful."

"Yeah. She's perfect." Jade kisses her again, then whispers to her, "You have to meet your daddy."

Jade hands her to me. I gaze down at her, cradled in my arms. She's so tiny. So sweet. So beautiful. I just met her and I already love her more than words can describe.

Later that day, Frank and Karen go back to the house and I stay with Jade in her hospital room. Grace was here, too, but she left with Frank and Karen so Jade could get some rest.

Jade's exhausted. She was taking a nap, but she's starting to wake up.

"Hey." I gently rub her arm. "How are you feeling?"

She sits up a little. "Sore. Tired." She gives me her sleepy smile. "Happy."

"Yeah. Me too." I take her hand and kiss it.

"We did it, Garret."

"*You* did it. And you were amazing."

A nurse walks in carrying the baby, all wrapped up in a blanket, a pink cap on her head. "Someone's here for a visit."

The nurse hands the baby to Jade, who smiles as she takes her. Jade smiles every time the nurse brings the baby in.

"I'll come back and get her later," the nurse says, but Jade's not paying attention. All her attention is on the baby.

I sit next to her on the bed and Jade holds the baby up for me to see. "Garret, look what we made."

"We did good." I lean down and kiss Jade, then gently kiss our new baby girl. "She's beautiful. Just like her mom."

"She has your eyes."

"You think so? I think she looks more like you."

We both just stare at her. It *is* kind of amazing we made something so perfect.

"Did you pick out a name?" I ask Jade. We decided we wouldn't pick a name until we saw our baby. Because what if we picked a name and it didn't fit? We wanted to meet her first and make sure her name fit her.

"Abigail Grace," Jade says without hesitation.

We talked about Grace for a middle name, but not Abigail.

"Where did you come up with Abigail?"

"When I saw her, the name just popped in my head. Look it up and see what it means."

I get my phone out and go to the baby name website we've been using for ideas.

When I find the name I smile. "It has a couple different meanings. One is father's joy and the other is brings joy."

"Then it's perfect." Jade talks to the baby. "You're definitely going to bring us joy. You already have."

"Abigail Grace Kensington." As I say it, she gurgles a little. "I think she likes it."

"Garret, we don't have to name her that. It's just an idea."

"It was the first name that came to you when you saw her. That means it's the right name." I put my phone away and scoot closer to Jade on the bed. I look down at our baby. Jade's looking at her, too. We can't seem to take our eyes off her.

"What name were *you* thinking of when you saw her?" Jade asks.

"I wasn't thinking of names. I was too overwhelmed by the fact that I have a daughter. And that I'm a dad."

"How does it feel to be a dad?" She hands me the baby.

"I'm not sure how to describe it." I look down at her, sleeping in my arms. "All I know is that I love her. I loved her before I even met her. And I'm already overprotective of her. She's never dating by the way."

Jade laughs.

I give her a serious look. "I'm not kidding, Jade. And she's going to an all-girl school."

"Let's worry about that later. She's only a few hours old. Born right on her due date." Jade leans her head on my shoulder, her eyes on Abigail. "Five years ago today you proposed, and I found out you were out of the organization for good. If they'd taken you, I don't know where I'd be right now. I wouldn't be married." She runs her hand over the baby's head. "And I wouldn't have her."

I hand Jade the baby again and put my arm around her. "But that's not what happened. Which means May 15th will always be a good day." I squeeze her into me and kiss the top of her head. "I love you, Jade."

"I love you, too."

The nurse comes in again to take the baby and Jade falls back to sleep.

My phone rings and I go out in the hall so I don't wake up Jade. My phone's been ringing all day. Sean and Harper called. Then Ryan and Chloe. Then Lilly, William, and Meredith. I haven't talked to my dad yet. He's flying back from Europe today, but he must be home now because he's the one calling.

"Hi, Dad."

"I hear I'm a grandfather."

"Yeah. You have a granddaughter. Abigail Grace."

"Congratulations. How's it feel to be a father?"

"Truthfully? Like I'll be worrying for the rest of my life."

He laughs. "Yes, I remember that feeling. But Garret." He sounds serious now. "Don't worry about things you don't need to worry about anymore."

He knows I still worry about the organization. He always tells me not to, but I still do. I probably always will, because I know it'll never go away. You can't defeat it. It's too powerful and the members are embedded in every facet of society. Large corporations. Judicial systems. Law enforcement. Government. And they'll do everything they can to stay in power, because they know if they don't, another group just like them will take over. There will always be people who crave power. People who want to control the masses. Control the system. It's always been that way. And that will never change.

Sometimes I wonder if the organization will come back for me when my dad and William are gone and I have no one left to protect me. I'm one of the few people who knows about them and that makes me think they'd want me back someday. I've told my dad this and he assures me it'll never happen. He says that so much has changed there the past few years, that it's nothing like it used to be. They recruit people now, instead of forcing people to be part of it. But I still worry.

"Garret, did you hear me?"

"Yeah. Sorry. It was a long day. I'm just tired."

"Get used to it. You won't be getting much sleep anymore."

"Did you get the pictures I sent?"

"Yes. And she's beautiful. Let me know when you want Lilly and me to come out there. We can't wait to meet her."

"Come out whenever you want. Jade was just asking when you guys would be here."

"Then we'll plan on being out there in a couple weeks."

"Okay, I'll tell Jade."

"Is she there? I'd like to talk to her."

"She's sleeping. She's really tired."

"Well, call me tomorrow when she's had time to rest."

"I will. Bye, Dad."

"And Garret?"

"Yeah?"

"Enjoy this time. It goes fast. And if you miss it, you'll regret it." He's talking about himself and missing all my teen years.

He still feels bad about that. He doesn't need to. I've forgiven him. "I'll let you go. Call me if you need anything. Goodbye, Garret."

As I put my phone away, I see Frank and Karen getting off the elevator. They brought the small travel bag Jade packed for the hospital. They were in such a hurry to get Jade to the hospital this morning that they forgot to bring it.

They come up to me and Frank hands me the bag. "How's she doing?"

"Good. She's taking a nap right now."

"It's good she's getting some rest," Karen says. "She won't be getting much sleep when she gets home." She smiles. "You should be taking a nap, too. You won't be getting much sleep either."

I nod. "Yeah, that's what everyone keeps saying. That's okay. I don't need much sleep."

"Well, we don't want to wake Jade up," Frank says. "We just wanted to drop off her things." Frank takes Karen's hand. "You ready to go?"

She tugs him toward the nursery. "We have to go see the baby first."

He looks back at me, laughing, as she pulls him down the hall. "I guess we'll see you later."

"Yeah, bye." I wave him on.

The next day after lunch, the nurse stops by with the baby. It's a different nurse than the one who was here yesterday. An older lady with gray hair. She gives the baby to me this time because Jade still has her lunch tray in front of her.

The nurse takes the tray away and says to Jade, "The doctor will be in to check on you later this afternoon. If all looks good, you'll be discharged."

"Really?" Jade glances up at the nurse. "That fast?"

She smiles. "You're young. Healthy. Didn't have any drugs. The delivery was smooth. No complications. So you'll be sent home. Unless you want to stay another night."

"No, I'd rather go home. But you're giving us the baby?"

The way Jade says it is so damn funny. Like she can't believe they'd send the baby home with us.

The nurse is trying not to laugh. "Yes. She's all yours."

"But is she ready? I mean, don't you need to check her over? Make sure she's okay?"

"She's already been checked. And she'll be checked again before you leave. She's a very healthy baby. I'll give you some time with her, then I'll come back and get her."

"Thank you," I say to the nurse.

She nods, and walks out of the room.

I'm still holding the baby and Jade points to her and says, "Garret, they're sending her home with us. Today!"

Now that the nurse is gone, I laugh. "Yeah. She's ours, Jade. We have to take her." I bring her over to Jade.

"I know. It's just that she's so tiny. We might break her."

"We won't break her. I read all the books. I'm ready for this. And so are you. You just need to get home and practice."

Jade looks down at Abigail. "I'm nervous, Garret. What if I screw up?"

I sit on the side of the bed, lifting her face up to look at me. "Everyone screws up. It's part of parenting. We'll just do the best we can. And you're going to be a great mom. You already are."

She gazes down at Abigail again. I know Jade's going to be a great mom. She just needs to convince herself of that.

We leave the hospital at six that night. Karen and Frank are waiting for us at the house. Karen had dinner ready for us, which was good because we were both starving. The hospital food was really bad so we didn't eat much while we were there.

After dinner, Karen gives us some tips on taking care of a newborn since she's an expert in this area. It's great having Karen here. She and Frank are going to stay another week to help us out. And Grace lives in the guest house, so she'll be a big help with the baby after Frank and Karen go home.

Grace is 76 now but you wouldn't know it if you saw her. She's young for her age. She doesn't have any health problems and she's in good shape. Probably because she stays active, gardening and taking walks. Sometimes I think it's also because she still has access to the clinic. Since Arlin was part of the organization and William still is, Grace will always have access to the clinic.

By nine o'clock, Jade and I are both wiped out and ready for bed. The baby's sound asleep in the bassinet, which is by Jade's side of the bed. Jade's lying there, just watching her.

I lie down beside her, my arm around her middle. "I thought you'd be asleep by now."

"I just like looking at her. Now I know how my mom felt when she wrote me that letter. She said that after I was born, it was like nothing else mattered. I get it now." Jade turns to me. "Garret, if they ever come after us again. If they ever even try to get near her, I'll kill them."

Jade and I never talk about this anymore. We don't talk about the organization at all. I know we both think about it, especially when William's visiting and he suddenly has to leave. He doesn't say where he's going, but we know he's off doing something for the organization. We just don't talk about it.

"Jade." I sweep my hand over her cheek and lock my eyes on her. "They will never come near her. And if they even tried, I would kill them myself. Nobody will hurt her or try to take her from us. I promise you."

Maybe it's too bold of a promise. Maybe I shouldn't have made it. Given our history and what we've been through, I never completely trust that we'll be safe. But what I said to Jade is true. If they even attempted to harm my family, I would kill them. Not just members of the organization, but anyone.

I haven't forgotten the rules my father taught me all those years ago. Rule number two. Protect your family above all else.

I shouldn't even be thinking about this. They're not going to come after us. And if they did, I know William would take care of it. Or my dad would. They'd never let anyone harm us. And I wouldn't either. I was already protective of Jade, and now that I'm a father, that protective instinct has kicked into overdrive. I would do anything to keep my wife and my daughter safe.

"She's so tiny," Jade whispers, her eyes back on the baby. "And sweet. I can't stop looking at her."

"I know. She's pretty damn cute. Just like her mom." I pull the blanket over us. "We need to get some sleep. She'll probably be up in an hour."

Jade falls asleep, but I stay awake, watching the baby. *Our* baby. We have a daughter. I'm a dad.

I tug Jade closer and kiss her head. God, I love her so much. And I love my baby girl. I love my whole damn life.

# Chapter 43

## Two Years Later

**JADE**

*I* love summer, because every summer we have both sides of the family come and stay for an entire week. We eat and swim and hang out on the beach. It's one of those big family gatherings I always wanted as a kid, and now I have them every year.

Everyone left last week, except for Lilly. She's living with us this summer. She used to come for just a couple weeks, but last year she stayed with us for most of the summer, so we invited her to stay with us again this summer. She's 13 now, almost 14. I think Garret secretly wants her here so he can keep an eye on her. Keep her away from boys. She's growing up and she's really pretty and boys are noticing. She's tall for her age and thin, but developing on top to the point that Garret keeps buying her baggy t-shirts and sweatshirts to hide her growing breasts. It's too funny.

This week, Sean and Harper are visiting. They only live an hour away but they come stay with us for a week or two every summer. They just had baby number three. Another boy. I'm starting to think Harper's going to keep having babies until she finally has a girl. Not that she doesn't love her boys. She totally loves them, but she'd still like a girl. Probably because she loves *my* girls so much.

Garret and I had another baby girl. We hadn't planned on having another baby so soon, but we felt like Abigail needed a little brother or sister and we didn't want to wait. It's funny, because for years I was so afraid to have just one child, but then I had Abigail and couldn't wait to have another.

It took me some time to get the hang of taking care of a baby. There's so much to learn. But Garret helped and Grace did, too, and eventually I figured it out. Now I feel like an expert taking care of Hannah. That's her name. Hannah Julia Kensington. Her middle name is in honor of my mom. She wasn't a good mom, but that wasn't her fault, and I know from that letter she wrote me that she never wanted to treat me the way she did. And now that I'm a mom, I feel even more sorry for my own mom and what happened to her. Royce took away her chance to be the mom she wanted to be. He drugged her to the point that she didn't even know I was her daughter. She missed out on all those moments that I now cherish with my own daughters.

"Jade, can you grab my bag?" Harper's sitting next to me on one of the lounge chairs on the back patio. We're in a shaded area near the pool, watching the guys play with her two boys out on the lawn. Harper's holding her new baby, who just spit up a little.

I hand her the bag. "You need some help?"

"Nope, I got it." She reaches in the bag and takes out a towel.

Hannah's next to me in her baby sleeper. It's like her own little lounge chair. She's sound asleep, the breeze blowing her wispy brown hair. Abigail's coloring at the patio table, still in her swimsuit from swimming with Garret earlier. She's only two and she's already a really good swimmer. Garret had her in the water when she was just a baby. And she loves it. She could live in the water.

Lilly's beside her at the table, working on a charcoal sketch. She draws and paints all the time and she's getting really good at it.

"Aunt Lilly!" Abigail shows off her picture. "Look!"

"Wow! That's really good," Lilly says. "I'm thirsty. You want to go with me to get a drink?"

Abigail nods and climbs off her chair, then takes Lilly's hand and they go inside.

"Lilly is so pretty," Harper says. "And so tall. She could easily be a model."

"I know. She gets prettier every time I see her. She already has boys asking her out, but don't tell Garret that. He doesn't even want to think about her dating."

"Does Pearce have an approved dating age for her?"

"Yeah, she has to be 16, but Garret's trying to get him to up it to 30."

Harper laughs. "What is he going to do when Abigail and Hannah start dating?"

"If he has his way, they never will. They'd live as old maids in our house for the rest of their lives."

We both laugh.

"So you think you're going to try for a girl?" I ask.

"Yeah. Probably in a year or so."

"Are you serious? I was kidding! You really want four kids?"

She shrugs. "Sure. Why not? I've already got three. What's one more?"

"Four kids? That's a lot. And they're all so close in age."

"So are yours. And I think it's good. My sisters and I are close in age. When we were little, my mom said we never got bored because we always played together and kept ourselves entertained."

"But what if you have another boy?"

She laughs. "I'm sure I will." She looks down at her baby. "But that's okay. I wouldn't mind another boy. When I'm in one of my girly moods, I always have your girls to spoil."

"Are you done after four?"

"Probably." She smiles. "But you never know. If we keep going, Sean and I will have our own sports team." She looks out at the back yard where Sean and Garret are tossing a kid football to Charlie and Tanner. "I hope they don't want to play for real someday. It's so dangerous. Those high school guys always get concussions playing football. That can cause permanent damage."

"You and Sean are huge sports fans. I'm sure your boys will want to play football."

"Yeah, I know. And baseball. And soccer. And basketball."

"They can't play every sport."

"Garret played all those sports in high school. And Sean played football and baseball."

"Then I guess in a few years, you and Sean will be spending all your time at games."

"We're actually looking forward to that. I can't wait to see them play. Any sport but football."

Her oldest son catches the ball just as she says it, then runs for a touchdown.

"I think Charlie's going to play football, Harper."

She sighs. "Then I'm getting him a double-reinforced helmet and wrapping his head in bubble wrap."

As I watch Garret playing with Harper's boys, it makes me wonder if he wishes we had a boy. I told him we were done after two kids, but I know he'd like one more. He always wanted three kids.

Lilly comes back out with Abigail, who goes over to Hannah and kisses her cheek. She does this all the time. It's too cute.

"Come see your Aunt Harper," Harper says to her.

Abigail toddles over and kisses Harper on the cheek. She loves to give kisses.

"You want to sit on my lap?" Harper shifts the baby to her other arm and sets Abigail on her lap.

Abigail leans over and kisses the baby a little too hard. He wakes up and fusses, which scares her.

"It's okay," Harper tells her. "His big brothers knock him around all the time."

Harper is such a relaxed mom. Her boys are always running around, getting hurt, and she just fixes them up and sends them back out to play. She doesn't overreact to stuff. Sean's laid back, too, so they work well together. I used to overreact all the time with Abigail. If she got a tiny scrape or the slightest fever I wanted to take her to the doctor. I'm way better now. Part of that is because of Garret, who is laid back like Sean. But also watching Harper has helped me calm down and enjoy being a mom instead of worrying about every little thing.

"Look what Uncle Garret gave me!" Charlie runs up to Harper with a plastic baseball and bat.

Harper's kids use the aunt and uncle titles for us since Abigail uses them for her and Sean.

"In case he gets bored with football," Garret says.

Sean's right behind him, and says to me, "I told him if Charlie breaks a window, you guys are paying for it."

Harper laughs and playfully hits Sean's shin with her foot. "Stop it. We would never do that."

"I'm just kidding." Sean picks up Tanner. "I'm going to get the grill going. These guys are hungry and so am I."

"I'll get the meat." I get up from my chair.

Lilly takes my spot. "I'll watch Hannah for you."

Lilly's a huge help with the girls. She loves taking care of them and playing with them. And the girls both love their Aunt Lilly.

Garret follows me into the kitchen, grabbing me around the waist and kissing my bare shoulder as I open the fridge.

I laugh. "Hey, I'm trying to get dinner ready."

"And I'm helping." He spins me around and shuts the fridge door, then gives me one of his kisses that still causes that hot, tingly feeling inside.

"We probably shouldn't make out in the kitchen with everyone just outside."

"Then you shouldn't walk around looking so damn hot. I mean, come on, Jade. You're wearing a sundress. You know what that does to me." He kisses my neck, then my shoulder.

"I wore it because it's hot outside."

"You still know what it does to me." He kisses my lips, his hand cupping my butt and pulling me into him.

He's got me so turned on I have to force myself to pull away. "We need to stop. But we're definitely continuing this later."

"I'm going to hold you to that." He kisses me once more and pats my butt.

Even with two kids, Garret and I still have an active sex life. Not like when we were in college, but as a married couple with kids, I'd say we do it a lot. I never want that to change. I love Garret and I love being with him that way, so I flirt with him and kiss him when he's not expecting it. And I wear sundresses. Yeah, I kind of lied about the hot weather. I wore the dress because I knew it'd turn him on and it's been days since we've done it and I want him. Just not right now while I'm trying to get dinner ready.

I open the fridge again. "So when did you get the ball and bat?"

"When I was at the grocery store yesterday. They had a big display of them. It was only five dollars. Sean said they already have a baseball set at home, but since they're here for a week I thought they might want one to play with. I didn't think the boys would want to play with the girls' dolls." He smiles at me as he gets the plates out.

I laugh. "Yeah, probably not." I set the platter of steaks and burgers on the counter, ready for Sean to grill.

"You ever wish we had a boy?" I ask Garret as I go around him to grab some napkins.

He catches my waist and pulls me into him, smiling. "Where'd that come from?"

I shrug. "I just wondered."

"I love my girls, so I don't think about it."

"I know you love the girls, but I think you'd like a boy, too."

"What are you saying?" He leans down and kisses me. "You want to make one tonight?"

"No." I smile. "Not tonight, but…" I kiss him.

He pulls back. "But what?"

"Maybe in a year or two, we should try for another."

"Are you serious?"

"Yeah." I try to go around him, but he's got me locked in his arms.

"But after Hannah was born you said we were done."

"That was the pain of childbirth talking. And that was months ago. In a year, I'll have forgotten all about it."

"But you always say three is too many and that we can't let the kids outnumber us."

I laugh. "Yeah, I do say that. But we're bigger than them so I think we could handle one more."

"When did you decide this?"

"I've been thinking about it for a while. And whenever I see you with Harper's boys, I always think it'd be nice to have a boy. Not just for you, but for me, too. For our family. I think the girls would like having a baby brother. And if they ended up with another sister, they'd be happy with that, too. Would you be okay with us having another girl?"

He smiles. "I'd be happy with whatever you give me."

"So we're going to try for a third? Not now, but in a year or two?"

"I would love for us to have another baby." He kisses me, then talks against my lips. "And we're going to practice making one tonight."

He's causing that hot, tingly feeling again, so I push him away before I end up taking him to the bedroom.

"Oh, I forgot to tell you, your dad called earlier. They're coming back to stay with us."

"Already?" He smiles. "They were just here. So when are they coming?"

"For the Fourth of July. I told them to stay for the whole week, or longer if they want."

Sean walks in. "You got the meat ready?"

"Right here." I hand him the platter and he takes off again. He insists on cooking whenever he comes here. He says it's his payment for letting them stay with us, but I know it's because he has to cook. He can't go a day without cooking.

"Daddy!" Abigail runs up to Garret with a drawing in her hand. "Look!"

Garret picks her up and kisses her cheek. It reminds me of when he used to do the same thing with Lilly. He checks out the drawing. It's a picture of the two of them in the pool. It's really good. Lilly obviously drew it and Abigail just ran some crayons over it.

"Thank you," he says to her. "I'll add it to my collection."

Garret has her drawings all over the wall in his office. He rents out part of a building in town where he has an office and a conference room for meetings.

"Where's your sister?" He sets the drawing on the counter.

"I've got her." Lilly walks in holding Hannah, who's awake now. "She needs to be changed."

"I'll do it." Garret sets Abigail down and takes Hannah. Lilly whips her phone out and smiles at whatever text she got. Garret notices, and from the look on his face I know he assumes it's from a boy. "Lilly, come with me."

"Why?" She follows him down the hall.

"I'll show you how to change a diaper."

467

"I already know how."

"Then you can help me."

He's just trying to distract Lilly from her phone. I agree she shouldn't be dating at 13 but he can't really stop boys from texting her. And he's not her father so he shouldn't be interfering, but he can't help himself. He's an overprotective big brother, just like Ryan used to be with me.

"I'm not dating him, Garret," I hear Lilly say. "We're just friends."

So it was definitely a boy texting her. No wonder she smiled. *Just friends.* That's the worst thing she could say to him. Garret and I used the 'just friends' line for months, even though we were definitely more than that.

I don't think Garret's going to survive the teen years with Abigail and Hannah.

## GARRET

I swear, these girls are going to give me a heart attack before I turn 40. Lilly already has guys calling and texting her, and before I know it, Abigail and Hannah will, too.

I already worry about their safety, but now I have to add boys to my worry list.

I didn't expect boys to be interested in Lilly this soon, but I guess I should've been prepared for it because she's gorgeous and developing in places I didn't think she'd develop until she was at least 16. She's only 13, but she turns 14 in a couple months. I was kissing girls when I was 12, so yeah, I'm freaking out that boys are calling and texting her.

My dad is pretty strict with her, though, and keeps a close eye on her. He won't let her date until she's at least 16. When she reaches that age, I don't know if she'll be able to pick who she dates, or if guys will be chosen for her. My dad wants her to be able to choose, but Katherine doesn't. This past year,

Katherine has taken an interest in Lilly again. I think she sees Lilly as her ticket back into high society. Katherine assumes her social standing will be elevated if her daughter is seen with the right people at the right events, and that includes dating the right guy.

"Hey." I nudge Lilly and wait for her to look at me. "You know I'm just looking out for you, right?"

"Yeah, but I swear I'm not dating anyone. And when I do start dating, I already know about sex and condoms and—"

"Okay, stop." My little sister did not just say 'sex' and 'condoms,' did she? How does she know about sex? "You're 13, Lilly. You shouldn't even be thinking about that stuff."

"I'm almost 14. Everyone my age thinks about that stuff."

"Yeah, well, you're not everyone so stop thinking about it."

I'm only 26 and yet I sound like some old-man dad telling his kid not to have sex. But shit, Lilly's way too young to be talking about condoms and sex. I know I had sex when I was 15 but that was a mistake. I should've waited longer.

"After dinner, will you race me in the pool?" Lilly asks.

I look over and suddenly she's a little girl again. Just like that, she switches. She's in that in-between stage where she's not sure if she wants to be a kid or a grown-up. Despite her excitement over a text from a boy, I think she wants to stay on the kid side a little longer.

"Yeah, we'll race." I hug her into my side. "But you know I'll beat you."

"You're old, Garret. I'll easily beat you."

"Hey! I'm not old!"

She laughs and walks out of the room, but I hear her talking. "Once you're a dad, you're officially old."

I pick up Hannah, holding her in front of me. "Do you think I'm old?"

She just giggles, drool dripping down her chin.

I kiss her cheek. "Promise me you'll never talk about sex or condoms when you're 13. Or 15. Or ever."

She giggles again, then stuffs her fingers in her mouth. I take her back to the kitchen. It's empty, so I walk to the patio door and see that everyone's outside. Harper and Jade are talking. Lilly is at the table, working on another one of her drawings. Grace is across from her, holding Abigail. And Sean is tossing the baseball to his boys.

I never thought this would be my life, at least not before I met Jade. Before that night in the parking lot when I first saw my future wife, I was lost and angry at the world. I was just going through the motions with no real purpose. I drank too much. I slept around. I went along with the fake life that was given to me.

Back then, I never thought I'd have a wife or a family. Or true happiness. I thought my life would be spent working, running a company. When I think about that, I almost sound like my dad. I never wanted to be like him, but the future I'd planned for myself was exactly his life. I just didn't realize it at the time.

But then that beautiful girl with the big green eyes who was just as lost as I was, came into my life and saved me from myself. And I saved her. Now we both have this life that's better than either one of us ever imagined.

Hannah squeals and takes her drool-covered fingers from her mouth and points to Jade.

"Yeah, that's Mom. You want to go see her?"

I kiss Hannah's cheek, which draws her attention back to me. She lays her head on my shoulder, her tiny hand gripping my shirt.

I kiss her again, this time on her tiny head. Then I look back out at the rest of my family, and our best friends, together and having a good time.

This right here? It's exactly what I wanted in life. I just didn't know it. Until I met Jade.

# Chapter 44

## Another Two Years Later

**JADE**

*I* cradle one in each arm, their tummies now full and their eyes sleepy. It's 2 a.m. and everything is quiet. The room is softly lit by a lamp next to the door.

The three of us sit on the small, light blue couch across from their cribs. This couch is my favorite piece of furniture, because every night Garret brings the girls in here and reads them a story before bed. He sits on this couch and the girls pile on him, one on each side, snuggled under his arms.

And I sit beside them, holding the newest additions to our family. They arrived ten weeks ago. That's right—they. As in more than one. We had twins. Twin boys, Ethan and Miles. I call them my mini-Garrets because they already look like him.

"Hey," Garret whispers as he walks in the room. He's shirtless and wearing white cotton pajama pants that hang low on his hips. His skin is tan, his muscles defined. Even after all this time, he still stirs something in me whenever I see him. Love. Heat. Excitement. Desire.

"You need some help?" he asks, sitting down next to me on the couch.

"I think we're good." I look down at our babies, watching their tiny chests rise and fall as they sleep.

"You're really getting the hang of this twin thing." Garret lays his arm over my shoulder and kisses my cheek.

"I'm trying to. I seem to have the sleep thing down but the feedings are still a little tricky. Two babies are a lot harder than one."

"Here." He puts his hand under Ethan's head. "Let me have him."

I lower my arm as Garret slips his hand under Ethan's little body. His eyes remain closed but he gurgles a little and his pink lips curl into a sweet smile as his daddy picks him up. He looks so tiny in Garret's big strong arms.

"Is that better?" Garret asks, cradling Ethan in one arm and securing his other arm around my shoulder again.

"Yeah, thanks." I glance down at Miles, who's completely knocked out. He's a deep sleeper. Both boys are, especially after eating. "You didn't have to get up. I was just about ready to put them in their cribs."

"I missed you." He leans over and kisses me, then looks at the babies. "And I missed them."

I smile. "You see us all the time."

"I always miss you when you're not next to me. You know that." I see him gazing at me in the soft light of the room, his eyes so full of love. He glances down at Ethan, then over at Miles. "And as for these two, they're brand new. I'm just getting to know them, and so far I think they're pretty amazing, so yeah, I missed them, too."

I laugh. "So far? You think you'll change your mind about them?"

"No. They're definitely amazing." He rubs his thumb over Ethan's tiny hand and leans over to kiss my forehead. "We're pretty good at this baby-making thing, aren't we?"

"Yeah. We are." I shoot him a look. "But we're done now, Garret. No more. We were only supposed to have three. And then you tricked me with the whole twin thing and we ended up with four."

He laughs. "You think I somehow had control over that?"

"Yeah. I do. You couldn't take being the only guy in the house, so you had to go and make two boys to even things out, and now we have four kids."

"What are you saying? Four's too many? Think we should return one?"

His face is serious and it makes me laugh. He lifts Ethan up a little. "This one cries more than that one. Maybe we should return him and keep *that* one." He nods toward Miles.

"Garret!" I whisper scream at him.

"What? You think we should return Miles instead? He *does* eat more than Ethan. Could make for an expensive grocery bill, especially during the teen years. Where exactly do you go to return babies, anyway?"

"Cut it out." I hold Miles even closer. "We're not returning either one of them. I love them way too much."

"I know you do. I love them, too." Garret kisses the top of my head. "I also love *this*."

"What?" I ask, leaning my head on his shoulder.

"Sitting here in the middle of the night, when everything's so still and quiet. The girls asleep in their rooms. Us here together with these two little guys sleeping in our arms. It's just...I don't know, peaceful."

"Yeah. It is." I turn a little to face him. "Garret?"

"Yeah?"

"Thank you."

"For what?"

"For giving me everything I ever wanted in life."

He gently squeezes my shoulder. "What did I give you?"

"A best friend. Love." I gaze up at him and smile. "A family."

"That's everything I wanted, too. You gave me way more than I ever thought I'd get out of life." He looks down at Ethan. "If anything, I should be thanking *you*. I mean, shit, I only asked you for three kids and then you went and threw in a bonus one."

I reach over and touch Ethan's hand, his tiny fingers, his baby-soft skin. "He *is* a bonus. A really great bonus."

Garret leans down and kisses the side of my head. "I love you, Jade. And the life you've given me. And our kids. I probably don't say that enough, so I'm saying it now. I love you, and I love everything you do for me and our family. You're such a great mom and you're an amazing wife."

I feel like denying it because I feel like I'm never a good enough wife or mom. Life gets busy and crazy and sometimes I feel like I can't keep up. But whenever I need help, Garret's there for me. He's always by my side, helping me, supporting me, loving me.

"You're not so bad yourself. You're an awesome dad. And the best husband ever. The hottest one, too." I glance down at his bare chest and those sexy abs that he's managed to maintain all these years. I reach up and give him a kiss, lingering at his lips.

"How about we put these two to bed and go back to our room?" I give him the smile I reserve only for him. He knows what it means.

He smiles back, nodding at the crib. "Go ahead."

I slowly stand up and take Miles to his crib. Garret appears next to me, putting Ethan in his. Then Garret puts his hand around my waist, drawing me into him. He reaches behind my neck and brings me in for a kiss that makes my whole body fire up with desire. Even now, he gets to me this way. A simple touch, a simple kiss, is so much more with him. My body comes alive, wanting to be with him.

He slowly pulls away. "Let's go."

I turn off the lamp by the crib and we walk out into the hall and down to our room. The window's open and a light breeze is blowing in.

"I wasn't planning on going to sleep yet." I give him my sexy smile and walk backward toward the bed.

"Damn straight you're not." He stops me, slipping off the straps of my nightgown and letting it fall to the floor. He picks me up and lays me down on the bed. Then he takes his pajama pants off and lies beside me, skimming his hand over my skin.

I close my eyes as he kisses my neck, sending a shiver down my spine. He continues to touch me, knowing every inch of me, knowing exactly what to do to make my body respond.

"You're so damn beautiful," he whispers.

I smile as I feel him lie over me. Garret always makes me feel sexy, wanted, desired. After having four kids, my body's not as great as it used to be, but he doesn't see that. He doesn't see the flaws. To him, I'll always be beautiful.

When we're done, he holds me in his arms and says, "I love you."

"I love you, too." I snuggle closer to him and whisper, "I will love you forever." It's the vow I made on our wedding day. But it's also what I said to him back in the woods when I thought I'd never see him again.

Even if that day in the woods had been the end for us, I still would've loved Garret forever. He helped me find myself when I was lost. He was my friend when I had none. He loved me despite all my faults. And he never gave up on me.

But that day wasn't the end for us. And every day, I'm thankful for that. I'm thankful we're together. That I'll always have my best friend next to me. The person I love most in the world. The person I will love forever.

As I lie in Garret's arms, I savor how it feels, and how I feel at this moment.

I do that a lot now. I live in the moment. I focus on it. I pay attention to all the tiny details.

Before I met Garret, I spent all my time being angry about the past or worried about the future. But I've learned that when doing that, you miss out on the here and now. And before you know it, time goes by and you don't even know what you missed.

I don't want time to just pass me by. I want to live it and be present for each precious day. I don't want to miss a single moment of my life with Garret and our beautiful family. It's too great. It's more than I ever imagined it could be.

And the best part is…it's only just begun.

Made in the USA
Lexington, KY
03 August 2017